"I am Aaron Lee Fairfax. I am forty-three years old. I am married to Janessa, but she wants a divorce. I work for Thagg, Morgan, and Edwards Brokerage Group in Kansas City, Missouri. I own a Maserati."

It all sounded so false, these big words coming out of a boy's mouth. He sat alone, small in the adult-sized chair, clad only in shortie pajamas with Peanuts characters rampant. His feet did not even reach the floor.

"Why did you go on the Holn ship?"

"Because I was curious."

"What happened in the Holn ship on June 10?"

He stopped, stared at the floor. He took a breath, let it out.

"They did something to us."

REWIND

TERRY ENGLAND

AVON BOOKS • NEW YORK

VISIT OUR WEBSITE AT
http://AvonBooks.com

REWIND is an original publication of Avon Books. This work has never before appeared in book form. This work is a novel. Any similarity to actual persons or events is purely coincidental.

From *Wonderful Life: The Burgess Shale and the Nature of History* by Stephen Jay Gould. Copyright © 1989 by Stephen Jay Gould. Reprinted by permission of W.W. Norton & Company, Inc.

AVON BOOKS
A division of
The Hearst Corporation
1350 Avenue of the Americas
New York, New York 10019

Copyright © 1997 by Terry England
Cover art by J. K. Potter
Published by arrangement with the author
Library of Congress Catalog Card Number: 96-96915
ISBN: 0-380-78696-6

First AvoNova Printing: February 1997

AVONOVA TRADEMARK REG. U.S. PAT. OFF. AND IN OTHER COUNTRIES, MARCA REGISTRADA, HECHO EN U.S.A.

Printed in the U.S.A.

RA   10 9 8 7 6 5 4 3 2 1

For LAURENE F. and ROBERT D. ENGLAND
I just wish you both were here to see this . . .

We came *this close* (put your thumb about a millimeter away from your index finger), thousands and thousands of times, to erasure by the veering of history down another sensible channel. Replay the tape a million times from a Burgess beginning, and I doubt that anything like *Homo sapiens* would ever evolve again. It is, indeed, a wonderful life.

—Stephen Jay Gould, *Wonderful Life*

Prologue

"They did something to us."

The voice was wrong—*his* could not have made that high-pitched sound. The naked, smooth, pink body could not be his, either—he was an adult, he had adult muscles, he had adult height—

The ground spun, he began to tremble. Two more high-pitched screams pierced his mind, then a curse, a moan, but they weren't his, they came from behind . . . he didn't look. All he could do was stare at his shaking hands, now so small and so close to the dirt his bare toes gripped.

A new sound, a shout, made him look up. Like cattle out of control, a gaggle of adults rushed toward him, led by a short woman, ponytail bobbing, trying to keep a vidcam balanced. The wave of men and women in business suits and coats and jeans and slogan-bearing T-shirts and shorts and dresses and pants but almost all shod in the same style of soft-sided shoe rolled down like an avalanche. For a second, he forgot his own predicament and gaped.

"What's your name son—" "Stop shov—" "Get some clothes on these kids, for chrissake—" "Here, son, let's put this on—" A tall man picked up a shirt and held it up so he could slip his arms in. It fell below his knees *(But it's my shirt . . .)*. "Where are the people who

1

disappeared into the ship—" "Did you come off the ship—" "One side—" "Fuck off, CNN asshole—" "ABC shithead—" "Who are you, kid—" "Where's the Holn—" "Was your mother on that ship—" "Where are your parents—"

"Yarrow! Cohen! Baker! Get some people around these kids!" The tall man shouted. "The rest of you clowns back off, goddamnit! You act like you've never seen naked children before."

"Who the hell are you?"

"FBI. Wanna make something of it?"

"Easy, sir, easy. We're just trying to find out what's going on, the same as you, I'm sure," said a tall—*(All of them are tall)*—black man in a light tan suit with muted red-striped tie. Next to him, a beefy bearded man in a Metallica T-shirt hefted a vidcam. The lens barrel swiveled to the FBI man.

"Don't get solicitous with me, Kinsea. You media gorillas are causing a lot of problems here. Officer! See if you can get that squad car over here. Clear the way! That means you!"

"Were you on the ship—" "What happened—" "Who are—" "Where are—" "How did—" "When did—"

All he could see were legs, torsos. *Once I could look a man in the eye. Once I could look down on a boy*—The ground tilted again; knees met dirt.

"Hey!"

The FBI man squatted, big face creased in concern. "Just hold on a second, son, we'll get you out of here." He stood and shouted again. "Clear the way for that car or I'll start punching!"

Stones pressed into his knees. The sun beat hot on his head and the ground still threatened to tilt. His breathing came in ragged gasps, the shouting now just meaningless sound hammering at him. He looked up to see the cyclops eye of Metallica T-shirt staring back.

"All right, son, come on." A strong hand pulled him to

his feet. He grabbed for, but missed, a pair of pants on the ground nearby.

"My stuff—" he croaked.

"We'll get them later."

As the hand moved him inexorably toward a black car, his last sight of his shoes were of them side by side, a pair of brown argyle socks folded neatly across the tops.

The car smelled of vomit. The door slammed shut. He kept his head down, but pushed an impatient hand through unruly hair.

Hair?

Before he could pursue the thought, the other door opened and a girl was pushed in. When the door shut, she pressed herself back against it, staring at him through wide blue eyes. One hand clutched a yellow wadded-up cloth against her chest; her other hand kept a tight grip on too-big blue jeans covered with dust and weeds where they extended beyond her feet. He'd seen her somewhere before—

—tall, slim and lithe, walking with an easy grace. Hair, dark as mahogany, flowing over her shoulders and back and down to her knees like a brown waterfall, framing an oval face with pert nose and angular eyebrows, high cheekbones and clear skin. Yellow pullover blouse in loose folds across her front, not completely obscuring a gentle swell of bosom; stonewashed jeans covering long legs; sandals on her feet. Her passing scatters a delightful aroma toward him—

—now she was small and frightened, hair in tangles across her chest but still long enough for her to sit on. Her face retained many of its striking features, although softer and rounder, like a portrait of a child.

Boy and girl stared at each other until a uniformed policeman got in behind the wheel, slammed the door and started the engine. The faces outside flinched as the electronic siren blared and the car began a slow trek forward.

* * *

"No one is sure where these children came from. Observers say most were found dazed and confused, and all were naked. The garments you see in neat stacks are adult clothing, although we are told the children claim them as their own. Some became rather upset at having to leave the articles behind, although police attribute that to confusion. Jack Theodoric, an FBI agent at the scene, had some choice words."

"A zoo. And you media types were gorillas. Of course, a couple of agents and soldiers acted like muddleheaded baboons, but given the utter hysteria of the place, I'm surprised we stayed on such an even keel."

"Do you have any idea what happened to the seventeen missing adults?"

"Not a shred. The ship took off, and that was that. We're trying to identify the children, and trying to find their parents. That's all we can do right now."

"The unknown children include this boy, who was discovered by a CNN crew not far from the spot where the Holn ship took off."

"They did something to us."

"If anyone knows who this boy is, please contact the FBI or your local police immediately.

"Marinka Svoboda, CNN, the Holn site, New Mexico."

Part I

Inception

One

June 11, 2008

"I am Aaron Lee Fairfax. I am forty-three years old. I am married to Janessa, but she wants a divorce. I work for Thagg, Morgan, and Edwards Brokerage Group in Kansas City, Missouri. I own a Maserati."

It all sounded false, these big words coming out of a boy's mouth. He sat alone, small in an adult-sized chair, clad only in shortie pajamas with *Peanuts* characters rampant. His feet did not even reach the floor. On the other side of a glass partition, formless adults sat in shadows.

"What were you doing in Santa Fe?"

He could not tell who asked the questions. "The firm wants to open a Southwest branch, Phoenix, Tucson, or Albuquerque. We had visited the other cities and it was Albuquerque's turn."

"Just yourself?"

"No, four officers from the firm."

"They did not go to the Holn ship?" The intercom suggested a feminine voice.

"No. I was the only one who wanted to see it. I was curious."

"You went alone?"

"I drove our rented car to the site." He looked down at his pale, thin legs. "A small car. I was too tall for it."

"We have reports that the children are claiming to be the missing people. Authorities are skeptical because the medical bulletins from St. Vincent Hospital say these are definitely children, all in excellent health.

"We asked Jack Theodoric, FBI agent in charge, about the coincidence that seventeen adults are missing yet seventeen children were found after the ship left yesterday."

"Very coincidental, don't you think?"

"That's all he would say. Meanwhile, authorities are trying to find parents or other relatives of these children. A source, asking not to be named, told me absolutely no one has stepped forward.

"Marinka Svoboda, CNN, Santa Fe."

And so it went:

Up on this table, please, take your top off, breathe deep, please, as hands encased in thin plastic touch a stethoscope along his back, his chest. Open your mouth, please, an eye peeking through a hood peers in, then into nostrils, ears. Lay on your stomach, please, thump, thump, thump; over please, thump, thump, thump. Remove your bottoms, please, as rubberized hands prod, push, separate. Stand still, please, and huge adult hands press childlike fingers into ink and then onto cards. Human faces anonymous behind swaths of green cloth say little to him but much to each other.

To X-ray: lie on the table, please, as he's turned, rolled and twisted into every conceivable position (don't move, please). In a white room, more poses for less penetrating photos, but naked again: front, back, sides, chest, legs, face, arms, feet, hands—every inch photographed from every angle.

"Am I posing for child porn or something?"

No one laughs.
No one says a word.

"Twenty minutes after departure from the New Mexico desert, the Arianespace DS1 satellite captured these images of the Holn lander linking with its deep-space engine array orbiting the Earth. Within five minutes, attitude control jets turned the linked ships and the massive nuclear engines roared to life. Scientists say the acceleration must be immense.

"All efforts to contact the ship have failed. The Holn have not answered, and the ship continues on a course away from Earth. One scientist suggests the occupants might already be in biological stasis for the trip back to the mother ship, which could take up to twenty years.

"Kinsea Lee, NBC News, Santa Fe."

"What happened in the Holn ship on June fifth?"

"We were inside, looking around at the displays. No warning or anything. I mean, no lights, no buzzers. The last thing I remember was looking at a holo of the Holn mother ship. Then I woke up on the hill, naked." He ran his hands down his thin chest, feeling ribs under cloth. "And—and . . . smaller."

"Do you remember anything in between?"

He stopped, stared at the floor. "Vague things. Shapes and forms. Long . . . tentacles, or wires. No one talking. Light overhead, soft sounds in the background. A curved wall, ceiling, overhead, I think. . . . Memory is a gap." He took a breath, let it out. "First thing I really remember is seeing an ant crawling along the ground. Then the ground started vibrating. I could barely get to my feet."

The anonymous green people later stuck his body into a dark tunnel. As he lay listening to the whirrings and poppings, he wondered if he would come out even smaller. . . .

"Dr. Rolstein, why, after six years of exchanging information, did the Holn do this?"

"The question of the decade don't you think? Only the decade, though. The question of the century is, why did they come in the first place?"

"You don't have any idea after six years?"

"We can give one answer, of course, the same answer to the question of why we went to the Moon. To beat the Soviets—I mean, to find out what's there. We did sort of advertise our presence, did we not, by beaming our TV signals all across the galaxy. Hogan's Heroes, Gilligan's Island, Howdy Doody. I wonder what they think of a wooden doll on strings pushing Nestle's chocolate, eh? So they came to find out what the Sam Hill was going on over here. Gave them an earful, I must say."

"What did we get in return?"

"The answer to Enrico Fermi's question: Where are they? Right there, Dr. Fermi, with a lot more out there, we now know. On a more prosaic level, some information on new metal alloys and rocket engines. No warp drive, sorry Captain Kirk. Their engines are practical examples of technology we've already thought about. Nice computers, though, machines that'll make ol' von Neumann green with envy. New polymers, some other stuff making DuPont go nuts. No cure for cancer, though, I'm afraid. Their physiology is much too different."

"What did we give them?"

"Ah, an interesting question. On the surface, not too much, no? I find it a wonder they didn't leave after—or during—the Millennium Riots of ought-4. Maybe they found tear gas tasty. Or perhaps they found it all amusing."

"In all the exchanges of information between Earth scientists and the Holn, there was no suggestion they would kidnap seventeen humans for experiments?"

"Not unless we missed something in the fine print. Besides, we don't know they did experiments. Maybe

they offered them a ride. 'Come wiz me to the Kochab.'
And the humans said 'Why not?' ''

''How do you explain the children?''

''I have an idea about that, but for now, I am keeping
my mouth shut.''

''Unfortunately, we cannot pursue that line of thought.
We switch now to Rolf Treadwell in Washington where the
president's spokesman is about to issue a statement.
Perhaps later we can discuss your theory, doctor. This is
Marinka—''

''If you pursue it too far, young lady, you'll be burned as
a heretic.''

"Aaron Lee Fairfax." The words swiftly faded to nothing.

He sat alone, legs dangling over the edge of the bed. Ages had passed since the day on the hill, but hospital staff kept telling him the rocket had left only yesterday. Now this day was fading to black. . . . another night of terror ahead. . . .

He glanced at the wrinkled paper in his hand, a photocopy of his driver's license. In one corner, an image of a man: strong chin, no folds of fat underneath; broad face; set mouth; receding hairline; looking out with confidence, perhaps a touch of arrogance. Vital statistics deemed necessary to know by the State of Missouri—Date of birth: 2-27-65; Height: six feet, two inches; Weight: 197; Eyes: brown; Hair: black; Physical Disabilities: none; Glasses: no.

"You continue to insist this man is you?" The gargoyle in the sterile gown had held the photocopy two inches in front of his face. "Look at yourself in the mirror, and tell me again: Is this man you?"

"Yes, sir." Meekly.

The gargoyle made a sound deep inside the mask.

"Look at yourself." A gloved hand thrust open his pajama top. "Where'd your muscles go? Look." He

poked with a finger. "Nothing there, just a kid's skinny chest. Your biceps." He pulled an arm out, squeezed with his other hand. "Nothing. Weak as a kitten." He pushed Aaron back, yanked down his bottoms. "Look at this. You call this a man's penis? And these genitals. These aren't a man's equipment, they've never been used. And not a hair on them, slick as a newborn's." He leaned forward until his masked face was inches away. Aaron could see only brown eyes glaring at him. "You still say you were once a man?"

"Y-yes. Yes. I was a man once."

"Shit." The gargoyle crumpled the photocopy, threw it down. "Get dressed." He stomped away.

Now alone in the cold, sterile hospital room, the boy wrapped his arms around himself, bent forward and took deep breaths.

I am Aaron Lee Fairfax, 43 years old; I own a Maserati. I am an adult.

He squeezed his eyes shut.

I will not cry. I will not.

"They did something to us."

A tear slipped out from beneath an eyelid and down a cheek, paused a moment at the edge of the jaw, then fell to oblivion.

Two

June 12

Miranda Sena had the distinct feeling she was arguing a lost cause. "I'm just a bit, uh, surprised to be asked."

"We've got to get order out of chaos, it's that simple." The sharp greenish eyes of Avram Rolstein, a prime mover in the Holn Contact and Study Group, remained fixed on her. "And we need your help."

"I'm only here a couple of days to gather a little more data on Holn brain configuration. I'm scheduled to present a paper at the neurological congress next month."

Avram smiled. "All I want you to do is listen and make suggestions if you see fit. I was very glad Franklyn told me you were here, and it goes beyond the artistic thing."

Miranda tapped a foot on the floor of the carpet and looked out of the window. Once again, the Holn were throwing everything out of whack. Her first word about them came from a fellow graduate student crashing into a lecture in the late '90s, shouting about an odd blip that had shown up in sky images and how this blip had changed course. Then the blip began sending messages. . . .

"Can you imagine what would've happened if they'd

just announced themselves in a blaze of light and pulsating music?" one of many scientists netted by TV had said during the ship's transit across the solar system. "They're giving us a chance to get used to them. If we can."

The calm voices of scientists (in public, anyway) did little to smooth the hysteria on the planet. Miranda's studies served to steady her own nerves as she followed the transit daily like a soap opera addict. She was in transit herself, from graduate student to postgraduate status and thus tried to bear down on her future. But the Holn had changed that paradigm forever. . . .

And the pulse of fear that had surged through her the first time Hubble telescope pictures came in of the ship shocked her so much she had to switch off the TV. Once the ship had landed, though, data about an alien physiology started trickling in. She dropped the line of study she'd pursued for six years like so much scrap paper and joined the tumult of scientists begging, pleading, conniving to get a piece of Holn research. When her number finally came up in the "contact lottery," she played a hunch—and it paid off spectacularly.

Now *this* new twist. . . .

With an inner voice warning she'd regret it, she turned to Avram. "Dr. Nakai warned me about you." She began stuffing wallet, hotel key, and change into pockets.

"Did he, now? I'll take that as a compliment."

Miranda followed the slight figure—she stood a head taller than he did—out of the room. Avram, now stuffing tobacco into his pipe as they walked down the three flights of stairs, had been the first scientist on the site. Not by design, though.

"You came up here just to get me?" She said as they crossed the lobby. She had to scramble to keep up.

"I'm surprised you got a room here. La Fonda is usually booked solid in summer."

"Luck," she said as he pushed a wooden door with

glass panes open, held it for her. "I called, they'd just had a cancellation."

Avram nodded as he scurried down a short flight of steps and got into position to hold another, heavier wooden door for her. He was supposed to be closer to seventy than sixty, but his pace made Miranda wonder what he'd been like at twenty-five. He crossed a street in the middle of the block, seemingly oblivious to the crawling traffic.

"Holn physiology," she started as they headed down a sidewalk under a long roof supported by upright logs, "is much different than human. So how could they pull this off?"

Avram swerved to avoid a camera-toting tourist. Indeed, weaving became essential in order to get around slow-walking people gawking into store windows. She caught her own reflection, a slim woman with dark hair cut at her collar, dressed in T-shirt, khaki shorts, and sport sandals.

"That question is number one." Avram went left to get around a coven of youths in red T-shirts; Miranda swerved right but other knots of bag-laden shoppers kept them apart for another quarter-block. "We don't have the faintest idea how or why it was done," he said when they could rejoin.

"I just don't know what I can add—"

He grabbed her left arm, pulled her around and pointed with his pipe stem at a newsfax-vending console in front of a Woolworth's store. WHO ARE THESE CHILDREN? blared *USA Today*'s headline window-screen with an electronic image below it of the children as they had been found on the hillside but with parts of their anatomies fuzzed over. SCIENTIST: CHILDREN "ALIEN" said the window-screen for *The Santa Fe New Mexican*, the local digi-paper.

"That's what we're up against," Avram said, as a man in a straw hat and yellow shirt stepped up and dropped

in a dollar coin and punched the buttons for the news
and sports sections of *USA Today*. "Rumors, speculation, fantasy, spreading at the speed of light all over the
world. Much faster than we bumbling scientists can keep
up with. And this," he gestured at the customer's facsim-
ile copy sliding out of the slot, "is mild compared to
some of the other stuff. We need ideas, direction, and we
need them now from anyone we can grab. Your mistake,
I'm afraid, was being within my reach."

At a newer—and to Miranda, uglier—hotel, milling
people crowded into the meeting room. Some were from
the contact group, others she recognized from television
appearances. She felt self-conscious among the suits and
skirts until she noticed a tall, broad-shouldered man.

"Greetings, Dr. Gunnarson, I believe," she said as the
man filled a plastic foam cup with cold tea. "Glad to see
someone else is casual."

The man turned to her, smiled. His eyes were bluer
and hair blacker than had been promised by video color.
"Name's Matt. Almost twins, I'd say, although you seem
to have more refined tastes in T-shirts."

"Umm, maybe." Hers said "Santa Fe Opera," his
"Old Santa Fe Trail Run." "I'm Miranda Sena, of
UCLA—"

"Ah, yes, the one who discovered the Holn have an
aesthetic side."

Miranda sighed, reached for a cup. "I guess that's
what I'm going to be known for."

"Nothing to be ashamed of. You shot up in esteem at
Princeton just for that one discovery."

Miranda shrugged as she plopped a couple of ice cubes
into her tea. "It just seemed a natural quest—"

"Can we get everyone to settle down, please?" a man
in a suit called out. "Chairs around the table are first-
come, first-seated. Otherwise grab what you can."

Matt's muscular build helped clear a path to the long
conference table. Through the introductions and re-

views, Miranda just sipped her tea. Almost immediately, complaints started flying about restrictions.

"You Americans have been hogging the good stuff all along, anyway," said an accented voice. Miranda knew the Australian Jake Skettles because he'd had the slot for the Holn audience right behind hers. "Now your FBI and your soldiers are telling us to bugger off—"

"All operations have switched back to the chaos and confused modes," said a sandy-haired man in his late thirties. "I'm Ben Danthen of the Jet Propulsion Laboratory and I'm here to tell you the situation is just like the days of first contact."

Ben took off his glasses, rubbed an eye, put the glasses back on. "The Holn breathe poison, methane and ammonia. They didn't poke their noses—such as they are—out in six years. For them, oxygen is both toxic and caustic. Indeed, they were quite shocked at the O_2 levels on this planet. So we had not a clue, not an inkling, not a warning, a premonition, anything, they would pull humans in beyond the museum. That's why we sent out the SOS."

"After the fact," said Skettles.

Miranda accepted an electronic notebook Matt passed to her containing preliminary reports about the children.

"Oh, man." Ben put his head in his hands. "You guys are sounding like the media. 'So—What were you talking about, the weather?' We unfortunately took a cue from the Manhattan Project and compartmentalized the research. Everything we know about the Holn is scattered among every state and twenty-one countries at last count. Everyone wants to be the first with the Nobel for Holn research, and the competition is nasty. Well," he looked around at the group, "speaking for a beleaguered JPL—help."

"We've declared a national emergency." Heads swiveled toward the voice at the head of the table.

The speaker was a heavy-set man in a tailored three-piece suit with the attitude of someone used to moving easily through the corridors of power: Harrison Conroy, the president's science adviser. "From what I can see, there's been no coordination between groups. A national emergency will allow us to at least begin sorting it all out."

"You mean knock anyone who isn't American out," said a French-flavored voice from Miranda's left.

"That's not our intent, Anton. We ask that you give us time to work the wrinkles out. This took us completely by surprise, too."

"We were like kids on a beach," Ben said. "Trying to gather up all the pretty shells before the tide came in and swept them all away."

"I think first we need to form some kind of central group to organize the data mountain and coordinate the teeming masses of scientists," Avram said between smoky pulls from his pipe. "But you'll have to cut the red tape, Harrison."

Murmurs of agreement passed around the table as Harrison leaned toward Avram and said something. Avram nodded, then Harrison faced the group.

"Our marching orders come from the President of the United States. She has made it clear she wants action right now. I, personally, see no reason to delay. As soon as this meeting's over, Avram becomes administrator of that committee and will begin picking the members—"

"It's too late."

Conroy searched the table for the source of the comment. "Excuse me? Who said that?"

"I did." Miranda waved her hand, suddenly feeling self-conscious again. "You people are discussing this like it's just another bureaucratic task to be done, another folder to be filed."

"Well, I haven't had time to review in detail the initial reports from the Santa Fe hospital—"

"Ladies and gentlemen," Miranda hefted the notebook, "I was told, as I was being herded to this meeting by a very insistent senior scientist, that we have precious little time. Well, he's wrong. That time ran out two days ago." She tapped keys. "A bladder removal remade. Amputated toes back in place as if they were never gone. Asthma cured, missing teeth regrown, missing tonsils regrown—"

"I'm sorry, uh, Miss—Ma'am," Conroy said. "That's all anecdotal at this point. There's nothing to support—"

"I see nothing yet refuting these 'anecdotal reports.' Somebody mentioned the Manhattan Project. From where I sit, the blast of the first atomic bomb will be a firecracker to the explosion *this* is going to cause.

"And, ladies and gentlemen, the detonation has already begun."

"In other developments related to the mysterious group of seventeen children, Health and Human Services Secretary Roberta Fletcher announced today the appointment of Radmilla Everett, an attorney and one-time social worker, as special liaison who will report on the status of the children. Everett will work with the New Mexico Department for Children, Youth, and Families to ensure, as the statement by a spokesman for HHS put it at a briefing, 'rights are protected and special needs of the young victims are met with immediate and fulfilling dispatch.'

"Also in Washington today, Harrison Conroy, special scientific adviser to the president, announced the formation of the Holn Effect Task Force, a panel of scientists who are, as Conroy put it, 'empowered to determine the facts behind the extraordinary events of June tenth, especially in relation to the group of seventeen children found after the departure of the extraterrestrial ship,' end quote. The main members of the task force will be made up of volunteers who will take leaves of absence from their respective institutions, Conroy said.

"The exact structure of the task force still has to be determined, but two appointments have been made already. Dr. Avram Rolstein, a neurophysiologist with Harvard University, has been named administrator, while Dr. Miranda Sena, a professor of neurological studies at the University of California at Los Angeles, has been named scientific director. Rolstein has been with the Holn project since the landing six years ago. Sena received some attention three years ago when she pointed out that the Holn have an artistic side.

"Rolf Treadwell, CNN, Washington."

The just-appointed scientific director of the Holn Effect Task Force stood at the head of the same hotel conference-room table Avram had brought her to two days before, idly tapping the surface as other people filed into the room. One of them was Matt, and by now she'd gleaned other facts about him, including his speciality— genetics—and the fact that he was not married, although she would not allow herself to see the relevance of that.

All members here had been pressed into service, and not so much "volunteers" as TV would have everyone think. Just like Miranda, they all had met the velvet-coated iron will of Avram Rolstein.

"You're doing this to get back at me, aren't you?" she had said. "You and that Harrison fellow."

Avram merely smiled. "Harrison has no say whatever in the formation of this group beyond my appointment. I want you because I think you are the best qualified. That will be true of everyone on the committee."

"But why in charge? We just met formally yesterday when you dragged me to the meeting."

"And what I saw there impressed me. Everyone read the same reports, yet you were the one who seemed to put it all into context first."

"Maybe I was just panicking first."

Avram shook his head.

"Yeah, well . . ." She looked down at her hands. "Dr. Nakai might not like me leaving at this time."

"I've already cleared it with Franklyn."

"But the neurology congress—"

"Has been canceled."

Miranda sighed. "The deck is stacked, isn't it?"

In the conference room, the group had settled down, each member looking at her with expectation.

"All right," she said as the murmuring quieted, "I declare the first meeting of the Holn Effect Task Force in order on June 14, 2008. Welcome to meat grinder."

Polite laughter greeted the remark. "As you know, the children were taken to the Lovelace Medical Center in Albuquerque late last night with so little fanfare more than one reporter was taken by surprise." She shrugged. "My first run-in with the press. Anyhow, this means a move for us also. Our new quarters will be at Sandia National Labs. We should all be down there by tomorrow night. Housing is being arranged. The lab is on an air force base, and that means security, and that means badges, and that means guards. A DOE rep will explain all this a bit later. I know many of you aren't comfortable with this, but look at the bright side: You won't have to dodge reporters every time you need to go to the rest room."

"Hallelujah," a voice muttered.

"Another advantage is proximity to the supercomputing facilities of both Sandia and Los Alamos, which means, in case you're unfamiliar with either, access to a whopping chunk of computer power.

"Meanwhile, JPL has formed a new data-search team. They have assigned a liaison, a Wanda Bettym—Bettermay"—she looked at the slip of paper in her hand—"Bet-te-mey-er, Bettemeyer, to the group. Until she arrives, though, Ben, Dr. Danthen, has graciously agreed to give us a quick review of the Holn contact. That might mean going over some old history for most of us—but, you never know, there might be a clue there somewhere. Lord knows we need a clue. And I need to sit down."

Matt jumped up, hurried over, pulled her chair out, held it as she sat down. "Thank you," she said.

"At your service." He stepped back to his chair.

"If you're sitting at this table, you're the head of a study group. Staff and technical personnel are being assigned to each group, along with a colleague representing other nations. Officially, that's so research information can flow freely back and forth. Unofficially, it's so we can dodge the charge of being selfish.

"Olive Greenlea, here on my left, heads the Psychological Study Group. She and her colleagues are the only direct transfers from the local hospital, but they did such an outstanding job we decided we needed them.

"The rest of you are fairly well known in your fields, but I don't know how much you know each other. Next to Dr. Greenlea is Dr. Timothy Jenkins, head of the Cardiopulmonary Study Group, then Dr. Constance Peterson, Genetics and Cells, Dr. Lindsey Rollins, Neurological, Dr. Randall Whitman, Nutrition and Metabolism, Dr. Orlando Tousee, Osteology, and Dr. Anna Lowry, Endocrine. On my right, the chivalrous gentleman in the Marvin Martian T-shirt is Dr. Matthew Gunnarson, at-large member, willing to work with anyone. Dr. Avram Rolstein, of course, is the overall head of the group and the one we all can blame for being in this fix, but right now, he's out sparring with the media."

"I heard Smilin' Sam Innes has been appointed," Matt said. "Is this true?"

"Dr. Samuel Innes of Florida is the other at-large member who will join us in Albuquerque. Is this a problem?"

"*He* could be." Matt shrugged.

Terrific, she said to herself. She turned to the group. "The other personage at the table is Jack Theodoric, FBI. You can relax, he's not here to check our loyalty. Jack?"

"Yes," the man said as he scribbled idly on a yellow pad. "I'm a liaison. My first report is that we should have information shortly on the fingerprints taken at the hospital."

Miranda nodded. "A start at last. Other data from the St. Vincent studies are being transferred to optical disk. We're also collecting medical records from family doctors, hospitals, whatever. We should be able to confirm claims of removed tonsils, say. Other suggestions?"

"We'll need sources of pre-event DNA," Matt said. "The famous strands of hair from hairbrushes and the like, and I suppose if there are toenails or fingernails lying around, you could collect those, too. Or favorite clothing that might have flakes of skin embedded, although if they've just been washed, it'll probably be no good."

"Right."

"Two of the people have claimed to have had surgery not too long before the event," Olive said. "Each said the hospital collected blood prior to surgery. We've contacted both hospitals and both blood samples are on their way."

"Excellent," Matt said.

"We're also checking the hotel rooms where some of these people stayed," Jack said. "Collecting personal belongings."

"Birth records?" Randall asked.

"As we speak," Miranda said. "We're going to the families first, but if they're lost or the families don't want to cooperate, we can go to county authorities."

"We'd better try to cut down on the number of people going to these families," Anna said. "They're already distraught, and all these people making demands could make it worse."

"Good point," Miranda said, taking notes.

"What, uh, what goals have you established?" Orlando asked.

"Avram and I have set down some priorities," Miran-

da said, scrolling back a couple of pages. "First, establish
the identity of the children. Second, decide if they are
human or alien. If we decide the children are who they
claim to be, then the priority is to find out how they got
into that state. Brain transplant? Transfer of personality
into another organism? Or have the adults been . . .
regressed . . . into children?" Miranda paused, frowning
at her notes.

"It sounds a bit unreal," Constance said.

"It sounds like bad science fiction is what it sounds
like," Miranda said. "Anything else?"

No one spoke.

"OK. Ben?"

"Can someone get the lights? Ladies and gentlemen,"
he said as a giant image of a Holn loomed on a wall
screen, "here are the beings most responsible for saving
the Jet Propulsion Lab from extinction." As the laughter
died, he added, "After NASA handed the project to us,
some of the staff suggested we change the name from
JPL to the Holn Analysis Lab, to be known to the world
as HAL."

That joke didn't go over as well, but Ben didn't seem
perturbed as he adjusted his glasses. "Some of this might
be old territory, but here's some of what little we know.

"About two-point-four meters total length, although
only one-point-five erect. About as wide as a human,
slightly thicker. Total body mass is approximately two-
and-a-half times average human male, but distributed
more evenly. Four sort of legs on the back section, with
hair covering the body. The triocular vision is a theme
common throughout Holn physiology. The body is divided into three segments. The larger pair of tentacles on
the second segment are quite powerful, the smaller on
the first are about the strength we have in our arms,
and the itty-bitty ones just above the second set divide
into three fingers for fine work. How many times have we
wished for more than two hands? They have six append-
ages of independent mobility."

"What they could do with a set of Lego blocks," Matt muttered.

"Or an erector set." Ben hit a button and the vidstill was replaced by an anatomical drawing. "Bilateral symmetry, plus a spinal cord that makes almost a ninety-degree turn here. I get a backache every time I look at this.

"Their brains are segmented into three pairs. One pair is in the upper segment, two pair are in the middle segment. As far as we can tell, each segment, or each nodule in a segment, handles different types of processing."

The drawing was replaced by a video. "Inside the control room, with Pip and Pop doing something." A titter passed through the room. "Yes, I know, those are silly names for ETs, but they didn't seem to have individual monikers, so we came up with our own for all six: Pip, Pop, Pup, Pook, Alpha, and Beta. The latter two were named by someone with a little more of a serious demeanor. Watch Pop, here—see how he just seems to climb up the instrument console? This is the scene that makes everyone compare these creatures to terrestrial centipedes. A superficial resemblance at best, but enough to give many humans the heebie-jeebies."

"Amen," said Constance, a slim blonde woman. "I had dreams of tiny Holn scurrying across my kitchen floor."

Ben chuckled. "You know, I don't think anyone asked if they have their version of cockroaches. Anyhow," the video froze, "nothing we've seen about Holn technology is beyond the realm of our own. The ships, the fuels—chemical in the case of the lander, fusion in the case of the deep-space boosters—the life support systems, the orbital mechanics, the mother ship—all are within Earth technological limits. Just a couple of generations ahead is all. Look at some similarities, such as the Apollo program and the late lamented Delta Clipper. We had trouble transferring data at first, but that was mostly equipment incompatibility, not anything so outrageous we couldn't find an accommodation eventually." He looked around at the faces in the room, "As for the seventeen, well, looking at what's being suggested as possibilities . . ." He took a breath. "I don't envy you people one little bit."

After a long silence, Miranda stood. "OK. Get moving ASAP. The children have been isolated not only from the outside but also from each other. Two days from now, we're going to bring them all together for the first time since June 10. Dr. Greenlea and her group will be observing, as will I. Anyone else is welcome to join." She closed the notebook. "Any questions?"

She waited a moment. "Any answers?"

Three

June 15

All eyes in the circle turned to Aaron as he stepped through the door. "Is this Ms. Phelps's fourth-grade class?"

"Right room, wrong year." The speaker was a gangly youth with flaming red hair flowing over his head like liquid fire. "Have a seat. The table and chairs are child-sized."

"How considerate," Aaron said as he stepped to the only empty chair left. The red-haired boy was on his left and the long-haired girl on his right. She smiled briefly as he sat down. Everyone wore the same outfit: blank white T-shirt, blue jeans. And sandals, although Aaron hadn't worn his.

"You know what this place is?" asked a thin-faced boy.

"Lovelace Hospital, or something," a girl answered.

"Yeah. When the original seven astronauts came here for medical evaluation, one of the things they made 'em do was walk up and down the halls with enema tubes stuck up their asses."

"They haven't treated me much better," said a girl with curls of bright blond hair. "All those needles and tubes. Ugh."

"I don't mind that as much as someone pulling off my clothes and demanding how I could say I was ever grown up," Aaron said. "Anyone else get that?"

Almost everyone nodded, including the women.

"Some old bat with a mole on her forehead," the blonde said. "Ooh, I wanted to belt her. But how could I? She was a hell of a lot stronger than I was. Am."

"An attempt to intimidate us into saying something they want to hear," said a boy just on the other side of the long-haired girl.

"At least they're leaving us alone for a while," said another girl to the left.

"Don't kid yourself," Aaron said. "See the big wall mirror there? You can bet psychologists and psychiatrists and psych-whatevers are gathered on the other side listening to every sound and watching every move and writing in their little electronic notepads."

"Maybe they're waiting for us to get overconfident and reveal how we're pulling a con job," said a dark-skinned boy.

"Or hoping we'll strip off our disguises and reveal ourselves as ugly, foul-smelling aliens bent on taking over the Earth," the redhead said. "Perhaps we should pull out our ray guns now and start blasting away."

A couple of the others tittered. The long-haired girl stirred.

"Are we aliens?"

The room fell silent.

"They did something to us, that's obvious," Aaron said. "None of us knows exactly what. That alone could make us alien, despite our Earthly origins."

Seventeen pairs of eyes glanced around, locked gazes with others a quick second, then darted away.

"Well," said the bright blonde suddenly, "even if we are all alien, we're in the same boat. It might be good for us to at least know each other's names. I'm Linda Rithen." Her face had sharp features with high cheekbones and pointed chin. "I was—still am, I guess—forty-nine years old. I'm from Teaneck, New Jersey, but we moved to Rio Rancho five years ago. I am—was—a hairdresser. We have one son, who works for the gas company in Amarillo." She jabbed the boy to her left with an elbow.

"Yeah, yeah, I'm the schlub who brought us out here." The boy had thick brown hair, wide face, large nose and thick lips. "I'm a construction worker, and I followed the work." He shrugged. "My name is Jerry."

"Guess I'm next," said the boy who had talked about the astronauts. "Perry Stangle, accountant, from California. Married, one kid on the way. My wife was visiting her mother in Montana when the boom fell."

"Pete Aragon, Albuquerque." The speaker had a handsome, dark face and jet-black hair. "Videocam operator for KALB, token minority."

"Eddie Thompson, second token, black, obviously." The boy's face was wide, with set-back eyes. His voice seemed to have retained some of its adult bass quality. "Sanitation engineer from Chicago. Garbage collector, as my old man would rag me. Guess I won't be tossing cans much now."

"I'm Sandra Mellinfield from New York." Brown hair tumbled around a long face. She kept interlacing her fingers, letting go, then doing it all over again. "My husband's a banker. He's not here. I was visiting my sister. She had—had stayed home with her baby."

"This is Pam Yolbin, KALB New Mexico News-Team." The thin shoulders shrugged. "Old habits are hard to break. Pete over there is my cameraman." She also was a blonde, but a more subdued shade than the girl across the table.

"Myra Caslon, Salt Lake City." Short brown hair, round face, receding chin. "I had come out representing a church committee studying the Holn thing for ourselves." She grimaced. "Bad timing."

"Harold Coner, Santa Fe, used cars. The Holn weren't buying." His sharp face made a little grin. "I came out here after my divorce to start all over again. Oh, boy."

"Charlie Romplin. I used to drive trucks, semi-rigs." The boy version carried some of the bulk of what the adult must have been.

"Tom Cathen, professor of humanities at UC-Berkeley." The boy was thin and wiry, with smooth, studied movements. "I was studying the Holn as part of my work."

"Marian Athlington," said the long-haired girl next to Aaron. "I work in the city planner's office in Bellingham, Washington."

"I am Aaron Lee Fairfax. I am forty-three years old. I own a Maserati."

"Think you'll drive that Maserati again?" Tom said.

Aaron sat up. "I doubt it. I have the same problem Charlie does: My feet won't reach the pedals."

The boy Charlie Romplin let out a bark of laughter.

"Earl Othberg," the redhead said. "Retired. Used to own a couple of movie theaters."

"Pardon me, but I don't remember seeing anyone with that color of hair in the ship," Linda said. "And I would remember hair like that."

"How about a white-haired, stooped old guy limping along?"

"That was you?"

"Indeed." He swatted at his hair. "The Holn gave me my youthful red back."

"How interesting." Linda lifted a lock of hers. "Mine used to be brown. I just dyed it blond. The doctors say it may be permanent now."

Earl grinned. "Be careful what you wish for."

"Oh. Uh, Paula Caulfield." The face creased in confusion. Her brown hair was cut close to her head. "I, uh, worked in a Wal-Mart. In Amarillo." She dropped her gaze.

"Cheryl Vroman, lawyer, San Francisco." Her heavy-lidded eyes gazed from under a tangle of light hair.

"A-Alisa Bardnoth, I work as a secretary in a church in Stratford, Texas. My husband was fishing. I didn't go." She rubbed her cheek, looked away.

"So, that's everyone," Linda said. "Pretty diverse group."

"Random selection," Perry said.

"Not that random," Aaron said. "No children, yet I remember some children in the ship with us."

"Good point," Tom said. "Also I just noticed another odd detail: It's almost evenly split between male and female. There's one extra man. I wonder how long they had to wait before they got that mix?"

"But like the gentlemen pointed out, there's very few other races here," Linda said. "Two, I believe, if you don't count the Anglos."

"Perhaps they don't consider race," Tom said. "I can imagine them not even dividing us into separate racial groups. To them, we're all alike, the way the six on the ship looked alike to us. The makeup of the group is balanced in the only aspect they saw as important: gender. Although"—he rubbed his forehead—"they might not have realized another division, that of homosexuality. I speak from personal experience. I am gay." He looked around. "Anyone else?"

No one spoke.

"Another minority represented," Pete said.

"If you remove the gay from the mix, you have an even balance in gender," Eddie said.

"I hadn't thought of that," Tom said. "I wonder if it's possible."

"How could they know?" Cheryl said.

The conversation took a surrealistic turn for Aaron. He could see sixteen children chatting around a low table. All they needed were large sheets of blank paper and lots of colorful Crayons and they could begin work on a project some adult would have in mind. Instead, words coming out of the child-sized mouths went far beyond coloring, or TV, or school.

"—what now?" Pete was saying. "I have two kids to feed. I can't just abandon them."

"That, in a nutshell, is our main problem," Tom said. "Ever since the Holn left, we've been at the mercy of the big folk. Simply because, as Linda pointed out, we're too small and weak to fight back. When do we get out of here? Not until they—whoever *they* are—decide what *we* are. And whether we pose a security risk to the country—or the world."

"How can we be?" Linda said. "We're the same people we were before. Just a little smaller."

"Against all the rules of nature and God," Tom said. "If we were true adults, we have no business being children again. What are the implications of that? Myra?"

"I don't know. It would have to be debated among the elders of the church."

"You could lose your family," Perry said.

"I-I know," Myra said, biting her lip. She looked down at her lap, close to tears, it seemed to Aaron.

"Cheryl, what about the legal end?" Jerry asked.

She made a wry smile. "You've heard of the proverbial can of worms? From a strictly legal standpoint, I'd say this constitutes a proverbial supertanker of worms."

"There's nothing wrong with their rationality," the sharp-faced woman said, tapping the rear side of the mirror window lightly. "Especially that lawyer. She shows no signs of incompetency to me."

"Their rationality has not been in question." As soon as Miranda had met Radmilla Everett, warning flags had gone up in her mind. "All show ability to reason, handle problems, comprehend reading material, and so forth. And all at levels higher than suggested by their physical bodies."

The woman turned from the window-mirror Aaron Fairfax had guessed researchers lurked behind.

"I had been led to understand their mental faculties had been impaired, that some were babbling idiots."

"That was started by one of the tabloid television shows," Olive Greenlea said crisply, looking over the tops of her half-glasses. "Some rumors, however, have a grain of truth in them, even that one." She stepped over to the window.

"There's no reason to get snotty," Radmilla said.

"Dr. Greenlea is distressed by the lies and rumors flying all over the media, and I agree with her," Miranda said. "If you are interested, if you have been told to be interested in this, then I suggest you be open less to the rumors and more open to the facts as we find them."

Radmilla gazed at Miranda for a moment, dim room hiding most of her expression. "Look, all I'm after is to ensure these children receive the best care, and that their rights are guarded. That is the charge I've received from Secretary Fletcher. The eventual goal, of course, is to return them to their families as quickly as possible."

"And if they turn out not to be children, what then?"

"Excuse me?"

"If these people turn out to be who they claim to be, what will your recommendation be?" Miranda shrugged. "Perhaps you could hire Ms. Vroman to help you sort it out."

"I see. Please continue, Dr. Greenlea."

Olive gazed out at the group for another moment. "What you see is the calm after the storm. Right now, the individuals are finding strength in each other. In fact, we brought two of them together early yesterday, the married couple on the far side, Mr. and Ms. Rithen. He was surly and uncooperative, she distressed and belligerent. Together, they're calm, cooperative and even show flashes of humor."

She consulted her notebook screen. "Their observed responses to the situation they're in are the sources of the wild speculations about their mental states. Disbelief, of course, colors everything. Also anger, which has ranged from screaming fits to belligerency to violence. Mr. Stangle yelled invectives at the medical staff and threw anything he could get his hands on. Mr. Thompson went on a rampage in both hospitals, throwing items around, breaking glass, upsetting furniture, tearing curtains off the windows. He misjudged his current size and strength when he tried to lift a television with the intent, we believe, of hurling it through a window. The result was severe muscle strain. Mr. Romplin also targeted the medical staff, sometimes being cooperative to a point, then punching and kicking when he assumed we weren't prepared.

"Shock has been another main response, such as Ms. Caulfield, who curled up into a fetal position for three days and sucked her thumb, and Ms. Bardnoth, who has wept nearly constantly since the tenth. Ms. Yolbin tore her bedsheets into strips, and refused to eat or take baths. Both of the latter behaviors have faded, fortunately. Mr. Aragon spoke only in Spanish, mostly obscenities, for most of the first three days. Then he asked for and received a Bible. He apologized for his behavior and has spent the rest of the time reading that Bible. Ms. Caslon has wept quite a bit, not over her condition, but over her family. She also has spent much time praying and reading the Book of Mormon."

Olive removed her glasses, rubbed the bridge of her nose, put the glasses back on. "Other responses include passive behavior, such as Ms. Mellinfield, who would just lie unmoving as the medical procedures were done. She does not move around much when left alone. Mr. Coner, however, has passive resistance down to an art. As soon as medical staffers would enter his room, he'd go completely flaccid. The staff had to lift him into a wheelchair or onto an examination table. One staffer said he'd had better responses from sacks of potatoes. Mr. Cathen was the exact opposite. He asked many questions about the test results and submitted to every test we requested without complaint but with insatiable curiosity. Overcooperative, if that's possible. Ms. Vroman hid under the bed the first few days, but took to wrapping herself tightly in the bedsheets and blanket. A couple of times we had to cut the cloth away. The calm persona you see here has manifested itself only in the last eighteen hours."

Miranda stepped up to the window. "And the three there, the ones closest to us?"

Olive looked at her over the tops of the glasses. "Ms. Athlington displayed no overt emotion, no physical reaction. She showed curiosity about her situation, taking time to examine herself in the mirror, an activity almost all of the others avoided. She seems to be the most introspective of the group." Her glance returned to the screen. "Mr. Fairfax also has been subdued, although he has wept quietly several times. He paces his room constantly."

Miranda nodded. "And Mr. Othberg?"

"Mr. Othberg." Olive's lips shaped into a slight smile. "Mr. Othberg has been somewhat mischievous lately."

"There's a shady table over there." Earl gestured at a round metal table with glass top surrounded by four white-painted metal chairs. The branches of an elm tree stretched over it, blocking bright sun. Earl, Aaron, and Marian each sat down at the table after much pushing and scraping of chairs.

"Everything's so damn big now," Marian muttered as she tried to find a comfortable position.

"They're probably still watching or listening," Aaron said.

"My, my, trusting soul, aren't we?" Marian brushed a long lock of hair back.

"We are dealing with government nincompoops, you know."

Earl leaned forward. "Just for the record," he said,

ducking below the tabletop, "and for any hidden microphones," he turned, spoke close to his chair back.
"Aaron Lee Fairfax, who owns a Maserati, said that. Me,
I'm just," he turned toward a *piñon* tree growing not far
from them, "an average Joe, smiling and waving at the
hidden cameras." He did both in the direction of the
tree.

Marian and Aaron chuckled, and when that died, all
three cast glances at each other.

"Why us?" Marian finally said.

Earl shrugged. "Maybe we said something to offend
them."

"Seems to me they'd be offended by that tent city at
the base of the ship," Aaron said, running a finger across
the glass tabletop. "There was some weird stuff going on.
I thought I'd time-warped to Woodstock or something."

Electronic music competed with sitar and African
chants as Aaron had approached the booths and trailers,
some of which had been around long enough to have
grass and wildflowers growing underneath. The June sun
beat down on him out of a cloudless sky. He'd had to
walk through an unpaved parking lot, and his dark-
brown shoes had turned grayish-white under a coat of
dust. (And yet, later, he would remember their shine as
they sat side-by-side on the ground.)

He barely glanced at a painting of a Holn standing at
the edge of a cliff above a group of nude humans, all
reaching upward to catch the light rays emanating from
the creature. However, a hefty chunk of smoky quartz
nearly a foot high in the next booth caught his eye. As he
turned it so the light reflected off the facets, a scrawny,
shirtless man approached, faded denim pants seemingly
hanging on the man's pelvic bone.

"It's the best chunk I've seen in a long time, man." He
pushed back his long, stringy hair. A matching beard fell
from his lower face to mid-chest.

"I agree."

"The energy vibes from the Holn ship have turned it this lovely color. It was clear when I brought it—"

"Bullshit," Aaron snapped. "It got smoky from being near a radioactive source."

A grin split the beard. "Yeah, OK, you know why it turned smoky, and I know why, but some people, man, just go ozone when they hear that. They think the thing'll mutate them."

"Well, I didn't come to buy crystals," he said, setting it down. "I came to visit the Holn."

"Yeah, go ahead, man. You need to do that. I'll hold it until you get done. Here's my card."

The Astral Dance, Sedona, Arizona, the silver-ink-on-blue card said, *Argon Donnell, prop.*

"Maybe the vibes'll add some more color while you're in there." Another grin.

Back in the courtyard, Marian stirred. "And you never saw the quartz guy again."

"Nope. Lost his card, too. It wasn't with my stuff when they gave it back. He'd probably be tickled to think the Holn still might have it."

"I came up the other side," she said. "Got stuck parking pretty far away, too. I was wondering what the hell was going on."

"Of course it's the last of the days, honey, it's in the Bible." The obese woman had sat on a tiny chair, knitting, folds of dress draped over her like a collapsed tent.

"The Bible doesn't say anything about visits from extraterrestrials."

"It does if they're devils."

"Or angels." That from a thin woman stepping through a curtain. "Soon the Holn will throw off their disguises and reveal their true selves as radiant angels.

Gabriel might even blow his trumpet from right on top of that space ship."

"I see."

"Devils or angels, we will soon know," the knitter said without looking up. "The end of the world is near and the Thousand-year Reign of Christ begins. Those who believe, who have always believed, will be taken up in the Rapture."

Marian moved on, finding only a few things of interest. In one booth watched over by a thin youth with a shaved head, a large, vivid painting depicted three slavering Holn-caricatures watching a fourth deftly strap a screaming, nearly-nude young blond woman down onto a table with one pair of tentacles while using a single tentacle to rip what was left of her shorts off and yet another to fondle a voluptuous breast. Marian had to leave quickly before she burst out laughing.

As she walked by the last booth she heard a man in a maroon beret over shorn hair, a green T-shirt that barely hid a mass of body hair, and the ubiquitous camo pants tell a rapt elderly couple, "When the time comes, this side of the road will be the first line of defense. We'll let the Holn have the space cases over there on the other side of the DMZ. It'll distract them while we establish a defense perimeter."

"Didn't buy anything from the guy?" Aaron said, still running his finger across the surface of the table.

"Ugh, no." Marian said.

"I didn't see any of that stuff," Earl said. " 'Cause I was handicapped, my taxi driver was allowed to drive me right to the Holn door. I mean, I saw the booths and stuff, but only through the windows. Never got a chance to see the charming denizens close up."

Aaron shifted in his chair. "Well, I'm sorry, it didn't look like a space ship."

In three minds, the image had to have been the same: The odd truncated flat-sided cylinder looming behind the "crew cabin" squatting on the ground in front, both with a dull finish of flat gray, but not metallic.

"I thought it looked like a hot dog stand, or a pizza place," Marian said. "The little part, in front."

The engine array stood five stories; the cabin two.

"Handicapped accessible," Earl said. "Easy on us old goats."

Marian stretched, shoved a lock of wayward hair aside. "I remember seeing Linda Rithen talking, I assume to her husband. Over by the comet display, discussing the merits of artificial turf on golf courses."

"I suppose all the group had come in by then," Aaron said. "Plus a few others, remember? The pregnant woman, for instance, and those three black kids."

"I remember seeing that woman on TV later, really agitated because of her narrow escape," Marian said. "'What would they have done to my baby?' she kept saying over and over."

Aaron turned to her. "Nothing. The Holn had no intention of taking her, or any of those kids. Don't you see? If we had left before the pregnant lady or those kids, we would not have been captured. She left, the kids left, and boom!"

"I remember you, too, Earl," Marian said softly. "You were—" She suddenly burst into laughter. "I was going to say, you were a completely different man then."

Earl and Aaron also laughed. "Ain't that the damn truth. Boy." He laughed again. "More than you know. I remember you, too. That kid in the glowing orange shorts bumped me and made me lose balance. I would have fallen on my fanny if you hadn't been there to catch me. You scared the hell out of me."

"I almost fell myself. I guess I yelped—"

"That's not what I meant. You were young, and, oh, man, so lovely—"

"I wa—am forty-one, Earl."

"So? I was almost forty when you were born. You were young to me, lady, young and beautiful. And I was positive young and beautiful women wanted no part of me. Old, and sick, and crippled, and dying, piece by piece."

Earl sat quietly looking at his hands. He was taking deep breaths and moisture rimmed his eyes.

"If I told you life was over for me, you might think I was just exaggerating. At seventy-nine years, it was a pretty good chunk. But now it was all behind me, and in front was just more pain and misery. I saw my wife and son die in a stupid car crash. First the arthritis, hobbling both knees, I couldn't walk, sit down, do anything without pain. Then the cancer came and they took my bladder out, and put in a new artificial replacement. Risky, they said, 'cause it was experimental, but what the hell, I was old and it really didn't matter if it failed, it would at least give my suffering a noble purpose. There was still a hole, though, plugged with a valve I had to operate by hand, so I couldn't pee like normal people did. It wasn't so bad I guess, but . . . never mind. Just another step toward putrefaction. I was rotting away like all the other near-dead corpses in the home. I'd had enough. If the Reaper wanted to come, then let him come, he wouldn't get any static from me." He clenched his teeth and uttered a strange noise.

"Earl—" Aaron started.

"No, no," he said with a quick snap of his head, causing strands of hair to fall across his brow. "Mark Twain called them the 'jimjams' and I get them every time I think about my life until June 10."

"Where did you live?" Marian asked.

"Oh, uh, Wisconsin."

"And you came all the way down here? In your condition? Why?"

Earl leaned back, but slipped and thumped against the chair back. He laughed softly. "Still not used to my new size.

"The one thing that snagged my interest during all of this bladder stuff was the Holn, the alien ship that landed in New Mexico, a place I'd never been. The operation took place soon after the ship landed, and I just devoured the news. I became obsessed with learning everything I could. I'm stubborn and singleminded. I glom onto something and I won't let go. This time it was worse. I limped out of the nursing home—without telling them where I was going—into a cab and onto a plane and found a cab driver at the Albuquerque airport willing to take me directly to the site. No hotel reservation, I'd get one later. I just wanted to get to the site before someone came after me."

He ran a hand through his thick hair, looked first at Marian, then at Aaron, who sat transfixed. "Did I have mystical calling to come? No. I just wanted to see the ship, walk on the ship, touch the interstellar spacecraft before I became too feeble to move. My first reservation was for the day after I actually came, but the airline called and said I'd save three hundred dollars if I went right away. The hell with the money, I just wanted to get here. And five minutes, *five minutes,* later and the ship's doors would have shut and I'd of been left outside."

He looked at Aaron.

"After the Holn left, they found the clothes I had worn—shoes, socks, pants, underwear, everything—in a neat little stack on top of the suitcase I'd brought. And nothing was missing from that. What they did not find, though, was my fake damn bladder and the valves and tubes. I have this picture of it on display in the Holn ship with a sign saying 'A Sample of Primitive Human Medicine.'" He laughed out loud, turned to Marian. "Fell out of bed this morning. Misjudged the size of the bed and the size of my body and just tumbled out, whump. A few weeks ago, that would have meant lying in a heap, cursing the pain, perhaps leaking from a bent pee valve. Instead, I leaped back onto the bed and started jumping up and down on it. The nurse caught me—and scolded me." He laughed again, a long laugh that echoed off the concrete around them.

"Mister Othberg," Aaron said in a falsetto voice, "you're acting like a child."

Earl whooped with laughter; Aaron couldn't stop himself from grinning as the red-haired . . . "boy" . . . leaped up, ran and jumped over a bush in the center garden, turned quickly on his heel and jumped back. Heads turned to watch as he jumped over another, then a rock, whooping and laughing, then he returned to the table.

"Aaron, Marian," Earl said, one hand on a shoulder of each, flushed face turning from one to the other, "at this point, I am not really concerned with what happens next. I don't even care if we ever grow up again." He ran both hands through his hair, emitting a half-laugh, half-sob. "Right now, right at this moment, I am whole again, I am lithe again, I am mobile again. And I love it. *Love* it."

Four

June 20

"You always were the one to cause problems." Arlene Bermond stood arms crossed just left of the exact center of the room, a bear in a cave.

"You think I asked for this?" Marian looked up and found herself once again a little girl under the stern gaze of the big sister. Looming as she always did in her mind—except now Arlene *was* huge, a physical confirmation of the mental picture.

"You couldn't have done better if you had planned it. Right at a critical junction in my life you come along with this and throw everything out of whack."

"For God's sake, Arlene." Marian stood up, to no advantage. "I did not—this, this . . . just happened."

"Just happened," Arlene snorted. She dropped her arms and stepped toward a wall. The straight blue skirt falling to her ankles made her figure almost a solid mass. "Nothing 'just happens,' dear sister. Everything has a reason—I've told you that a thousand times. You consciously decided to go see this thing. Probably another whim." She let out a long sigh. "You are so irresponsible."

Marian felt a flush grow on her cheeks. "I have not

43

bothered you for twelve years. I would not bother you
now except for . . . for this."

"Oh, you'd think of something." Arlene adjusted her
glasses. "Christ, Marian, what am I supposed to do
now?"

"There's been some suggestions we should be released
to the custody of our closest relatives—"

"Custody?" The word flew out like a chicken bone
suddenly freed from her throat. "I'm supposed to take
custody of you? Blast, Marian, I am in no mood for you
again. I've just got Micah at home, I'm about to see him
off to college, and Faith and Daniel are off on their own.
The farm is clicking along very nicely, thank you, after
years of sweat and meticulous planning. And now you
want to throw *this* wrench into the works."

Marian fought to keep the tears back. "I can't hold a
job this way. I can't drive a car, I probably won't be able
to buy a beer. I don't think the government, or somebody, is going to let me live by myself. I need your help.
It won't be like raising a child. I won't need
schooling—"

"I heard the scientists haven't decided on that. And if
you don't go to school, that means you'll be underfoot
and in the way. You can't drive a car, you can't drive a
tractor." Reflections on Arlene's glasses blocked any
view of the eyes that regarded her. "For the love of
Christ, Marian, why did you have to go into that space
ship?"

She looked at the floor again. "I was . . . curious."

Arlene snorted. "Curious."

"Look, I have some money saved, not a lot, but
enough to ease a financial burden on you. For a while,
until we can figure something out—"

"We have to figure something out damned quick. Too
many details are waiting for me at the farm."

"Please, Arlene. I need your help."

Her sister continued to glare down at Marian, feet
planted, arms crossed again.

I'm an adult. I do not need to fear her.

"Yes," Arlene said. "I'm going to have to figure something out very quickly."

When the door began to open, Aaron had to quash a wild impulse to hide, or to seek a better spot to stand on, or lie down on, or sit on, or lean against; perhaps he should strike a cool pose and act nonchalant. Instead, he rooted himself to the spot next to the bed. He faced the door and hoped the panic in his head was not molding the muscles in his face.

Janessa wore a light white skirt, slightly pink blouse, and white jacket. The ensemble was cool and summery. She stopped short when she first saw him and stared a second. Then she deliberately shut the door and walked slowly to a chair opposite and sat down in a careful sweeping motion. She crossed her legs and regarded him a moment, clicking some keys together and tapping the air with the suspended foot.

"Your hairline has advanced," she said finally.

"Uh, yeah." He ran a hand through it. "Don't know how long I'll be able to keep it, though."

She smiled slightly. "I—" She shifted position. "The divorce proceedings have been put on hold."

"Yes, I imagine this complicates things."

"What am I supposed to do?"

Aaron stepped over to a chair and pushed himself backward into it. "I don't think there's much you can do. Under the circumstances, I think the divorce should proceed, but on different grounds. 'Incompatibility' could be a good generic term." He scratched a cheek. "I wouldn't think you'd want to stay married to a child."

"Are you, uh—"

Aaron shook his head. "The scientists and doctors keep hedging, but I'm pretty sure I know who I am in this child's body. A prepubescent child's body, as they say on TV. I can't respond to certain stimuli. I've, um, tried."

She straightened. "I guess that leaves the division of property, then. What will you do after?"

"Hope that dear sister Adrienne still has a spare room. And a bit of patience for notoriety. I'm famous, you know."

She grimaced. "Don't I. Ever since the news broke that you were among the Group of Seventeen, my phone has rung off the wall. I had to hire private security to keep the property clear."

He got up and went to the window. Outside, Earl was walking with a man with red hair, although a much more subdued hue. "One thing you need to remember as you proceed, Janessa. While I have the body of a child and will be unable to satisfy some basic lusts, I still have pretty much the mind of my adult self and remember many things. Don't think you can pull anything over on me. I'll be watching every sticky move you make."

He heard a long exhale of breath. "Out of the mouths of babes. We'll see—"

He turned and faced her. Because she was sitting down, it was easier to look directly at her. "Christ almighty, I always knew you were a cool babe, but will you look at me? Something has happened to me, something fairly traumatic. No 'How are you? Are you in pain? Can I get you anything?' Has emotion and caring hardened in you that much?"

She didn't answer, but the keys did stop clicking.

"I'm not sure yet whether I should be afraid of you."

Earl smiled. "Your father always said I got all the genes to match the hair. I guess that should tell you something."

The man stretched out on a bench. Walter Othberg turned out to be as restless as Earl, so by mutual agreement they had gone back into the courtyard.

"Dad seemed to have taken the advice seriously. When you came over, he'd hide his prize ceramics."

Earl snorted. "I know. I'd planned to break one just

out of spite, but your father up and moved all of you to Hawaii."

"Mother wasn't in favor of the move, but it turned out OK in the end."

"Still live there?"

"Yes. On Maui."

"Near a beach?"

"We're surrounded by them."

"Hmmm. Still want to take me in?"

"We made up our minds to do so if the decision goes that way. Just give us a little slack. My youngest child is eight, you know. He's going to have a hard time accepting that you're his Granduncle Earl."

"*I* still have trouble accepting I'm Granduncle Earl."

Walter Othberg studied his uncle a moment. "Why did you go, Uncle Earl? Cousin Dora said your health was failing. What made you just leave the nursing home and fly down here on your own?"

Earl met the gaze of the tall man. "Something my father used to tell me. Never give up assimilating what's around you, he'd say. Never stop looking, observing, always be curious about the world and what's going on. Once I got into the habit, it was hard to break. One day I said the hell with it—I was going to see the ship from space before I die." He shrugged. "The rest is history."

He stood up, faced Walter, clasped his hands behind his back and rocked on his feet. "An interesting turn of events, don't you think?"

In the hallway, Aaron leaned against the wall just outside of the door to the room. Janessa remained inside, intractable both in spirit and chair. Love and respect had been draining out of the marriage for years, slowly, like sap oozing through a gash. He still couldn't believe what had happened to him; he still waited for the alarm clock to ring and end the nightmare. Divorce— yes, a certainty now, he didn't expect her to keep this marriage. But, Christ. . : .

He let himself slide down the wall until his butt hit the floor. *What makes a woman change like that? I was in love with her once.* Or perhaps blinded by it—or the milk-white breasts and shapely thighs. *So I couldn't see the real aspects of her character. Oh, hell.*

A noise echoing down the hall caused him to look up. A man in his early thirties walked quickly toward him; the first thing Aaron noticed was how bald the man was. As he approached, though, Aaron saw the man's eyes staring straight ahead. One hand dragged a crying little girl of about five, the other arm supported a boy of about two, not crying, but little face creased with confusion. The man half-ran by Aaron, even though at any second the girl could lose her footing. Figures in white intercepted the trio, and two other people Aaron recognized as psychiatrists stepped forward quickly. After several gestures and gentle prodding, the man allowed himself to be led away. Two of the white-clads hurried down the hallway and entered the room where the man had come out.

Someone's reunion didn't go well.

He ignored more scurrying in the hallway as he studied the pattern in the tile floor. After a moment of this, he heard the sound of cloth sliding against cloth. He looked up to see a woman squatting next to him—not an -iatrist, this one, but an -ologist.

"Are you having problems, Mr. Fairfax?"

" 'Fraid so."

"Would you like for me to talk to her?"

"I don't know if there's anything you can do, but yes, I would like you to do that."

"Certainly. I'll be back." She stood.

"I'll be here," he said as the door closed behind her.

He decided to move, though, got up and went back out to the courtyard. Earl was gone, but Aaron saw Tom leaning with one arm against a rock sculpture, head down.

Aaron stepped up to him. "All right?"

Tom looked up with moist eyes. He nodded, then took several deep breaths.

"I'm emotionally wracked, that's all. My spouse refuses to listen to me. I don't want him burdened with this. It's bad enough being gay, but now it'll be worse with what looks like a boy in the house."

"Didn't you say you were from California?" Aaron perched on the edge of a low wall. "I thought that state passed a cohabitation law."

"Oh, yes." Tom rubbed his jaw, then looked at his hand. "Huh. I keep forgetting I don't have a beard anymore. Anyway, yes, you're right, and Mark and I had ourselves declared married cohabitants. But the law does not change eons of prejudice. And you know us fags. Always on the lookout for sweet young boys to seduce into our perverted lifestyle." He extended his arms. "And I *look* like a boy. There's trouble ahead. So what does Mark say? 'We'll bar the door together.'" He shook his head again. "And you?"

Aaron grimaced. "Dr. Wellborn is at this moment speaking to Janessa. She'll need a sledgehammer to break through that woman's indifference."

"Indifference? Even after all this?"

"Indifference before, indifference after. All this does is give her a chance to speed up the divorce." Aaron shrugged.

"Hard to believe," Tom said almost to himself. He dug his hands into the jeans pockets and bounced on his toes. He closed his eyes. Aaron thought he saw tears. He walked over to Tom.

"What is it?"

"I'm scared, Aaron. I had a pretty good life. I was in love, and I was loved in return. We're still in love, we're pretty sure, but we cannot do a thing about it. We're too frightened to even touch each other."

He turned, took two steps, turned back.

"But that's not the worst of it. I have my tonsils back. A scar on my leg from a hiking accident is gone. What else did they fix? What did they do to my brain?"

He stepped close to Aaron. "Don't you see? What if they 'fixed' my homosexuality, just took it right out of me the way the pediatrician yanked out my tonsils?"

He stepped back, gestured with his arms.

"What if I am incapable of returning Mark's love?"

"The seventeen people who had been caught in the Holn ship, the so-called Group of Seventeen, are the center of hearings by a special three-judge panel made up of two federal judges and one Supreme Court justice as chairperson, appointed last week by the U.S. Attorney General. Discussions today are preliminary because, first, the scientific task force has not yet made any conclusions about who these people are, and second, no one is sure who speaks for the seventeen. Health and Human Services attorneys presented arguments that the federal government could and should represent the interests of the individuals. Justice Alger Alden said that was patently absurd because—and he pointed to the empty table across from the government attorneys—no other party was present to offer counterarguments. The judges ordered the government to expedite the sorting out of the problem. Meanwhile, they did accept briefs that review the arguments that could come up in relation to the children. Avram Rolstein, administrator for the Holn Effect Task Force, said today his panel was not yet ready to theorize about the children's status.

"Meanwhile, although most officials connected with the Holn Effect Task Force are remaining mum, CNN has learned from inside sources that attorneys who won visiting rights for families of the Group of Seventeen have already petitioned the Alden Commission to release the children into the custody of their loved ones. A spokesman for the Holn Effect Task Force says release of any of the group is premature. However, as one woman, a

relative of one of the children and who asked not to be named, put it, whole lifetimes have been thrown right out of kilter and they need to start rebuilding shattered lives.

"In other words, confusion reigns as the common denominator in all aspects dealing with the Group of Seventeen.

"Rolf Treadwell, CNN, Washington."

"The religious world is in ferment over the evident disagreement over the significance of the Group of Seventeen between Reverend Lakewood van Kellin of the Church of Encompassing Faith in Magnolia Springs, Tennessee, and Reverend Jim Brigman, pastor of the Faith Christ Evangelical Ministry of Waterhaven, Oklahoma. Both ministers announced to their flocks today that they spent the last three days in isolation, praying and fasting—Reverend van Kellin in his soaring glass cathedral and Reverend Brigman at the top of his spire. However, they came to radically different conclusions.

"This is the word from Reverend van Kellin:"

"The Lord says those aliens do not know His glory and have placed among us homunculi that look like human children, sound like human children, but they are not human children. They are agents of a great evil, an evil that seeks to turn us away from the Resurrection, the Life Eternal, and accept a false god and false religion the like we have never seen before."

"Meanwhile, across Interstate 40 in Oklahoma, the Reverend Brigman had this to say:"

"These seventeen people, these children, are messengers of hope. They are messengers of life. They are messengers of faith. The Lord our God has sent them to enlighten us, to aid us on our journey. They are Angels, my friends, come to enrapture the faithful and gather us into God's bosom, to teach us how to become like them, like children, God's messengers."

"Asked about this apparent dichotomy, Reverend van Kellin blamed the secular media."

"It is just another pathetic example of the left-leaning media reporting what they want to hear, not what they actually heard."

"Reverend Brigman was a little more circumspect."

"I am sure we can reconcile these differences, if any really do exist. I have not heard Brother van Kellin's statement myself and I really doubt the veracity of what I have heard through secondhand sources so far."

"What do you think? Is the Group of Seventeen made up of devils or angels? Let us know. Call the number on the screen, then press one-asterisk if you think the children are devils, or two-asterisk if you think the children are angels. Results will be announced on News-Overnight, ten P.M. Eastern Daylight, nine P.M. Central.

"This is Hope GoForth, CNN Religion Today, Waterhaven, Oklahoma."

Five

August 14

"Are these folks children or not? Are they the missing people?"

From the podium, Miranda Sena could not see the face of the reporter who had asked that question. Too many faces packed the Sandia labs auditorium, too much glare from the forest of TV lights. She stood alone, although other members of the task force sat at a long table to her left. She sighed inwardly and poured ice water into a glass from a pitcher on the table. She had worn the wrong clothes for this task; the dark suit sucked in the heat from the TV lights like a sponge.

"As I have said, we are willing to say they are the essence of the missing people. They retain all memories of their past lives, all memories of their families, their childhoods, the schools they attended, the cars they drove, the jobs they had. The memories are complete in the sense that long-term memory is selective where only bits and pieces are recalled and a spouse or parent has to fill in the missing pieces. This is normal in a human mind. It can retain only so much. If every chi-person in the group could remember every little detail about their lives, we would be suspicious. To reiterate: Yes, the individuals in this group are the missing adults, in a different form—"

"Are they human?" She didn't see the questioner on that one, either, but she didn't need to: Allan Goth, commentator/reporter for one of the Christian networks whose voice was heard by ten million people daily (he said).

"In many physiological terms, yes," she said, noting in a corner of her mind the cold of the water glass against her palm. "The trouble is, those systems are not at the point they should be in terms of chronological age. Every physiological system—endocrine, digestive, cardiopulmonary, reproductive—has regressed, or has been regressed, to the developmental stage of about a nine-year-old—no younger than eight, no older than ten. This includes sexual organs, which are now in prepubescent states. All but one of the women had had sexual relations pre-incident, and their hymens have not been replaced, but that's a poor indicator anyway. Circumcised men have not had foreskins replaced. In all other aspects, however, signs of sexual intercourse and childbirth have been eliminated, including secondary sexual characteristics—beards, pubic hair, some muscle development. No wrinkles, no scars, no moles, no acne, no blemishes of any kind. Better than newborn babies, even. Vision for each is rated at 20/20 or better, so none need glasses or contact lenses anymore." She sipped some water.

"Some of the factors do not match completely what you would expect to find in a nine-year-old child. Tonsils removed from ten of the people have been restored, but appendices removed from four of the seventeen have not. This seems to suggest the Holn couldn't find a use for the appendix, either." She was surprised at the low laughter that greeted that remark.

"What about the thymus?" The question came from a Swedish medical reporter Miranda knew only by accent.

"Good question. The thymus is one of two main

factors showing no differentiation. The gland in each of the seventeen remains shrunken as we would expect in adults, although the tissue itself has been devolved back to the lymphoid type instead of the fat cells of maturity. T-cell production is at the balance required, with lymphocyte production nominal. Some numbers show the immune system response perhaps a little sharper, a little more aggressive, but we still aren't—"

"The bones! Why don't you ask about the bones?" The shout came from a man with thick gray hair and mustache at the opposite end of the table: Dr. Samuel Innes, at last showing up as a member of the task force.

"What about the bones?" an AP reporter asked.

"Ask her, ask her."

"Dr. Sena?"

"Well, the bones are smaller—"

"Piffle!" Dr. Innes exploded. The lenses and faces turned away from her to him. "Science fiction! Fantasy! You cannot shrink bones and maintain integrity! You cannot scale back a femur and expect it to function. It is impossible! You cannot change an adult into a child!"

"Dr. Sena?" The lenses and faces swung back.

"Not only are the bones smaller, they have changed form." She deliberately refrained from looking at Dr. Innes. "In babies, bones are mostly cartilage, soft material, because a growing human needs flexibility. Cartilage turns to bone gradually as a child grows. Final ossification doesn't start until maturity, when the body reaches full height. In these seventeen people, the bones are cartilage where we would expect it: at the ends of the long bones, for instance, and in the fingers. The sacral vertebrae have been separated into the individual bones of childhood. Plus, the ends of the ribs where they meet the sternum are cartilage again. The sternum itself—the breastbone—is nearly the last bone to stop growing and ossify. Careful examination shows this bone, this large, protective structure, has been renewed into flexible cartilage with the potential for regrowth. Even the fontanelles, the seams in the skull that allow a brain to grow, show the flexibility we lose as adults."

"That is amazing. Really amazing." Dr. Innes began the statement glaring at her, but as the lenses and faces again focused on him, he turned in their direction. "The Holn visited this planet for what, six years? And in those years, the suggestion goes, they learned enough about humans to turn some of us into children. This is outrageous! Why would they do such a thing in the first place? They never left the ship in all those years. For the love of God, will you people begin to look at this seriously? We don't know what we're dealing with here." Dr. Innes slowed to take a breath. Miranda surprised herself by jumping in.

"Actually, they did these people many favors." The focal point shifted back. "Other than the tonsils, a woman who had had her gall bladder removed now has it back, and a man has three toes back he lost in his first childhood. The most amazing case is the man who lost his bladder to cancer. Removal of the bladder often takes more than just that organ. Sometimes the prostate is removed or damaged so the patient becomes impotent. This man has it all back—his bladder, his prostate and all connecting tubes and vessels. And all organs are organic—no artificial material was used whatsoever. There's no sign the operation ever took place. We have not found anything artificial or mechanical in any of these bodies. Nothing exotic. All cells, all tissues, suggest human origin."

"Very miraculous. Very heartwarming, indeed," Dr. Innes said, and the focus swung again. "Have you pointed out that all of these children are exactly the same height? Fifty-two point one inches, four feet and a tad more than four inches, a hundred and thirty-two and a tad centimeters. And they all weigh within a few grams of each other. This suggests to me they were poured into molds like . . . like cookie-cutter kids."

"For what purpose?" asked Marinka Svoboda of CNN.

"To spy on us, maybe? To report on the condition of the planet to the mother ship as advance preparation for an invasion, perhaps?" Dr. Innes mopped his brow. "Or, more likely, to plant seeds that will grow like weeds and spread among the population until we humans have been replaced with—with whatever it is they left here. The important question, the *only* important question, is, are these people really human, do they think—"

"That question touches on the other factor I mentioned as seemingly unchanged: their brains." Miranda straightened, set down the glass and put both hands on the podium as eyes organic and inorganic swung back to her. "Let me tell you another thing about the gentleman who got his bladder back. As we age, our brains lose neural cells because those cells do not regenerate. By the time you're in your seventies, you might have lost five to twenty percent of these cells. This man is seventy-nine years old. However, PET, CT, MRI, MFM, and other scans show he has regained brain mass. *Regained* it. He has the brain of a nine-year-old, a young, healthy brain. What does this mean for him? A new life—"

Dr. Innes jumped to his feet. "Even more proof he's an alien—"

"I wish you would refrain from using that word." Miranda, staring directly at Dr. Innes, was testing her mother's axiom that a calm, steady voice could outshout a screamer. "We do not know for sure if these are their real bodies or something manufactured."

"*Are* they human?" Goth again. "Please answer the question. You have been talking like you believe these . . . these children are—have been the people who are missing. Will you state right now, before God and all these witnesses and the witnesses across America and the world, that you believe those people now inhabit childlike bodies?"

"I have come very close to saying that many times, I believe. The reason—"

"Will you state—"

"The reason," she said louder, "I don't say it outright is because I'm not sure yet. We have only two months' study so far, too soon to be taking rock-hard positions. That's one of the vexations of science. I can't make a flat statement like that until I study more evidence. However, I will say I'm leaning in that direction, barring evidence to the contrary."

"We have heard the reunions with families didn't go very well." The Svoboda woman again.

"What did you expect? Whatever else these people are, their physiologies have changed drastically. Some parents look younger than their children. Wives, husbands, suddenly find themselves married to children. Parents who had raised their children to adulthood are faced with the possibility of starting almost all over again. Yes, the reunions didn't go well, but some wild and deep emotions have been washing over those people. Actually, it's a bit encouraging that the emotional blowups weren't worse than they were."

"And what happens now?" Kinsea Lee of NBC shouted. "Are you going to release the group? If so, into whose custody?"

"That question hasn't been resolved yet. We on the task force would like to continue observation for a while longer, first to make sure each individual has recovered enough emotionally to handle the new situation, and second, to make sure there are no physiological difficulties that might crop up." Now *that's* a nice way of dancing around the central issue. "Plus, there's a raft of legal questions that have to be answered. Dr. Rolstein and I have been consulting with HHS attorneys who are reviewing the situation with the Alden Commission. As a personal view, I do not think it is wise to let them out into the mainstream just yet."

"Well, at least we agree on something," Dr. Innes said.

"We have too many questions as yet unanswered. And we don't know the long-term effects of the procedure, whatever procedure it was, on the psychological stability of each person. And we should isolate them anyway because they are aliens and should not be let loose into the general population."

"Are you suggesting they be kept locked away for the rest of their lives?" A CBS reporter asked.

"Not 'locked away,' certainly, but kept isolated, probably for a long time, until we can determine if they pose a threat to society. We should not let them breed with any humans, because, you see, that's how they'll eventually replace the human race. It would take hundreds of generations, but it would be inevitable."

"Dr. Sena, do you agree?"

"So far, though we haven't found evidence to suggest an alien physiology—"

"We haven't found anything to deny it, yet, either."

"True—"

"But the result, the organism we see as a result of the experiment, is an alien concept. A turning back of the biological clock? That goes against everything we've known about the workings of the universe, both in science and religion."

"You have to ask—" But Allan Goth cut her off.

"The fact that the main scientists of the task force disagree so sharply seems to show you know nothing and are floundering about—"

"And I can see from that statement, sir, you are totally ignorant of how science works." Miranda turned so she faced the direction of the voice. "It would be a lot more dangerous if we scientists sat up here in perfect harmony. Then there would be no information forthcoming because we would not consider any data or theories contrary to our stated position. The fact that Dr. Innes disagrees with me, and is not shy in saying so, is evidence that we are exploring every question, every angle possible because we are seeking truth. An egghead concept, I know, but that's the way science advances, that is the way we will advance. If for no other reason than those seventeen people whose lives have been turned upside down deserve the truth." She took a breath, let it out. "From the big folk who now control their destinies."

"Video Journal *captured this exclusive video of three of the Seventeen relaxing in a courtyard at an Albuquerque hospital. They have been identified as Perry Jerzy Stangle, by the tree, Sandra Denise Mellinfield and Edward Samuel Thompson. At the time these pictures were taken, they were eating lunch of grilled chicken, corn on the cob, a salad, and chocolate cake for dessert. A real child-pleaser.*

"Our source tells us that the one who calls himself Eddie Thompson also calls himself the 'token black,' and was fifty-two years old at the time of capture by the aliens. We also have learned that one of the so-called children is gay, but we haven't been able to identify him. Spokespersons for the Holn Effect Task Force say nothing is ready to be announced yet, but that something could be forthcoming soon.

"Video Journal will keep abreast of the latest developments, and as soon as we can get some more clandestine pictures, we'll damn sure show them to you."

Six

September 12

"I'm tired." Marian half-sat, half-fell into the chair.

Aaron looked up from the thinscreen. "Why? You haven't done a damn thing all day."

Marian fixed him with a glare.

"Oh, that's right, you were on the treadmill today."

"Yeah." She leaned back, letting her arms flop to her sides. "'A little faster, now, Marian, just a bit faster, thank you, please concentrate and breathe deeply, thank you, a bit faster now.' Linda was absolutely a hundred percent right. I want to slug 'em. So what torture did they have for you?"

Aaron grimaced, held up a hand with two bandaged fingertips. "Blood alley."

"Eeeeyew." Marian hugged herself. As bad as running the treadmill was, having fingers pricked and those huge needles shoved into an arm time after time was far worse. And this had been going on for three months.

"What'cha readin'?" She came around beside him as much to change the subject as to find out anything.

"New York Times." He pushed a button and the front page formed—minus about a third, as if someone had cut the lead article out. "The new news unfortunately was about us. So, naturally, they zapped it all out."

61

"Even with the hole, it's still strange to see a color photo in the *Times*," she said, picking up the thinscreen, the size, shape and weight of a standard print page. Marian touched the controls on the debit card-sized news cartridge and zoomed in on the photo, which showed a banner someone had draped on the Statue of Liberty.

" 'Free the Chunnel 7,' " she read. She looked at the gray hole. "I wonder what they're saying about us we don't need to know."

Aaron snorted. "Probably more crap. Cheryl says the censorship is one of the levers the lawyers are using to pry us free. I like having my bed made up every morning and all, but I feel like a prisoner."

"I suppose. But, Aaron, where do we go? You want to be released into your wife's custody?"

"I—" Aaron looked away. "I'd rather go with my sister. But she's out of touch in the depths of Alaska. They won't let me use the phone so I can't call her." He looked at her. "Where would you go? Your sister?"

"I'd rather be released to the custody of my cats." Marian closed her eyes. "I miss my cats. And I can't call Shirley to make sure they're all right—"

Aaron nudged her, pointed. Earl was walking slowly, barefoot, head down, face creased in a frown. She glanced at Aaron, then stepped over in front of Earl, who kept going until he bumped her. He looked up, startled.

"Penny for your thoughts," she said.

"I'll double her price."

"Still the big spender, eh?" Earl said to Aaron.

"You just look so deep in thought. Is something wrong?"

He looked directly at her a few seconds, then let out a half-laugh. "No. Just . . . puzzled, worried. I was thinking about, about something . . . when this memory intruded. I was eleven years old when I saw this . . . big, black locomotive chugging along, indistinct in shadow of the full Moon. In my mind I saw a monster, hulking, dark, forbidding—and yet pathetic. It was old, snuffling along, looking for morsels, too old and tired to chase me. I thought I could hear it weeping as it passed, forlorn and alone, looking for shelter, a place . . . a place to die." He crossed his arms, looked into the distance. "I was thinking about that tiny room again, the egg-shaped room of the Holn, the place of formless specters and soft rustlings. I saw shadows moving around me again, but they changed into this engine-shadow and the sounds of it cut through as sharp as a knife—why, with nearly eighty years of memories in my head, does that particular one suddenly spring to mind? It's so real, I can feel the rumble of the machinery, smell the smoke, taste the metallic tang of the air. They must have messed with my mind, stirred it up like a bowl of blue Jell-O—"

"Gosh," Marian said quickly, "they had trains when you were a kid?"

Earl looked at her.

"Probably hadda walk ten miles to school every day, too," Aaron said.

Earl moved his gaze to Aaron, who grinned.

"You young whippersnappers," Earl said in a quavering voice, waving a hand, "no respect for your elders. In my day, they'd of tanned me alive if I'd-a talked like that. Young hoodlums."

"That's all right, old man," Marian said, taking his arm, "come and have some tea. And tell us all about your boyhood."

"Aren't we lucky that an HDTV crew happened to be there when the Holn landed?" Ben Danthen gestured toward the wall monitor. "Otherwise, we wouldn't get to see the twelve-millionth replay."

Members of the task force were slipping into the other chairs in the conference room, some watching the commercial-station's replay. Miranda was already there,

half-listening to the conversation as she stared out of the
large picture window on the opposite wall where Sandia
Lab's namesake peaks rose in rugged splendor under an
intensely blue sky. She'd tried to sketch the scene, but
the lines on her notebook screen weren't taking the right
form.

Avram, across from Ben at the table, scraped his pipe.
"Believe me, no video in the world holds a candle to the
real thing."

"Oh, yeah." Ben sat up. "You were there. I never did
hear how that happened."

Avram shrugged. "Just another random event. My
eventual destination was the Santa Fe Institute, and my
wife and I used the trip as an excuse to take a leisurely
drive through the Southwest. Just as we came over the
top of this long hill, I saw something spitting fire in the
sky. Damn near drove under a big truck watching it."

On the screen, the ship split apart as the crew
section—and, later, museum—slid down the boosters
to ground level. "When we heard the ship had landed,
we asked where, and someone said some rangeland just
off Interstate 25 toward Waldo, New Mexico. Our next
question, of course, was, 'where's Waldo?'"

Avram and several eavesdroppers laughed. "I took the
nearest exit but it wasn't marked, so I didn't know the
name. I didn't have to drive very far to find the rather
astonished, and somewhat frightened, astronomy club,
watching that ship descend with gaping mouths." He
shook his head. "What a sight."

Constance leaned back in her chair. "I never quite
understood how one small group of people could get
them to land when all those government officials were
making all those grandiose plans."

"They lost patience, essentially," Ben said. "That's
what they said later. They were ready to land, but the
squabbling on the ground kept them orbiting a week.
With the exceptions of Iran, Saudi Arabia, Singapore,

Rwanda, and, for some reason, Wales, every country wanted the first alien contact to be on its soil. Our own government had prepared an elaborate site at Edwards Air Force Base where access could be controlled despite pleas from scientists, New Agers, UFO believers, science fiction writers, and the Dalai Lama. So, when that amateur astronomy club simply invited the Holn to land, they accepted. Much to the chagrin of everyone else."

"There's the traffic jam on I-25 just after," Orlando said, jerking a thumb at the TV.

"You mean the I-25 parking lot," Avram said. "I couldn't get my car out for a week."

"And then we had, of course, a Holn on the range."

"Ben, if you don't stop that, I'm going to swat you." The speaker was a dark blonde with thick shoulder-length hair cut in bangs across her forehead, long face and an overbite that put just a touch of lisp on her S's. She dropped a shoulder bag on the table and pulled out the chair next to his.

"Before you sit and swat, let me introduce you to Dr. Sena. This is Wanda Bettemeyer, your new liaison."

"Please, my name is Miranda." She stood to shake the other woman's hand. "Welcome to the pit."

Wanda smiled as she sat. "We were the center of the universe for a while. I guess it's your turn."

Miranda gave a small snort. "No thanks for that." She raised her voice. "All right, everyone seems to be here." She introduced Wanda. "We'll put her on the hot seat immediately."

"Well, the JPL gang loaded me down with all sorts of stuff. I sorted through it, and decided to start with the computers—"

"Does that have anything to do with us?" Dr. Innes said from his seat down near the end.

"We think it forms a base for Holn philosophy and biology," Wanda said, evidently not rattled by the interruption. "It has to do with the basic operating functions of their computers. Human-made computers use a binary system, ones and zeros, off or on, yes or no, male or female. The Holn have a trinary system: on, off, and neither on nor off. One, zero, neither one nor zero."

"Neutral," Lindsey suggested.

"In sense, yes, but maybe not. Hmm, I'll use Dr. Gottleib's metaphor of a computer—the machine itself as a whole. In one state, it's on, being used; in another state, it's off, not doing anything, just sitting there. According to the Holn, though, there's a third state, when it's no longer being used at all, as when it's obsolete. It can still function, but no one has a use for it because the programming or the hardware is no longer needed. That made things complicated. Neither side could make sense out of the other's computations because the systems are so different. Right now, there's only one human computer on Earth that can compute like a Holn machine. Sort of. Just up the road in Los Alamos. A polyglot affair, with boxes and wires and circuits all over the place. And frazzled programmers."

She studied her notebook screen a moment. "Now, I'd like to slip into biology," she said, tilting her body slightly as if actually prepared to do so."

She reached into the bag, pulled out several optical disks in cartridges and dropped them on the table. "The details are in these reports.

"Holn cells come in threes. They operate only as a triad; if just one is missing, the tri-cell does not work. In the center are their DNA connections. Now understand, I'm using the word DNA as a label, not a description. Holn structural molecules are different, forming different bases, but we call it DNA for simplicity. Where ours is a double-helix strand, theirs forms a triangle. A triangular helix? Anyhow, when you look at it end-on, it forms an equilateral triangle. Human DNA uses four molecular combinations to form the chain, the Holn chain uses six. With six basic molecules and three strands to connect to, think of the combinations possible."

Matt whistled. A couple of others let out their breaths. Even Dr. Innes raised an eyebrow.

"It gets more interesting." She pulled a glass toward her. Timothy poured water from a pitcher.

"Thanks." She drank half the glass. "Three cells, right? OK, in one cell is the DNA code from the father carried in the sperm, in another is the DNA code from the mother carried in the egg. The third is an amalgamation unique to the individual Holn. One question we have yet to solve, though, is in replication. The Holn cells lack mRNA. From what we can gather, replication is assisted by protein chains. The sticky part is those mama and papa cells. The way it looks now, they replicate exactly the same every time without the faults you'd expect from being zapped by errant gamma particles, say. The offspring cell, however, is subject to random errors.

"Anyhow," she said, still peering at the screen, "gestation is approximately twenty-six months, and one mother bears two young but they are not identical twins." She looked up. "Again, we run into this triad business. The embryos form in three discrete parts and join into one unit only after fourteen months. A child Holn reaches adult size in about eight years, but not adult maturity for another thirty to thirty-five years. However—and this might be a key—they are not gender specific. Primary and secondary sexual characteristics do not show up until maturity. Although the children have ninety-nine percent of the physiology of the adult, they do not know if they will be male or female until they reach their form of puberty. In other words, there are three parts to the whole: male, female, and neither male nor female."

Matt straightened. "On, off and neither on nor off."

"Precisely."

"So you're saying," Miranda said, looking up from the scribbles that were evolving slowly into the form of a

Holn, "they might have turned the human adults into children thinking they were studying a third and separate part of human culture."

"I don't think it can be discounted. This seems to suggest bias might have entered their studies, just as contemporary anthropologists sometimes let cultural bias creep into theories about earlier civilizations."

"I am puzzled about something," Dr. Innes said. "Dr. Danthen—"

"Ben."

"Ben, thank you, in one of your reports, you said no Holn came out of the ship and nothing was taken in. Is this possible for six years?"

"Yeah, we kept asking if they wanted anything, perhaps a snort of fresh ammonia, but they always declined. Said all they needed they had on board."

"Food?" Constance said.

"The Holn didn't eat, at least in our sense of sitting down and masticating bulk material. Refueling was more direct, nutrients in discrete packets." He shrugged. "Quantum eating, we dubbed it."

"Nothing was left at the site?" Matt said.

Ben waved hand. "Not a thing. And nothing entered or left the ship the whole time." He scratched his bearded chin. "Except the children."

"Did they take off and come back to leave the children?" Lindsey said.

"No," Wanda said. "The children were removed from the ship just before takeoff."

"An air horn or something started blasting about ten minutes before ignition." Ben shifted position. "And that sucker was loud, driving back the National Guard troops. Sometime during that period, the children were deposited in a depression well away from the ship's exhaust. How, when, we don't know. Nobody saw it. Any tracks left by tires or runners were obliterated by the rocket blast and later the trampling feet of the people at the site."

"What about before?" Dr. Innes said. "Just before they trapped the people inside, I mean."

Ben reached over to a flat notebook computer and pushed a button. The picture on the monitor switched from talking heads to a shot of the flat cabin. "Video from one of our surveillance cameras, this one pointed at the door of the museum. See that kid in the fluorescent orange shorts? He was the last human to get out before the door slammed shut. Indeed, in slow-mo, we can see the door slide right behind him, almost catching an ankle. Then the cabin immediately starts to rise, but it was halfway up the booster array before anyone realized there were still people—humans—inside. You can see some of the shouting and gesturing beginning here. Confusion quickly gave way to panic, mostly out of fear the ship was about to take off with them too close."

No one spoke as the cabin reached the top of the boosters and settled on top. "This is the way the ship sat for four days, June 5 to 9. The morning of June 10, they took off."

"Communications?" Miranda said.

"Not a peep after, but forty-five seconds before the doors shut, the datastream they'd been sending since a week after their landing stopped. Last words were 'The home grows distant.' A reference to the mother ship, we think."

"I'm still reluctant to accept that the Holn could learn enough about human physiology in six years to pull off a feat like this," Dr. Innes said. "As has been pointed out, we have been studying this subject for thousands of years and still do not know all its secrets."

"Time," Wanda said.

"Pardon me?"

"You need to understand the time frame here," Ben said. "The original race left the original planet in the original mother ship—a term, by the way, the Holn find highly amusing—about the time the Earth had cooled enough to allow single-cell organisms to survive. By the

Cambrian explosion, the Holn had joined the original race on the ship, which had added two more species by then and added four more after the Holn joined. About the time ol' T. Rex was chomping around, the ship had changed course, eventually bringing it to this sector of the galaxy. About the time Socrates was trying to convince everyone they didn't know anything, the ship made another shift in course because the stellar group wherein our Sun resides showed promise. This decision paid off a couple thousand years later when they began receiving coherent energy waves—our radio broadcasts, the first echoes of what was to become an electromagnetic beacon in the wilderness.

"About the time we landed on our Moon, the Holn left the mother ship—destination, they weren't sure. It wasn't until they got close to Pluto's outer orbit before they were able to resolve the size and location of their destination. On the long trip in, they analyzed the by-now thousands of signals and picked what they thought was the dominant language. Their English is astounding."

Ben rubbed his nose. "So you see, they've had plenty of time to cogitate and learn. Many of those coherent energy waves contained information about human physiology. They've had a lot more than six years to learn this stuff. What's a few years taken off of a human being to them? Nothing. They did some research into the human form but—unlike us—they're too kind to kill their lab animals. So they just let them go, not realizing what they had done to them."

"Welcome to Crosshairs, *I'm Maynard Allbright, the right guy on the right, and he's Kensington Turrell, the wrong guy on the left. In the crosshairs is Dr. Avram Rolstein, administrator of the Holn Effect Task Force, back in Washington after meeting with his task force last week. Dr. Rolstein is a popular man these days and it's only with difficulty we've managed to sit him down between us in*

this studio so we can wrest some information out about an event that's reverberating around the world. And in this country, the debate is so intense it's shoving the presidential campaigns right off the TV screens.

"So, doctor, about those seventeen people, and the fact that all you scientists agree they are human—"

"We have not reached a consensus on that, although we are close. Besides, if three scientists ever agree completely on anything, it's a cult."

"I see. As I was saying, what's missing in these discussions, so far, and in general, is an examination of motive. What possible reason would visitors from outer space have for turning adult humans into child . . . somethings?"

"Some people would have you believe it was an experiment on laboratory animals, some would have you believe, as you've said, to plant some kind of alien life form on the planet. We don't know. We're searching all the records to see if the Holn mentioned something, dropped a subtle hint somewhere we missed—"

"Benign, you still say?"

"So far, Mr. Turrell. Six years they sat on that patch of New Mexico soil and didn't do a thing except talk. Never a threat, never a sign of weapons, although we certainly pointed a few at them—"

"You don't think they brought their own?"

"Undoubtedly, but we never saw them."

"All right, you're saying they sat out there for six years without giving a hint of what they're doing. Surely, though, they were aware of what their presence was doing to us. The Millennium Riots of 2004 should have been a clue. What have they said about that, Dr. Rolstein?"

"They asked many questions, and we explained as best we could. We tried to be honest about how the two groups who'd been camping out by their ship disagreed—"

"Two groups of whom?"

"*The Enlightenment Network, Mr. Allbright, is certain these are the Wise Old Aliens come to solve all of our problems. The other, the Armageddon Group, is convinced the landing is a sign of the Last Days of Man. Their disagreements sparked two days of riots, forcing the arrival of the third group, the National Guard with their canisters of tear gas. Well, the Holn mulled it over, but never, ever made any judgment about what they were seeing. They just said it was all very interesting.*"

"*Interesting enough to capture innocent humans and make them inhuman—*"

"*Come, Maynard, don't bring up that alien life form folderol again. We're trying to figure motive here—*"

"*It's simple, Kensington, when you strip it all down to basics: subjugation or eradication of the human life form. And here NASA sits on its collective posterior and refuses to go after them—*"

"*With what?*"

"*Dr. Rolstein, NASA is supp—*"

"*No, wait, you tell me how we're supposed to chase the Holn. We're down two shuttles and the others fly irregularly. The Delta Clipper and its successor programs have been abandoned, the so-called international space station is unmanned more than it is manned and moon bases remain a pipe dream. Plus, the SETI project that might have given us an earlier warning of their approach was hobbled back in 1993.*"

"*It wasn't a good expenditure of taxpayer money—*"

"*Mr. Allbright, after all that's happened, are you going to sit there and say the project was a waste of money? After the Cold War was over, Congress kept prattling on about how space projects are too expensive and should be cut so we can rid ourselves of the big bad deficit. Well, the space budget was torn to shreds and we still have the damned deficit. The reason the space program is dying is because chowderheads like you two and your clones in Congress don't think there's anything out there worth studying.*"

"Dr. Rol—"

"You've got it backward, Mr. Not-so-bright. There're plenty of things out there for us to know. It's just that, as the Holn might have discovered, there's nothing down here worth studying."

Seven

October 2

"What we have to do is leave this meeting with a decision." Miranda said. "The pressures from all directions are at the breaking point, partly because of the elections. So—the question is: Are these the missing people?"

Miranda waited as the others shuffled papers and glances. Outside, an early fall storm sent clouds pouring over the rugged peaks.

"Well, Dr. Greenlea," Dr. Innes said, "I'm afraid this puts you on the spot."

"Yes, we saw this coming. Our general conclusion is that each person of the group carries the characteristics of the concomitant adult."

"And the families?" Constance said.

"Rejection is giving way slowly to acceptance." Olive tapped her notebook. "Very slowly."

"We ought to hold off," Matt said. "Ask for a delay of, say, two weeks so we can hash this out some more."

Miranda shook her head. "We've asked. The answer is no." She sighed. "I wonder who's really in control here."

Olive pushed herself erect. "I can give you a confidence factor of ninety percent that these people are at least the personalities of the missing adults."

74

"Really?" Miranda raised an eyebrow.

Olive shrugged. "As I said, we've been hashing this out, to use Matt's terminology, already."

"And if what she just said gets out," Dr. Innes rumbled, "God forbid, we could find ourselves on a very hard spot."

"All right," Miranda said. "Are there any hard objections to this task force saying we believe the children carry the personalities of the missing adults? Lindsey, Anna? Neither of you have said anything."

"We can't find anything to object to right now," Lindsey said. "I'd urge we keep the option open for changes, though."

"Right." Miranda picked up a stylus and began scribbling on her notebook screen. "Anna?"

"I defer to Olive's group, with Lindsey's option."

"OK. We'll say each . . . 'child?' " Miranda looked up.

"I don't like that term," Olive said.

"Agreed," Dr. Innes said. "And 'victim' is too pejorative."

"We could go with what the police use," Randall said. " 'Subject.' "

"Each . . . 'subject' . . . carries the full personality of each missing . . . each adult reported missing." Miranda looked at what she had written. "Nice and passive."

"We should make it clear we are reserving judgment on whether the 'subjects' are alien or human," Dr. Innes said.

"OK. Let's see . . . Although we feel the subjects carry the . . . something . . . of the adults." She looked up again.

"What was that word you used at the press conference?" Constance asked. " 'Essence'?"

"A relic from the New Age," Matt said. "A more common usage would be 'personalities.' "

"Umm, OK. We're at least highly confident, barring any changes through subsequent research, that these . . .

subjects carry the personalities of the missing people, but we reserve judgment on the other issues, including the humanity, humanness, humaneness of the individuals of the group. Anything else?"

After a moment, Dr. Innes said, "Just make sure Carson doesn't put anything in the press release we haven't said."

"Roger knows better than that," Miranda said. "I've shown him the two-by-four I'm going to thump him with if he screws up."

"The hearing before the Alden Commission today was going along smoothly until an attorney for the Department of Health and Human Services turned against his own agency.

"The three-judge panel, after again denying a request for video cameras to be allowed to record the proceedings, heard arguments about the status of the Group of Seventeen, including questions about the legal issues surrounding each member and whether they should be released into the care of so-called designated guardians to be appointed by the HHS.

"The questions came up after the panel heard the statement from the Holn Effect Task Force, or HETF, that the individuals, whatever else they were, do carry the memories, behavior and personalities of the adults termed missing at the site of the Holn landing. Once the panel accepted this, two motions were presented that no one had indicated would come up: a motion by HHS for a ruling on the legal status of the children and a motion to allow the members to leave confinement in custody of their respective guardians. The latter motion was made by Robert Carlisle, the well-known rights advocate and de facto head of the lawyers representing relatives of the missing people. Justice Alger Alden asked the HHS group if they had any objections, and Radmilla Everett, chief counsel, said no.

"At that point, Jason Kylie, a career lawyer for the

*department, stood up and said there were plenty of
objections. When Federal Judge Brandon Catlin asked
Ms. Everett about this, she stated she was not aware of
any objections nor of any plans to make any. Federal
Judge Anthea Tallulah, widely regarded to be in line as
the first black female judge to be nominated to the
Supreme Court, asked in her soft Mississippi-accented
voice who, exactly, Kylie represented. Kylie then said,
and I quote, 'I guess I represent the scientists because
they don't seem to have a voice here.' He then explained
that several issues had yet to be resolved before a
decision on releasing the group could be made, but
Everett said that was not true and HHS was ready to
proceed. The judges, after advising the HHS lawyers to
get their house in order, took the motions under consideration, again over the vigorous objections of Kylie.*

*"At this point, it's still not clear who Kylie was speaking
for. None of the participants had any comments after the
hearing, but it seems clear there have been some behind-
the-scenes negotiations. The other question, of course, is
the possibilities of appeal if Mr. Kylie or someone else
decides it's necessary. With a Supreme Court justice
sitting on the commission, however, there might not be
any avenue.*

"Rolf Treadwell, CNN, Washington."

"That was real slick, Radmilla, real slick, indeed."
Miranda paced the floor between the desk Avram sat
behind and the couch Radmilla sat on. On the opposite
end of that couch sat Harrison Conroy. Miranda already
had bought her airline ticket when Avram called. "Your
ability to spring unannounced surprises is quite impres-
sive."

"The sarcasm does not help," Radmilla said, toying
with a long gold-colored chain around her neck. "We
have had many discussions about the situation and
believe we have found the best solutions for all involved."

Miranda stopped, looked at the sharp-faced woman who parted her brown hair down the middle and cut it off at the ear lobes. "Define 'we.'"

"In the department—"

"Who?"

"You are not the only people involved with the group," Conroy said. "Several agencies—"

"Who? CIA? FBI? NSC? NASA? NOAA? NTSB? CDC? FAA? FDA? HHS—well, that one we know. NBS? OSHA? DOE? DARPA? NRC? NAS? NIMH? The President's Council on Physical Fitness—"

"Please, Dr. Sena, can we ease off a little?" Conroy's right hand fluttered in the air. "Just say that representatives from many agencies, including some of the ones you mentioned, have been meeting to provide guidance. The consensus brought forward is reflected in the motions presented to the Alden Commission."

"You didn't ask us about those motions. You just asked if we could say the missing adults could be the mysterious children. You did not ask if we were ready to let these people walk off. Our answer would have been no. Flat, unequivocal, no. *Hell* no."

"Look, you've been studying them for nearly four months. You should have been able to make some decisions by now. We feel, partly, they should not be held in an institutional environment any longer."

"Oh, I agree, absolutely." Miranda leaned against the desk. "Get them out of this hospital. But find one place to house them, a bed-and-breakfast inn, or a motel, one of those all-suites jobs. Put them all together in one wing where they can interact with each other. They're getting along fine because, as one of them put it, they're all in the same boat. Let the families move into another part of the motel where they can visit or not. In other words, do the assimilation slowly, day by day. Let them get used to each other first, instead of jamming them together at once."

"How long do you envision this taking?" Radmilla said, frowning.

"At least a year."

"A year!" Conroy snorted. "We don't have a year."

"Why not? You had six years with the Holn. You, the government, whatever, can spare the time for these . . . citizens."

"I'm afraid not, Dr. Sena. The president has made it very clear she wants this taken care of as soon as possible. With as little fuss as possible, with as little cost as possible. The president would like to clear this issue so she can concentrate on the main issues of the campaign. Your proposal goes way beyond any fiscal sense. We've advised the president the best path is to allow the families to take the children into custody, take them home, try to reestablish a normal life as much as possible. Meanwhile, you can continue your studies."

"Normal life?" Miranda resumed pacing. "Look, there's still a lot of fear out there, unsettled minds grasping for explanations. Listen to the TV. Hear the uncertainty, look at the questions in their eyes. Most of the people in this country—and maybe the world—still haven't made up their minds about the Holn, much less this. We need time—"

"You yourself said time already has run out. Change your mind?"

"Of course not. The deed has been done, and that's the problem. We need the time to absorb this—"

"We don't have time to go slow. Perhaps if you can't understand that, then we need someone else who—"

The sound of a hand slamming down on a desk top made everyone jump.

"Is this a threat I hear?" Avram surged to his feet. "Is this a threat issuing from the lips of the adviser to presidents and hobnobber with makers of law and dinner-party goer with chief executives of giant corporations?"

"Now listen, Avram—"

The scientist pointed a finger at him. "Harrison, for God's sake, dig into your psyche and call up the fragments of your scientific background you've buried under the bureaucratic persona. *Think,* man! I'm telling you, this thing could blow up in your face a lot worse than it has so far. Go back and tell your president she thinks she's got problems now, wait until she releases these people on an unprepared world."

A flush had flowed across Conroy's face at the beginning of the outburst, but he had regained control by the finish. "You don't understand all of the factors at work here," he said with a definite chill. "You are not the only group undertaking to resolve the situation. You are an advisory group, and only an advisory group. The final decisions on all aspects of this will come from elsewhere."

"Where?" Miranda said. "CIA? FB—"

"Please, Dr. Sena. That is not—"

"Harrison."

Miranda suddenly thought that if the two men got into a contest on who could chill their voices the most, Avram would win hands-down.

"The President of the United States and her Cabinet. Satisfied?"

"Only if they get good advice."

"Avram, damnit, I'm getting tired—"

"All right, all right, all right." Miranda put heat into her voice. "We're getting wrapped up in our own power plays and forgetting the seventeen people whose lives have been tossed upside down. We're supposed to be helping them, you know."

Radmilla opened her mouth, but Miranda pushed on. "I'm willing to compromise here. If the court rules in favor of the guardian motion, then fine. Let the group be released into the guardians' care. But—keep them in one place. Here—I mean, in Albuquerque, or here in Washington, or wherever. In a place like I described earlier, where we can separate them if necessary. That way, we will be able to monitor them instead of having to chase them all over the country."

"That makes sense—" Avram began, but Radmilla finally cut him off as she stood up.

"Actually, I believe you people have very little foundation to stand on."

Miranda and Avram blinked at her.

"Attorneys for the families say they have evidence of mistreatment."

"What!" Avram exploded.

"Surely, Dr. Rolstein, you yourself remember the comments by some of the group about how they had been confronted by someone wearing masks, stripping off their clothing and shouting questions at them?"

"That was—" Avram began.

"That's just a start. There's the enforced medical tests you've been performing, most without their permission. There's the issue of withholding information—"

"Withholding and not knowing are two different things," Miranda said. "They've been informed of all we've learned—"

"I think we can successfully challenge that, but that certainly isn't all. We can show how you've denied them televisions and other electronic media, such as how all forms of newspapers and magazines have been censored of all articles about the Holn and their own situation. In addition," she said to Miranda's shocked face, "these people have not been allowed to make phone calls, to contact loved ones and assure them they're all right."

"In other words," Conroy said as he, too, got to his feet, "you have not been treating these people very well, and the families are getting quite upset about it. Their attorneys are prepared to raise a big stink about it, and in the interest of justice and fair play, we have come to the conclusion we'd better go along with their requests."

Miranda stared at Conroy, then shifted her gaze to Radmilla. "Damn, all right, listen. If what you say is true about the news censorship, although I don't know why it should be"—she glanced at Avram, but he had his head down and was pinching the bridge of his nose with a thumb and finger—"we'll back off from all of that. We'll give them each a stereo HDTV with remote control and we won't deny them access to any magazine, book, or tape. We'll give them two-line telephones. We'll stop the testing except for standard daily vital sign collection. We'll promise we'll do no more testing without their permission and we'll explain everything we do and what we find out in writing if necessary. But please, don't let them scatter. We cannot let these people out. Nobody is ready for them. Not us, not the government, and certainly not their loved ones."

"You make a compelling case," Conroy said evenly. "We will consider the proposition."

"One more thing, too. Please, bear with me." Miranda planted herself in front of Conroy. "We have no way of determining yet if these people are going to mature in the normal human lifespan or even if they'll mature at all. In other words, are they going to grow up again? If they're going to be stuck at this size and maturation level for the rest of their lives, what kind of burden do you think that will cast on their designated guardians?"

Conroy stepped aside. "Important issues. They will be included in the deliberations."

Avram looked up. "Harrison, I'm depending on you to shake the movers and shakers into doing the right thing. This goes far beyond us, the government, or even the Group of Seventeen. This has repercussions that'll reverberate for generations."

Harrison Conroy buttoned his jacket, smoothed the lapels. "All aspects will be considered," he said.

"The Alden Commission has just released rulings related to the Group of Seventeen. A preliminary statement sent by fax to CNN gives just a few details. We expect a full brief will be released later today.

"Briefly, the commission accepts the scientific findings that the seventeen children are, in fact, the missing seventeen adults because their personalities have been carried over intact, quote, by whatever means was carried out, endquote. In that vein, the commission says, because these people are not the physiological size that they were, and because scientific findings show they have the physical maturation level of nine-year-old children, these people cannot function as productive members of this society. Therefore, all rights they heretofore had gained are to be transferred to the designated guardians as determined by the Department of Health and Human Services. This includes property rights, custodial rights, and any other rights normally assumed by adult citizens. They are children—I'm quoting now from the press statement—and should be treated as such. The commission further urges that the transfer of property and financial assets be expedited as quickly as possible so all legal matters can be cleared up quickly.

"In addition, the commission rules there is no reason to detain any member of the group any longer because they have been shown to be healthy and do not pose a health risk to others. The court says once the proper U.S. government agencies determine who the guardians will be, all individuals must be allowed to leave forthwith if that is the wish of the guardians. All of these rulings are unanimous, according to the statement.

"When CNN tried to get a comment from the scientific board, the person who answered the phone, upon being told of the rulings, uttered a curse and hung up.

"Rolf Treadwell, CNN, Washington."

"Theodoric!" The FBI agent jumped at Miranda's shout.

"I'm just a poor, innocent field agent," he said, pressing himself against a wall in the conference room, holding up his notebook computer and peering over the top. "I got a phone call fifteen minutes before that

Treadwell guy went on the air. It was a done deal. They didn't ask for my opinion. Honest."

Miranda let out a breath, turned away. She tended to believe him, but she still turned back and shook a finger at him. "If I found out you had anything to do with any of this, or I find out you've been skulking around behind my back, I'm going to flay you alive. You got that?"

"Oh, yes, ma'am."

Miranda headed to the table. The others quickly and quietly took their places, some suppressing grins.

"All right, this meeting of the toothless and impotent Holn Effect Task Force will come to order." She sat down. "The first thing you have to realize now is just how powerless we are. Exhibit A: The rulings by the Alden bunch. Not one cautionary step we recommended was adopted. Exhibit B: Jason Kylie, the attorney who had the audacity to speak for us at the hearing, has been kicked off the HHS lawyer team. Exhibit C: Our orders to transfer to California posthaste." She looked down at a sheet of paper. "Part of the organization will be at UCLA, the other part at USC. Headquarters will be UCLA because that's where my office is. You will be allowed to go to your respective home bases and do work from there, but group leaders must be ready to fly to L.A. at a moment's notice. Comments?"

"Dr. Sena," Dr. Innes said. "I feel like we must try at least once again, and strongly, to get some of these decisions reversed, or at least modified."

"I can practically guarantee the answer, but, yes, we can try. Is there something specific?"

"While you were in Washington, we put our heads together and wrote a position paper," Constance said. "It contains a one page abstract and ten pages of discussion about where we are with the research and extrapolations as to why the group should be kept together. Dr. Rolstein told us of your compromise, so we included that in our call."

"We've included some of our findings, mostly what JPL had found out," Lindsey said.

Miranda leaned back in her chair. The lack of rest from flitting to and from Washington had begun to work at her, making her limbs lethargic. She was impressed, though; she wouldn't have given a wooden nickel on the chance the group would knit together so tightly.

"And all of you are supporting this?"

"We've all signed off," Matt said. "Mr. Theodoric also, and Dr. Betterm—Wanda, by fax. Only one signature line is empty—yours."

"It won't stay that way. This is terrific. Thank you."

Dr. Innes rubbed his chin. "It doesn't mean we all see eye-to-eye, you understand." He glanced over at Matt.

"Oh, absolutely, I wouldn't have it any other way." She felt like smiling.

"We were wondering if we should ask Roger to prepare a version for the press," Constance said.

Miranda considered. "No. This document is to stay within the task force and go only to HHS. I think we'd be better off if we're not seen as trying a runaround of the decision process."

"You mean an end-run," Matt said.

Miranda waved a hand. "Whatever."

"Miranda," Orlando said, "who decided to censor the news for the group? And make them incommunicado?"

Miranda's eyes went to Jack, who put up both palms. "Not guilty. We concerned ourselves with security, nothing else."

Olive Greenlea stirred. "I think," she said slowly, "that came out of a consensus among us. At the Santa Fe hospital, before the task force was formed. We thought that if the people saw what was being said about them, the trauma could be worsened." Her hands fluttered. "I-I'm sorry—"

"Your decision was made only for the first days," Miranda said. "And, as far as I'm concerned, it was the right one. I confronted Avram—who, after all, was in this from the beginning. He knows exactly who made the order because he took the phone call. He says it was a mistake, he's sorry, but it was one of those things that got started and then fell aside forgotten."

"But HHS is using that against us as evidence of our . . . cruelty," Olive said.

Miranda was pained by the hurt and confusion in the other woman's eyes. She sat up, shaking off the tiredness trying to steal over her. "More evidence of our power-lessness. HHS is responsible for all those decisions, but HHS is shoving that blame back on us. The behind-the-scenes negotiations Mr. Treadwell mentioned are to make us the scapegoats."

"Why?" Three voices demanded at once.

"A hotheaded journalist coined the phrase in the '60s," Matt said. " 'Fear and loathing.' "

"And as much as I disagree with this brash fool," Dr. Innes said, "he is correct in this case. Ladies and gentlemen, I suggest we tread very lightly from here on."

The members of the task force fell silent.

"Agreed," Miranda said, "but don't let it interfere with your work. We have been given a charge to find out what happened and why. We cannot drop the ball now. Just remember, we're not doing this for the government. It's for those seventeen people. Be wary, but bear down on your work.

"People, we've got to get those answers."

"Many of the children belonging to the so-called Group of Seventeen have left Albuquerque, the first time many of them have been away from any kind of hospital since the day the Holn ship departed four months ago.

"The individuals are leaving in the custody of desig-nated guardians, such as Harold Coner, seen here leav-ing in the company of his sister, Janet Caperton of Wilmington, Delaware. To be a designated guardian, the applicants must show proof they are related to the child,

they are gainfully employed and can provide all amenities, and that they are of sound moral character. A special committee appointed by the Department of Health and Human Services handles the applications and makes the decisions.

"Some confusion has been noted in the identifications of the children. For instance, Eddie Samuel Thompson, the only African-American in the group, nearly slipped away without anyone noticing, but a CNN crew taped him with his brother Michael, of Chicago. Michael apparently bought Eddie a beer in a hotel bar, but was warned by the Albuquerque policeman seen here with the pair that the Alden Commission ruling makes it illegal to buy liquor for the children of the group. Michael Thompson, saying he didn't realize the ruling went that far, apologized and said it wouldn't happen again.

"Other members of the group seen leaving today include Myra Caslon, here leaving with her husband and six children. She originally had been identified as her own granddaughter. In this still frame, however, Ms. Caslon can be seen between her youngest son, Sydney, eleven, and daughter Linette, in her twenties. Of all the images seen so far, this one seems to illustrate clearly what has befallen these people. Caslon, fifty-four years of age, is the mother of six children, and yet here she is, not even as tall as her youngest child.

"Other members of the group have left already, slipping away unnoticed, including the oldest member, Earl Jackson Othberg, seventy-nine. A spokesman for the hospital says three will remain there tonight and leave tomorrow, but the hospital has declined to identify them. More than likely they are Cheryl Vroman, thirty-five, a former San Francisco lawyer, Pablo 'Pete' Aragon, thirty-two, a former video operator for a local CBS affiliate, and Aaron Lee Fairfax, forty-three, a former stockbroker.

"CNN also has heard reports that the scientists of the Holn Effect Task Force attempted one last time to delay or stop the release of the group. The scientists allegedly

*signed a petition which was presented to HHS Secretary
Roberta Fletcher yesterday by Avram Rolstein, the administrator of the task force, but the petition was rejected.
Spokespersons for neither the task force nor HHS will
comment, however.*

"Marinka Svoboda, CNN, Albuquerque."

"It wasn't a petition," Olive muttered. "It was a
desperate plea for sanity."

"We lost," Constance said.

"Reason usually does come out second-best," Matt
said, flicking the TV off with a remote. "Or third, or
fourth."

Miranda stirred herself in the chair next to the hotel-
room desk. She, Olive, Constance, and Matt had gone to
lunch together, then had come back to Miranda's room
to watch the scattering of the Group of Seventeen.

"We lost a little," she said. "But they, the children,
whatever you want to call them, just lost a hell of a lot."
She ran a hand through her dark hair. "I'm frightened,
folks. Frightened for them, frightened for us, because
God knows what's going to happen now."

Part II

Diaspora

Eight

October 18

Earl stepped into the warm humidity of Maui from the controlled environment of Walter's house and looked around at the cozy suburban street. Despite an occasional palm tree, the scene could have been taken from any housing development in any part of the United States and dropped here.

Of course, the weather was a clue, too—Halloween was two weeks away, yet the ambient temperature now would be a Wisconsin summer. Just more unreality in the dream he sometimes thought he must be dreaming.

He wandered over and sat on an enormous chunk of lava plunked down where sidewalk met driveway.

"Escaping" from Lovelace had been easier than anticipated. Walter had brought his youngest son, Lucas, an eight-year-old just a bit taller than Earl (more surrealism, as he remembered himself staring at this kid right in the eye). The boy pulled off his Random Noise T-shirt and Earl put it and the boy's Ultron Enervator cap, a soft combat-helmet affair that hid most of Earl's hair, on. Earl and Walter simply strode through the phalanx of cameras and reporters and into a van; only one or two cameras followed their progress. Walter called Lucas on an EnviroPatrol walkie-talkie and the boy, now hatless and wearing a white school shirt, simply walked out. Later, in the hotel room, Lucas washed black coloring out of his hair. A redhead too, but still no match for Earl.

Earl's first meal with the family had been the weekly Sunday dinner. Earl had to give Walter's wife, Marcia, credit for the time needed to make the meal of roast beef, mashed potatoes, spinach, a tossed salad, rolls, cake for dessert—nothing came out of a can or package except the rolls—but it was all served with an undercurrent of tension. Marcia did not seem overly pleased to see him; the oldest boy, Tom, seventeen, was sullen, but how much of that was normal teenage angst Earl couldn't tell; and the daughter, Jennifer, fifteen, barely glanced at him and said even less.

"Did you enjoy your little excursion, Lucas?" Marcia said as she passed him the peas, which he took reluctantly.

"It was fun," the boy said. "There sure were a lot of reporters and stuff."

"We saw you on the news," his mother said. "They said they think you were a decoy for someone else, but they didn't know who."

"Did you really see me on TV?"

"We almost missed you," Tom said. "You didn't look the same with black hair."

Lucas giggled.

"About settled in, Earl?" Walter said, passing a plate of sliced meat.

"I think so. Nice room. Nice house."

"We'll have to take you up to Haleakala Crater sometime," Walter said as he sliced his meat and vegetables into bite-sized portions. "Spectacular place."

"Yeah," Lucas said. "One of the highest and driest places on Earth. A big volcano, and hills and dunes everywhere. There's this weird plant that grows up there, the silverfish—I mean—"

"Silversword," Jennifer said.

"I was going to say that."

"It's the state flower. You ought to at least get it right."

"I—"

"Never mind," Walter said. "We can take Uncle Earl to see all the sights upcountry, right, dear?"

Marcia glanced at him. "Yes, of course."

She thinks it's a lousy idea, Earl decided. Marcia kept her hair cut short, businesslike, although Earl wondered how she got all the individual strands to move as a unit.

"So, what is it exactly you do, Walter?" he said into the stiff silence.

"I'm associate director of operations at the Hono-kohau Haven Resort, part of the Adkin Lodging Group."

"Big hotel?"

"Fifteen hundred rooms. Divided into six clusters with three swimming pools apiece. Six restaurants, a movie theater, several small stores, a full-function post office, three excursion boats."

"Which one is it?"

"Farthest end, Kihei side. Marcia works at the Maalaea Hilton at the Kamaole end."

"And what do you do, Marcia?"

"I run the registration system." She didn't look up.

"I understand ten years ago the Maalaea Anchor complex didn't even exist."

"Some close-the-gate-behind-me types wanted to stop the project, but the possibility of a thousand-plus jobs in these hard times won out over antidevelopment senti-ment," Marcia said.

"They're just afraid the hotel complexes will fill up all the spaces between Kihei and Kamaole," Walter said. "That's not the intent of the project at all. There are height restrictions and design conditions to be met. It'll look great when it's done."

"I see," Earl said turning his fork into a mound of potatoes. "And the native people? I mean, the real Hawaiians?"

"No—"

"Pass the potatoes," Walter cut in.

"The bowl needs refilling." Marcia carried the bowl into the kitchen.

"Actually, we hope someday to open our own business," Walter continued. "We've been saving for it."

"Oh? Something people need, I hope?"

"A small grocery store, perhaps with a pharmacy. Ellis Silverstein runs the hotel pharmacy but would like to have his own place." Marcia returned and handed the filled bowl to Walter, sat back down. "Kihei or Kamaole aren't that far away, but it would be more convenient."

"Where?"

Walter ladled out a portion of potatoes, then offered the bowl to Earl, who took it and scooped out some.

"We're looking at a small store near the intersection of the Kihei Road and the main road into this housing area."

"Near the poor side of town," Tom said.

"'The poor side of town'?" Earl thumped the bowl down on the table. "This place isn't even ten years old and you're already declaring class warfare?"

That last comment, Earl reflected back on the lump of lava, probably hadn't been a good idea.

His eye was caught by Lucas expertly guiding a skateboard around a parked car and up the driveway, stopping a half-meter away from Earl. A foot clad in layers of polymer shoe clumped on the ground while the other stopped forward progress of the board. Lucas regarded Earl through pale eyes set in a face speckled with freckles, which continued down the boy's neck, across his arms, and on down legs sticking out of multicolored shorts. The pattern was unbroken under the bright yellow T-shirt, Earl remembered.

"Hi, grandnun—grun—"

"Call me uncle."

"Yeah." The boy looked at him a moment longer.

Now that the excitement was over, he'd had time to consider this strange being who'd moved into the room next to his. "Granduncle? Is that right?"

"Well, let's see." Earl counted off on his fingers. "I had a brother, Sam, who had a son, Walter. That son is my nephew, and I am his uncle. Walter grew up and had a son, you, making you my grandnephew, so yes, I am your granduncle."

"You look like a kid."

"Looks are deceiving. I'm seventy-nine years old."

"Wow."

"This your board?" Earl jumped off the rock and nudged the board with a toe of his sandal.

"Um, yeah."

Lucas took his foot off and Earl picked up the skateboard, a sculpted flow of aerodynamic plastic. "Interesting." He set it down again. "Just step up here and—woop."

"Put this foot here," Lucas said, squatting and pushing Earl's foot. "The other here, so you can balance."

"Ah. Ready to rip now." He crouched. "Flying down the highway—" He looked at Lucas. "How do you turn this thing on?"

Lucas laughed.

"Let's see, foot power 'stead of horsepower." Earl pushed a couple of times, then went back into the crouch. "Look out, here comes the board-skate terror, tearing up the landscape, brummm." The board slowly rolled to a stop. Lucas giggled again.

"All right," Earl said, turning the board so it faced down the driveway, "time to get serious." He got on, pushed hard several times.

"Good," Lucas said, jogging alongside.

"Now we're m-m-moving—" He nearly lost his balance where driveway met road. "Pocket of turbulence, there." He pushed a few more times and rolled swiftly across the street. "Oop, wait, how do you turn? Quick!"

"Shift your weight—"

"Too late! Abandon ship!" He jumped off the board, which smacked into the curb. "Sorry."

Lucas shrugged. "It didn't hurt it. Shift your weight to turn."

"Oh. Sounds easy."

"Like this." The boy took the board to the other side of the street, pushed off hard. "This is the way you turn." He made a graceful sweep up a driveway, around and back.

"Ah."

Lucas demonstrated a few more times, then Earl got back on. The first few attempts were rocky, but soon Earl began to get the knack of it.

"Not bad," he said about an hour later, "but I wouldn't want to make a living at it."

"Some thrashers get big bucks."

"Is that what you want to do when you grow up?"

The boy shrugged.

"Well, don't worry about it now. What's over here?" Earl crossed an empty lot shorn of vegetation, passing utility hookups sticking out of the ground.

"One of the new golf courses," Lucas said as they reached a fence.

"Jeez. Pretty soon this island will be nothing but fairways and greens. I suppose it's part of that new hotel complex thing your parents work for." Across the expanse of links, he could see flat shapes like a low pile of boxes.

"Yeah."

"The ocean's on the other side?"

"Yeah."

"I haven't been there yet. Let's go." Earl climbed over the fence, just a low chain-link affair. He held the skateboard as Lucas scrambled over.

"Um, they yell at us if we walk on the grass and stuff," Lucas said.

"Well, I suppose you could get hit with a ball," Earl

said as he strolled across a fairway that angled off in a different direction. "There's one now. I wonder where the owner is." He couldn't see anyone back along the flat, grassy corridor.

"This dips in the middle, you can't see them."

"Ah." Earl heard a sharp intake of breath from the boy as he picked up the ball and hurled it into the bushes next to the fence. "I hate golf." The boy tittered.

The rest of the journey was mostly on access roads, passing groups of bare-kneed, sweating, huffing golfers. Eventually, they came out on a hill that had been sliced into and lined with concrete to allow a two-lane road to pass below.

"The highway," Lucas said. "They moved it back from the beaches so they could put the hotels in. This way." He led Earl to a pedestrian crossing over the road, fenced on both sides but with flowers along the edges and grass in the middle. On the other side, the grass turned into a macadam path angling between two hotels built low and spread out. The path widened into a sort of mall with carefully arranged gardens bounded by low walls, benches, and sidewalks divided up into geometric shapes differentiated by color and texture. A McDonald's restaurant was tucked into one corner.

Finally the paved mall ended in bright white sand. Earl's feet sank as he trod across, weaving around ozone shelters squatting like misplaced mushrooms. A trade-off between wanting to bask on the beach yet reduce risk of skin cancers, the shelters generally formed a half-dome, the open side facing the waves. Those who didn't have the shelters oiled themselves to a bright sheen in liquid sunscreen; only a couple of diehards allowed themselves to roast to brownness. Blaring portable radios competed with blaring portable TVs or even the rapid-fire beeps of video games; an occasional beach ball or Frisbee or the person chasing them threatened to collide with Earl, but he simply dodged and kept going. The ocean edge was only a little less crowded, mostly

with parents holding wriggling tots as the waves glided
in. He didn't stop, but waded in until his polymer-and-
Velcro sandals were covered in churning water, soaking
the cuffs of his new jeans. He stopped, looked out toward
the horizon.

"Uncle Earl, what are you going to do now? Are you
going to go to school or something?"

Earl looked back at the boy at the edge of the wet,
holding skateboard nose down in the sand. Lucas, the
youngest, seemed least bothered by him. Of course, the
boy was too young to remember the snarling, gnarly old
man he'd been so recently.

"A loaded question, Lucas. I don't have the faintest
idea. There's a bigger question that has yet to be
answered. It affects my whole future. And that is, am I
going to grow up again? Or am I going to be this size the
rest of my life?"

The boy's eyes widened. "You mean you might stay a
boy forever? Wow."

"Yeah, wow." He looked around at the beach, the
hotels, the ocean, the rippling flesh of near-naked humans, then looked back out toward the sea. His mind
wandered back to the night before he left the Albuquerque hospital, sitting in Marian's room with her and
Aaron. They had talked way past midnight about things
they had avoided before, their past lives, their families—their future.

They had been reluctant to say good-night, and stood
in the center of the room, looking at each other.

"Well, take care of yourselves." Earl saw the moisture
in Marian's eyes and barely could restrain his. "Don't let
the big folk let you down—"

He found himself being crushed in an embrace; the
sensation startled him because all of the group scrupu-
lously had avoided such contact (except maybe Linda
and Jerry). As Marian hugged him, Aaron awkwardly
stepped forward and joined in.

A wave rolling in toward a Maui beach shoved at Earl's knees. He took a deep breath.

"I seem to be only like a boy playing on the seashore while a great ocean of undiscovered truth lies before me." He laughed lightly at his pretension, kicked the water. "Wonder what ol' Newton would make of all this."

"Arlene, what's going on? I thought you wanted to get back to the farm. It's been nearly a week since they released me from the hospital."

Marian shrank inwardly from Arlene's gaze over half-eaten scrambled eggs. "I have to make absolutely sure everything is in proper order. The farm can wait a couple of more days. Elisha says everything is running well."

"Well, it's just that we seem to be wasting time. And running up a motel bill."

"That is unavoidable." She touched her napkin to her lips three times, then tossed it down and stood up. "I have an appointment." She reached into her fanny pack, tossed a twenty on the table. "Pay the bill, then go back to the room. I hope to be done within the hour."

Marian watched her sister stride off, moving between the tables like a cement truck through traffic. Marian's trip wasn't as steadfast—one person shoved a chair back into her path; a waiter laden with tray did a quick and graceful swerve; three boys wouldn't yield space for her to pass by.

"How're you doing, honey?" the cashier said, ersatz smile splitting the makeup coated face.

"Fine," Marian said, knowing the woman couldn't give a damn. She knew the attitudes of most of the staff by now; Marian and Arlene had eaten every meal at this plastic-and-veneer restaurant attached to their motel. Marian was sick of the bland, textureless food and constant smell of something being cooked to rancidity.

At least now, though, her fame as a member of the Seventeen had faded; only occasionally would someone take a quick snapshot.

She didn't bother to zip her coat as she walked across the motel parking lot. After a three-day spell of cold rain, Albuquerque's October had warmed again, so she'd gone back to the sandals they'd given all the Seventeen. Arlene had bought only a few items of clothing for her, including one pair of clunky and uncomfortable shoes. The sudden drop from the frenzy of the last couple of weeks to idle waiting for Arlene to do whatever Arlene was doing made her listless. She felt a vague unease thinking about that, and she unconsciously hurried up the external stairs to the room. What to do now? Watch soap operas or talk shows? She was sick of the misery and neurosis—

Something to do offered itself when the phone rang.

"It's Shirley."

"Oh, good. It's nice to hear a friendly voice. How's things?"

"At home, OK. Merlin and Phoenix are fine, although they miss their mistress. Last night I found them sitting in your chair again, looking eagerly at me, then being very disappointed when I wasn't you."

"Oh, they're just being ornery again. When I get back, they'll sulk because I was gone so long. I can't thank you enough for taking care of them, and watching the place."

"My pleasure, I keep telling you. Any idea yet when you'll get home?"

Marian sighed. "Arlene keeps delaying our departure, I don't know why. I think she's— Oh, I shouldn't say that. This has been a shock to her."

"Not as much as to you, I'll bet. Anyhow, the other news is that Dave has accepted your resignation. He says the city manager has agreed your situation is unique and is giving you a year's severance pay. I'll get the check and hold it for you. Dave helped me clear your desk. The stuff's in your house."

One part of a past life gone. "Thanks. How's your mom?"

"Pretty much the same. The doctor says she's at the point where anything could happen." The line was quiet for a moment. "I think I've said this before, but I don't know what else to say. I'm sorry about what happened to you."

"I know, but no use stewing over it. I would feel better if Arlene did something. This is so unlike her."

"Well, forgive me, I'll never say this again, but watch out for her. See you soon, I hope. Keep your chin up."

After hanging up, Marian again gave serious thought to asking Shirley, her friend in Bellingham for six years, if she would take her in . . . but again, she shook her head.

I can't ask that of her.

She picked up the thinscreen, pulled the cartridge out of the receiver, and attached it. She chose the local paper from the menu and noted news about the Seventeen had moved to page three, now that they'd all scattered. Her own departure had been, like everything Arlene did, carefully planned. They waited until ten at night—Earl already having left, Aaron scheduled to go the next day—and walked out while the few media people were off to the side interviewing some politician who'd dropped by. Straight to this motel, a standard low-cost chain.

After about a half-hour of desultory clicking through pages, Arlene returned. A man and woman in business suits followed her in.

"It's all set. You're going with them." Arlene went to the closet, grabbed a suitcase and tossed it onto the bed.

"What do you mean?" Marian jumped up. Both the man and woman stood between her and the door.

"I mean, everything's settled." Arlene scooped clothing out of the dresser drawers and into the suitcase. "I have assigned custody of you to these people. You'll go with them. They'll give you room and board."

"For what?"

"For—they have their reasons." Arlene stepped into the bathroom, returned with Marian's toilet items and dropped them in. She pushed on the lump of clothing and began to close the suitcase.

"I'm not going anywhere with them. What are you doing?"

"You'll go with them because it is my decision. It's been made legal. This will allow me to go back to the farm with minimal disruption. Please go, and don't make a scene."

Marian stared as Arlene zipped the suitcase closed. The woman stepped forward and took it.

"I don't believe this, Arlene."

"Listen to the one who suddenly doesn't believe. As if I'm supposed to believe what happened to you. Just a whim of yours. Lord."

Marian felt her face go hot; her heart thudded in her chest. "I am your sister!"

She thought she saw an opening in the way Arlene turned away and fumbled with a pillow.

"Arlene." Marian stepped forward and touched her forearm. It jerked like it had been zapped with electricity. In the next instant a hand slapped across Marian's face with enough force to make her stumble back and fall. Fighting against shock and pain, she looked up. And froze.

Anger and fear rippled across Arlene's face—and hate, washing across the muscles, setting her mouth and settling into a wide-eyed stare. Arlene's hands clenched and her body shook.

"Don't—you—ever—touch—me—again." The words came out low, even and cold.

Marian trembled as she pushed herself to her feet. Arlene continued to loom over her. Marian understood, now.

"You coward—"

Arlene raised a hand and took a step, but the woman

interposed herself between the two. "That's OK, we'll take her now."

"I'm not going—don't touch—leave me alone!" But the man's grip was strong as he pinned her arms. She felt herself lifted.

"Arlene! Don't do this! Help me! Arlene! For God's—" She continued to shout and struggle, trying to twist and kick, but she was aware of being carried out of the room, down the steps and toward a car. Every move she made was met with a countermove, even in the car where she was pressed into the seat between the man and the woman. Her struggles diminished—until she saw something thin and shiny in the woman's hand.

"This will calm you."

"No!" Marian shouted, yanking her arm free and nearly knocking the syringe out of the other's grasp.

"Whoa, easy," the man said, pinning her head against his shoulder.

She barely felt the prick; she concentrated on screaming and trying to twist out of the stranger's grasp. Rage and humiliation were all she had to power the effort, but even that soon drifted into a contradictory mishmash of sound and light until everything just faded away.

"Set: time." No response.

Aaron sighed. Yesterday, his office computer had responded immediately to his command "Break wind" by giving him a flatulent reply even though the timbre of his voice had changed. The VCR, on the other hand . . . he began tapping at keys on the remote control.

Yesterday had been an entirely different day. First a visit to the suddenly larger mall to get new clothes (in the children's department, of course, where he turned down an Automatic Enema T-shirt in favor of more mundane shirts and pants, although he did buy some purple undershorts), then a visit to Thagg, Morgan, and Edwards in downtown Kansas City. The place came to a virtual halt—"Are you for real?" Merilee, the receptionist, had blurted—as he made his way to his office. As he cleaned out his desk—a huge, flat surface to him now—some of the staff had surprised him by presenting him with a boy-sized T-shirt with the motto "I survived the Holn" emblazoned across the front.

"Of course I don't expect the firm to keep me on," he told Forrest Thagg, senior partner. "I, as a customer, would find it a bit difficult to take me seriously anymore. Now that it's apparent my . . . condition . . . is somewhat, um, permanent, I see no other recourse."

Thagg's muscles registered just the tiniest fraction of relaxation. *Not long ago, I towered over this dried-up gnome.* "Just so. Although we held your position until we heard something different, we decided it would be difficult to maintain decorum under the circumstances. However, we do appreciate all you've done for us, Mr. Fairfax, and we have determined a fitting severance bonus."

That bonus, Aaron had to admit, was most generous. However, as they walked out of Thagg's inner sanctum, the old man did an odd thing.

"Ah, Mrs. Fairfax. May I see you for a moment?"

Aaron watched quizzically as Janessa walked past. Then, he'd dismissed it as Thagg's wish to comfort the bereaved wife. That night at dinner, though, Janessa had said Horace Duncan would be over at eight A.M. the next day. Aaron had pressed her to say why "Horseface" Duncan, her divorce lawyer, would be making a house call. She'd been evasive, though.

Between Thagg and Horseface, Aaron couldn't shake the suspicion something was up, which was why he was climbing shelves stringing camcorder wires and programing a balky VCR. He had to bend almost double to see his watch face on the shelf below so he could confirm the time. He hadn't had time to get the band shortened to fit a thinner wrist yet, so now it was mostly just a nuisance.

Please, lord, let Horseface be on time. And please make this jury-rigging invisible to the eyes of mine enemies.

The VCR's digital clock said 8:04 when Horseface followed Janessa into the entertainment-center den. Aaron already had taken a chair on one side of the room. Janessa did what he expected by sitting behind the low, circular glass coffee table.

"That him?" the attorney said as he placed a briefcase on the table.

"Him," Janessa said.

"Boy, they really did make him into a rugrat." His thick, long face, which inspired the nickname, split into a grin as he sat down next to Janessa. "I can see why you want out of this mess."

"Will it be easy?"

"Easy as pie, my dear, easy as pie. The ruling simplified things tremendously."

"What's easy as pie?" Aaron said. "Are you going to let me in on your little game, or are you going to continue to play screw the husband?"

"Oh, dear," Horseface said, opening the briefcase and extracting a sheaf of papers, "they didn't do anything to blunt that tongue, did they? That's too bad."

"As part of the process, the Holn cut away diseased tissue. If you'd been there, Horseface, they wouldn't have had enough left to do anything with."

The attorney grinned. "Such talk from a brat. Maybe you need some discipline." He spread papers out on the table, addressed Janessa. "It's all here. You sign these papers, and everything's yours. The house, the car, the property, the bank accounts, everything."

"What if I refuse to sign?"

Horseface turned his head slightly to look at Aaron. *"You* are not allowed to sign."

"Now wait a minute. Some of this stuff is mine, and there's damn little in any of the bank accounts that's hers."

"Sign here, here, here, and here." Horseface stood up and walked around the table toward Aaron. "Didn't you hear what the judges said, little boy? You are the size of children, you *are* children, you do not have the maturity to act as adults. Therefore, as children, you do not have any rights. And there ain't a thing you can do about it."

The attorney lunged and knocked Aaron off of his chair. He hit the floor with a grunt, and when he rolled over and looked up, Horseface was leaning over, leering at him.

"Not a goddamned thing. Little boy."

Aaron's body shook as he stood up. "That is the damndest piece of melodrama I have ever seen, but somehow it fits coming from you, shit-for-brains." He turned to Janessa. "Now I know why you were so fucking anxious to deposit that severance check."

Janessa looked up from the papers. "Of course. We can't allow children to handle that much cash." She shrugged. "Besides, I would have gotten it anyway. This just makes it quicker."

"Jesus. Don't I get anything? Bus fare to—huh. Where do I go from here?"

"Oh, that's been taken care of, too."

"What?"

"Horace, be a dear and take him to the utility room, make sure he stays there."

"Of course." He came at Aaron, who tried to turn, but felt a hand on his shoulder. He twisted but Horseface grabbed again. Aaron struggled, but could not prevent being dragged from the room. He raged at his helplessness, and Horseface actually chuckled as he pushed him into the small room with the washer and dryer. Aaron lunged at the door, but the lawyer already had blocked it. His rage continued as he paced in front of the appliances, muscle spasms threatening to make him kick or lash out at something. He kept himself from doing so, but just barely.

Now what is she doing? What arrangements? She's been planning a lot, this "wife." And that goddamn lawyer—acting like the curly mustachioed character in a melodrama where they tossed peanuts at the bad guy.

The most maddening thing was that Janessa and her shyster knew, where he did not, what was going to happen next.

Finally Horseface opened the door. "You can come out now, little boy. Janessa says to meet her in the living room."

Aaron dashed into the den. No one was there, and the VCR was still running. He cut the recording, rewound the tape for a quick moment, played a second to confirm he had something, hit the rewind button. He had to climb up on the shelf and stretch to get the camera. He yanked the cable, pulling it free of the tape he'd used to press it into the edges along the large-screen monitor. Jumping down, he stuffed camera and cables into a cabinet below the VCR.

"Aaron?" Janessa.

He stabbed the stop button, yanked the cassette from the machine and slipped it into a cardboard sleeve.

"Coming." He tried to act nonchalant as he stepped into the hall.

"What were you doing?"

"Looking for tapes."

"You don't have time for that." She led the way into the living room. Three men glared down at him; Horseface smirked from the couch.

"There's your stuff." Janessa pointed to a suitcase. "You're going with them."

"Them who? And where?"

"I have signed custody over to their organization."

"What organization? Who are these people? Where are we going? *Answer the goddamn questions.*"

"They are your guardians now."

"But—"

Janessa nodded at a tall thin man, who in turn nodded to a bulky man of medium height, who leaned over and picked up the luggage.

"Let's go," the thin man said, placing a hand on Aaron's shoulder.

He twisted away. "Just a fucking minute. Let me get this straight. You stole my house, my car, my stuff, all my money, then you signed away my rights to a trio of thugs? Damn you, woman, bitch!"

"*Au contraire,* my little friend," Horseface said. "She is within her legal r—yow!" Horseface dived to avoid a candy dish that hurtled by the spot his head had been.

Someone shoved Aaron against a chair, pinned his arms. The thin man kneeled in front, pulled out a flat box, opened it and took out a syringe.

"This is a sedative. You can cooperate and walk out of here on your own power, or we can carry you out. It makes no difference to us."

"I guess it does to me. You have all the cards."

The man nodded, stood up. "Let's go. Give me that." He took the tape from Aaron and stuffed it into a side pocket of the suitcase.

Aaron was guided firmly out the front door and toward a long car. The thin man drove, the bulky man sat on his left and the third man, only slightly less bulky, sat on his right. As the car backed out of the driveway, Aaron leaned forward so he could see the house, roosting elegantly on top of the highest rise in the Briarwood development. In the closed garage sat his Maserati. He sighed, sat back.

No one spoke on the trip up Interstates 635 and 29 to Kansas City International Airport. Aaron had to put aside plans to shout how he'd been kidnapped in the crowded concourse because the car went to a commercial area and the three silent ones guided him to a private jet.

Once airborne, he asked, "Can you tell me where we're going, now?"

No one answered. That almost was worse than being beaten. He flicked his wrist to check the time, forgetting again he didn't have a watch there. He patted his shirt pocket before remembering where he'd left it: on the shelf below the VCR.

So she got that, too.

Thinking of the VCR made him look at the suitcase in the seat next to him. The rectangular bulge of the tape still showed through. He slumped back, felt sleep sneaking up on him. He'd been up early, setting up the vidcam and VCR, climbing up and down the shelves—"Like a monkey," his mother would have said in the days when he was a boy and did such things as a matter of course.

The background roaring of the jet lulled him toward sleep, and his mind drifted to the day he left Lovelace. He'd watched the man Earl had said was his grandnephew and a boy walk into Earl's room, and a few minutes later man and boy walk out. Except there was something about the boy—Aaron grinned. Earl looked so natural in contemporary kiddie-character-tie-in clothing. Aaron slept in the hospital room one more night, and when his turn came, Janessa simply asked if he was ready and they walked out the door and past the army of media. The bright sunshine blinded him, making the figures indistinct in his peripheral vision. He heard them muttering until a bright one finally caught on and started calling "Mr. Fairfax! Mr. Fairfax! Any comment?" The name rippled through the crowd as they all suddenly remembered the naked boy on the hill, and for a fleeting second, Aaron discovered what it was like to be a megacelebrity. As he walked, eyes on the ground in front of him, he noted Janessa was as cool as ever in the tumult, even though someone occasionally called her name. By this time, an impulse that had been building in him became overwhelming. When he noticed the eye of a telephoto lens pointed right at him, he gave in. He lifted his left hand, three fingers and thumb curled, middle finger sticking straight up. The image, like the one in June, went out, but in the taped replays he saw later, the gesture was buried under electronic fuzz.

Someone shaking his shoulder brought him back from sleep he hadn't been aware of falling into. "We're landing," a gruff voice said.

After checking his seat belt, he looked out. The plane
was in final approach, and the ground below looked
vaguely familiar. It didn't click, though, until the plane
glided over the runway and he saw the terminal building
flash by.

"Hey, this is Albuquerque. What's going on here? Are
you people from Lovelace? The government? *Who the
fuck are you people?*"

All three glanced at him, but all three turned away.

Aaron slumped. After the long taxi to a general
aviation terminal, they walked straight through to another long car. He watched listlessly as the streets and
building zipped by in an unfocused blur. Finally the car
turned into a nondescript driveway past a long cinder
block building painted a sick mustard yellow and pulled
up in front of a nondescript gray building, also cinder
block. Inside, blue linoleum stretched before him, cinder
block walls painted dark blue halfway up and white the
rest of the way hemmed him in on both sides. About
halfway down the long corridor, Less Bulky opened a
door with a foot-tall *6* stenciled at an adult's eye height.
Aaron stepped into a small room of white cinder block
walls and brown linoleum. A window framed in gray
metal broke the solidity of the blocks; below it, a
floorboard space heater ran the length of the wall. A
desk, chair and lamp stood against the wall to his left,
and a bed to the right. A chest of drawers faced the foot
of the bed against the wall of what turned out to be the
closet.

"Your room," the only words spoken by Less Bulky.
"Key on the desk." Bulky dropped the suitcase in the
middle of the floor and both men left, shutting the door.

Opposite the closet, to the left of the hall door, was the
bathroom: toilet, sink, shower stall, all perfunctory,
nothing fancy. He noted wryly among the supplied toilet
items a can of shave cream and a razor. The first couple
of days he'd automatically stepped to mirror, but the
face looking back always reminded him of that futility.

Actually, he'd quickly gotten used to not having to shave.

He stepped to the window, but had to pull the chair over and climb up. A gray cinder block wall filled the view left to right, top to bottom. Across four feet of asphalt-covered ground, one clump of crab grass grew defiantly from a crack where wall met asphalt.

He got down, went over and sat on the bed, staring at the brown floor until the door opened and a hefty woman in a white nurse's uniform stepped in.

"Aaron? I'm Ms. Ames. We need to get you signed in and all, but right now, I imagine you're hungry. Please come with me, and we'll get you some lunch."

He stood, began moving toward the door.

"Don't forget your key."

A large metal tag with 6 stamped on it hung from the key. He stuffed it into his pocket. He followed her down the corridor to a point where another branched off.

"This is the dining room," Ms. Ames said. "Please go in and have a seat. Jerry will bring you a lunch in a few minutes."

He watched as she strode down the branch corridor, took out a key. As she twisted the key in the lock, Aaron noted a dark blotch on the back of her left hand. He stepped into the dining room, actually just a longer version of his room. More cinder block walls, egg-yolk yellow bottom, white on top, dark-green linoleum floor. Fluorescent light glared from fixtures imbedded in the false ceiling. A rectangular metal table with a fake wood-grain pattern stood in the center with plastic chairs in disarray around it. The only other furniture was a soda-pop machine in the far corner. No pictures broke up the unrelenting flat expanses of the walls, not even a clock.

Someone else sat at the table, head down, but there was no mistaking the cascade of auburn hair flowing down over the shoulders. She did not move until he stepped close. The head came up and Marian Athlington fixed him with her eyes, not fearful, just tired.

The two stared at each other—so much like their first meeting in the patrol car all those seeming years ago—for several seconds.

"I am Aaron Lee Fairfax. I am forty-three years old." He took a deep breath, let it out. "I do not own a Maserati anymore."

Nine

October 19

Miranda started to brush some lint from her skirt, but glanced quickly at a monitor. It showed her looking down, but not what she was doing. She straightened. The main monitor did show what Dr. Samuel Innes was doing: talking. He'd talked—and remained on screen—most of the show, leaving her to roast gently under the lights of the Time/Warner/Tribune Multimedia News affiliate. The late-night news show had wanted Avram, but he was scheduled for someone else, so they took the second banana.

"Dr. Sena," the host said, evidently remembering she had another guest, "how do you respond to Dr. Innes's comment that you and most of the task force believe the children are human?"

"That conclusion is not set in concrete." A monitor showed Dr. Innes comfortably ensconced in an office instead of an overheated studio. "We tend to emphasize that because we have found no evidence to the contrary—"

"What evidence do you have for your position?"

"Minds, in particular, memories. These people remember—"

"A false lead," Dr. Innes said. The main monitor

113

quickly switched to him. "These memories have been transferred from the source. These are not the same people they were before—"

"Of course not!" The words came out with more heat than she intended. "To assume these are cell-for-cell, thought-for-thought copies of themselves as youngsters is absurd. Look at photos of them when they were young the first time. There's superficial resemblance, but there are also larger differences. Where one was obese as a child, she isn't now. Where one had asthma as a child, he doesn't now. Where one had brown hair as a child, she doesn't now. Their body shapes are different—"

"Cookie-cutter kids," Dr. Innes said.

"That was amusing the first time, but isn't it getting a little stale now?" Miranda flashed what she hoped was a friendly smile. "And their minds are not cookie-cutter because they all retain their memories. I might add," *before the host cuts to a commercial,* "that culture itself has changed. The oldest member of the group was born ten years before the outbreak of World War II, the youngest four years before the collapse of the Berlin Wall, and in neither case has society remained stagnant. The families have changed; some parents are no longer alive, brothers, sisters have grown up, the members of the group have had children of their own, grandchildren in a couple of cases.

"Stephen Gould argues that if the tape of life were rewound, the repeat play would go off on a totally different plot and the rise of humans would not necessarily follow. Of course, he's talking billions of years. But this group, these people, have had the tape of their lives rewound, just a hair in geological time.

"Their lives have been rewound for a fraction of a second, but the plot has been changed forever."

". . . the victim has been identified as Charles Thomas Romplin, one of the so-called Group of Seventeen. We are—yes, we are cutting now to a live press conference

being held by police detective John Barker at Tempe, Arizona, police headquarters."

"We, uh, we have a confession from the father. Henry Romplin has stated he shot the boy at about ten P.M. last night with an older model double-barrel sixteen-gauge shotgun. Mr. Romplin said the boy tried to run, but, I'm quoting here, I got him anyway. Both shots came from a distance of about four feet. The first shot evidently slammed the boy into the front door, which was closed at the time, and the second shot was fired before the boy hit the floor, according to the father's statement. The medical investigator has said death was instantaneous. After the alleged shooting, Mr. Romplin placed the shotgun on the dining room table, left the house through the back door, and upon seeing a neighbor looking over the back fence, stepped over and told him he'd better call the police because there'd been a shooting. Officers found the elder Mr. Romplin sitting at a table on the back patio smoking a cigarette and drinking a beer. He offered no resistance to arresting officers.

"As for motive, Mr. Romplin has not said much upon the advice of his attorney. However, Judy Romplin, Mr. Romplin's daughter, has stated to investigators the elder Romplin was quite upset over what happened to his oldest son. According to Judy Romplin, Mr. Romplin said several times over the last few months that Charles, the victim, was not his son, that, quote, something else had been put in his place.

"That's all we have for you now. We will not take questions."

Miranda bit off a curse as the top paper notebook fell off the stack. With both arms holding other documents, she couldn't see how to retrieve the errant book.

"Allow me." Matthew Gunnarson picked it up. "May I help with some of the others?"

"Your chivalry is not going unnoticed. I would appreciate it."

In order to transfer documents, they had to get close, and again she noticed the clear, blue eyes. They often belied the continual smirk, a trick of his she had trained herself to look out for.

Now the face smiled at her, eyes twinkling . . . *Stop it.*

"Didn't see you in the hall," she said as they started moving.

"I was in the copy room. Stepped out just in time to see that thing leap from the top of the pile. What are these?"

"Some of the data on brainwave studies misplaced in the move. I just now found them."

"Yeah, it's too bad we had to leave Albuquerque. New Mexico in the fall can be quite delightful. Instead, we're back to the Santa Ana-driven heat and dust of Los Angeles. I'm a bit vague on the reasons why."

They pushed through a door into the standard-issue conference room: long, no windows, pictures of famous alumni on the walls.

"Politics, Dr. Gunnarson, pure politics." She set her load down at the end of the table. "California wanted First Contact on its soil. State officials planned for it practically from the first Holn signal. Then the Holn crossed them by landing in New Mexico and they were angry and jealous. That jealousy finally found a venue of revenge when the House and Senate, spurred by the entire California congressional delegation, went to all the bother of passing resolutions that suggested the Holn Effect Task Force would be better off in California despite pleas from us that moving would be an unnecessary disruption. California was determined to get back some of the glory stolen by that upstart state, so it flexed muscle the puny New Mexico delegation couldn't match." She shrugged.

Matt lifted an eyebrow. "I see."

She grabbed some notebooks. "You also might want to remember we're pawns, Doctor, vulnerable to all sorts of political machinations. Now will you place one of these notebooks at each chair, please?"

"I hear and obey, O Great Leader."

She fixed him with a look, but he just chuckled as he walked along the oblong wooden table, tossing a spiral-bound book at each spot. She sighed, smoothed her blouse and skirt, then snapped her electronic notebook on and arranged some of the papers before her. *If you want to impress the guy, that's not—oh, shut up.*

By now, other attendees began to enter, find a place, and thumb through the notebooks they found there. Miranda had called the meeting because she wanted at least one face-to-face contact with the scattered group. Even Avram showed up, taking a seat to her right, calmly chewing on an unlit pipe.

"No TV shows today?" She regretted it the instant she said it.

He just turned a bemused face to her, eyes glinting under the bushy eyebrows. "That's why I'm here. I've been in front of cameras so long, I figured I'd better find out what I'm talking about."

"I wonder if we have any idea ourselves." She watched Dr. Innes walk past without a greeting and take a spot midway down on her left. She also noticed Matt took the chair directly opposite.

"Just what do you think you're doing?" Dr. Innes said.

"Making sure you don't steal the limelight." Matt smiled a fake smile. "Or the funding."

Miranda watched as they seethed at each other for a moment. "Avram, I'm still going to get you for this."

Avram smiled his smile again.

Miranda poured a glass of water from the pitcher, then sat down and moved the tray to her left so she could see down the whole table. Until now, displays of animosity between Dr. Innes and Matt had been kept submerged under the effort of forming the task force and struggling just to find where to start. Now that the work was becoming routine, though, emotions didn't have the detours they did before.

"All right." Miranda put her elbows on the table, leaned forward. "As you know, we've lost one of our subjects, Charles Romplin, shotgunned to death by his frightened father. We all knew something like this would happen, and it did, but it won't be the only one. This points out better than anything I can tell you what we're up against, the time we don't have, the reason you're being ridden so hard.

"The notebooks contain the missing EEG scans. OK, we'll start with status reports. Tim?"

Timothy's Cardiopulmonary Group reported on healthy lungs and hearts "with nary a trace of clumped cholesterol, damaged alveoli, clogged veins, blocked arteries, or arrhythmic heartbeats."

After punching keys on the notebook, he said, "No signs of surgery, either. No incisions, sutures or scar tissue. This is consistent with all organs we've studied, but I'd be willing to bet no one else has found any indications of manual surgery. Any takers?"

Anna's Endocrine Group was eating up supercomputer space trying to determine how chemical reactions could be reversed, speeded up/down or otherwise modified to remake glandular response and control. Randall's Nutrition and Metabolism Group reported no change in the dietary preferences of the subjects and no indicators in changes in metabolism rates of what was ingested. "No ulcers, either," he said. "Mr. Romplin had been a heavy drinker, but his post-event liver was as healthy as it ever was." He paused. "Too bad he didn't live to enjoy it."

"In the initial examinations, one area was overlooked," said Orlando of the Osteology Group, "and that was the teeth. No thorough exams were done, no X-rays made. We have had to fall back on pre-event X-rays and dental records. In all cases, cavities are gone, fillings, crowns, bridges, false teeth, and, in one case, braces have been removed, but none of that stuff is needed anymore anyway. All subjects have a full complement of thirty-two teeth—that much we know—and they seem to be adult teeth."

"What size?" Dr. Innes said.

"Scaled to jaw size. The skulls are about ninety percent adult size, they won't have grown much—"

"You mean, the enamel was cut back without destroying the tooth?"

Orlando stroked his walrus mustache. "In recent examinations of two cooperating subjects, we found perfectly formed teeth with no signs of the wear you would expect in adult teeth. These are not refiled or reground, these are brand new, complete teeth."

"I see."

Lindsey used Earl Othberg as a base of discussion in her report from her Neurological Group.

"We keep coming back to him because he's an interesting case neurologically as well as physiologically. Fortunately, a PET scan had been done of him three years ago. His total brain volume has increased, but this cannot be attributed solely to replacing losses due to age. This new matter is made up of neurons and glial cells, and of the correct structure for brain location. The usual brain defenses against aging—growth of dendrites, for example—are present in some of the neurons. This almost allows us to differentiate between new and old neurons. Plus"—she referred to her notebook screen—"signs of dementia—senile plaques, vascular amyloid deposits, neurofibrillary tangles and such—are erased. Gone, removed, disappeared. Now, our question is, is he smarter than he used to be? He was pretty intelligent before, so it might be just icing on the cake."

It was left to Constance's Genetics and Cells Group to drop the real bombshell.

"The female side of the family of Linda Rithen, maiden name Cole, has a case history of breast cancer." Constance sat straight up in her chair and read from her notebook screen like it was a school report. "Ms. Rithen's mother and grandmother died of it, an aunt has had a radical mastectomy, a sister is undergoing chemo-bullet radiation therapy in hopes of avoiding surgery. A check of this sister's DNA shows the one-base switch in genes in chromosome seventeen so prevalent in inherited cases of breast cancer. Ms. Rithen, pre-event, had had her DNA checked, and she also had this combination." Constance looked around at the table, took a deep breath. "Subsequent analysis of her post-event DNA shows . . . shows a change in that combination, a switch of an adenine and a thymine. We feel the risk of Ms. Rithen now developing the cancer has dropped by a magnitude—"

"What!" Dr. Innes's shout echoed off the walls. "You're now telling me these—these aliens from another world fixed it so this woman won't get breast cancer? That is absurd! Ridiculous!"

Constance's face went deep red. "We have looked again and again and reconfirmed it once, twice, three times. The numbers are there—"

"Suppositions, you mean. You've led the charge to find out how to prevent and cure breast cancer, Dr. Peterson, and I think you're letting your obsession lead you by the nose. Obviously someone has misread the data."

"I said, we have checked again and again—"

"Preposterous!"

"Dr. Innes, that is enough." Miranda glared down at him, but he concentrated his fury on Constance.

"Look for yourself! Here!" She tossed an optical disk at Dr. Innes. "It's all there, the Cole family data, Rithen's test results both pre- and post-. Find our mistake. Or find the mistake in the original analysis. Here, all of you!" She dealt disks off a stack like cards from a deck. One came skittering down the table and stopped next to Miranda's hand. "That's all the data. Biopsy samples are available at USC if you want some.

Please, find where we went wrong." She glared around at the table. "If you can."

"But how . . ." Timothy picked up a disk, looked at it as if it could answer his question. "How does an ET know where the cancer-causing genes are?"

"There is one possibility," Avram said quietly. "Linda Rithen might already have had a tumor forming, too small to be noticeable. The Holn found it, analyzed it, compared it to the other females of the group, and took the necessary corrective switch."

"We have considered that," Constance said. "Another possibility is our own research the Holn studied."

"Still," Randall said, "that's quite a stretch."

"Wanda, how much information about human physiology was given to the Holn?" Miranda said.

Wanda ran a hand through her hair. "Just about everything we know."

"Was that really wise?"

"In the interests of intragalactic relations, Dr. Innes, it was deemed the proper thing to do. The Holn gave us a lot of information about themselves, and about the other beings on the mother ship. Data we haven't even touched yet."

"And how can you be sure that information is valid, that they weren't feeding you garbage?"

"That's the old Cold War mentality, isn't it? Our decision was based partly on the Holn's actions as they arrived, not being clandestine, letting humans traipse through part of their ship and all. Plus, we decided to put a little trust in them."

"Aside from all that," Matt said, "could they in six years learn enough about us to know when to reformulate the base pairs?"

"Not to mention regrowing organs," Lindsey said. "What, a bladder, a prostate, a gall bladder, some toes, and several pairs of tonsils."

"And hair," Olive said. "Our Mr. Othberg had thin, white hair; now look at him. And Mr. Stangle, Mr.

Fairfax, both losing quite a bit of hair in the standard male pattern. Both with thick heads of hair now. Question is, will they get bald again? I know Mr. Stangle is anxious about it."

"We've talked about scaling, how the extremities and inner bone structures are scaled to the correct proportions for ten-year-olds," Constance said. "This applies to hair, too. I keep thinking of Ms. Athlington's lovely tresses. Pre-event, she cut it just below the knee. Post-event, it is just that long despite her being that much shorter."

"What about the structure of the hair itself?" Olive asked.

Constance gave her a sidelong glance. "Exterior structure matches pre-event samples minus signs of damage by aging. Cellular samples show matches in DNA, except, of course in Ms. Rith—"

"Oh, come on," Orlando said. "We're talking millions of combinations of DNA, plus the chemical formulae for growing cells. Even in six years that would be impossible to learn."

"Remember their computers," Wanda said. "Those machines are miles beyond anything we have, including all the Crays and Thinking Machines and Sunrooms and Deep Blues and CubeLinks and whatnot. In addition, JPL is studying something we haven't mentioned here: nanotechnology."

"Molecular manipulation," Timothy said. "Do we have anything to suggest they used it?"

"Not explicitly, no."

"It certainly would explain the lack of surgical signs," Randall said.

"How have the psychological studies progressed since the release of the group?" Avram asked.

Olive tossed her stylus on the table, frowning. "Our group has come nearly to a standstill. Some of the families are flat barring us from getting anywhere near. Mr. Romplin's family being one."

Miranda took another sip of water in the short silence that followed.

"Well, does that leave nanotech as the main engine of manipulation?" Timothy said.

"On the whole human genome?" Orlando said. "We don't even have the total DNA sequence for ourselves in ten, fifteen years of effort."

"Because the budget keeps getting sliced," Matt said. "We're almost there now, but the last pieces are in limbo because some congressmen don't see the need for it. As far as Connie's results go, I've been working with Dr. Philmont at Harvard and we are getting some confirmation."

Dr. Innes snorted. "Next, you're going to tell us these people are human right down to their bones."

"What's the big deal about bones?" Lindsey said. "You have osteoblasts to build up material and osteoclasts to take it away. So the Holn jazzed the 'clasts to shrink 'em."

"You, too, then, think all humans are, are just a collection of chemicals that can be stirred up in a cauldron like a witches' brew. Add a little eye of newt here, a little toad mucous there, a pinch of salamander lungs there and poof! a human, right? Not enough, my friend, not enough. There's something in the human, something intangible, that gives us spirit and intelligence. It resides in everyone and I'm afraid the Holn or whatever they're called removed it with the excess bone."

"And this spirit resides in the pineal gland, no doubt," Matt said.

Dr. Innes waved a hand. "Make your jokes. But we have no proof any of the original material is still in these people, that the spirit could survive the transformation."

"What is your suggestion?" Miranda said.

Dr. Innes turned a stony face toward her. "I've explained it a hundred times. The-the creatures put the brainwaves, the individual patterns, into humanoids

they grew in a tank. Are these simulacra, incompletely
grown and given the attributes of these people while the
real humans are being taken to the mother ship?
Possibly—this is how they populate the thing, don't you
see, and leave seeds of themselves behind, animated
bodies with memories impressed within, but without—
soul. Yes, I'll use that word."

"Piffle," Matt mumbled. "Science fiction. Fantasy."

"It's a damn sight better than anything you've—"

"You grant-sucking worm!" Matt jumped up, climbed
up on the table and glared down at Dr. Innes. "Tell us
what the answer is, Dr. Innes, you're the only smart one
here. Lay those pearls of wisdom on us—"

"You smart-ass little—"

"I'm not buying it, Doctor. I'm not one of your
political worshipers, licking your shoes, the ones you use
to make end runs around the budget process and steal
money from other projects so your Florida university
can build you a big, nice new lab—"

Dr. Innes jumped to his feet. "I do legitimate research,
you jackass—"

"According to the gospel of St. Innes." Matt jabbed an
arm at him. "You can't do that here. I'm not going to sit
and listen to it. Do some thinking for a change, leave
your fucking prejudices behind and approach this like a
scientist, not a preacher—"

"You whining baby! You're still mad at me because
they chose my project over yo—"

"And sixty oth—"

An explosion of glass made everyone jump, then stare
down at the head of the table.

"Sit down and shut up!" Miranda glared down the
table as water and glass dribbled down the wall to her
right. Hurling the pitcher had pained muscles in her
arm, and in the arc, water had sloshed out and caught
Avram. Her whole body shook and she had to lean on
the table to keep control. "You, off. You, down."

Matt was off in a flash, but Dr. Innes remained standing.

"Down!"

He sat.

"Too bad the TV crews aren't here to capture this. It'd be a great show. Scientists standing around screaming at each other. How entertaining! We have nothing, *nothing* except a dead man killed by fear and the rising of a new superstition. 'Something else had been put in his place,' the father said after pulling the trigger. *On his own son.* Soon we'll have more dead people and all we can think of is grant money? Damnit, if you can't leave your arguments and your grudges outside the door, or sweep them away, or throw them in the trash, then get out of here! *Right now!"* She grabbed Constance's disk. "This is what you are to concern yourself with from now on. You are here to analyze and research this phenomenon, find out what the hell's going on.

"I want this nanotech business pursued. Wanda, that's you. Those of you with alternate theories have ten days—ten days—to provide a solid base for your theories. The rest of you, stop yammering and give me some results—quantifiable and substantial. If—"

Dr. Innes yanked his briefcase open. "I don't have to put up with this. This is not the fifth grade." He jammed papers and disks—except one—into his briefcase, slammed it shut, stood up.

"You step out that door and you're fired. I will have security escort you from the campus."

"Really—"

"Sit down!"

"Avram, for God's sake—"

Miranda paused, surprised Avram didn't answer. She stole a glance at him and stopped in shock. The hard look he had fastened on Dr. Innes sent chills down her spine; she wondered why the water droplets in his hair didn't freeze. Dr. Innes took one step, faltered; then stepped back, turned away, set his briefcase down on the table and flopped into his chair.

"The disk, doctor." Miranda kept her voice even.

Dr. Innes picked up Constance's disk with two fingers as if it had slime all over it, opened his briefcase slightly and shoved it in.

"Dr. Innes isn't the only one under the gun, people." The fury had blown itself out, but the residual anger still tightened her voice. "All we have now are suppositions, guesses and maybes. Not good enough. Answers, people. We have to have answers. Other people are going to die and it'll be our responsibility." She let her gaze linger on each person for a second. "Meeting adjourned."

She leaned against the table as the silent scientists passed by. Most didn't look at her, but Constance flashed a brief smile while Wanda gave her a quick thumbs-up. Dr. Innes strode by quickly, eyes locked front. Water drops sliding down the wall reflected points of light into her peripheral vision. *Poor innocent pitcher. All it ever wanted to do was serve.*

Avram patted her shoulder. The left side of his shirt clung wetly to his skin.

"I'm sorr—"

He put up a hand. "Never mind. An occasional cold shower does the soul good."

"I lost control. You want my resignation?"

Avram laughed. "My dear Miranda, whatever for? You did not start the shouting match. I must say though, your method for ending it is rather unique. See you tomorrow."

"Yeah. Better change before you get a chill."

Some leader. She would have lost Dr. Innes if Avram hadn't been there.

Matt stepped forward slowly, stopped at the corner of the table.

"Didn't know you were still here."

He shifted. "Guess I owe you an apology." He pulled a white handkerchief from a lab-coat pocket, began wiping water off of the table. "I just felt that Sam was going off—"

"Never mind. An explosion of some sort had to happen sooner or later. Now that it has, perhaps we can settle down." She rubbed her forehead. "Or, maybe not."

She began collecting the scattered papers. "I see you're aware of politics, too."

Matt grunted, stuffed the handkerchief back. He drummed his fingers on the table, looked around, studied the pattern of water on the wall. She expected a sarcastic comment about her pitching ability, but instead he said, "Speaking of the pineal gland, what do the data show?"

"Oh, um, they're clear, little if any pineal sand visible. They've been enlarged slightly, like they are in children, but no other changes have been noted."

"No souls showed up in the X-rays, huh?"

"We're hoping to see changes if the group reaches maturity. If their internal clocks have been reset, then that's likely where. Assuming they grow up again, of course."

"God, it must be frightening not to know that."

"I think it's one reason Mr. Romplin was killed."

Matthew shook his head. "Poor guy."

"Yes." Miranda finished gathering her material. "I daresay his death got to all of us more than we care to admit."

Matt drummed a little more, then said, "Doing anything this evening? I know a great restaurant off the Strip."

Talk about audacious. This man screamed, stood on a table, disrupted a meeting because he's aggressive, boorish and opinionated. Another Samuel Innes in the making.

"You're on. I just hope you're bringing a lot of money."

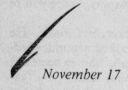

Ten

November 17

Marian felt a hand on her shoulder. "Tonight, if you're ready."

"I'm ready."

"And willing?"

"Not a shred of doubt."

Aaron nodded. "Four, then."

She nodded in turn, watched him jog down the corridor. A shiver washed over her at the thought of what they were about to do.

She hurried to her room. The technician had botched the blood collection again and the spot on her left arm throbbed just a bit. Another big purple spot likely would form. Almost like Lovelace—blood tests and X-rays and treadmills and stationary bikes and immersion into pools of water while breathing into tubes. Three weeks of this, day after day, so much blood being drawn they talked about installing a shunt so they could tap her like a beer keg.

And nothing could be done—except plan. One of the first things Aaron and Marian discovered was the lax security. They studied every detail of the routine and layout. Sunday turned out to be the best day; two medical technicians came in early, did the perfunctory data gathering, then left. That left two guards whose routine was as predictable as clockwork.

She pulled the chair over, climbed up and looked out. "Aw, shoot," Aaron had said, "you got the view." Some view: the west wing to the left, a large parking lot of patched asphalt, the ugly yellow building beyond. The parking lot was the "prison yard" where they were allowed to walk in counterclockwise circles—except once, when the guard made them go clockwise—like dogs on a leash. The gate always was closed and locked, but on the other end of the yellow building, the fence left a gap where it didn't meet wall.

A child-sized gap.

Marian tried to see as much of the lot as she could, but it was in its usual Sunday state: empty and lifeless.

She jumped down, went to the closet and pulled out a backpack, three shirts, and three pairs of jeans. She tossed the stuff on the bed, went to the chest of drawers and yanked on the drawer that always stuck. Here she grabbed T-shirts and underwear and tossed them onto the pile. She went into the bathroom and gathered soap, shampoo, and skin cleanser, a towel and washcloth. She gave a wry glance to a box of menstrual pads given to her "just in case something unexpected happens." Fat chance. She left it. When she picked up her toothbrush, her reflection in the mirror caught her eye—again. Once more, she studied the small face. The same child's face of four decades ago? She couldn't tell exactly—she'd forgotten what her childish face had looked like. She watched the girl in the mirror move a hand up to shove aside errant strands of hair. Marian Anne Athlington on this side supposedly was doing the same thing—but was she a copy? Then the mirror would be reflecting a copy of the copy of the real Marian—

"Oh, brother," she muttered, grabbing the toothpaste and dashing out of the bathroom.

"Something evil is going on," Aaron had said the day after his arrival. They had expected more of the group to

appear, but no one else did. The only people they saw
were three nurses, two doctors, three beefy orderlies, six
guards, and Dark Suit and Slick Suit, two men who
strutted like groomed poodles on the days they allowed
themselves to be seen. They always arrived and departed
together in a baby-blue Lexus with Texas plates.

She shoved the stuffed backpack under the bed. After
changing clothes, she punched the TV on and sat down
on the bed. The TV images made no impression, however. Other images began to form, images that intruded
into dreams and at moments when her restless mind
would allow them in. The Holn museum, with holo-
graphic scenes of a sun orbited by planets not in the
familiar configuration. *Alien suns,* she had thought,
*different worlds—I'm looking at something that exists
billions of miles away.* She saw herself turning, spotting
an odd bluish plant in a corner, heading toward it,
walking by a man in a white shirt . . . Aaron, he confirmed, much, much, later . . . but she never makes it to
the plant, instead the room twists and she falls. Muffled
sounds, she feels herself moving . . . no, being
moved . . . through a dark place. Quiet shufflings, a
light, an unreal light, glowing all around her, a close
ceiling or wall . . . a touch of a breeze on bare skin. . . .

In the room, alone, she placed her head in her hands.
She'd been wrestling with the shadows off and on since
arriving. Aaron, too, and they had talked about them,
and agreed that Earl hadn't made up the egg-womb. It
was real . . . perhaps. No matter how much they talked
about them, tried to grab them, the shadows remained as
elusive as leaves in a wind.

Her alarm beeped: Four P.M. She slipped her coat and
backpack on. She opened the door slowly, peering out.
The only person in the hallway was Aaron, peering
around his door. He walked quickly over to her, wearing
almost the same thing she did: backpack, denim coat, T-
shirt (his black to her tan), jeans, and almost-new
athletic-styled shoes.

"OK?" he whispered.

She nodded and shut the door softly, muffling the TV. They hurried down the hall, Marian stepping ahead to the locked double-doors. Through the small window, right on schedule, she saw a guard carrying a steaming bag of microwaved popcorn and a soda in a can into a room where football played on a TV. The pair moved on past the examining rooms.

They reached a metal door and Aaron handed her a pair of wirecutters with taped handles he'd stolen from a tool box, then knelt on the floor. She climbed up as they had rehearsed and clipped a wire leading from the door and saw the red warning light on the alarm blink out. After jumping down, Marian pulled out the key she had stolen the day before from a careless guard. The lock clicked and both pushed gingerly on the release bar, but the door swung open easily and quietly.

"Small favors," Aaron muttered.

They ran along the building, stopping at a corner. Aaron peered around, nodded, and they scurried for a dumpster looming large and green about ten yards away. They scrambled along the wall behind it to the next dumpster, then stopped. Marian's heart was beating fast. The longest run lay before them, about fifty yards with nothing between them and the windows of the clinic's west wing.

"In the movies, I think they'd run across one at a time," she said in a low tone.

"Meaning someone is left behind. I say we stay together."

"Let's go, then."

He dashed out, and she jumped practically on his heels. Their footfalls echoed off the wall like shots. Aaron hardly hesitated, scrambling up to the gap and out. Marian pulled herself up and through. They dashed down and across a street, the sinking sun angling shadows across their path.

They slowed their run a bit once they turned a corner,

but Marian kept straining to hear shouts or a car engine. They trotted across another street, then up another block to a wide, four-lane road with the first traffic they'd seen. They slowed, looking for signs.

"There." She pointed.

He nodded. "Fifteen minutes."

"We'd better stay out of sight while we wait."

The bus stop had a sheltered bench, but they slid behind a bush growing beside a building entrance.

Marian breathed deeply, turning her face, trying to keep her hair from being snagged by twigs and dry leaves. "Been a long time since I've run like that."

"Yeah. At least we're able to do that much."

She had a hunch she knew to what he referred. "The wiggling fannies in the *Playboy* videos didn't help?"

Aaron snorted. "I didn't expect them to. What about you? Any responses?"

"I haven't tried that hard." *I didn't try that hard when I was an adult.* "You have the quarters?"

Aaron reached into his pocket. "Yup."

They sat in silence for a few moments, then Aaron nudged her, pointed.

They crawled out from behind the bush, waited until the bus was a half-block away, then dashed to the stop. The bus stopped with the door right in front. Marian misjudged placement of a foot and went down on one knee on the now-larger steps.

Aaron dropped the quarters in for two fares. "Can we get a transfer for downtown?"

"Sure." The driver pulled two slips of paper off a pad. Aaron and Marian took the seat one down from the driver. Two other people were on the bus, and one more got on before the driver called out "Transfers for downtown." The next bus started off almost as soon as they were aboard. Marian, next to the window, watched the buildings and streets of the strange city pass by, although many of the places had the familiar names and designs she knew from Bellingham. Different climate, same architecture, same products.

"Downtown, Civic Plaza." Aaron and Marian looked at each other; first he shrugged, then she did, then they stepped off the bus.

A flat concrete expanse stretched away from them, broken up by trees growing from small plots of grass. A pile of giant concrete blocks dominated one side, and a few people sat around the base. Tall buildings of concrete, steel, and glass edged the square, except on one side where a block-long slab lined the street as if one of the buildings had toppled over. Not too far away, a man and woman sat on a bench, the woman peering into a Burger King bag as if looking for stowaway French fries.

"Well, we have reached the point of asking ourselves 'now what?'" Aaron stuffed his hands into his pockets as he looked around.

"Find a phone." The adrenaline from the escape had faded. Now Marian began to feel hesitant.

"Yeah. Looks like there's some over there."

Aaron had to stretch to drop coins in. She held the phone book for him as he dialed.

Looking around, Marian saw the man and woman moving across the square; as they passed a trash can, the woman tossed the bag in. Marian felt a pang in her own stomach.

Twenty minutes later, they sat down on a bench. "Three of them thought I was some kid playing a joke and hung up," Aaron said.

"One did that to me. Three wanted my parents' names. This is a problem we hadn't considered. It could be touchy when we go to register."

"If we go to register." He sighed. "The cheapest motel is going to take most of our eighty dollars in one swoop. And that's just for tonight."

"One night might be enough, assuming I can get into my accounts from here."

"The big if again."

"Yes," she said, doubt now creeping into her mind like a cold fog.

"One night stand, maybe a burger between us." He opened his hand. "I have four of our quarters left."

They both sat silently. The shadows had engulfed most of expanse; only the tops of the taller buildings still remained in direct sunlight. A November breeze swept across the concrete. Marian pulled her coat together but couldn't keep the chill out.

"I thought this place was a desert."

"Deserts can be quite cold, I hear."

"Aaron, we've got to do something."

"The cheap motels are several blocks, miles, away from here," Aaron said. "The ones we see from here would charge eighty dollars just to ride the elevator. We came to the wrong place." She felt his eyes on her. "Think we made a mistake?"

"I won't go back. No." She felt a chill not from cold air. "I am not a laboratory animal."

She felt a hand on her shoulder again.

"I understand the feeling. I wonder if there's some fleabags around h—"

Two persons sat down on the bench, sandwiching them. At Aaron's end, a man with uncombed graying hair, gray beard stubble, and a broad, lined face turned his shaded eyes on him. The man's open black coat showed a slight bulge pressing against the dark-green knit pullover shirt at his waist. His clothes were well-worn and his leather shoes were falling apart, showing red socks underneath. At Marian's end, a woman had a similarly well-worn appearance, but her brown eyes had a sharper focus. Her short brown hair was better combed, and her long tan coat and faded jeans looked worn, but not greasy, from long periods without wash water. She wore sandals, but long white socks extended beyond the tops of short, patched, off-white socks on each foot. Marian caught a whiff of alcohol, but she wasn't sure from who.

"Name's Ken," the man said.

"Virginia," the woman said. "Who're you?"

"Umm, just a coupla kids running away from the boring decadence of middle-class suburban life," Aaron said.

"Seeking thrills and glamor from the big city," Marian said.

"Hoping to fall into a life of drugs, alcohol, and sexual depravity."

"Tasting the sleazy side of life, planning to write a best-selling book about it later."

"See, they don't talk like children."

Ken stretched, rubbed his hands on his khaki-coated thighs. "Right again, Doctor Virgie. They sure look like kids, though."

"They ran away all right, that much is true," Virginia said. "They have eighty dollars and some quarters between them. They used to have more, but they wasted a bunch trying to find a motel room."

"Eavesdroppers," Aaron said.

"We've been watching you since you got off the bus, actually."

"You had a sack from Burger King, over on the bench," Marian said.

Virginia laughed, stood up. "I'll tell you who you are. You're part of that group that was caught in the spaceship and made into children. I recognized you as soon as you got off the bus, although I don't remember your names. You have no friends, no family available to take you in. And no shelter. You'd better come with us."

Aaron and Marian looked at each other.

Ken jumped to his feet. "This place ain't safe at night. 'Specially for people your size. What're you gonna do when a three-hundred-pound gorilla with a taste for young flesh nabs you? Now come on."

Marian looked down, a helpless feeling rising again.

"We could outrun them," Aaron said. "Just take off—whang!—and they won't be able to catch us."

"True enough," Ken said. "I've lost my youthful football-captain physique. Someone else will, though. Even Albuquerque loses the night to the thugs, thieves, and drugs. Or maybe the people you're running from'll catch you."

"Look," Virginia said, sitting back down next to Marian, "I heard that comment about how you're not a lab animal. That sent chills right up and down my spine. I don't know what trouble you're in or who you're running from, but we're offering you a place to stay, with some food available, among people who do not desire to hurt you. That's the truth." She shrugged. "All I have to offer in the way of security is my word."

Aaron and Marian again looked at each other. Marian shrugged, Aaron shrugged.

"What choice?" she said.

"Not much," he said.

They both stood and adjusted their backpacks.

"Good." Virginia stood again.

The pair led them across the plaza, down a street between a hotel and a bank, around a corner and toward a construction site. A half-block-long skeleton of a building jutted skyward, crisscrossed by heavy rust-red girders. Some of the floors were closed off.

"Home, all twelve stories of it," Ken said. "Grid Manor, we call it. Ain't much, but it keeps the rain out." They passed through a gate in the surrounding fence, then stepped into the open bottom floor. A metal staircase led to the next floor, where a wooden ramp took over. The ramps angled on up the floors, and on each people watched as they climbed.

"Spread the word," Virginia had said on the second floor. "General meeting."

A gangly youth had sped up the ramp ahead of them. The ramps seemed endless—they'd top one, just to find another. During the climb, a few individuals joined the group. They gave them curious glances, but said nothing. "Ninth floor, the great room," Ken finally said.

The room was about the size of a basketball court and lit by fluorescent lights hanging from the exposed ceiling and by tungsten from several lamps scattered across the floor. Couches, chairs, tables, and cushions were set in groups, some covered with bright cloth. To one side, two bearded men sitting at an aluminum picnic table looked up from a chess game. The walls seemed to be made of plywood. On one side, rugs hung from the plywood while another wall was papered with photos cut from magazines and a third was covered in bright scenes painted directly on it. To the left, a stack of boxes and boards closed off a separate space, where the sounds of a television could be heard. Virginia steered them toward a spot where several couches and chairs had been placed in somewhat of a square. A solid-looking wooden rocking chair sat unoccupied by the couch Aaron and Marian were led to. The couch itself was soft and springy, although it tilted toward one corner. More people gathered around, some taking seats, others pulling chairs over while some stood in the background. Conversation was muted.

"The center of social activities." Ken giggled.

"We're calling a general meeting to discuss your situation," Virginia said. "The people here deserve to know what's up."

"And if they don't like it?" Aaron said, pulling off his backpack and setting it on the floor. Marian did the same.

"We are not hateful people."

The "we" of that statement formed a fair-sized crowd now. The individuals came in various sizes, colors, and shapes, most dressed in seemingly whatever they could find: flannel shirts, jeans, khaki pants, blouses, faded and torn jackets, dresses over hiking boots, shorts over sweat suits. Two of the faces made immediate impressions on Marian: a heavyset woman with her hair pulled

back in a neat bun that contrasted to the ripped and
resewn dress she wore; and a youth whose brown hair
was combed neatly in place like a first-grader's first day
at school. That and his torn blue-and-red checked flannel shirt made him stick out, and when he caught her
looking at him, his face creased into a toothy grin and he
stuck a thumb up. She turned away quickly, hoping the
flush she felt on her cheeks wasn't noticeable.

Ken plopped down next to Aaron, making the couch
bounce. Virginia remained standing as some of the
group parted for a tall, thin man whose shaggy jet-black
hair and thick stubble beard shot with gray framed a
rugged face where dark penetrating eyes peered out. He
wore an off-white shirt buttoned from collar to belt, dark
trousers, and laced boots that gleamed in the light.

"What's up, Virginia?"

"Tontine, I'd like to present . . . well."

"Aaron."

"Marian."

"Aaron and Marian—sounds like a movie. Anyhow,
they need shelter, if the group agrees."

"Runaways?"

"Right, but not what you think." She told them of the
Holn, and how Aaron and Marian were part of that
group, and how she and Ken had found them.

The man called Tontine whistled. "You brought us
some live ones this time, Virginia." He turned to them.
"What are you running from?"

"Not sure." Aaron explained everything—the clinic,
the physical exams, the escape.

"Why did you end up there? Where are your par—uh,
relatives?"

Aaron told him about his wife; Marian described what
happened with her sister. At first, she was reluctant, but
Aaron had been frank, so she followed his lead.

"What were you planning to do?"

Aaron shrugged. "Find a motel, where we could relax

a while and plan what's next. I know it sounds like poor planning, but, well . . ."

"We had to get out," Marian said.

Tontine nodded.

"And what about you people?" she said. "Who are you?"

Tontine regarded her a moment longer. "Homeless, but not helpless," he said. "Most of us. We share this place, live together, help each other out. They stopped work on this building five years ago. It was just sitting here, so we moved in. Put up temporary walls, built the ramps, brought in furniture, the like. We're not leeches, though. We have electricity here because we pay the bills. Same with the water and cable TV. Some of us have jobs and contribute to the general fund. Like Miguel over there, Miguel Ruiz." He pointed to a slim, dark youth. "He works at the Hyatt just down the block. And Eddie and Alice, and Frank, all have jobs. Some of us get temporary jobs to help bring in money. We make enough to get by, just not enough to get out."

"I see," said Aaron. "We've fallen in with one of those secret underground societies, the favorites of fiction writers, where a mixture of society's outsiders band together."

Tontine shrugged. "We have banded together out of self-preservation. We protect each other and keep the wolves at bay. Do you have a problem with that?"

"Only if we can't stay. I think I can speak for Marian when I say we're in a bind and need help. I have eighty dollars I'm willing to donate to whatever fund you have. It's all I can offer right now." He ran a hand through his hair. "As you can see, we have no place to go."

"It's up to the group." Tontine stepped aside.

Murmuring spread through the crowd. Marian saw the portly woman step up behind her. She touched a wayward strand of Marian's hair, then grasped a long lock in slender fingers and began stroking. "Lovely," she said, releasing the hair. She turned and stepped through the crowd, which parted for her. Marian leaned toward Aaron.

"You think this is a good idea?" she said in a low voice.

"It's the only alternative we have. Unless we just walk back out into the street. Virginia seems straight enough, and this guy Tontine seems to have a lot on the ball."

Marian nodded and was about to speak when a clatter cut her off. The crowd parted again, and the woman emerged, pushing a metal grocery cart ahead of her. She parked it directly behind Marian and began rummaging through one of the bright cloth bags she had stashed in the cart. She pulled out a flat black box, opened it and took out a comb, scissors and brush. She sat down next to Marian, held the implements up. They gleamed in the light.

"Clean," the woman said. "Fine." She slid fingers down the long length of Marian's hair.

"This is Betty," Virginia said. "She's a trained beautician, although her mental condition prevents her from holding a job. She's very good at it, and she keeps her equipment spotless. That's what she meant."

"Tangled," Betty said, grasping a thick lock. Agile fingers worked at a knot.

"It's not in good condition. I, um, sort of haven't had a chance to take care of it." Marian looked at the woman's face lined with wrinkles while her forehead creased in concentration. Her hair was all gray, going to white, but every strand was in place and the bun sat neatly at the back of her neck.

Betty glanced up, met Marian's eyes for a moment. "Bad times," she said, picking up her brush. "Tangles out." She began brushing with steady, confident strokes, holding the hair so it didn't pull. Marian felt tense muscles begin to relax.

"We ought to get her and Linda together," she said to Aaron, who smiled.

"It's settled," Tontine suddenly said. "Welcome to the secret underground society."

"I have adopted these children in order to save them. In turn, they can save us. They have been blessed by God, touched with the miracle of the Word, the wondrous miracle of His love. They are victims of fear and hate, but God has sent them to us as a sign of his love and commitment to give life eternal to those who accept Jesus Christ into their hearts. Amen."

"That was the taped statement from The Reverend Jim Brigman on why he has become the custodian on record for Alisa Bardnoth and Harold Coner, two of the so-called Rewound Children who were caught by the extraterrestrials and apparently turned into children. One of the children Brigman adopted, Alisa Bardnoth, apparently cut her wrists in a gas-station restroom in Stratford, Texas on November fifteenth. A patron discovered her immediately and paramedics were able to stanch the bleeding. Bardnoth, twenty-nine at the time of her capture, had been a church secretary married to Archie Bardnoth. She told police her husband had physically thrown her out of their house on the day she tried to kill herself. No action has been brought against Mr. Bardnoth, and he has refused to comment to reporters. The couple had two children, a boy, two, and a girl, five.

"The other Rewound Child, Harold Coner, thirty-one, had been a used-car salesman in Santa Fe, New Mexico, near the site of the Holn landing. He had been living with his sister, Janet Caperton, of Wilmington, Delaware, after the Holn incident, but as Coner reportedly told state child welfare officials, one day he came back from a walk to find his clothing and other belongings piled on the sidewalk in front of the house. Ms. Caperton also has refused to talk to reporters. Coner is divorced.

"No other information is available, either from Brigman's statement or from his church, the Faith Christian Ministry. A reliable source in the church, however,

told CNN Brigman had heard of the plight of the two and
immediately started adoption procedures.
   "Brent Caseman, Time/Warner/Tribune Multimedia
News, Waterhaven, Oklahoma."

Aaron whistled what he thought was a happy tune as
he walked up the ramp to the ninth floor. As he got to the
top, he realized it was the melody for the heavy-rock
group Bent Photons's controversial song "Jesus Had No
Legs." He grinned, surprised that under the screaming
guitars and pounding beat there was even a melody
there.
   Mild weather had allowed the window covers in the
great room to be removed, and sunlight flooded the area.
The "windows" were little more than heavy plastic
stretched from floor to ceiling girders, but they did let
light in.
   In the two days they'd been here, Aaron and Marian
had begun to settle into the routine, pulling various
duties, including "KP" in the ground-floor kitchen of
two camp stoves, three hot plates, and an electric skillet.
That, and the old refrigerator, were not enough to feed
the thirty to fifty people who might be staying at the
manor at any one time, so full-blown meals were eaten at
the Salvation Army food kitchen in an abandoned
department store three blocks over. The food was tasty,
but Aaron couldn't resist seeing the irony of him eating
in a soup kitchen.
   Today, he had accompanied Tontine on "fire warden"
duties—Tontine being the person who established the
fire rules in the first place. Aaron had been impressed—
the preparations even included alternate staircases and
chain-and-bar ladders coiled on three floors.
   "This place is a firetrap," Tontine had said. "Flames
would shoot straight up the ramps. All I want to do is
give everyone a better-than-even chance."
   Off the kitchen were the showers, one for men, the
other for women, and makeshift as they were, they did

have hot water. The toilets, however, were outside of the building in the auto-privies set up on the sidewalk. Rules controlled these amenities, also. Because the toilets were outside, women had to have an escort. At night, temporary toilets were set up in the showers. So far, he hadn't pulled "honey pot" duties.

Aaron marveled at how well Grid Manor functioned. Some residents came in just for a few days; some had been there almost from the day they had started enclosing the spaces.

"In winter, we get pretty crowded," Virginia had said. "It gets chilly, but it beats trying to stay unfrozen on the streets."

The only cloud had come the day before as the group had walked back from a Salvation Army dinner. Aaron had spotted a van waiting at a traffic light—a van like the one he'd seen parked at the "prison" when they'd "exercised." He'd pulled Marian aside and explained to Tontine. The van had turned a corner at the green light, but five minutes later Ken abruptly pushed him and Marian into a bank alcove.

"That van again." He placed himself in front of Marian, Virginia in front of Aaron. Tontine and the chess players—who played so much they were known as Black King Leo and White King Sam—watched as the van drove by slowly.

"As if looking for someone," Virginia had muttered.

When it turned a corner again, Tontine signaled and the group scurried down the street, everyone searching for signs of the van. Once inside the construction fence, Marian kicked an empty bean can.

"So, this is how it's going to be, huh?" she said. "Every time we see a white van we're going to cower."

"Don't forget blue Lexuses, Lexi, with Texas plates," Aaron said.

"We're going to have to be more careful," Tontine said. "It might be that your friends haven't quite given up."

Marian had pegged Tontine as the most enigmatic of the group.

"Yeah, I know, the name sounds like something out of a bad World War I flick. What can you expect from shavetail soldiers on their first drunk? We swore undying allegiance to each other, lubricated by bottles of Kentucky Beau, the worst rotgut crap you'll ever find on a legit liquor shelf. Anyhow, one of the guys took our last unopened bottle home to Omaha and put the damn thing in a safety deposit box. The last survivor of the group has to chug it. He won't be a survivor for long."

The others weren't so reticent.

Such as Ken: "High school hero gone bad. I dated the head cheerleader. I cared nothin' for college, to the dismay of my parents. They gave up on me and I gave up on them. They had my little brother, who did them proud, so that relieved me of 'sponsibility. What the hell." He shrugged. "Just another incomplete pass."

And Virginia: "Phud from Duke, research at Fermilab for a while. The death of the Supercollider pretty much decimated particle physics, too. Too many phuds, too few accelerators. When Fermilab cut a bunch of us, I panicked. Traveled everywhere, to CERN, to Japan, to Livermore, back to Fermi, to Brookhaven, to Cal Tech— resume in hand, humble pie for lunch, looking, hoping, talking. *Nada*. I didn't have the right connections, the right specialty, the right racial mix. Came to New Mex, talked to Sandia, planned to go to Los Alamos, but Los Alamos was pretty well chopped up by then. I never made it up there. These people found me crying myself to sleep on a bench in the plaza." She shrugged.

In the great room, Aaron found Marian where he expected: in the rocking chair, legs curled under as she worked with needle and thread, flowing hair glistening. Betty's tender ministrations had brought back its luster.

"Hey, windee." He sat down on an ottoman.

"Hey, wound up," she said, with a quick glance. News

shows already had taken a scientist's description and dubbed the group the Rewound Children.

"Who's getting his buttons back?"

"Kilkenny." She snapped a thread. "What have you been doing?"

"Checking for fire violations in the men's quarters." The men slept on the floor below the great room, the women a floor above; married couples had partitioned rooms on the sixth and seventh floors. "When I was little the first time, I wanted to be a fireman in the baddest way."

"You still might get your wish—"

"Marian." Tontine called across the room. He carried what looked like a pet carrier in one hand and a large envelope in another. "These have your name on them."

"What?" Marian tossed the sewing on the couch as Tontine set the carrier on the floor next to the chair.

Marian unlatched the top and a furry head immediately thrust through the opening. "Merlin!" She reached in and gathered a large cat, coat splotched with browns and whites, into her arms. It meowed lustily and rubbed its face against hers. Marian looked up at Tontine. "Where did you find him?"

"I stopped by to see a friend who works at Lovelace Hospital, just down the road from the VA hospital. The cat arrived in this about a week ago, addressed to you, care of the hospital. The staff didn't know where you were, but they fed it and watched it, but weren't sure what to do with it. I told D.J. I'd take it. I didn't tell him why."

"I don't understand. Was there just this one? What about Phoenix? There should be another cat."

Tontine held out the envelope. "Maybe this will help. It was taped inside the box. D.J. said they had plenty of arguments about opening it, and had just about decided to."

"I—here, hold him." She thrust the cat into Aaron's arms.

"Whuoof." The force of the thrust and weight of the cat almost knocked him backward. "Man, you are one big cat." The animal looked straight back at him from chest level, one green eye surrounded by brown fur, the other by white. "A nice one, though." Aaron scratched gently behind an ear. After a moment, the cat condescended to enjoy the scratching, blinking and tilting his head slightly.

Marian, meanwhile, had torn the envelope open. As she pulled out a folded paper, a bundle fell and scattered. Money—Aaron could see at least three five-hundred dollar bills in the pile.

Marian glanced at the cash as she unfolded the sheet. "It's from Shirley."

Dear Marian,

I am so sorry, but I have bad news.

Two days ago, your landlord cleaned out your house. Just cleaned it out. Didn't call, didn't tell me. Sold what he could of your stuff, gave away what he couldn't. Chopped up that old bureau you never knew what to do with for firewood. Last time I saw the place, he was redoing the floors and repainting everything. Not a thing of yours is left. He chased the cats out of the house. I don't know how long they were out. I found Phoenix on the road, hit by a car, killed. Merlin was sitting by her body. Not making a sound, just sitting there.

It gets worse. Your sister claimed all of your savings and checking accounts. It was done by an electronic fund transfer. I couldn't figure out what was going on, so I had a friend at the bank check for me. It was all gone in two hours. Even your 401 (k).

Marian rubbed a cheek with the back of the hand holding the letter.

* * *

Inside the envelope is your severance pay from the city, plus an extra bonus they stuck in. I know we're not supposed to send cash through the mail, but after what happened to your accounts, it's all I could think of.

I don't know what else to do. Mother is dying and the doctors want me to come to Minneapolis right away. I can't contact you and your sister slammed the phone down on me twice. I'll send the cat and your money to that hospital you were at and hope they can forward it.

I am so sorry. I have failed you in the worst way.

Marian rubbed her eyes. "Oh, Shirley—"

The letter fluttered from her hand to the floor. Marian covered her face. Aaron got up, stepped over and gently placed the cat in her lap. She wrapped her arms around it as it let out a quiet meow; then Marian pushed herself back in the chair, head down, hair hiding her face, weeping.

Aaron sat back down hard on the ottoman, barely aware of Tontine gathering the money and letter, folding it all back into the envelope, placing it on the ottoman next to him, then quietly walking away. Utter powerlessness washed over Aaron. He wanted to touch Marian, comfort her, but what could he say? It'll be all right? That would be a lie—and he would not pretend otherwise. She'd lost everything, just as he had. So? That could be no comfort to her. Anger sprang up in him, hot and fast, and he wanted to hit something—but to what end? All of his manly power was gone—the power to get forces in motion that got things accomplished. He shook his head, looked at his sneaker-clad feet resting near the runner of the rocking chair. He pushed his left foot forward until it touched, then slid it up on the runner. He hesitated a moment, then gently pushed down. The chair tilted forward, then back when he relaxed. It took a couple of times, but he got a steady rhythm going, not too fast, not too far forward or backward, just a gentle swaying. The cat watched him through heavy eyelids.

Marian didn't look up, but the weeping diminished. Aaron sat as unmoving as the cat, except for his foot gently rocking the girl in the chair.

Eleven

"New York police have identified the victim as one of the so-called Rewound Children, Sandra Mellinfield, who was thirty-four at the time of her capture by the Holn. Her body was found in her bedroom late Sunday. Police say she apparently took an overdose of sleeping pills.

"Her husband, Paul, has said Sandra was despondent over what had happened to her. Mr. Mellinfield admitted the couple's marriage had been in trouble before, partly because of Sandra's inability to conceive. He also said she suffered from severe arthritis, although a spokesman for the Holn Effect Task Force said all signs of the disease had been eradicated. Presumably, the Holn also might have corrected the reproductive problem. Mr. Mellinfield, a top manager for the Global Bank of Commerce in New York, said the situation had caused difficulties that spilled over into his job. He did not elaborate.

"Marinka Svoboda, CNN, New York."

November 23

"Why are you such a hardass?"

Earl looked up at Walter, who regarded him calmly. "If I am, it's because I still have remnants of what I was before. I was a pretty sour old man, you know."

"So I've heard tell." Walter sat down at the kitchen

table opposite where Earl sat slathering peanut butter on a banana. "You still blame yourself for the deaths of Aunt Edna and cousin Freddie."

Earl stared at the coated slice. "My whole family, dead long before I was, will be. If I had been a better father, a better husband . . ."

"The accident wasn't your fault."

Earl dropped the banana, leaned back in the chair. He wore only a pair of shorts, a mode of dress he'd adopted quite readily. "I blamed *Star Wars,* but of course, that's stupid. I had wanted the film for my theater because the buzz was so good, but Halyard beat me out. Freddie, being that age, was about to die if he didn't see it, so Edna took him to Superior. I stayed because we had a show, too. I don't even remember anymore what film it was." He ran a hand through his hair. "The old story, a drunk crosses the center line and death takes all." He jabbed the knife into the peanut butter. "They didn't *need* to go to Superior, she just wanted to get away from a surly husband. At least Freddie got to see *Star Wars* before . . ." He pushed the knife to the bottom of the jar. "Anger and sorrow have been constant companions."

Walter looked down, then back at Earl. "I'm sorry."

Earl shrugged. "If what has happened to us is supposed to be a reward, I'm the wrong guy."

"Is that what you think?"

"No." He straightened. "No. My number just came up in a strange lottery, is all."

Walter remained silent. Earl reckoned his nephew had reason to be upset. Two police officers had just left; they had been seeking a redheaded boy golfers were complaining was disrupting games. Lucas had been the prime suspect until Earl had entered the room. He refused to apologize, saying at seventy-nine, he didn't have to account for his actions. An officer countered with the possibility of trespassing charges.

"Between this and the Halloween incident, I just might have to toss you out."

"So a televangelist can swoop me up and put me on display as a Miracle Child?" He picked up the banana slice. "Oh, please, I'll be good."

Walter tried to bury a smirk by rubbing his chin. "This goes beyond tricks and trespassing, though. Many people I work with are religious and they seem to be finding you somewhat unsettling. At work, in the neighborhood, among the kids' friends, at school, we can feel an unease."

"Why do you surround yourself with assholes like that?" He shoved the banana slice into his mouth.

"I work with them, go to church with them."

Earl had to drain the milk from the glass before he could speak again. "What was the reaction of the family when your father up and brought his pregnant wife and four-year-old kid to Hawaii?"

Walter shrugged. "Not much, from what I understand."

"Because it was totally in character for an Othberg. We get tired of the status quo and often chase dreams. It's a big reason I ended up in the Holn ship, because it was new, and fascinating. I also did it for Freddie, but still, if this"—he gestured at himself—"had never happened, if I had dropped dead right afterward, I would have died happy. You have a dream, too, you told me. *Do* something about it."

"Earl, I'm quite satisfied. Marcia and I have good jobs, the kids are in a good school. It's not easy making ends meet in this place—"

"That is not an Othberg talking. For some of us, the dream comes first, the consequences later."

Uncle and nephew looked at each other for a moment, then burst into laughter.

"The death of Perry Jerzy Stangle marks the third of the seventeen among the Rewound Children. Stangle, twenty-eight at the time of capture, allegedly was killed by his nephew, Hugh Stangle, who then apparently fatally shot himself.

"San Bernardino police say ten years ago, on Thanksgiving Day, Perry Stangle allegedly sexually molested Hugh Stangle when the boy was eleven and Perry Stangle eighteen. When Perry Stangle was turned into a child, Hugh Stangle apparently saw a chance for revenge, police said. Today, again on Thanksgiving Day, Hugh Stangle allegedly raped and sodomized Perry Stangle, then strangled him and threw the nude body down a staircase into the living room where family members had gathered for the annual dinner. Hugh Stangle shouted 'The circle is complete,' according to police, and then ran back to his own room and shot himself in the head with a .357 Magnum pistol. Police said a note left by Hugh Stangle detailed the years of sexual abuse and blamed the rest of the family for letting Perry Stangle get away with it. Family members deny knowing of the abuse before today, police said.

"Hugh Stangle was not married, but Perry Stangle leaves behind a wife with a three-month-old child.

"Brent Caseman, Time/Warner/Tribune Multimedia News, Los Angeles."

"Three down, fourteen to go. If this goes on, we'll be free of the scourge soon. And I'm telling you people here in the studio and those listening in my vast TV audience, it cannot come too soon.

"Good thing the wife was pregnant before her husband went to the Holn ship."

"Where to?" Earl, biting into a flat piece of white-meat turkey, followed Lucas out the front door.

"Other Worlds," the boy said. "Jasper, Frank, and Carl are meeting us there."

"Indeed. And what other world are we going to?"

"That's the name of the place in Kihei. It's got VR games."

"Oh." Lucas was free because it was the day after Thanksgiving. Just two boys out on holiday, both in the off-duty uniform of T-shirt emblazoned with some kind of pop character, shorts and sport sandals.

And why am I doing these boyish things? Did I really never grow up? He shrugged, stuffed the rest of the turkey into his mouth.

During the ride on the electric bus, Lucas asked about Sandra Mellinfield.

"No, I hardly knew her. She and the others, Charlie and Perry, we met at times in the hospital. I struck up friendships with a couple of others."

And how are they doing, Marian with her cold sister and Aaron with his cold wife? He hadn't heard from them, to his dismay.

"Are you scared?"

"No, except for Sandra, they were killed by family members. You're not planning to do me in, are you?"

. Lucas grinned. "Heck, no. Not when you're getting so good on a skateboard."

Other Worlds was jammed with youngsters, and the only game available was Battle for the World, and the only reason that was open was because the Maui champions, a loose group of nine wild-haired youngsters ranging in age from nine to fourteen who called themselves the Barracudas, were waiting for someone to accept their challenge "to be wiped all over the VR map." Lucas and his friends reluctantly agreed, so Earl paid for four hours.

"You'll be dead in twenty minutes, you redheaded deadhead," sneered one of the younger Barracudas.

"You need an alias," Lucas said as they headed for the dressing room. "Like that kid who razzed you, he's called Sharkjaw."

"Sharkjaw, lovely. OK, how about"—he looked over at the pugnacious young Barracuda—"Redhead Deadhead?"

Earl studied the suit studded with wires he had to put on, then looked askance at the central control loop. It looked like some hacker's idea of a high-tech torture chamber. He'd read about virtual reality, of course, but as an arthritic old man, he hadn't expected to participate. Except—here he was, being wired in like a computer peripheral.

Once hooked into the scenario, he nearly got killed right off the bat. Lucas had to save him.

"Pay attention, will you?"

"I've never done this before, you know. I was sightseeing."

"That can get you killed real quick."

To eyes not used to digital sophistication, the scenes around him were remarkable, obviously influenced by the old movie *Blade Runner*. Rising around him was an odd intermingling of futuristic and medieval architecture. Also lurking in the shadows, though, were several VR soldiers wanting to blow his image into itty-bitty pixels.

Earl found himself picking through a blasted landscape when he heard a low roar off to the left. The vehicle rumbling into view stunned him, bristling as it was with missiles and cannons and radar and IF and UV scopes.

"Analysis of vehicle."

COBRA, MAIN BATTLE VEHICLE OF BARRACUDAS a perisplay—"Peripheral vision display," Lucas had explained—informed him, then proceeded to display what was known about the structure. Earl thought he saw a flaw. He squeezed his VR self into a corner between two massive blocks of marble and sighted down the laser-guided missile launcher until the metal beast rolled into position. (And again, an old memory of a cold night and a metallic beast shuffling along a track played in the recesses of his mind.) He let fly with a Slimline Lo-Profile solid-fueled smart missile carrying a Hi-Ex shaped-charge MK-4 warhead. Flame lashed out everywhere around him, the light blinding him. Concussions hammered at his ears; he even could feel the pressure waves slamming at his body. He began to wonder if he'd included himself in the destruction. Finally the roaring diminished.

COBRA DESTROYED

"Way to go, Un—Deadhead!" Lucas shouted, seemingly right into his ear.

In the perisplay, six of the nine figures representing Barracudas went black.

"Calamitous!" another teammate shouted. "Everyone's been trying for months to bash that thing."

"Oh."

"And you ripped six 'cudas!" another voice shouted.

"Oh, my."

The Barracudas quickly showed why they were champs with the remaining three dispatching Earl's four teammates in quick order, leaving him to face the last one alone. Earl took stock of himself and decided he needed to beef himself up, although he already stood fifteen feet tall with arms the size of tree trunks and a punch able to knock holes into brick walls.

Wait a minute. In one world, I'm an adult inhabiting a kid's body, but in another world, I'm a kid with an adult's mind playing an adult operating a body three times the size of the biggest adult. This is getting confusing.

The battle got nowhere until Earl was warned the structure they were fighting under was close to collapse. He sent a couple of well-placed missiles in and brought the whole edifice down on the enemy.

A glum bunch of Barracudas met them in the changing room.

"I have a confession to make," Earl said. "I'm not your average kid. I'm actually seventy-nine years old, so you were battling a mind with lots of experience."

"How—" began a tall, skinny youth in black leather, "wait. You're one of those rewound dudes, aren't you? Now I remember. I saw pictures of you on TV."

"Yep."

"Were you in the army or something? I mean, you pulled some nasty tricks in there."

"A couple of years in the early fifties chasing and dodging tanks in war maneuvers. Nothing to qualify me for generalship or anything. As I said, just experience in the real world. So, actually, you guys are still tops. You very nearly got us anyway."

"Wow." All of the Barracudas looked at him differently.

"Here y'are, boys, the disk on your late Cobra," said an obese youth with bad skin from behind the counter. "Heh, heh."

"Don't worry, jellyass, we'll reprogram it and wipe you right out again."

"Next time put your fuel tank in a better place," Earl said. "That was your weak point. And try a different fuel. Gasoline is inefficient and too volatile. Even hydrogen stored in a solid medium would be better—"

"Uncle Earl, don't give them hints. We're going to have to fight them again some day."

"Boys, boys, boys. If there's one thing you should be learning from this machine it's that for every new weapon you devise, your opponent eventually will figure out a way to defeat it. How do you think we won the Cold War? We built a system, they built a countersystem. We built a counter-countersystem, they made a new weapon, we countered, they counter-countered, and so it went until someone raised a hand and said meekly, 'I quit.'"

Earl treated all of them—including the Barracudas—at the nearest ice cream salon, and they asked him a lot of questions, some about his first childhood.

"No computer chips when I was a kid. We were lucky to have anything that moved without a spring. Everything was made of metal and all seemed to have bad paint jobs. I had a good collection of comic books, though, including several first editions."

"And your mother threw them all away."

"Nope. I kept them. When I sold the collection, I made enough to help start my business."

"You saw the birth of rock'n'roll, too," said a boy with green hair (which, against Earl's red, fit in perfectly with the Christmas decorations draped everywhere).

"Yep, although I was a big-band fanatic in youth.

Benny Goodman, Glenn Miller, Louie Armstrong, guys like that. I know this'll age me when I say I had a thing for the before-TV Dinah Shore."

"I heard being a kid growing up during World War II was kind of cool," another Barracuda said.

"Oh, it was fun in a way. We were too young and dumb to know what was really going on, the slaughters and mass killings and all. We were protected. No bombs fell on Wisconsin, no armies trooped through. Blackouts were a hoot. One time we set off Roman candles near a big gear factory during one. We nearly died laughing watching all those old coots in funny hats running around hollering and carrying on. 'Course, if we'd been caught, I'd still be in jail."

He was not surprised when the subject turned to sex. "What's it like?"

"Well, remember, this is a seventy-nine-year-old man telling you this, not a ten-year-old schoolboy. There's sex and then there's sex. I mean, you can ram yourself in and dump your load, but what's the fun? I'll tell you where the fun is, and that's when you and your partner take your time and make every move count. Right from the beginning, when you're undressing, especially if you undress each other. I'm telling you, one of the biggest turn-ons in life is s-l-lowly slipping a blouse off the shoulders of a woman and sliding it down her arms and back. And don't be afraid to get naked. The idea is to get as much of your skin in contact with hers as possible, skin against skin. Yeah. You caress her slowly, taking in the smooth feel of her skin and the sound of flesh rubbing against flesh and the smell and taste of her body. You've got five senses, use them. When the time comes for the main act, you're both so turned on every nerve is jamming your brain with signals. You start making those panting noises that sound so hokey in the movies but you can't help it because you're concentrating so hard and you get more and more excited and the action speeds up until the bedsprings are squeaking and she's twisting and moaning and you realize again this beautiful woman is naked and you're naked and you're together and you get even more excited until the climax comes and you fall right off the bed and lie in a heap, exhausted. But happy. Very, very happy."

He found himself surrounded by utterly still listeners with glassy stares and slack jaws, one boy with his cherry-laced cola halfway to his mouth.

Uh-oh.

"Uh, none of you guys are going out on a date tonight, or anything, are you?"

After the group came out of their reverie, the Barracudas went their way with some friendly words and short waves.

"That was weird," one of Lucas's friends said. "Usually they're bullies."

"They're just like you guys, they just like to show off a bit," Earl said. "Maybe your next game won't be so antagonistic. Any of you have a watch?"

One of the boys had a pocket radio that showed the time in the dial when a button was pushed. "Shit," he said when he did, "I have five minutes to get home."

All three bid hasty farewells and hurried off across an open-air mall.

"Guess we'd better head home, too," Earl said. "Your mom will have both our heads if we're too late. Where's the bus stop?"

Lucas pointed and they headed in the opposite direction. "Do all your friends use four-letter words?"

"Oh, yeah, once in a while."

"Do you?"

"Um . . ." Lucas looked at his feet. "Mom makes me go to my room if I do."

"Well, try not to. Not because it's so bad, but because it's unimagin—"

"Evil one!"

Earl turned to face a thin man in white shirt and pants

pointing at him. His face was red, seemingly from exertion, but Earl couldn't tell from what.

"One of the evil ones! I saw him on TV! Mr. Goth said one was in Hawaii! Here he is! Evil!"

"Come on, Lucas, we'd better get out of here—"

Two more figures in white blocked their way. "Evil!" said an emaciated young woman with stringy blond hair. "He's been remade evil!"

"Save the boy, the one in the red shirt! He's an innocent being corrupted."

By now, the strangely garbed people had surrounded them, and a couple grabbed for Lucas. He dodged them, but others moved toward him.

"Get away," Earl snarled. "We aren't dealing with you."

"Save the boy, the real boy!" someone half-chanted, half-shouted. "Get him away!"

A hand gripped Lucas by the wrist. "Leave me alone! Let go!" he shouted.

Earl grabbed the arm, but someone bumped him hard and he lost his grip, at the same time the one holding Lucas twisted away, hauling the boy around. "Let go of me!" The boy screamed as another man grabbed his other arm. Earl was being bumped and pushed farther and farther away from the struggling boy. A hard shove sent him against a raised planter and he half-fell into a spiny bush.

"Let him go! Right now! Move!"

The new voice was different, not the high-pitched chant but one carrying authority. Earl saw a dark figure flash by while the white ones suddenly yielded. When he managed to struggle out of the planter, he saw a policeman in dark shirt and shorts facing the pair who held Lucas. Immediately, another cop rode up on a bike. The policeman jumped off, letting the bike fall over next to his partner's.

"Let him go," the first officer said in an even voice.

"We are trying to save this boy from evil." The

speaker was the one who had first pointed at Earl. "You cannot expect us to—"

"One more time. Get your hands off that boy."

"Officer, we are on a mission of mercy."

"We have witnesses to an attempted kidnapping of a juvenile," the second cop said, sweeping his arm around at the small crowd watching. "That and a charge of child abuse will bring the roof right down on your heads."

"We cannot—"

"All right." The first cop pulled out a pair of handcuffs, the second a nightstick. "Take 'em." Both started toward the captors.

Immediately, the pair released Lucas, who ran over to Earl, tears in his eyes.

"What's going—"

He grabbed the boy's shoulders. "All right. It's all right now. It's OK." The boy snuffled, turned toward the cops.

"OK, fine," the first cop said. "Now disperse. Clear the area."

No one moved.

The first cop raised his handcuffs. "Call for backup. We'll arrest all these bozos."

As the second cop reached for the radio switch on his belt, all of the white-garbed figures, as if on cue, whirled and disappeared in seconds.

The first cop let out a breath as he replaced the handcuffs. Then both came toward Earl.

"Are you all right?" The first cop's name tag said Leong.

"Who the fuck were they?"

"One of the religious cults that have sprung up on the Islands. That one is a little more, uh, intense, than the others."

"They usually don't cause this kind of trouble." The second cop's name tag read Amalu.

"I guess they recognized me—"

"I do, too" Leong said. "You're Othberg of the rewound group. I visited your house last week."

Earl looked away, clenching his hands into fists. He
had to take three hard breaths before turning to Lucas
and looking into the frightened face, the wide eyes with
moisture still threatening to spill over where earlier tears
were drying against the freckled cheeks.

"I-I'm sorry, Lucas. I couldn't help you. I couldn't do
anything." He looked down at the two rows of toes lining
the fronts of his sandals. Tiny toes, now. He looked back
at the boy. "I'm no longer a man and I don't have the
power of a man anymore. I'm sorry."

"I-it's all right, Uncle Earl. You tried. I-I know how
you feel." The boy's gaze fell toward the ground.

He probably does, Earl thought. He himself probably
had felt this kind of powerlessness before, but for Earl,
that had been so long ago he'd forgotten.

"Where are you going?" Amalu said in a not-unkind
voice.

"Home," Lucas said. "We have to catch the bus to
Maalaea Anchor."

"We'll accompany you," Leong said. Both picked up
their bikes. With the action over, most of the watchers
had left.

Earl forced his fists to relax. He looked at the sky
where thin clouds traced narrow patterns. The innocence was over, if there ever had been any. Charlie,
Sandra and Perry dead; Harold and Alisa tossed out of
their families' lives—Earl had a sudden feeling that
leaving the Lovelace Hospital, leaving the group behind,
had been a big mistake. Just being who he was had
placed Lucas into danger. He would not do that again.

"Coming Uncle Earl?"

"Yes," he said, and fell into step behind the protective
shadows of the policemen.

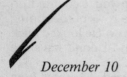

Twelve

December 10

"You want chocolate raspberry swirl or mint chocolate chip, or you want to tell me what's bugging you?"

"What?" Marian stared at Aaron who gazed back through the rapidly fogging glass of the door to the ice cream section.

"Ever since the library, you've been as antsy as a nervous cat."

Marian jammed her hands into her pockets. "Mint chocolate chip." She watched as Aaron grabbed the package. "And Nurse Ames."

Aaron stepped back, let the door slam, looked at her with a raised eyebrow.

"As we came out of the library I saw a woman several yards away in a brown coat. She was as um, hefty as Ames."

"That doesn't make her—"

"She turned and walked away, but then turned back. She had her coat hood up so I couldn't see her whole face. But she kept looking in our direction and followed us as we headed toward the car. I don't know, Aaron, maybe I'm just paranoid."

"Yeah, uh, um, wow. Cold." He set the ice cream into

the crook of his arm, rubbed his hands together. "Let's go find Virginia."

"Tell her?" Marian said as they walked along the frozen-food cabinets.

"You bet."

Marian felt foolish casting glances along every aisle until a woman in a brown coat halfway down the candy lane looked up as they passed. Marian grabbed Aaron's coat, pointed at the aisle.

"There. Surely two women can't have the same awful hairstyle."

"Let's do it this way." They ran down the next aisle, slowed and went around the end by a display of Christmas beers. Aaron stopped, carefully peered around the corner. "She's headed for the other end. She—damn! We've got to find Virginia."

They found her on the other side of the huge store examining cabbage heads.

"We think one of the people who held us is here," Aaron said.

She tossed a head into the basket, swung it around. "Let's go. Aaron, why don't you put the ice cream in?"

Aaron looked at the package like he'd never seen it before. "Uh, yeah."

They got into a line with three people ahead of them. "Stay alert," Virginia said. When the line was down to two, Marian stole a glance.

"Express lane, five down. Watching us."

Aaron turned and brazenly looked in that direction.

"Her," he said.

"You're sure?"

"Mousy hair, heavyset, double chin, usually a barrette where head meets neck."

"That could fit anyon—"

"Brown spot on the back of her left hand," Marian said.

"Confirmed," Aaron said.

"I can't see it," Virginia said, "but then I didn't get my eyes fixed, either."

Marian turned. The woman wasn't looking in their direction now, but the hand holding the giant Hershey bar had a brown splotch almost the same color as the wrapping. The chill of knowing that was indeed Nurse Ames was ameliorated a little by being able to see such detail at that distance.

"Let me know when she gets to the register."

About the time the person in front of them began to send his cart through the scanner tunnel, Aaron said, "Candy bar scanned."

"Go." Virginia shoved the basket aside and they hurried through a closed check-out station and out through the automatic doors. "Left, Aaron." Virginia headed toward the next store, an office supply warehouse.

"Over here," Aaron said once they got inside.

"Good thinking. You two stay behind the desks and stuff." As Aaron and Marian ducked behind a large wooden desk, Virginia positioned herself so she could see the front doors. "Yep, here she comes." She moved slowly around behind a bookshelf. After a moment, she shrugged. "Let's try it. On this side of the store if we can."

They ran straight for Tontine's balky, smoky '78 Ford Fairmont whose odometer read 72,876 miles but was rumored to be on its third trip around.

"Come on, come on," Virginia muttered as the engine took a few seconds to catch. Smoke billowed from the exhaust as she backed out; she jammed the car into gear and headed for an exit. Just as the traffic light went from yellow to red, she gunned the engine. The car jerked in response and almost died in the middle of the intersection. Finally she got it going at a good clip, but exhaust smoke left a well-marked trail.

"Check for cars that might be following us," Virginia said. "I wonder if she knows this one."

"I think she was at the library," Marian said.

Virginia grimaced. "All right, keep a sharp eye out. Who is she?"

"All we know her by is Nurse Ames," Aaron said, looking out of the window next to him. "Never told us her first name, never heard anyone call her anything except Ames. Except when Marian called her Nurse Igor."

Marian wasn't sure if any of the other vehicles were tailing or not; all seemed to go around or turn off as usual. Finally, Virginia pulled into a driveway on the north end of Grid Manor.

"You still have the keys, Marian?"

"Yes." She jumped out of the car and ran to the gate, grappled with the large lock until it snapped open. As the car passed, she cast furtive glances around, but saw nothing. She pulled the gate shut, made sure the lock was secure, then ran into the "garage." Aaron and Virginia already were piling barrels and sheets of wood and metal behind and over the car.

"Let me get the books out," she said.

Aaron pointed. "They are."

"York, where's Tontine?" Virginia said as soon as she saw someone inside.

"Workin', second floor," answered a man in overalls.

"I'll get him," Aaron said.

"Right. Big room."

Virginia faded by the fourth floor and Marian slowed to her pace. Once on the ninth floor, she went to the picnic table and dropped the books on it. She sat down and almost immediately, Merlin jumped to the bench next to her. She idly began scratching his ears.

Virginia dropped onto a couch. "Whoosh! If we're going to play skullduggery, I'll have to get into shape."

Within a minute, Tontine jogged into the room, Aaron at his side. Ken followed, then Black King Leo and White King Sam.

"Aaron's filled me in," Tontine said as he sat down

next to Virginia. "You're absolutely sure about this woman?"

Marian nodded.

"Damn good at drawing blood," Aaron said as he sat next to Merlin. "She could hit a vein from a mile away."

"I don't know if we lost her in Office Depot," Virginia said. "And I have no idea if she followed us back."

Tontine nodded. "All right, neither you nor Aaron will leave this building unless both Ken and Virginia and either Leo, Sam, or I are with you. When you go out, wear clothes and hats to obscure your faces. We'll pretend Ken and Virginia are your parents. Use different names."

"You be Suzie and I'll be Frank," Aaron said.

"You're already too frank," she muttered, causing him to lift an eyebrow.

"We can hook up the interior restrooms," Black King Leo said. "There's a new guy, Albert, used to be a plumber. He says he can do it."

"Good," Tontine said.

"All we need to do is scrounge the fixtures," White King Sam added.

"I'll buy the stuff," Marian said.

"We don't want to deplete your cash," Tontine said.

"I want to. You people are doing all this for us, I want to help out as best I can." She shoved hair aside. "A couple of toilets aren't going to drain me."

Aaron raised his eyebrow again.

Tontine nodded. "We're also going to beef up the night watches and start a daytime patrol."

"OK, Tontine, fine, but what's gonna prevent someone from sneakin' in?" Ken said from the rocking chair. "Strangers come in and out all the time. Unless you start givin' out badges or somethin' you can't stop 'em."

"I know." Tontine sat a second, gazing at the floor. "That's going to have to be an honor system, with us at the core. Keep your eyes open, recruit people we know we can trust, and stay alert."

Aaron stirred. "The next question is, why are you d—"

Tontine stood up abruptly. "Because it's necessary." He turned and started walking away. "We're starting now. Let's draw up a schedule." As he headed for the ramp, the others got up and began to file out, including Virginia and Ken. The two kings each winked at them, Black with his left eye, White with his right.

Marian looked at the floor as the steps descended the ramps. Events completely out of her control blew her along again, just like when she was a kid. The adults then made the decisions, the adults now made the decisions. *But I am an adult. I have not died and been reborn, I have been—*

A thump startled her. Merlin had jumped off the table and seemed to be scratching at the floor. Then he reared up on his back paws and swiped at something in the air. He jumped back up on the seat, then leaped up on the tabletop. The cat hunched down, staring intently at a bright red spot that quivered and shook. Merlin lowered his head, gathered himself, then pounced with a resounding thud.

"Merlin, you're acting like a kitten." She reached over and rubbed his neck.

"Well, if his mistress can be a kid, so can he."

The cat sat down, acting nonchalant. "Mrow."

She put her face next to his, rubbed his back. "You are a silly cat."

"Mrrow."

She straightened. "What was that, anyway?"

"This." Aaron pointed a penlike device at the floor. A red dot appeared and began to move in patterns. "Virginia's laser pointer. We discovered Merlin has a thing about itty-bitty red dots."

"Well, at least you two are getting along." She pulled off her jacket.

"I've always liked cats, but I avoided them like the plague because of allergies. In my normal life, right now

I would be half-dead from finding said cat sleeping next to my face this morning."

"I guess the Holn cured you of that." She shook her hair to free tangles.

Aaron toyed with the pointer. "That's amazing enough, but what really gets me is, how did they know I had allergies in the first place?" Aaron pulled the pile of books toward him. "I didn't know you checked out Tony Hillerman. *Seekers of Spirits*. 'Belagana faith-seekers start turning up dead.' Dibs."

"Not so fast. That's a new one, and I saw it first. Virginia has seconds. Remember, it's her card."

"Yeah, yeah. So what else is there? Human physiology, astronomy and *A Tale of Two Cities*. Hard, harder and hardest. Thanks."

Marian stepped over to a box on the floor. "No one's left any mending. Good. I'll start the Hillerman." She snatched it from Aaron's hand. "Thank you very much."

She gave Merlin another hug and headed toward the rocker. The cat had earned room and board by catching his first mouse the day after his arrival. That spurred Tontine to come back from a shopping trip with canned and dry cat food, water and food bowls, a litter basket, a package of cat litter, and three cat toys.

She settled into the rocking chair not too far from one of the new space heaters bought with her money. In addition to the heaters, the cash bought some extra blankets and bedrolls. It also had bought a catered Thanksgiving dinner to the mansion, an incongruity she had found delightful.

She had just opened the book when she noticed Aaron standing to one side gazing at her.

"Yes?"

"You look so imperial in that chair. The Queen of the Underground on her throne."

"Don't be silly." She set the book down. "My grandmother had a rocking chair. Big, covered with cushions she made herself. She taught me to sew. She was every-

one's typical grandmother, plump, curly gray hair, twinkling eyes and an easy and gentle laugh. I used to sit in
that big lap a lot, in that rocking chair. We'd rock back
and forth as she read to me, or showed me how to thread
a needle, or just talk to me. When the diabetes killed
Mom, she moved in with us and lived long enough to see
a heart attack kill her son, my Dad. As a child, I used to
get jealous when Arlene would be in the lap instead of
me. I was always jealous of Arlene." *And Arlene damned
well knew it.*

She shook her head. "That was another lifetime." She
looked at her small palm, stopped rocking. "What would
it be like to live like this for the rest of our lives? This
size, this shape? How long would we live?"

Aaron grimaced, sat on the footstool. "Not too long if
Charlie and Sandra and Perry are indications."

She wrapped her arms around her. "I can see Perry
and Sandra, but Charlie I have a hard time getting a fix
on."

"He sat to our right at the round table. A truck driver,
the one I compared myself to when I made that joke
about the Maserati."

"Oh, yes . . ." A picture of the burly child formed in
her mind. "Poor Charlie. Why did his father do that?"

"His father feared what Charlie had become."

Marian sat with that cold thought in her mind, hugging herself a little tighter.

"I don't even know if I'm divorced, or whether
Janessa simply annulled the marriage. She signed all the
papers, then had me out of there before I could see
them."

"Conrad, at least, was spared this."

"What would he have done if the plane crash hadn't
killed him?"

"I don't know." She shook her head. "I like to think
he'd be brave and kind, because that's what he was. I
just—" Conrad's round face formed again, hovering in
her mind, image captured and held from the last time

they had made love and he'd propped himself on an elbow and looked down on her, fingers gently tracing a figure on her abdomen, both bodies shining with sweat, sunlight cascading in the open window—

She snapped her head around, hair flying across her face, breath ragged. Tears threatened to overflow.

"I know the feeling," Aaron said softly.

She looked at Aaron, who slowly reached out and touched her forehead with a finger, then moved it down her face, pushing hair aside. *How could he know?* The touch was gentle, and once the hair was clear, he retracted his hand.

She in turn reached out and gently pushed an errant lock of hair back. "Are we—" She shook her head. "No. Forget it."

"Oh, for a good jolt of gonadal juices right now."

"You'd embarrass us." She smiled.

"Yeah. So?" He got up, walked over and picked up one of the books, came back and flopped on the couch.

"'It was the best of times, it was the worst of times, it was the age of wisdom, it was the age of foolishness, it was the epoch of belief, it was the epoch of incredulity—'" He closed the book, looked at the cover. "Is this guy writing about us?"

"The Alden Commission issued two rulings today pertaining to the Rewound Children, as the Group of Seventeen are now being called. These are the people the extraterrestrial Holn are purported to have turned into children.

"The court, a three-judge commission empaneled to hear legal questions surrounding the group, met in special session last week to hear the cases.

"The first case is out of Berkeley, California. Tom Johannes Cathen, a Rewound Child, sued the state of California seeking the right to register to vote. His argument was that he still is thirty years old and he has the mental faculties to make careful decisions. The state

denied the petition, but attorneys appealed to the commission. That ruling went against Mr. Cathen, with the judges citing their own ruling that everyone in the group was a child in stature and nature. Come back in ten years, the court, in essence, said.

"Meanwhile, in Amarillo, Texas, two of the Rewound Children, Linda and Jerry Rithen, were sued by their creditors, including three credit card companies and two banks, over nonpayment of debt. Federal court in Texas referred the matter to the commission. The Rithens, who had been married before metamorphoses but whose marriage has since been annulled, used that same commission ruling as a defense, asking how they were supposed to pay their bills when they were barred from working. The creditors argued that the debts were incurred before metamorphoses. The commission sided with the Rithens, saying that even though the debts had been incurred before the change, they were incurred when the Rithens still had had a reasonable expectation of being able to repay."

"Rolf, excuse me, this is Kerry Sherman in Atlanta. What do these rulings say as a whole?"

"Very simple. The judges are saying you can't have it both ways.

"Rolf Treadwell, CNN, Washington."

Thirteen

"The story is just a bit strange and has Amarillo, Texas, usually a staid oil and farming community, abuzz.

"Apparently, one of the Rewound Children, Paula Katherine Deborah Caulfield, was abandoned by her legal guardian, her sister, Georgeanne Dumas, at the behest of the two women's mother, Henrietta Caulfield. This would make the third Rewound pushed out by family, but this case was a bit unusual. Ms. Dumas took Paula to the Amarillo Wal-Mart store on the pretense of doing some Christmas shopping and abandoned her there. Paula panicked at first, wandering the aisles crying and confused, according to Texas family welfare officials, but she was afraid to approach strangers. Now, Paula had worked at this store as a cashier for fifteen years, and knew the place pretty well. Well enough, in fact, to find a niche to hide in when the store closed. She avoided the security guards, who never did figure out she was there. For five days, she lived in the store, borrowing fresh clothing off the racks and food from the snack bar. This is Wal-Mart, after all, and she should have been able to find whatever she needed. And, apparently, she did.

"Wal-Mart officials have said with the Christmas crush keeping store associates busy, it probably was easy for her to go unnoticed. As for her former co-workers, none recognized her because, as one pointed out, asking not

172

to be put on camera, Paula Caulfield used to be heavyset, moved rather slowly, and always complained about her feet. How could we, the co-worker said, recognize her as a small child?

"No one can say how long things might have remained this way if two other Rewound Children, Linda and Jerry Rithen, hadn't accompanied their son, Dale, to the store. Paula saw the Rithens and told them what was happening, and Dale Rithen agreed to take her home. Store officials still haven't discovered where she hid all this time. Dale Rithen and his wife, Sue, designated guardians for Linda and Jerry, have officially petitioned to be the designated guardians for Paula, which is how the story finally came to light. The final decision will be made by the Alden Commission.

"Dale Rithen, who works for a local natural gas company, has declined to be interviewed. The Rithens also were in the news lately after winning a case against former creditors. Texas authorities say no action will be taken against Ms. Dumas or Henrietta Caulfield because of the extraordinary circumstances surrounding the case. As one social worker put it, Paula's mother is eighty-six years old, and just how much of a burden can an elderly woman be forced to take?

"Marinka Svoboda, CNN, Amarillo."

December 18

I don't yet completely know how this works in a normal human, much less someone who's had their cells rejiggered by an offworld visitor.

Miranda stared at the single neuron and its attendant dendrites and axons floating before her in virtual three-D. This particular neuron was an assimilation of data from various noninvasive scans of one of the Rewound Children, combined into a graphic representation by a supercomputer chain at Livermore and Los Alamos.

"Rewound Children." She grimaced inwardly every

time she heard it. She was responsible for the name, which made it worse, but it also trivialized them.

She sat back, stared at the image, mind drifting to other neurons in other heads, and wondered how the personalties of, say, Sumo and the Harpy, could emerge from the tangles.

She could see Harrison Conroy—Sumo—wrapped in his suit of brown as immovable as one of those bulky wrestlers on the couch in Avram's Washington office. On the other end was the Harpy—despite all her efforts, Miranda could not shake the image of a bird with a woman's breasts and Radmilla Everett's face flitting around the stoic mountain of a man screeching and berating. The names had popped suddenly into a tired brain suffering from having to fly an all-nighter to another meeting.

"I can understand your distress, Dr. Sena—" Radmilla had begun with the smooth tones as she always used, but Miranda's perkiness refused to be roused.

"Distress my foot," she had snapped, rousing a different emotion. "Three deaths and three disownings. I would say that constitutes an emergency."

"Aberrations, Doctor. Overall, the success rate of assimilation has been successful."

"It ain't over until the fat lady sings. And in this case, she's going to be singing dirges for seventeen innocent lives lost because of bureaucratic ineptitude—"

"Really, Avram," Conroy said from the couch, "I don't know why you insist on bringing Dr. Sena to these meetings. We can't get much done because of her, well, her—"

"Hot Latino blood?" Miranda said.

A red flush chased a look of shock across Conroy's face. Avram chuckled.

"I need an ally," the elder scientist said. "Dealing with you two is like swimming in gravy."

"Look," Conroy said, pulling himself erect, "I've told you before, the consensus is we're on the right track. A couple incidents are to be expected. Not with quite the deadly force expected—"

"The coroner's report on Charles Romplin said because of the close range, the pellets did not have time to spread," Miranda said. "Many of them ripped through several organs before imbedding themselves in the door."

"What is your point, Doctor?" Radmilla asked, black-stockinged legs clamped together with knees at the apex of a sharp angle at the edge of the couch.

"Your complacency is what's aggravating. Two violent deaths and a possible suicide and you treat it like normal everyday circumstance. We warned you this would happen."

"What would you have us do? Assign a psychologist to each one?"

"I return to the idea I had before of the central place to let them stay and—"

"Dr. Sena, you don't understand," Conroy said. "The world is more complicated than that. Such a project would be a drain on our resources. And, frankly, there are more important things for this government to consider. The President just came off a bruising campaign and will face a Congress split between three parties. She is sympathetic and wants to help your group of people, but for God's sake there are only fourteen of them. She has to deal with many issues that affect everybody in the country, not just a small group, no matter how unfortunate recent events have left their lives."

"You're the one who missed the point, Mr. Conroy," Miranda said, rubbing the back of her neck. "This goes beyond a third political party or any other issue the current president or any current member of Congress thinks—"

"I fail to see how this small group—"

"It's not just that group, damnit. It's the Holn, man, you have no idea what they represent for every man, woman and child on this planet. No idea whatsoever."

Conroy stood up, and a half-second later, Radmilla shot up as if a broken spring had stuck her. "I think this conversation is ended," he said. Sumo lumbered out with the Harpy at his heels.

Miranda watched the door close, then said, "You think they're lovers?"

Avram burst into laughter.

He wasn't finished with her, though.

"All entreaties to the Holn are going unanswered. They're ignoring us, absolutely, completely. Desperation calls for any idea, no matter how wild. Ben wants you to send a message."

She stared at him. "Me?"

"Not as scientific head of the task force, but as the human who discovered their creativity. We think you made quite an impression and they might remember— and respond."

"Well, I . . . if you think it has even a slight chance of helping."

"We have nothing to lose by trying."

Back in her office, still staring at that same neuron, Miranda sighed. She had written and rewritten the message. Then she set it all aside.

"Rotate, all axes," she said. The pyramidal neuron slowly presented all its prickly sides like a chicken on a rotisserie. A comparison routine against a standard neuron had found polarization–depolarization occurring within normal chronological and chemical/biological parameters.

Still, the Holn could have introduced a subtle change, say a variation in the way the transmitting neuron jumped its signal across the synapse, or perhaps the way the chemical ions bound. Such changes almost would have to be that tiny; nothing on a larger scale had been discovered. These brains seemed to process information the same way "normal" brains did. The trouble was, the picture of how "normal" brains operated still was incomplete. On top of that, each person's genetic legacy caused variations in the thinking processes, and so did experiences and so did environment, adding a thousand more pieces to the puzzle.

She sat back. Perhaps she was letting Samuel Innes apply blinkers to her thinking, insisting something had to be different about these people.

The neuron still spun slowly before her. Just one, isolated, separated from its kindred.

"End rotation. Back seven." The single cell shrank and was joined by others until it disappeared into a net of ropy connections like Spanish moss hanging from a tree.

What do I see here? A personality, a character trait, an aberration?

The cells floating in front of her have been tampered with by agents of the same God the sisters the Catholic girls high school she had attended in San Antonio believed in so fervently as the prime mover of all in the universe. She put her elbows on the desk and rested her head in her hands. Back at the apartment complex where she lived, holiday lights snaked around the buildings and up the naked trunks of palm trees. Christmas—a celebration of the birth of the Lord Jesus, or just a myth sprung full-blown from a tangle of neurons, dendrites and axons? Where do the Holn fit into the Christian pantheon? Or—where does Jesus fit into the Holn pantheon?

Miranda pushed herself erect. Too many undisciplined thoughts rumbling through her brain. She took several deep breaths, stretched her legs and arms, tried to focus her mind on the task at hand.

You don't know what you're looking at.

She sighed, angry at the refusal of those thoughts to go away.

You don't even know who *you're looking at.*

A physical jolt snapped through her body at that thought. This could be one of the dead ones—

"Reference: Name of subject."

A blue window popped out of a corner: SUBJECT NO. 2 stood out in white letters.

"Cross-reference," she snapped. "Personal data."

Three seconds passed.

SUBJECT: MARIAN ANNE ATHLINGTON

AGE: 41

FORMER OCCUPATION: PLANNING ANALYST, CITY OF BELLINGHAM, WASHINGTON

"Marian Anne Athlington." She tasted the syllables with her tongue.

?? COMMAND.

"Buzz off." The window disappeared.

Somewhere in the real brain, represented here only by a computer-generated tangle, neurons were firing in a constant pattern, delineating all of what Marian Anne Athlington was—personality, curiosity, fear, love, hate, her vision of the world, the way she reacted to stimuli. Unique, at least as far as any measure now known could tell. Her past determined everything she was now—and a whole new set of conditions, never before encountered in any shape or form by any human, were creating new patterns that would take her life in totally new directions.

Who is *this person?*

Miranda realized she could not put a face to the name. Suddenly, it wasn't enough.

"Back, next stage."

The tangle coalesced into a solid mass of cells. The view switched to the outside, where the smoothness of the surface became convoluted with fissures and curves that folded and refolded around each other. Movement stopped.

"ID portion."

LEFT HEMISPHERE
FRONTAL LOBE
INFERIOR FRONTAL CONVOLUTION

* * *

"Total hemisphere."

The brain moved away from her while adding more mass to itself until the left hemisphere cortex had formed, with the striated cerebellum just visible underneath.

"Rotate."

The right hemisphere was missing, exposing the thalamus, hypothalamus, fornix, amygdala, hippocampus, limbic system, pituitary gland—connections, wiring, transmission circuitry. Plus the pineal gland, where the soul once was thought to inhabit.

"Where has the romance gone?" a pre-event Dr. Innes had asked at a symposium in Switzerland.

Gone to MRI, CT, PET, and computer crunching.

"Complete brain."

The right hemisphere's convoluted form quickly spread into its niche, obscuring the inner parts, snuggling up against the other hemisphere, forming the "two brains" of humans. The whole structure rotated to a bottom view. The midbrain formed, the pons swelling to fill the cavity, then extended downward to form the medulla, the vital switching center for so many automatic body functions. The brain stem continued downward to form the head end of the spinal cord. More rotation, and the occipital lobe came into view, cerebellum fitting snugly below. The right auditory nerve extended out and stopped, and as the frontal lobe again swung into view, the olfactory nerves grew, stopped in bulb-shaped ends. Then optic nerves, originating in the lateral geniculate nucleus, extended outward, crossed and swelled. The white sclera formed spheres, with the irides showing their lack of melanin in the bright blue rings surrounding the black dot of the pupil.

Rotation stopped. The brain of Marian Anne Athlington stared back at her.

The naked eyeballs began to make her nervous. Out of all the dissected heads and brains she'd seen and handled in her career, only this configuration ever gave her the willies. She felt she was being mocked: *How can you know me?*

Sometimes she wondered.

"Finish."

The pia mater began to form over the convolutions like Spandex. At the same time, nerves extended outward like live tendrils. Olfactory. Oculomotor. Trigeminal. Glossopharyngeal. Growing, splitting, reaching everywhere. Now blood vessels, tiny, hairlike at first, swelling as they formed branches and grew into more branches. The arachnoid membrane blanketed the pia mater; then the dura mater—now, finally, bone began to form, cranium first, coming together at the fontanelles. The Holn had left the edges soft, telling Miranda they expected growth.

Swelling into the domed heads of bug-eyed men of science fiction, minds seizing control of hapless humans, making them do vile things—

"No," she said softly.

The cranial bone swept forward to the face, wrapping sockets around the eyeballs, building up into the nasal passages, sweeping down into the jawline. Teeth appeared in the upper and lower jaws, giving the old grin of death—until things like worms began to wriggle out of the orifices, squirming and spreading; more blood vessels, nerves, and the beginnings of tissue, attaching first to the seven bones of the face and spreading upward to the cranium. The tissue spread into striated muscles, wrapping over and around, turning red with the iron oxidation of the blood. Now these began to disappear in turn under the subcutaneous tissue, fat cells and dermis, in turn erupting into sweat glands and hair follicles, nerve endings and capillary networks, turning the whole head into a grainy mass of wriggling tissue. Then the epidermis spread, smoothing and covering, softening the edges and giving definition to the face. The auricles took shape on each side of the head as darker cells filled into lips.

Now the face looked human, or at least not something out of a horror vid-play. Clusters of hair formed into eyebrows as eyelashes grew out of eyelids that finally reduced the wide stare into a steady gaze. Long strands of dark brown hair by the millions sprouted out of the scalp and flowed down each side of the face like a scarf.

The machine beeped.

COMPLETE
ELAPSED TIME: 3 MIN 22 SEC

That long? A face now peered out at Miranda, who unconsciously touched her own hair, cut short at the base of her neck. The face carried all the attributes commonly associated with beauty—clear skin, high cheekbones (which she had noted back in the skull stage), lustrous hair (she impatiently let go of her own locks), firm mouth.

"Reference, this subject, image before June 10."

Several seconds passed until the computer beeped, opened a new window next to the simulation.

PHOTO TAKEN 1-17-03.

Definitely. Both as child and adult, this woman was a classic beauty.

But—

Who is *this person?*

Miranda decided to find out. She would talk to them, discuss their situations, let them know what the task force was finding out, what the future might hold. It wouldn't be much, but it would open lines of communication.

Before they all die.

She grimaced. "Reference, this subject, current status."

She'd ask a couple of the others if they wanted to go. Matt, Constance, Randall, Olive, for sure, maybe Wanda. Dr. Innes? She smiled at the response she might get from him.

The computer beeped and she froze halfway toward standing up. Her smile disappeared. A chill swirled over her body like a blast of icy wind. She stared hard at the words on the screen:

STATUS: UNKNOWN

Fourteen

December 24

"Mashed potatoes?"

The bent man squinted through bloodshot eyes at Aaron, who stood ready with an ice cream scoop full of spuds. The scrunched-up face lined with gray stubble leaned toward him, which caused the man's body to stumble to keep balance. Aaron waited, amused not at the man but his own patience.

The man looked down at his plate. "Y-yeah."

Aaron plopped a potato igloo on the plate. The man peered at the mound, then up at Aaron again.

"Another? Sure." Aaron rolled another load into the scoop, dropped it deftly onto the plate. "Gravy?" With his right hand, he lifted the loaded ladle. At the man's nod, he poured the giblet gravy over both mounds, but they looked a little dry, so he ladled out another portion.

The man grinned, front teeth missing in action. "Th-thanks, kid."

Aaron nodded, turned his attention to the next person. *Christmas Eve, and here's Aaron Lee Fairfax in a church building doling out portions of mashed potatoes and gravy to homeless people.* The irony was doubled because he—and Ken, Virginia, Tontine, Miguel, and

Marian—technically also were homeless, but better off, so the destitute haves were helping serve the destitute have nots. The Salvation Army had found itself strapped and put out a call for volunteers. Because it was Christmas Eve, and because it was in a church, and because the Army wanted to send them 60 miles north to Santa Fe, they figured it was safe enough. The Army provided the electric van and Tontine drove.

"As a bonus, we get to see the *farolito* display there," Virginia had said.

"You mean *luminaria*," Ken said.

"No, I mean *farolito*."

"Luminaria."

The argument had continued off and on the whole trip, but Aaron had no idea what they were talking about. Part of the meal they were serving was fairly traditional—turkey roast, dressing, mashed potatoes, cranberry sauce, and the like—but also spiced with a different tradition: posole, tamales, enchiladas, sopapillas, carne adovada.

"This sure ain't Taco Bell," he had said of that spicy cuisine while getting his third serving from a beaming cook.

"Aaron, I'll take over now." Beth, one of the local volunteers, smiled down at him.

"Is my shift up already?"

"No, but something's on TV Virginia said you might be interested in. In the library downstairs."

"OK." He handed her the ice cream scoop and dashed down the stairs, where he found his group gathered around an HDTV flatscreen monitor.

"What's up?"

"Look who's on," Marian said.

"Well, well. Alisa and Harold. On display again?"

"If Brigman ever gets through sermonizing," Virginia said. "He's been going on for an hour. Really inspired, though. The congregation has been responding like an old-time revival."

"That should not be surprising," said a slim woman in an elegant skirt and blouse, light hair framing a wide, sculpted face and sharp blue eyes: the church's minister, The Rev. something Rose. "Jim Brigman started preaching in front of abortion clinics at the age of ten. By the time he was fifteen, he'd started his own church, the results of which you see around him."

Indeed, the monitor showed arching metal beams sweeping upward out of sight toward the ten-story spire, the icon of the church. Three-story-tall stained-glass windows rose above the Choir of a Hundred Joyous Voices, one window showing the Nativity, the other the Resurrection, each window glowing with light. A cross as tall as the windows hung on the wall between; the figure of Christ and the vertical post were said to have been carved out of one California Redwood tree.

The view switched to a tight shot of Brigman, clothed in blue, left arm extended, palm out, head bathed in a cone of light.

". . . must ignore the detractors." His oration flowed as mellifluous as audible wine. "We live in the pinnacle of the times described in the Bible, the culmination of the plan as set forth in that Great Book. These children are the embodiments of God's will. They are the living proof of the majesty of His love, the power of His word, the glory of His Kingdom. Through them, we will live again; through them, we will find the way to life eternal; through them, we find the Glory of God."

The camera pulled back enough to show Harold seated in a white chair behind and to Brigman's right, Alisa to his left.

"Welcome these children into your hearts." Brigman stepped back, arms spread. Both got up and stepped to his side. "Welcome them into your lives as symbols, as miracles, as true light to redemption."

"Look at that dress," Marian said. "I haven't seen that many frills on a Barbie doll. And that pink bow on her head—ugh."

"Yeah," Aaron said. "And how did a former used-car salesman allow himself to be talked into wearing a white suit with short pants and knee socks? I wonder what he really thinks about all this."

"You are seriously underestimating Reverend Brigman," said Rev. Rose. "He can be very persuasive. The Miracle Children and Time of Touching have pulled in about a thousand followers a week, but I assure you, that is not Reverend Brigman's intent despite what others say. He fervently believes in what he is saying. That power of that belief is what makes him so effective."

Brigman guided Harold and Alisa to the edge of the raised stage, then again extended his arms. He looked up into the heights of the cathedral and closed his eyes. "Let us pray," the voice boomed.

The camera angle switched to the right and behind the trio. In the background, the many faces out of focus formed a rippling tapestry of shape and color.

"Sounds like there's goin' to be another time of grabbin'," Ken said, slurring slightly.

"Time of Touching," Virginia said without taking her eyes off the screen.

"Whatever. What's the idea?"

"To pass the healing done to the Rewound Children to sufferers." Rev. Rose wrapped her arms around herself. "The scientists are saying now a woman who might have had breast cancer not only has been cured, but her genes have been fixed so she'll never get it again." She rubbed her neck. "Can you imagine the hope and longing that creates in the souls of ordinary mortals, those who can't walk, can't move without aid, can't control their own bodies? A mighty powerful inducement to believe in miracles. All you need is someone who can help you believe."

Aaron suddenly felt very uncomfortable. The expression on her face seemed a mixture of loathing for the person who was doing the exploiting—and yet a yearning to believe it was all possible. He glanced at Marian, but he couldn't read her face.

"Something's going on," Tontine said.

The activity still was out of focus but agitated nonetheless. Brigman prayed on.

"Looks like a bunch of 'em 're jumpin' the gun," Ken said.

A knot of people spread out of the background, headed toward Brigman.

"Oh!" Virginia said. "They knocked that man in the wheelchair over—"

Shouts began to filter through the prayer.

"Oh, God in heaven," the minister said. "He's worked them into a frenzy."

Now the surge reached the stage. Alisa stepped back, but someone grabbed a foot. She in turn grabbed the pulpit, tried to kick her way free.

"For the love of God, get those children out of there." Rev. Rose's hands clenched into fists.

Brigman began to realize something was amiss. More hands grabbed Alisa, yanking her forward. Others snatched at Harold, who dodged while he moved toward Alisa.

"Brothers and sisters, please, the time has not yet—" An elbow knocked him aside. Blue-coated figures tried to push the crowd back, but they might as well have tried to push back a wall of water.

"Look, even the choir is gettin' into this," Ken said as green-and-red robed figures leaped over a small bannister.

"On whose side?" Tontine said.

The blue-clads battled to form a circle around Brigman, who was bent over holding his face, blood spurting from under a hand. Screams, shouts, and curses reverberated from the cathedral walls as the mass behind pinned the people in front against the stage. A blue-clad grabbed Alisa's arms, but she was torn from his grasp.

Harold hadn't even gotten near her; now he tried to run
off the stage toward the camera, veering as someone
charged in. A flying tackle by a man in a checkered coat
brought him down hard on the stage. In the next second,
he disappeared under a squirming mass of bodies. The
camera suddenly jolted askew, but it still caught Alisa
who was borne aloft by hands grasping and ripping her
dress and pulling the bow from her hair. A few blue-
clads slugged and flailed as they tried to get at her, but
they made no headway against the tide. Long and
piercing screams sounded over and over, and curses
never uttered in that place before blasted out of the
speakers. Brigman disappeared from view, and a surge
carried Alisa toward the pulpit, her legs kicking feebly.
Arms grasping like tentacles yanked and pulled at her in
every direction, and the microphones at the pulpit began
to pick up her thin screams. She let out one long wail,
which cut off suddenly. Her body jerked up and flipped
over, then disappeared behind the pulpit.

"Dear God—"

"Jesus—"

"Motherf—"

The room spun around Aaron. He heard a sound
behind him and turned to see Marian dashing through
the door.

"Marian!" He followed, but she had fled into the
night. Before the front door had swung shut, he was
through it and running hard.

"Marian!" He forced himself into a faster pace, but if
there was one thing he found out about her now, it was
that she was swift. One block whipped by, then another
and she didn't slow one step. She cut down a different
street, and Aaron pulled out all stops, trying to get
around that same corner. She weaved and cut through
knots of strollers, hair flying behind her like wings. He
gasped when she leaped over a street barrier without
even slowing.

If she can, I—

"Arrghuh!" He cleared it with room to spare. *Earl's onto something here. . . .* He shoved the thought aside, dashing through a line of slow-moving cars, concentrating on his zigzagging quarry, now crossing a parklike area. He feared losing her in the milling crowd, but she suddenly pulled up, took two faltering steps and collapsed on a park bench. He dashed to the bench, sat down beside her, pulled her into his arms—

And found, again, he had no words of comfort. "Marian," he said lamely. Alisa's last scream tore through his mind again and again, Harold's last desperate dash played again and again. "Oh, Marian, Marian. MarianMarianMarianMarian."

She sobbed into the crook of his arm; he buried his face into her clean-smelling hair, tears wetting the strands. He tried hard to keep the sobs in check, not because he was a man and was supposed to, but because he would lose control completely if he didn't. He felt her trembling as she wept, but was she trembling any worse than he was? *This makes five. Five down, twelve to go. Even in the church, there's no safety.* "Marian, Marian, Marian," he murmured softly.

Eventually her sobs softened, and he felt her relax, although she didn't lift her head. He held her against him as they rocked slightly on the bench. He took a deep breath, slowly opened his eyes and lifted his head. As he did so, he became aware of a soft glow around them. The glow was more than just the multicolored lights in the two evergreen trees standing like sentinels to their right and more lights spiraling up an obelisk opposite, culminating in a blue-light star.

The glow seemed to come from thousands of lanterns set along the walks of the park. Aaron looked into one near the bench and found a paper sack, top edge rolled partway down, filled partially with sand where a votive candle had been placed, flame flickering lightly.

"Marian, if you possibly can, take a look." He continued to gaze around him. "I mean, *look* at this place."

She sniffed, raised her head, glanced at him, cheeks wet. She dried her eyes on her sleeve, then turned her head. She sat stock still a moment, then stood up, turning in a slow circle. The moisture in her eyes reflected scattered pinpoints of light.

"How lovely." A short, sweet laugh escaped. "How extraordinary."

"I wonder— ah, over there." They stepped over to a man in a denim jacket scratching a kitchen match on his pant leg. He stuck the match inside a bag until the candle caught.

"Excuse me," Aaron said, "we're from out of town. Can you tell us what all of this is?"

"Well," the man drawled in a scratchy voice as he straightened, "they're called *farolitos.* Spanish for little lanterns." The man wore a battered cowboy hat above his weatherbeaten face. Strands of dark hair stuck out from underneath. He wasn't as tall as most adults, but it was hard to judge because of his stoop. He wore a denim jacket over a shirt with diamond-shaped snaps and jeans faded to near-white. A wide, hand-tooled leather belt with a large metal buckle held up those jeans. Pointed cowboy boots, needing polish and with heels worn down on one side, completed the outfit. "Tradition hereabouts." He squinted, reached into a shirt pocket and pulled out a battered pack of cigarettes. "Every Christmas, the town puts on a big display. One of the things that draws tourists, though plenty of folks around here don't like 'em." He pulled out a bent cigarette, slipped the pack back. He tore the filter off and stuffed it into a jacket pocket, then tapped the untorn end. "The tourists, I mean." He waved a hand at the scene around them. "This is the Plaza. Used to be the center of town. Now the center is out at one of them malls." He stuck the untorn end in his mouth, reached into the shirt pocket again and pulled out a kitchen match. "Anyhow, tradition says the *farolitos* lit the way for the Christ child, but that's a little farfetched, eh? They didn't have paper sacks in those days." He whipped the match across a pant leg, lit the torn end of the cigarette, cupping it with hands roughened by much manual labor. "Supposition here is that they're imitatin' Chinese lanterns." He blew the match out, stuck it into the jacket pocket. " 'Stead of stringin' 'em together and hangin' 'em, we just put 'em on the ground. And on the buildings, 'cept those are electric. Cheap way out. These things are, how do they say, labor intensive, y'see." He knocked an ash into a patch of snow. "Worth it, though. I like 'em. They're soft, not like those garish things they stick in the trees like over yonder. Small breezes cause the whole shebang to waver, like a living thing."

The man was right. The light danced gently around the rows of sacks.

"Amazing."

Marian shivered. "They don't put out much heat, though."

Aaron suddenly felt the cold, too. "Yeah. Maybe we'd better get back."

"You kids all right? Y'looked kind of upset over there. Is anythin' wrong?"

"We, uh, received word tonight some, um, friends died. It was quite a shock."

"That is too bad. And on this night, too. I'm really sorry. Your parents around?"

"Um, back at the church, probably."

"Well, look, why don't I give you a lift? My pickup ain't much to look at, but it warms fast enough—"

"Over there!" Miguel's voice. He, Tontine, Ken, Virginia, and the minister ran toward them from across the Plaza.

"That won't be necessary. Here they are now," Marian said. "Probably a little upset with us. Thanks so much for the offer."

"Good, good. Well, take care now. Don't let life get

y'down too much." He pointed with his cigarette. "I see another candle's gone out." He ambled off.

Virginia held out Marian's coat and Tontine Aaron's as they stepped up. "You guys certainly could've outrun us if you'd wanted," Virginia puffed.

Marian slipped her arms into the jacket. "I'm sorry. I shouldn't have run away like that. It was a stu—"

"Forget it," Virginia said, helping her pull her hair out from underneath the jacket. "I know exactly why you did. No more need be said."

"Yes," Rev. Rose said. "Only prayers will help your friends, now. I just don't believe—" She shook her head. "If there's anything I can do, please let me know."

"Thank you," Marian said.

"We got sidetracked by the farl—what did he call them?" Aaron said, working his body into the down jacket, another prize from Marian's largesse.

"Farolitos," Virginia said.

"You likely got an earful," Rev. Rose said. "That's one of our town characters."

"Mmmmhmmm." Marian smiled.

"Except they're *lumin—"* Ken began.

"Pipe down." Virginia jabbed him with an elbow. "Here, they're called *farolitos.* This, however, pales to the real show up along the Acequia Madre. If you're up to it, we'll take the walking tour. It's the only way to go. They block the streets off." She placed a hand on Marian's shoulder. "It'll help distract from some disturbing images."

"I'm game."

"I must get back to the church," the minister said.

"Oh, we must help—" Marian started.

Rev. Rose waved her hand. "Never mind. The crowds are thinning. We can finish." She took a deep breath, looked around at the hundreds of glowing sacks. "Out among the rows of *farolitos,* perhaps you'll find comfort. And evidence of the true Christmas spirit."

* * *

". . . the Tulsa hospital just issued a terse statement confirming the deaths of Harold Coner and Alisa Bardnoth. The statement did not give a cause of death for either. Coner, who had just turned thirty-two, and Bardnoth, twenty-nine, were among the Rewound Children. Reverend Brigman had adopted them, and lately had been claiming they were signs of miracles from God with the power to cure.

"Although no one at the church has issued a statement, CNN has learned both Coner and Bardnoth died at the scene. Sources say Coner was asphyxiated when several people fell on top of him. In Bardnoth's case, she was the victim of a tug-of-war, and the source said her neck was broken.

"Three other people also died in the melee, said the source, including two who had been confined to wheelchairs. Thirty-six injuries of various degrees are being reported, more than twenty of those requiring hospitalization . . ."

Marian closed her eyes and tried to imagine herself in the back seat of her parents' car, traveling through the night, Mother and Father talking in low tones in the front seat as the air rushed by the windows. Opening her eyes destroyed the illusion. For one thing, she was facing backward, looking out at the lights of Santa Fe receding into the night. Still, there was security here as Miguel guided the van along the highway.

Virginia was right—the residential *farolito* display had been spectacular: little glowing sacks by the thousands, along the tops of walls, the edges of all the streets and driveways, along the roofs and some even resting in tree branches. A small elementary school had been transformed into a wonderland of flickering lights. All candle-powered—no electricity allowed. Occasionally the group came across a blazing fire of short logs stacked in a square, sending fragrant smoke out into the neighborhood now crowded with sightseers.

"*That* is a *luminaria*," Virginia had said as they approached one. Ken didn't answer; he was too busy accepting a paper cup of hot chocolate from the keepers of the flame.

After the midnight service back at the adobe-styled church—now adorned with its own *farolitos*—she had asked Aaron, "Did you feel anything at the service?"

"Safe," he said. "Not worried that anyone was going to grab me and try to make me cure their psoriasis."

"That's all?"

He turned to her, breath fogging in the cold air. "I've always said church is a place to go to be with people like yourself, where you don't have to worry about being politically correct in what you say, or worry about sitting next to persons of different races, or have to grit your teeth in order to be tolerant of someone else's faith. A sanctuary against the real world, in effect. Tonight, though, I felt at peace, surrounded by friends. Despite certain events in other so-called churches." He rubbed his nose with a gloved finger.

"Some people call it love, Aaron."

The mood lingered even now in the van. She hadn't been much of a churchgoer before June, and she wasn't sure if there was anything there that could help her now. Aaron was right, though—just being surrounded by friends eased the pain of seeing two more die.

As they had prepared to head back to Albuquerque, Tontine had approached.

"Um," he'd started with uncharacteristic awkwardness, "we, um, would like to give a lift to Sam and Louise. They need a ride home. It's, uh, it's right on our way."

"Where?" she had asked.

"Off the highway."

"Where?"

"We won't be there long."

"*Where?*"

"Waldo exit."

"Oh, you mean the Holn landing site. I didn't know anyone still lived there."

His face relaxed. "A few who haven't decided when, or if, they'll leave. You don't mind?"

"No. What's there to be frightened of, now?"

The road to the site had been paved when the state realized the Holn were going to be a big draw. Instead of the jam of semipermanent buildings, however, only a few mobile homes now huddled together against the cold.

"We'll be a few minutes," Tontine said. "We want to do some trading."

Marian saw Aaron look down the road where it disappeared into darkness. "Is that flashlight still here?" he blurted. "I'm going over to the landing site." He reached under a seat and pulled out a long, black tube.

"Me too," Marian said.

"All right," Tontine said. "Miguel, go with them. We'll honk when we're ready."

The flashlight beam illuminated a spot of road before them as they walked. A few scattered *farolitos* sat around the dwellings, and a small tree glittered with tiny lights. The air was crisp and the sky clear. Aaron pointed the light at the solid yellow line down the center of the road.

"The DMZ," he said.

"Did you ever come see this, Miguel?" Marian asked.

"No. I had to make sure I got a green card first, find a job. I'm trying to save enough to bring the girl I want to marry to the United States."

"How sweet," she said.

"This is the side I came up on," Aaron said, sweeping the circle of light among the low brush and grass. "The optimists. There was a whole community over there." Now the flashlight just showed scraggly bushes, an occasional rock, but mostly flat, unadorned ground.

They crunched their way through a patch of snow.

"May I borrow that?" Marian took the flashlight and played it along the road to their right. Gone were the camo man and his knives, the youth with the lurid paintings, the Bible ladies.

"I wonder what they felt when they watched the ship leave," she said. "Sorrow, anger, disappointment?"

"Poor," Aaron said. "Their money was fleeing."

"And their way of life. And their hopes, their dreams." She handed the flashlight back to Aaron.

He played the light ahead of them, catching a gray boulder the size of a picnic cooler in the beam. "That rock marked the food court. The carnita stand was back there, whatever a carnita is. I can still smell the aroma."

"So can I. Made my stomach rumble."

Another twenty meters and the pavement came to an abrupt halt. Ahead was emptiness.

"I will wait here," Miguel said quietly.

Aaron handed the flashlight to him. "It looks pretty smooth. We're not going far."

Their hands found each other's as they stepped forward.

"I said there wasn't anything to be afraid of now," Marian said, "so why is my heart beating so fast?"

"It's the thought of them returning suddenly and landing in this very spot, burning us into crispy carnitas."

They walked down into a shallow depression that had been scooped out by the blast from the ship.

"Where were we found?"

"I don't know. They keep saying on a hillside, but I don't see any hills. I remember a mound the newspeople charged down, I think, maybe, over there."

"Where our lives were changed. And where Charlie, Perry, Sandra, Alisa and Harold began their journey toward death."

She saw Aaron's head shake. "Alisa and Harold—what was that all about? I just can't—Christ."

"The faces of those people—animals." Marian shivered, unconsciously taking a step toward Aaron. They bumped, and Aaron slid an arm around her shoulders. She slipped one around his midback, pressing her body against his. Marian closed her eyes.

"Who's next? Who'll be the next victim of the crapshoot—"

Aaron kissed her forehead. "Hush."

She put her head on his shoulder, his hair tickling her nose, and took several deep breaths. She opened her eyes and raised her head, then stepped away.

"At night, before I go to sleep, I get scared. I see the glowing ceiling of the museum, the light blue walls and the silver floor. All nice and human. Then I see awful shapes and my body shrinks and I scream in pain—"

"Is it just the dreams?"

She stepped away, started walking in a circle, Aaron at its center. "I think I remember a room without corners, curved ceiling not far above, glowing the full length of my body. I envision arms without bodies, lights pulsing in my eyes. I'm on my back, I can't move . . ."

"And there's a soft chiming coming from behind."

"Yes. The sound of moving air."

"A quiet whirr, like machinery."

She stopped. "Then I woke up, sunlight beating down on me, roaring in my ears and the ground shaking. I'm naked, my blouse and pants folded neatly next to me."

"I can feel a touch, in that curved room, something warm and yielding against my neck. Then I woke up with all the world's media staring at my bare butt."

She kicked at the ground. "I don't know who I am anymore."

"Your cat does. From the moment you opened the carrier, he had no doubts you were the mistress who had given him food, shelter, and love. Even if you weren't the same size."

"Yeah." She started her circling again.

"I lost everything I owned, everything I'd built up, everything I had been," Aaron said. "I have nearly gone crazy. But the one thing I do not regret, the one thing I see as good coming out of this, is knowing you. I have drawn strength from you."

"How can you do that? I get mine from you." She reached out and fumbled for his hand. "Now I'm just waiting with fear as the future comes hurtling at me."

Aaron pulled her into his arms, and they embraced, hard. "I know that fear," he mumbled into her hair.

After a moment, he pushed her to arm's length, evidently studying her in the dark.

"Marian, marry me."

"Aren't we too young, or immature, or something?"

"Probably. But if—when—we grow up again, and you once again become the lovely woman I saw in the Holn ship, just remember who asked you first."

"I will remember." Marian wasn't sure if he could see the smile in the dark, so she wrapped her arms around his neck and embraced him; his return embrace was strong. Their cheeks slid together, and lips met, briefly, but she turned her head.

"I-I'm not ready."

"The hugs are plenty for now."

A soft laugh escaped her as they tightened their grips on each other. She looked up past his shoulder.

"Oh," she pushed back, "look at the stars."

Aaron craned his neck. "Whoa. Let's see if I can remember Virginia's astronomy lessons."

He pointed toward the glittering array. "North, Big Dipper, yes, bowl stars pointing to Polaris—"

"And Ursa Minor—"

"With Draco snaking around along there—"

"Cassiopeia over there, the big W—"

"Right, and Pegasus, but can't quite see Andromeda Galaxy—"

"And look, the Milky Way crossing along here, and Orion over—oh."

Orion dominated the southern sky. Marian had not paid attention to the constellations before, but this one pattern snared her and held her, glittering perfect against the black sky.

"And under that line of stars of his belt," Aaron said softly, "is where new stars are being born. And new worlds."

"New worlds," she repeated softly.

After a moment, he said, "This is a good spot to contemplate the mysteries of the universe." He slowly turned, looking up. "Such as, what's Tontine's real name?"

Marian giggled. " 'Yes, we're just tiny specks on a planet particle, hurling through the infinite blackness.' "

"That sounds so glum. Who said that?"

"Calvin."

"The theologian?"

"No, the boy in the old comic strip. He and his tiger were contemplating the heavens just like we are. After a few more minutes of gazing, Calvin demands they go into the house and turn on all the lights."

Aaron laughed. "Star light, star bright. They've touched us, Marian, you and I. Maybe that's why we're so bedazzled by them tonight. They've reached across the vast distances and touched us—" He laughed again. "Yeah. Look who's waxing poetic."

Marian fell silent. Nothing moved around them, no breeze ruffled hair, no animal skittered in the brush, no vehicle rumbled on the distant interstate. Just the two of them, linked together, sharing warmth, staring into the flickering depths of night.

Five minutes later, when Miguel came to get them, they were still staring skyward.

Fifteen

"If there is anything that proves these so-called Rewound Children are the instruments of Satan this is it. So powerful, so subtle are these agents that they seduced Brother Brigman. And look at the result. Even now, Brother Brigman is fighting for his very soul against other personifications of Satan, the anti-Christ, the Destroyer of Worlds. Brother Brigman was lulled into believing their serpentine persuasion partly because of the anti-religious left-leaning media, which have tried to make these abominations into victims or have us believe they have been returned back to the innocence of childhood. Innocence! The very thought makes my blood run cold. We must act to eradicate this menace to humanity."

"That was part of the statement released by the Reverend Lakewood van Kellin through his Church of Encompassing Faith based in Magnolia Springs, Tennessee, but no one at the church will answer questions about it. CNN has left messages asking if Reverend van Kellin, in saying—quote—We must act to eradicate this menace to humanity—end quote—is calling for the destruction of the Rewound Children. No one from the church has responded to repeated phone calls.

"Meanwhile, in Oklahoma, three weeks after two Rewound Children were killed in a mob scene at the Faith Christ Evangelical Ministry, there is still no word about

200

*Reverend Jim Brigman's status. He has not been seen,
nor have any services been held in the House of the
Spire, the main sanctuary for the church. Sources have
told CNN that the building remains as it was after the
incident, with smashed pews, damage to the pulpit and
choir area, and three wheelchairs still lying where they
fell. The two great stained-glass windows also reportedly
suffered damage. Associate pastors have been conduct-
ing services in other buildings.*

*"Jasmine Chastain, CN-what? Oh, yeah. CNN is doing
another telephone poll about whether you believe the
children are devils or angels. To record your vote . . ."*

January 24, 2009

Earl was going his usual speed on the bike—very
fast—and everything would have been fine if the car had
stayed on its side of the road. It didn't, though—at the
last second, it swerved right at him. Startled, he jerked
the wheel and the back end skidded around. Earl fought
the skew, managing to stop the slide to the right, but he
overcompensated and it started going left. By this time,
he'd managed to slow the forward momentum, and,
again, all might have come out OK if the county had
repaired the pothole his front wheel now hit. The bike
twisted right and fell over. Earl managed to break his fall
with a padded elbow. His helmet hit the pavement. After
a moment, he pushed himself up. The car, back in its
own lane, receded rapidly.

He untangled himself from the bike, took account of
his limbs. The elbow padding showed where it had taken
the punishment, and his head seemed OK, but he figured
his shoulders were going to be sore. He felt a jab on his
right knee. A pad had slipped and bare knee had made
contact with pavement. Blood oozed from multiple
microscopic cuts.

I scraped my knee. I scraped my stupid knee.

He stood, hauled the bike erect. Something had

jammed the front wheel and it scraped the side of the fork. The chain on the derailleur hung loosely in back. Outside of some paint left on the asphalt, he could see no other obvious damage. He'd bought it for himself—that is, Walter had withdrawn the money from Earl's account because Earl was not allowed to handle his own funds—and it had become an instrument to release tension. Except for that last car.

Marcia had taken a couple of days off and was in her sewing room working on a new dress for Jennifer's birthday. Earl walked into the room timidly.

"Mommy," he said in his best little-boy voice, "I hurts my knee. Can you make it all better?"

She looked at him, looked at the knee, back at him . . . and burst into laughter. She even played the game: "It won't hurt, will it?" "No it won't hurt." "Don't put that stuff on me, it'll sting." "It won't sting." "You sure?" "Sure I'm sure." "Ow! Ow! Ow! Ow! Ow! Ow!" "I haven't even put the stuff on yet." "Oh. Well, be careful, 'cause it'll sting, and I'll yell and cry and everything. When are you going to put the stuff on?" "I just did." "Oh."

She put the bottle down and looked at him as he sat on a kitchen stool. "You are amazing."

"Oh, come on, I'm just an average guy caught up in outrageous circumstances."

"Bullshit."

Earl stared at her with upraised eyebrows. "And Lucas gets sent to his room for that."

"Lift your shirt, let me look at your back." She pressed at various points. "Does that hurt?"

"No."

She nodded. "No broken skin. There might be bruises tomorrow, and stiffness." She put the antiseptic away. "Every family has a wild card. You are it for the Othbergs."

"Black sheep, you mean."

"No, I don't. What other seventy-nine-year-old man

stricken with arthritis among other things would get up and leave a comfortable nursing home and fly across half the continent just to see a space ship?"

"And if I'd done it earlier, we wouldn't be in this fix, either."

"That's under the bridge now." She crossed her arms, looked at him. "You want me to kiss your knee?"

"You know, Mom used to gross out when I suggested that."

She gave a short laugh. "Yeah, well. How did this happen?"

"I—oh, boy." He told her about the car.

"Silver foreign job?"

"With a chrome Christian fish symbol on the trunk."

She turned away, threw the wrapper for the adhesive strip into the trash below the sink.

"You know who it was?"

"Possibly."

"I'm really getting to be a real pain in the neck, aren't I?"

She looked at him a long moment. "Among the many strange things that have happened to you, one of the most is my seeming ability to accept it all with a degree of equanimity. I'm not sure how or when this started."

"Well, however you do it, thanks."

As she headed back to her sewing, he went out on the patio and sat down. Raindrops starting falling among the blossoms of her colorful garden. The scene with Marcia hadn't been possible two months before. As for the kids—he found out how well they were doing on New Year's Eve.

"MTV again?" Earl had said as he licked powdered sugar off of his fingers left behind by the pecan ball. "I'd thought modern teenagers would've gone on to something else by now."

"I suppose you want to watch Dick Clark," Tom said.

"Please. He makes me feel old."

The two teenagers actually smiled at that feeble joke. Lucas looked confused.

"Not too exciting a New Year's Eve to be babysitting your granduncle, is it?"

Jennifer shrugged. "There wasn't much going on around here anyway. All the good parties are in Kahului." She turned to him. "What do you want most from the new year, Uncle Earl?"

"To grow up. Sounds strange, doesn't it? After saying what a blast it is to be young of sorts again. But I cannot spend the rest of my life like this." He shook his head. "I just wish I could know for sure one way or another."

She jumped up. "We can measure you!"

"What?"

"Yeah, we can get the tape measure and see if you've grown. I remember what that-that scientist said, the old guy. All of you were the same height, he said. What was it, what was it, c'mon—yeah! Fifty-two point one inches."

"Well—"

All three kids jumped up and ran shouting into the kitchen. Earl followed, slightly dazed at the explosion of energy, particularly from the older two. What was in that egg nog, anyway?

"Here it is!" came Tom's triumphant shout.

"Okay, Uncle Earl, stand here." Jennifer pressed him against a blank section of kitchen wall. "You have the pencil and straight edge, Lucas?"

"Yeah."

"Heels against the wall, shoulders back." Tom inspected Earl's stance. "Stand relaxed, that's it. All right, Jenny."

With a few giggles and false starts, she finally got the flat piece of metal where they wanted it.

"All right now step away," Tom said. "Don't let that thing slip—damn!"

"Sorry," Jennifer said sheepishly.

"No problem." Earl stepped back up against the wall.

This time the edge didn't slip and Lucas was able to mark the spot. With breathless anticipation, the kids carefully measured the height of the mark.

"Uncle Earl," the girl said somberly, "our measurements show you're taller by three-quarters of an inch."

"A definite change," Tom said.

Jennifer again took Earl by surprise, this time with a ferocious hug.

"Hey," Lucas blurted, "it's after midnight. We missed the countdown."

"Don't worry," Earl said, touching the mark lightly with a finger, "a new year definitely has arrived."

A thump loud enough to reverberate through the house broke his thoughts. He dashed to the living-room window, but saw nothing. He went outside and found a white lump on the lawn near the door. He glanced up and down the street, but saw no one. The lump was a stone wrapped in blank newsprint held on by an elastic band. GET OUT, ALIEN was scrawled on the paper by what looked like a child's Crayon.

"What is it Earl?" Marcia asked from the porch.

"Pretty hokey," he said, handing her the rock and paper. "Must think I'm from Mexico or something."

She opened the paper, immediately scrunched it up, tossed the stone into the garden. Earl walked out to the center of the yard, looking around at the houses, the other lawns, the street curving by. A breeze ruffled his hair and drops of rain began to hit his shoulders and legs.

Something's got to give. I cannot let this family remain in danger. I've got to go, I've got to figure something out.

The rain increased in intensity.

But what, lord, what?

"The FBI is calling the death of Myra Caslon, another of the Rewound Children, a ritual murder. Caslon's age was listed as fifty-five, although records indicate her birthday

was two days ago. Caslon was the mother of six children, all but one grown and living away from home. She had been living with her husband, Haley, and their youngest son, Sydney, eleven, here in Salt Lake City. According to a family member who asked she not be identified, Caslon had attempted suicide not long after being released from the Albuquerque hospital, but, as that relative put it, faith and family saved her. As recently as New Year's Eve, said the relative, Caslon had pronounced herself optimistic about the future and had renewed her faith in God whatever the church elders might rule. That ruling, on whether she still had the blessings of God and was therefore a member of the human family or was an alien outside of God's grace, went against Caslon, according to the relative, but we have been unable to confirm that with Mormon Church officials. We now switch to the scene where an FBI spokesperson is making a statement."

"We are calling it a ritual killing at this time because of the evidence found. Uh, Ms., uh, Caslon's body was found in the middle of the living room floor, on its back, arms extended outward, feet together. The body was clad in a long gown, white in color, and a cord, purple in color, was found wrapped around her neck. No other clothing was found on the body, but no signs of sexual molestation are indicated. The medical investigator says preliminary indications show the victim had been strangled. Forensic tests will determine if the cord was the instrument of death. Several objects of apparent religious significance were found in a circle around the body, but we are not describing those objects pending further investigation. Ms. Caslon apparently had been dead about six hours. The body was discovered by the youngest son, Sydney, who collapsed upon finding the body of his moth—the, uh, the woman who had been his mother.

"That's all we have for you now. A press conference will be held sometime tomorrow."

*   *   *

"Ah, here we are at six. My friends, we are making progress. Just as I said, too, that if you wait, things will take care of themselves. The Mormon Church itself wasn't so sure if this woman was human, so the Almighty, of course, answered for them. He will end the threat, in his own time. You will see."

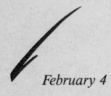

Sixteen

February 4

"Aaron, Marian, it's time—hey, come back here!"

Neither had any intention of doing so because it had been Nurse Ames who had yelled. As soon as they'd seen the blue Lexus, they both took off.

The snow on the ground from an early-February storm slowed them, but they pushed harder, running across an untrampled open area and across a street and toward another building with a steep roof. The outing to get away from confining walls and shadows of Myra's death suddenly had gone real sour.

Aaron glanced back.

"They—they haven't left that other lot yet. Go for the main entrance."

They dashed between a couple of school buses idling in the driveway. The sidewalk here had been cleared of snow, making it easier to slip past the statue of a dinosaur and through the front doors. More dinosaur models leered at them inside the open foyer, including one with a huge wingspread diving from the ceiling. Aaron just glanced at them as he looked wildly around for a corner, a niche, to hide in.

"This way." Marian led him around a corner behind

one of the displays, where they had a clear view of the front entrance.

"They'll be here any second," she said between pants. "Blocking all the doors."

"I know. We've got to get back to Ken and the others. Somehow."

"How are we going to get out?"

"I don't—" An explosion of sound cut him off, young voices, expanding in volume as the ranks kept swelling: Kids of all sizes, from high school to about their height, jabbering, laughing and playfully pushing each other.

Aaron turned to Marian and grinned. "Camouflage."

Marian grinned back, pulled out her bonnet. As she gathered her hair, he took off his jacket and reversed it so red replaced blue. He pulled his soft cap down farther.

They waited until the flow was at its greatest, then stepped out behind two stocky young men in jackets with "Matadors" printed on their backs. They were outside before they saw Nurse Ames trying to buck the tide. They slipped to the right, keeping the Matadors between them and Ames. Aaron began to angle between two yellow buses—of which there had to have been a dozen—and into the parking lot. However, he spied Slick Suit scrutinizing the students as they passed.

"Into the bus," he said quietly. The bus was filling with loud kids about their—age? Hardly, he thought. Size, yes. Aaron tried to keep a watch out windows on both sides. Once he caught a glimpse of Nurse Ames stretching to see in.

"Down," he whispered, and both sank into a crouch.

"Hey, you guys aren't assigned to this bus." A boy in military-style overcoat looked down at them from his seat.

"Uh, no, we aren't even assigned to this school. We're from out of town."

"You wanta transfer?" Scattered laughter greeted the remark.

"Perhaps. We're hiding, actually. A coupla guys out there are after us."

"Why? You drug dealers or something?" A girl with short hair and rings on every finger said. "You got some?"

"No to both questions. One of those guys made a trashy comment to my fr-sister M-Suzie, then tried to grab her and pull her into his car."

"Really? Molesters?"

"I guess. He was pretty crude about what he wanted to do to her."

"Ms. Briggs!" The girl's shout pierced right through the noise—and Aaron's ear.

A woman with short brown hair, long green coat and jeans stepped over. "Yolanda, was that you shouting again?"

"Yeah, these kids are in trouble."

Aaron went through his concocted story again.

"Well, we'd better call the police."

"I imagine our parents will. They're over at the other museum. If we could, uh, maybe ride your bus over there, I'm sure we'll find them. We could dodge the bad guys, too."

Ms. Briggs looked at Aaron a long moment, then at Marian. *Shouldn't have said "bad guys."*

"All right. Stay crouched so they won't see you."

"Thank you," Marian said.

Aaron couldn't see out so he had to take her word that's what she told the bus driver to do. He heard the engine rev and tires crunch through snow and felt the bumps of motion, and by the time he chanced to look out, it already was turning into the other parking lot. He spotted Virginia and Ken standing near a curb. Aaron pointed. "That's them," he said to the teacher.

The two watched in confusion as the bus pulled up to them and Aaron and Marian tumbled out.

"Mom, Dad," Marian said.

Ken looked confused.

"Da-*ad!*"

"Oh, M-honey, where have you been?" He kneeled, put an arm around Marian. Virginia came over and embraced Aaron.

"Why did you run off like that, son?"

"Some guy tried to pull Suzie into a car. We ran and they chased us all the way over to the other museum." It struck Aaron that he might sound too young; how did the current crop of ten-year-olds talk, how sophisticated were they?

"Oh, my God. And these people helped you escape?"

"Yes, this is Ms. Briggs, of . . . some school or other."

"Thank you very much."

"I would call the police."

"Damn straight we will."

Ms. Briggs gave Virginia an odd look. "Well, look, we can't stay. We have to get back to the school before it lets out. I'll give you my card. If the police need to talk to any of us, we'll be available." She pulled a card from her pocket.

"I can't thank you enough," Virginia said, taking the card. "You can't trust anybody these days."

"True. You never know. Good-bye, Suzie, and—"

"Uh, Frank," Aaron said.

"Frank." She gave him and Marian one last lingering look, then glanced first at Ken, then Virginia. Finally, she climbed aboard the bus.

"She's suspicious," Aaron said as it pulled away.

"She saved your asses," Ken said.

"Yeah, 'Dad,'" Marian said.

"Come on, let's get inside," Virginia said. "We'll wait for the city bus in there. I can't see them."

More school buses were pulling out of the other lot, but no sign of a blue Lexus.

"Ken, find Leo and Kilkenny."

"Right."

"They're off looking for you," Virginia said. "Told us to stay put in case you showed up. We didn't know you'd gone clear across the street."

Black King Leo was angry.

"Played us for fools," he scowled.

After assuring himself they were OK, Leo stayed outside with Kilkenny, scanning for the car. When the city bus rumbled up the driveway, he gave a signal and the rest of the group dashed out and into the bus. As they waited to drop their quarters in, Leo whispered, "Take a quick look at the other passengers."

Only three sat scattered along the seats and none were familiar. They sat together in one of the seats facing the aisle near the mid-bus doors. The trip was slow because many of the streets hadn't been plowed or sanded. The bus itself had no trouble, but the driver had to dodge a constant stream of sliding cars. At each stop, new passengers were given careful scrutiny as they knocked slush off their shoes and brushed new-fallen flakes off their shoulders.

"All right." Leo crouched in front of the seat. "I'm not positive we shook those people. They're smart and determined. Kilkenny."

The young man slid off the seat, bright eyes anticipating adventure.

"Kilkenny, you get off at Fifth. Go to Grid Manor. Don't dawdle. Find Tontine. Tell him we're in trouble. We'll get off at Second as usual. Understand?"

"Off at Fifth," he said. "Don't dawdle. To Grid Manor. Get Tontine. You off at Second. We meet you."

"Right." He slapped the young man's shoulder. "Good show."

Kilkenny grinned as he took his seat again.

Leo stood, grabbed a pole. "See anything, Ken?"

"Nada."

"They knew where we were," Marian said. "Exactly where and when."

Leo nodded. "Someone ratted."

Aaron frowned. "But how did they make contact? How did those assholes find someone who knows about us?"

"Homeless have a network, too," Leo said. "We wander all over, observe, tell each other what's goin' down. Some of us know this city better than the legits who run it. News travels pretty much on its own until the proper connection is made. Monetary inducement often diverts a wanted piece of information to those eager for it. The talker at the manor likely will be someone needing artificial help to make it through one day, much less a life."

Leo made sense, of course, but that also was the longest speech Aaron had ever heard him give.

As the bus approached Fifth Street, they all craned necks looking for the car. No sign, and Kilkenny jumped off almost before the doors had opened. By the time the bus was rolling again, he was out of sight.

As they stepped off at Second, Aaron found his heart pumping a little harder in his chest. *At least I don't have to worry about heart attacks.*

"Stay together," Leo said. Virginia took up a post to Marian's left, Ken to Aaron's right, Leo in front. The first block passed uneventfully. Snowflakes fell softly but in profusion, tickling Aaron's nose as they landed and melted. At every step, their boots crushed the crystal piles into hardened lumps impressed with brand names on the soles.

The Lexus flashed by just as they turned a corner and slid to a somewhat uncontrolled stop. A door flew open and Slick Suit jumped out while Nurse Ames carefully stepped out of the passenger's side.

"Aaron and Marian, now you must come with us." Nurse Ames pulled her coat around her as she stepped around the car. "You gave us quite the slip, but now it's time to go back. We have more data to gather."

"Fuck off, Ames," Aaron shouted from behind the wall of Virginia, Ken and Leo.

"Just get the hell into the car," Slick Suit shouted. "You don't have any choice. You belong to us. The Alden Commission says so, and in your case, your ex-wife agrees. Now come on." He opened the back door. "Get out, you."

A cowering man in torn overcoat half-fell out.

"Our quisling," Leo said.

"Yep," Ken said. "Wanted a drink, no doubt."

"Do I get my money now?" Like a child whining.

"Yes, yes, you get your reward." Slick Suit's long, goateed face frowned at the sniveling man beside him. He pulled out a money clip, pulled off a bill, then pushed the man aside. "Liquor store two streets down."

A thought nagged at Aaron's mind. Nurse Ames, Slick Suit . . . where was Dark Suit? He turned just in time to see the man rushing in from behind.

"Marian, look out!"

The warning gave her time to turn but not avoid the grasp. He grabbed her coat, then an arm.

"Stop the crap an—oww!" Aaron's boot heel clamping down onto his instep caused the howl. "You little shit! I've had enough of your crap!"

Aaron dodged but the kick got him square in the back. He felt himself flying forward and hit face first into snow. He rolled over quickly to see Dark Suit struggle with a kicking and twisting Marian. Leo jumped in front of him.

"Let her go," he said in a quiet voice.

"Fuck—"

"Now!" Leo swung a huge fist. The blow staggered the man, and if the street hadn't been icy, he might have recovered. He didn't; a leg slipped and he fell, pulling Marian down with him. Instantly, Virginia was on him, twisting fingers. He yelped until Marian broke free, scrambled to her feet and ran over to Aaron. Both stood together, snow clinging to their clothing. Her bonnet had been torn off and her hair covered part of her face. Ken stepped over and planted himself next to them. Dark

Suit heaved and Virginia fell over into the street. Dark Suit scrambled to his feet and backed up two steps, eyeing Leo warily. Virginia got up and hurried to Marian's side.

"Ain't that sweet?" Slick Suit said. "The drunken bums defending the little bast—"

Something suddenly hurled itself against the car door, slamming it on Slick Suit. He yelped in pain, but before he could fall, hands grabbed him and yanked him upright.

"Fucking bastard!" Tontine growled. "Tell me who you are. Right now!" He slammed the man against the car, face first. Slick Suit grunted. "Who the hell are you?" *Wham.* Tontine grabbed his collar, put his face next to the goatee. "You shit-faced bastard. Who the hell gave you the right to experiment on humans? Answer me!"—*wham*—"Or I'll break every bone in your slimy body!"—*wham*—"Tell, me goddamnit!"—*wham*—

"Hey! Hey!" Dark Suit had pulled out a pistol and aimed it at Tontine, who immediately spun the groggy and whimpering Slick Suit around and pinned an arm behind. Tontine wrapped his arm around the man's neck, began pushing him forward.

"You point that thing at me, you'd better shoot, asshole," Tontine shouted. "Go on, shoot, shoot, you mangy son of a back-alley bitch! Brainless coward! Shoot! Shoot!"

Dark Suit let the muzzle drop and Tontine hurled Slick Suit at him. Slick Suit went down on his face, but Dark Suit was only staggered. Nurse Ames, meanwhile, had taken three steps, perhaps to try to assault Tontine, but she suddenly was pummeled by a bevy of snow-balls, including three in the face at high velocity. They had to have stung. When she dodged another volley, she went down like a sack of potatoes. Aaron saw Kilkenny and Miguel among the hurlers.

Dark Suit snarled as he tried to find the pistol, which had fallen into the snow. Leo grabbed his collar, hauled

him around and punched him hard. The man's head
snapped around and blood spattered the snow.

"All right, stop, that's enough." Slick Suit had managed to find the pistol and rose shakily to his feet. "I'll
shoot the next idiot that moves. Enough of this crap."
He pointed the pistol at Tontine barely two feet away.
"As for you, I'm going to—"

"Curt, look out!"

The shout by Nurse Ames was too late; a burly figure
clipped Slick Suit's feet out from under him and he fell
on his side with a heavy grunt. The pistol bounced back
into the snow. Dark Suit let fly another kick at the new
arrival, but White King Sam merely grabbed the foot
mid-kick, twisted it and Dark Suit yelped and fell flat.
Sam grabbed the man by his coat, lifted him and carried
him toward the car, blood dripping a trail into the snow.
He tossed Dark Suit, who landed on a shouting Nurse
Ames and both fell into a heap next to the car. Leo
grabbed Slick Suit, dragged him over and shoved him on
top of the other two.

After a few seconds of shoving and cursing, Slick Suit
sat up and glared at the chess kings. Dark Suit also sat
up, holding his bleeding nose. Nurse Ames tried to
stand, but fell to one knee. She stopped, turned to see
what the others were doing. Another surreal scene for
Aaron, heightened by the snow swirling down, coating
the figures even as they remained utterly motionless for a
moment. Then Slick Suit began to struggle with something in his overcoat.

"We're taking those two brats," he said, "and
there's"—he jerked at the balky item—"nothing you
can—"

He stopped as Tontine bent over and slowly picked up
Dark Suit's gun. His hand shook as he gazed at it.

"I . . . think I'd . . . uh, have to stop you."

Slick Suit sneered. "Is that so? Come on, you two, we
can take that alky shaker. Just as soon as I get—"

Tontine suddenly dropped into a shooter's crouch and three sharp cracks sounded. For a split second, the suits stared at each other, then turned slowly to gaze at the car door, where three neat holes in a tight grouping had suddenly appeared—right between their heads.

"Damn," Tontine rasped. "My DI was right. Alcohol does throw off your aim. Lez'ee if I can't hit something this time." He pointed the muzzle directly at Slick Suit, who shouted and rolled under the car. "Ah, fuck," Tontine said, swinging the muzzle to Dark Suit, who suddenly had an urge to scramble to his feet and dive into the driver's seat. Nurse Ames grabbed the back door, yanked it open—and fell again. She was up in a flash and had climbed in by the time the other front door had opened and Slick Suit had clambered in, keeping his head low.

The Lexus's wheels spun as it backed, then the whole car spun completely around in the snow and slid slowly toward Tontine, who hadn't lowered the gun. He turned slightly so it pointed directly at the driver, who frantically turned the steering wheel. The car slowly turned aside, then moved forward. The muzzle of the gun was less than a foot away from Slick Suit's window; he was cowering in the seat, hands over head. The back end slid to one side, then swerved back and clipped a pickup parked at the curb. It whipsawed a half block, then turned about ten degrees less than completely sideways, still moving away.

"Turn into the skid, idiot," Tontine muttered, lowering the pistol.

The back end hit another parked car and the recoil sent it around into a more or less straight line as the car disappeared into the grayness of the falling snow.

Tontine let out a breath. "They ain't mafioso, and they ain't drug lords. I don't know what the fuck they were, but I wish I could've found out." He did something to the pistol. "Nine millimeter," he said to Sam, holding what Aaron guessed to be the cartridge. "Semi-auto." He removed the last bullet from the chamber and dropped the gun into the snow.

A warbling began echoing in the distance.

"Police," Sam said. "Too late, of course."

Miguel and another man Aaron recognized as Eddie from the manor came up to Tontine, the bleating man in torn overcoat between them.

"How much?" Tontine demanded.

The man just whimpered and stammered. Tontine reached into a pocket and yanked out a bill.

"Fifty bucks?"

"They were s-supposed to give a hundred," the man whined.

"Oh, well, that makes it all right then, doesn't it?"

"Pl-please, T-Tont, I d-didn't want to hurt them, I just wanted a drink. Thas a-all. I didn't w-want to hurt anyone."

"Yeah, sure. Go buy your fifty bucks worth of shit." He jammed the bill back into a pocket, but grabbed the man by his collar and pulled his face close. "If I ever catch you within five blocks of Grid Manor again, I'll tear you apart." He jerked on the collar. "Got that, you sniveling bastard traitor?"

"Yes, y-yess, I-I p-p-promise—" the man gurgled.

"Sure you do. Until someone offers you another fifty. Just remember, I'll tear you to shreds." He pushed the man away. "Now get out of here."

Tontine turned away and crunched his way toward Aaron and Marian. He knelt down in the snow next to her.

"Are you two OK?"

"Fine," Marian said. "All we got was a little snow in our faces. You guys did the rest."

"Uh, good show," Aaron offered.

"You've seen the other side of me now, the dangerous, maybe psycho part. The part that sends me to the therapist. Still want to—"

"You don't fool me for an instant, Mr. Tontine whatever-your-name is," Marian said. "What you did here wasn't fueled by anger or alcohol. It was fueled by outrage." She stepped over, kissed him lightly on his stubbled cheek. "Thank you."

Tontine stared at her, an odd look in his eyes. Softer, as if all sorts of gates had been left open. Then he sort of laughed and stood up.

"Take them to the manor," he said to Ken. "Before the police get here. We'll take care of the rest."

"Right."

The snow kept falling on the trek back, softening the hard edges of the city.

"You broke through Tontine's facade," Aaron said as they approached Grid Manor's gate. "Congratulations."

She looked up, smiled. "I know."

They didn't say anything as they shook the snow off their coats and headed up the ramps. Miguel and Eddie ran ahead, then came back and affirmed all was safe inside.

In the great room, Marian stripped off her coat and tossed it on the couch. Aaron did the same, watching her out of the corner of his eye as he went to the space heater and turned up the controls. She knelt by the ottoman where Merlin lay in feline comfort.

"Hello, Merlin. How's the boy doing?" The animal answered with a quiet "mrow" as she stroked its fur.

Aaron knelt down beside her and saw what he had expected. All through the incident, she had been collected and brave. Now, though, her hands shook as she petted the cat. He took one hand in his.

Marian drew a deep breath but did not retract her hand. She put her forehead against the ottoman and a rush of air escaped, almost a sob. Aaron put his other hand on her hair, but didn't stroke it—too much like petting a cat, he suddenly felt.

She looked up at him, then gave him a small but lovely smile.

"Thanks for your part," she said.

"My part was rather limited because of my limited physical abilities."

"They were enough."

"Yeah."

After a moment, she withdrew her hand and said, "Aaron, this can't go on. We've endangered these people, and they're turning against themselves."

"Well, fine," he said. "But where, and who, and what?"

"Written to your sister lately?"

He looked away. "No."

"Uh huh."

He looked back at her. "And surely Shirley has heard from you, *que no?*"

Marian studied the cat as she massaged its neck. "No."

Aaron made a noise. "Aren't we the brave ones."

"After the way Myra died, do we really want to expose anyone else to danger? Your sister, perhaps?"

Aaron ran a finger along Merlin's paw. "My sister." He waited another moment, Marian eyeing him. "First, no, my sister doesn't deserve to be exposed to danger. She has two kids, a husband, six—at last count—Siberian huskies and a ferret."

Marian looked down. "And Shirley's out, too. She's a dear friend, but she would just fall apart." She shook her head. "God, we're pariahs."

"Also because we're chicken."

She blinked at him. "Pardon me?"

"We don't *want* to leave. We've found security, a soft bed, food to eat, a few friends. We don't have to put out an effort to do anything so we've just kind of melded into the structure."

"It's the only structure that would take us in."

"So we think. We haven't really tried to find out, have we?"

Marian twisted around, put a hand on a hip. "So where do we start?"

"There has to be someplace." He leaned in toward her. "We've got to start thinking and stop hibernating."

"Oh, the old capitalist is rising again."

"More than you know. It pained me right in the heart to watch Tontine shoot that lovely Lexus. Such delicate curves—aack!" She had pushed him, but because of the awkward position of his legs, he had to roll sideways.

He straightened, gazed at her.

She didn't say anything, just kept petting the cat. "Ah, Merlin, your life is so uncomplicated. Sometimes I envy you."

"Mrow."

She started to say something but was distracted by the entrance of Virginia, Ken, and Tontine, the latter's hair still damp.

"Hi, everyone," she said as they jumped up and headed toward them. "How'd it come out with the police?"

"The police didn't find a thing," Virginia said. "Except the gun. We placed it so it'd be found. But everyone had disappeared, so there's nothing to investigate."

"No witnesses?"

"Maybe. Fortunately for us, the snow obscured everything."

"You mean you slipped away without telling them anything?" Aaron said.

"Yes," Tontine said.

"I'm not sure I like the moral ambiguity here."

Marian fixed him with a sharp gaze. "As if you've never run into moral ambiguity. Or been the force behind it."

"For your information, Ms. Smartypants, I was an honest trader. I suppose you never ran into an ambiguous situation."

"I smoked pot."

"Oh, lord." Aaron put his hand over his eyes. "All this time I've been consorting with a dopehead."

"That doesn't—" She stopped, turned to the others. "What's wrong?"

"Uh, actually, it was something we were going to bring to your attention anyway," Virginia said. "Before the, uh, incident . . ."

"What?" Marian said.

"Something, we, uh, found," Tontine began.

"Hell, just give it to them," Virginia said.

"Cold turkey?" Ken asked.

"Yeah. Give it to them, Ken."

"So the delivery boy can get whupped?" He pulled something out from under his jacket. "We, uh, we found this on the newsstand."

"You know, at the grocery check-out," Virginia said.

"Among the UFO reports," Tontine said.

With a puzzled look, Marian took the item, a *National Sensation,* a hyperactive tabloid and one of the few newsprint holdouts. STARTLING PHOTOGRAPHS OF POSSIBLE "ALIENS" screamed the headline.

"Hey, that's Linda Rithen," Aaron said, stepping up next to her. "Nude as a baby."

"More photos, page ten through sixteen," Marian read, stomach beginning to clench. She turned to the inside, and sure enough—

"Charles Romplin, Sandra Mellinfield, and—oh, God." She stared at herself standing arms wide, back against wall, hair pulled back so a flat, small chest could be seen unobstructed. She let go of the paper and turned away. Aaron snapped the next page over. "Yup. There I am in all my glory. And there's Earl. Look at the headline." He held the paper up. She glanced over. HUMAN OR MADE TO LOOK HUMAN?

She dug her hands into her front pockets, turned away again.

"All here, even Harold and Alisa, Charlie and Myra,"

Aaron said. "All seventeen of us, in bright four-color display. Naked as the day we were born."

"What are all these?" Virginia said.

"The doctors or whatever took them," Aaron said. "Close-ups of every part of our bodies. You know, I asked them if I was posing for child porn. I guess I know the answer now." He waved the paper.

Marian grabbed at it and managed to come away with part. She ripped it in half, then again and again, ripping and tearing. "How dare they! Bastards! First I'm made into a child and then presented as meat for pedophiles. Damn those bastards!"

Aaron ripped his portion of the paper, and both grabbed the shreds and tore them into smaller shreds and scattered them. She kicked and stomped the pieces, started jumping up and down; Aaron joined in and they jumped and stomped as they shouted obscenities, pieces flying everywhere. Marian couldn't stop the rage from screaming out of her, couldn't stop the desperate urge to jump, stomp, hit, smash something, but ended instead by bumping hard into Tontine, who placed a hand on her shoulder. She stopped, gasping for breath, pushing slightly upward to heighten the pressure of the touch, and focused on it. She wiped a sleeve across her eyes as hot tears burned them. The hand she leaned against pulled her gently against him, like a father comforting a daughter. Marian didn't look up, but she found solace in the gesture, allowing the rage and hurt to be subsumed.

"What a life!" Aaron shouted in the meantime. *What a goddamn fucking life!*" He kicked at the footstool Merlin had been on, sending it tumbling. The cat, however, wisely had abandoned it long ago.

Seventeen

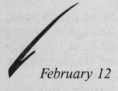

February 12

"Jack Theodoric."

The clean-shaven wide face and a portion of sport-shirt collar formed on Miranda's computer. "It's me again."

"Hello, Miranda, you're looking very well today. New outfit? Looks very nice. That color looks well on you—"

"Jack."

"Nothing personal, Miranda, it's just that I hate to talk to you. I seem just to have bad news. Maybe I should say things are just hunky-dory."

Miranda rubbed her forehead. "Six have died, two are missing, a cult is out for blood and that Allan Goth guy is counting down the deaths. And you say everything's hunky-dory."

"I don't say, Ms. Hawk-beak does. Her exact words."

Miranda smiled sourly. "Ms. Hawk-beak" was Jack's name for Radmilla Everett.

"I believe you said some strong emotions were going to be washing over everybody. You were right."

She stood up, paced the floor. "Wonderful. I predicted open season on Rewound Children."

"Could be. Romplin, Stangle, and Caslon were murdered, plain and simple. We have the perpetrators in the

224

first two cases, a pretty good idea in the third. Coner and Bardnoth died under extraordinary circumstances."

"That leaves only Sandra Mellinfield who died by her own hand."

The silence made her look back at Jack's image. "She did, didn't she?"

"What I'm about to tell you does not go beyond your office door, at least for now. We are suspicious of Mellinfield's death."

"Suspect?"

"Her husband."

Miranda shook her head. "You said you were fairly certain about Myra's killers?"

"The cult or whatever left enough clues a blind person could follow. You heard what we said about the religious objects? Dead give-aw—uh, I mean, solid clues. We expect to announce arrests within the week. We are pressing the case, Miranda, in order to thwart copycat killers."

"Oh, lord." Miranda sat down at her desk, picked up a pen and began scratching at her desk blotter with it. "Jack, is the fact that all six v—of the dead individuals were cremated rather quickly coincidental?"

Jack's image regarded her for a moment. "Not in the least. Just as many funeral homes still refuse to embalm AIDS victims, funeral personnel will not touch these cadavers and insist on cremation. And in all six cases, survivors did not object. We managed to do some preliminary tests on Caslon's body, but we were not allowed to do a full-blown autopsy. Despite it being a homicide, state and church authorities stepped in and said no." The image looked down, then back up. "Is it important for you?"

"Yes, of course, so we can slice and dice them and stick the pieces in jars of formaldehyde and label them and show them to all our friends and charge admission—"

"Miranda, I'm not accusing you of anything, I'm not making any judgments. Honest. Would autopsies have been helpful?"

"The bodies of the deceased would have been good resources for further study. I cannot—and will not—deny that. But I am not a ghoul." She took a deep breath. "Despite what the Caslons say. And I'm damn sure not conspiring with the killers so we can get body parts. They've even accused me of setting this whole thing up with the Holn in the first place."

"I know. They've asked me to press charges against you. Nothing will come of that, of course."

"I'm not so sure," she muttered low enough so the microphone couldn't pick it up. Then, to the image, "I guess they figure we deserve it after the reports got out about the radiation studies. I suppose I should not be surprised at being told to go to hell when I contact the family."

"I'll talk to the Caslon family, ask them to back off a bit. We have six dead now, we don't need any more. They, uh, also keep asking me about the tabloid photos."

Miranda made a sound in her throat. "What about them?"

"Some, um, people are asking about pedophiles on the task force—"

Miranda didn't say a word, just stared at the image.

"Mir-uh, Ms-uh, Dr. Sena, our information suggests those photos came out of the task force, uh, some-where."

"I will take care of that," she said evenly. "What about the missing two?"

The eyes in the image glanced downward. "In neither case have the ex-custodians told us to whom they assigned those rights. None of our business, both have told us. We finally got ahold of Adrienne MacQuarrie, Aaron Fairfax's sister, but she has not heard a thing from him. She only found out what the Holn did to her brother six weeks after it happened, believe it or not.

The MacQuarries don't keep up with everything. Barring any proof of anything amiss, we cannot pursue the matter very far. Although MacQuarrie has asked us to."

"You think something is not right."

A hand rubbed a cheek in the image. "In both cases, ex-custodians suddenly came into a lot of money."

She leaned toward the monitor. "You're going to tell me those people were *sold?*"

"Dr. Sena, I hope to hell I never have to tell you that."

Miranda pushed herself back. "I think you will in the end. And, possibly, that the count will be eight."

"I will not say that until I see undeniable proof the missing two are dead. Meanwhile, I'll keep looking." The image's head turned away for a moment, then back. "I have a personal interest in those two. I think about them often, I don't know why."

"Jack, why weren't we told Myra Caslon had tried to commit suicide? TV is where I heard it first, and I called Olive and she said she hadn't heard a thing. A friend of a friend of someone in her group found out that in the high ranks of HHS, someone did know."

"Did you know Haley Caslon is related by blood or marriage to no less than three congressmen and at least six high-ranking officials in the government that I know of? The reason you didn't find out, Miranda, is because someone didn't want you to."

"I see."

"Go easy, Miranda. At the risk of sounding paranoid, there are a lot of people in the government who want this swept under the rug. Forgotten, shelved, filed under *S* for suppressed. In fact," Jack dropped his voice a notch, "some government people would like to see every one of the Rewound Children dead."

"Members of the cult who are suspects in the death of Myra Caslon have all pleaded innocent to charges of first-degree murder. FBI officials and Salt Lake City prosecutors are remaining mum about the indictments. However,

someone in the Soldiers of God, the group claiming credit for, as they call it, the kill, sent out vid-DVDs to several media outlets. On it, Meg Parker, one of the suspects who still remains in jail, explains why the killing took place. This is an excerpt from that disk."

"You cannot accuse us of murder. We cannot murder that which is not human. Father van Kellin has no doubts, why should we? Did not the Elders of the Mormon Church decree Myra Caslon outside the province of God, unable to receive His blessings? Did not the Pope himself say that these beings cannot be true to God's creation? Are there not scientists who are saying these people cannot be human because you cannot make an adult into a child? These minds do not doubt. We should not doubt. We will not doubt. We will take the action that God has demanded of us."

"There's much more to the message, about four hours worth. FBI agent Jack Theodoric has been assigned to the investigation. Jack, does the FBI have any doubts about what 'replacement' means?"

"None whatsoever, Marinka. It means make them dead."

"What's the status of the Soldiers of God now?"

"We have most of the group in custody charged with murder and conspiracy to commit murder. There's about four more people we're searching hot and heavy for."

"Is it a safe assumption some of the evidence the agency declines to discuss led you to this group?"

"Better than safe, it's a fact. I'll go ahead and give you an example. A lock of hair was removed from the victim. We found that lock in a silver dish on an altar in the room the group uses as a church. These are not professional killers. This is one reason we think we can nip this group before they bud out."

"I understand there's a mixture of religious affiliations in the group."

"Eight Protestants of various stripes, three Catholics,

*two Jews, one who calls himself a New Age minister,
three Mormons."*

"No Muslims, as prior reports had indicated?"

"No Muslims, no Anglicans, no Unitarians."

*"Thank you. We now switch directly back to the Senate
committee hearings on the National Comprehensive
Health Care act.*

"Marinka Svoboda, CNN, Salt Lake City."

"Why were those stupid photos taken in the first
place?"

Avram's image on the computer screen was as placid
as ever. "Miranda, we were faced with a total unknown.
You know the procedure. Collect as much data as
quickly as you can. The physical structure of those
people was as important as anything else. For comparison, so we could go over inch-by-inch to see if there were
any obvious changes. Such photos were needed and I
will not apologize for that. Don't get too haughty; they
have been part of the database you've been using yourself."

The image of Marian Athlington on her computer
screen flashed through Miranda's mind. "All right. I see
your point. I want authority to root out the people who
sold them."

"And I want you to do that. Fire them. I'll see if we
can't bring charges of some kind."

Miranda leaned back. "From our preliminary checks,
we could lose most of our clerical staff."

"Lose 'em. Hire replacements. I want those people off
the project. Now," he stuck the stem of his pipe in his
mouth, "you had another question?"

"Jack tells me certain persons in HHS knew about
Myra's suicide attempt almost as soon as it happened.
We did not know a thing about it until we saw it on TV.
Why the hell not? And what else are we not being told?"

Avram nodded. "I know. A friend of Jack's in the

agency told me. I'm meeting Harrison tomorrow and I'm going to protest and demand they give us all they know—"

"Tell them this, too." Miranda leaned forward again. "We're not going to put up with this. I have some angry people working for me right now, Avram, believe me. And some of those people represent foreign scientific groups who are positive this is more information we've been hoarding. I've had a few offers from people with friends in high places, both foreign and domestic, to play some hands of our own. I will if I have to."

"I believe you." The eyes seemed to twinkle, but Miranda was inclined to put it down to noise on the line. "I will so inform Sumo and the Harpy."

"In San Francisco Tuesday afternoon, two men broke into a house and tried to assault Cheryl Vroman, one of the Rewound Children. Ms. Vroman, a former attorney for a prestigious law firm in that city, evidently turned out to be more than the alleged attackers had bargained for.

"San Francisco Police Captain Don Smith described the events this way":

"When Cheryl Vroman called 911, the dispatcher thought she was talking to a child and tried to calm her down, but Vroman said she wasn't going to wait. Apparently, shortly after that, the perpetrators broke through the front door of the residence. Vroman found an aluminum softball bat belonging to her brother-in-law. One of the alleged assailants grabbed her, but she hit him with the bat, breaking his hand. The other assailant came in but Vroman ran into the kitchen and hid under a table. When the second assailant entered, she attacked and they fought. Sometime during this fracas she managed to break his right leg, but he in turn broke her right arm. We're not completely sure of the chain of events here, but both assailants suffered many hard blows from that bat. After breaking free, Vroman smashed out a dining-room window and was running away from the residence as the

first squad car arrived. Uniformed officers quickly arrested the assailants, who were still in the house, nursing their wounds."

"No motive for the attack has been ascertained by police, but police said they found nude photos of Vroman that had appeared in the National Sensation, a supermarket tabloid, in the suspects' pockets.

"Vroman is resting in the hospital. In an exclusive, Pacific Regional News taped a short statement."

"It was the death of poor Myra Caslon that woke me up, finally. I'd been in pretty bad shape over the last few months, as my sister, Grace, here, can attest. In fact, I celebrated New Year's Eve by getting so drunk I passed out and poured expensive Scotch on her new rug. After Myra was killed, I realized the trouble we are in and how vulnerable we are. I stopped drinking and straightened myself out because no one else is going to help us."

"The day after the attack, Harry Lanker, the editor of the National Sensation, defended the decision to publish the photographs, saying they were a bona fide news event and therefore fall under the protection of the First Amendment. Even so, two national grocery chains have announced they will no longer carry the tabloid, a development Lanker calls cowardly. He had this to say about the controversy":

"Ask those sicko scientists what they really wanted with those photos."

"Well, Roger Carson, a media spokesman for the Holn Effect Task Force, said today four people employed in the administrative offices and three technicians have been fired because they supplied the photos to the tabloid. Carson admitted, however, that they probably won't be lacking for money because he said the tabloid paid, quote, many dead presidents, end quote, to each.

"It might be a case of too little, too late, however. The images, uncensored and unretouched, have turned up on the Internet, the computer network that links millions of people all over the world. A spokesman for the FBI's

Computer Crimes Division said criminal charges can be brought in this case.

"Tamara Chin, Pacific Regional News, for CNN, San Francisco."

"Jupiter, Florida, police have asked the FBI for assistance in investigating an incident where a crowd of people threw rocks, bricks and sacks of animal feces at a house belonging to the mother of one of the so-called Rewound Children. Police said the crowd shouted obscenities and derogatory names, and many in the crowd carried pipes, clubs, and torches. Police arrived and managed to break up the crowd before any real violence occurred.

"The owner of the house, Joanna Yolbin, and her daughter, Pamela, age twenty-five when she was captured by the aliens, were not home at the time. Apparently, they received a warning from a sympathizer earlier in the afternoon and managed to slip away. They are reported to be in hiding and were not harmed.

"Police say several windows in the house were broken and exterior paneling was damaged, but they did not have an estimate on the damages. According to police sources, the Yolbins have been receiving threatening phone calls and letters over the past several weeks, and a neighborhood association reportedly has passed a motion to seek eviction. Joanna Yolbin is the designated guardian for Pamela, and the two women lived alone. Joanna's husband, William, passed away six years ago.

"We'll be taking a commercial break right now, and when we come back, we'll ask singer-performer Tish Goodbody how she answers critics who say her Body of Works *album, video, book, and virtual-reality game have gone beyond the bounds of good taste and are unfit for children. . . ."*

Eighteen

March 15

"Happy birthday to you, happy birthday to you, happy birthday dear Ear-ul, happy birthday to you."

Earl could feel the heat from eighty candles as Marcia placed the cake before him on the table.

"All right, stand back," Earl said, getting to his feet. "This is going to take some extra effort." He took careful aim, filled his lungs in a long inhale. He blew for several seconds, sweeping the air stream back and forth until every candle winked out. Cheers erupted and he grinned as he sat down again.

"Last year at the nursing home, they had four candles on the cake," he said. "I couldn't get all four in one breath. Now look: eighty, all at once." He flexed his arm. "Anyone wanna arm wrestle?"

Everyone laughed but there were no takers. Marcia began removing the candles as Earl picked up the cake knife. He cut off a small corner, placed it on a paper plate festooned with printed flowers. "You all can share this. *This* piece"—he indicated the main cake—"is mine."

"Now Earl," Marcia said with mock severity, "be nice now and share."

233

"Don't wanta."

"Well, you hafta."

"Oh, all right." He pretended to grumble as he began slicing the cake into squares. He glanced at Marcia, who smiled.

This whole shindig had its genesis about a month ago during a Sunday dinner when Walter had said, "Beware the Ides of March."

"Why?" Marcia asked.

"Earl's birthday."

"Oh." She got a strange look in her eye. When the time came, she had invited perhaps thirty people, friends, neighbors, colleagues, co-workers. Outside of the family, a total of eight showed up.

Even so, someone laughed and others talked as he continued to cut the cake, a good-sized chocolate rectangle with banana cream sandwiched between the two layers. Marcia doled out chocolate ice cream, the good kind, unadulterated, heavy on the cream.

Just as he began slicing through the *E* of his name, a loud crash rattled through the house, followed by another. Something small but heavy whizzed through the dining room above Earl's head and thumped off of the wall. More glass crashed in a constant chorus.

"Everyone down!" Walter shouted. Tom and a teenage friend crawled through the living room, avoiding the shards of glass spread across the rug from the shattered living-room picture window. They opened the front door slowly; the glass in the storm door already had been knocked out. Suddenly, Tom and the friend leaped up and charged out.

"Be careful!" Marcia's voice quavered just slightly as her oldest disappeared.

"Back, too," Walter said, and he and two male friends crawled to the sliding doors, then dashed out.

"Dad, be careful," Jennifer hollered.

After a couple of minutes in which no more crashes were heard, Marcia stood slowly. "All right. Keep an eye out. Jennifer, Lucas, put on shoes, go upstairs. I think I heard glass breaking up there, too."

The other guests slowly got to their feet, began taking stock. Earl emerged from under the table, stuck the knife into the center of the cake and sat down heavily. More and more and more. . . .

Walter stepped back into the room.

"Some boys, young, maybe teens, maybe a little older. They climbed over the fence and ran off through the Brantlys' yard."

"Look." One of the men who'd run out with Walter held a small, barrel-shaped lump in his hand.

"Yes," one of the women said. "We found them in the living room, too."

"Strong glass in your patio doors. They didn't break."

"Lead pellets," Marcia asked, holding one up. "From guns?"

"No," said the visitor, "probably slingshots."

"Every window upstairs is broken," Lucas said as he came around a corner.

"Even the bathroom," Jennifer said. "And in my room." She handed her mother a pellet. "They hit the glass vase grandma sent me from Switzerland."

"Oh, honey, I'm sorry."

Lucas held up a piece of plastic. "Shot down the *Enterprise* I had hanging from the ceiling."

"Sounds like they target—"

A clamor from the front door cut the visitor off. Tom, sweating and breathing hard, dragged a swearing youngster into the living room. He had a strong grip, and needed it, because the boy flailed and kicked.

"The o-others got away, but we—ow—managed to catch this one."

"They had a car waiting," Tom's friend said. "They sped off when they saw Tom tackle this runt." He handed Walter a sculpted red-plastic slingshot with a wrist loop for stability. "That's what they were using."

Walter showed it to his friend.

"Take him out to the patio," Marcia said. "I don't want him in my house."

"Sharkjaw!" Lucas blurted.

The boy stopped struggling, glared at Lucas.

"You know this brat?" Walter said as Tom pushed the boy along.

"Yeah, he's one of the Barracudas we play VR games with in Kihei."

"Well, that'll come to an end," Marcia said.

Earl watched as Tom and his friend forced the Barracuda to sit in a chair next to a round table. Tom leaned forward and showed the boy a fist, and it took no imagination to figure out what he was saying.

"Oh, Marcia, I'm so sorry. I didn't realize it was so bad. What are you going to do?"

"Call the police, I guess."

"Wait a moment." Earl stepped out onto the deck. The boy stared down at his lap while Tom and friend kept vigil on each side. Earl stopped near the table, continued to look at the boy. Finally he looked up, then away.

"Sharkjaw, what the hell are you doing?" Earl said.

No answer.

"Who put you up to this?"

Nothing.

"Well, we'll call the police, and then tell them you're a Barracuda. They'll go out round 'em all up, of course, and then you'll all be together at juven—"

"The Barracudas didn't have anything to do with this!"

"Oh, sure."

"It's true! This was—was something else."

"Who then? Who told you to come over here and smash windows with your fancy slingshot? You and your hoodlum friends got every window in this house. Does that make you proud? And someone who's a real good shot broke Lucas's *Enterprise*." He leaned closer to the boy's face. "How'd you like it if someone came over to your house and broke *your Enterprise,* eh? You little shit. You act so tough. But this wasn't tough, this was cowardice. You're a coward, you're yellow."

"I am not!"

"Sure you are. Who put you up to it? Not the Barracudas, then who? Your father?" The boy's hand jerked. "Uh, huh. And the minister at your church? Told you I was a monster, didn't they, said a monster lived in Lucas's house. They said you could send a message to the monster that he wasn't wanted, so they gave you a slingshot and told you to smash the windows at Lucas's house, didn't they? So you came, you and your yellow, cowardly, chickenshit friends. They all got away, but you didn't. We got you and you're going to pay for every broken window and Lucas's *Enterprise* and Jennifer's vase. You, all by your little self."

The boy's lower lip quivered. Earl had seen it a hundred times—when resistance fails, the lip goes first.

"And I know what you've been doing, too, you dirty-minded little sot. You've been on the net, haven't you, and you found those photos of me and the others. And you downloaded them and you and your friends sniggered and giggled over them, didn't you? Oh, boy, naked girls, yes, sir. And you can see everything! Did you get a good look, Slackjaw? Did you see how tiny my thing is now? And all the other guys, huh, all puny and useless? Did you get a good look?"

"We d-didn't mean any harm—" Tears flowed down the boy's cheek

"Oh, of course not. They were available so you peeked. Giggle, giggle, snigger, snigger." Earl straightened. "What else did you see?"

"What d-do you mean?"

"Well, we're monsters, right? Did you see the horns sprouting from our heads? The claws between our fingers? The tails sprouting from the bases of our spines? Did you see my forked penis?" He slammed his hand on the table. "Well, did you?"

"N-no—"

"What did we look like? *Well?*"

"You looked like us—"

"Like you? Then why in God's name did you come over here to smash windows, scare Lucas and his sister and his mother and his father and his brother and all the guests? You could've hit somebody with those goddamn pellets, hurt someone. You could've put Lucas's eye out. *Why?*"

Sharkjaw looked down, stifled a sob.

"We played together, Sharkjaw." Earl softened his tone. "Remember when I blew up your big armored vehicle in VR? With·you in it? What did we do afterward? Went out for sodas. We talked about many things. You gave me skateboarding tips, remember? I taught you how to play marbles. We hung out together. For a while, anyway. And then they started telling you I was a monster, that the aliens did something nasty to me, that I'm going to gut someone and eat their liver raw and suck on their intestines. Yum."

Earl heard Jennifer gag, but he kept his eyes on the boy.

"Look at me."

No response.

Earl slammed both hands on the table. *"Look at me!"*

The boy jumped back, stared with wide eyes.

"What do you see?"

"Uh, uh—"

"What—do—you—see?"

"I see a boy with red hair!"

"What have you been *told* you see?"

"A-an a-al-alien." He burst into tears. "Dad t-told me you were evil, that the a-aliens had done something awful and you weren't a man any m-m-more—"

"Wrong, Sharkjaw. I am just that: an old man. Someone, something, somehow reversed the tape of my life and now it's playing forward again. But I'm still an old man. That's all." He put a hand on his shoulder. "You have nothing to fear from me."

Earl stepped away from the sobbing boy, past the silent observers and into the house. Walter followed. Earl took two plates, grabbed the knife and sliced his name in half, which still left two fairly good-sized pieces for each plate. He checked the ice cream; it had melted around the edges but the core still was solid. He scooped out a couple healthy dollops for each plate.

"What do you want us to do with this shark character?" Walter asked.

Earl shrugged. "That's your decision. I suppose we should call the police. After all, they did do a lot of damage."

Earl picked up both plates, two spoons.

"And you? What happens to you now?"

"I give this family peace. I pack my bags and leave."

As he reached the patio doors, Walter said, "Fat chance." Earl looked back, smiled slightly, headed on out.

"Here," he said, placing one of the plates in front of Sharkjaw. "It's my birthday today, did you know that? Eighty years old. Eighty candles, can you imagine?" He pulled a chair over, sat down. "Cake looked like a brush fire. Damn near set the whole place ablaze."

The boy giggled through his tears.

"Dig in. Mrs. Othberg makes the best chocolate cake this side of the Pacific."

The boy tentatively scooped out a small dab of ice cream, slipped it into his mouth.

"So Sharkjaw," Earl said, swallowing some cake, "tell me about yourself. Your real name, for instance. You have any brothers?"

"I feel like we did when we ran away from the clinic," Marian said as she finished fastening a flap on her backpack. "Only a lot more guilty."

"I know," Aaron said, setting his backpack on the floor. "We're not running from enemies this time."

Marian didn't answer; instead she concentrated on adjusting a strap for the fifth time.

"Time?" Aaron said.

She pulled her watch out of a jacket pocket. "Four thirty-three."

"All right. The bus leaves at six. That gives us a little time. The station is just a couple blocks over so we can wait a while longer."

"We still have to get past the sentries."

"I know." He looked at her. "It won't be as easy as last time. In more ways than one."

Tontine had clamped down hard since the kidnapping attempt, and for good reason—two weeks later the captors tried again. This time they had worked more subtly, recruiting allies within Grid Manor. Aaron, playing poker in the women's floor with Virginia, Miguel, and a former card dealer just laid off from one of the local Indian casinos, hadn't even been aware anything was wrong until Slick Suit, Dark Suit and two orderlies walked in, Dark Suit with a firm grip on Marian and Slick Suit prodding Tontine with a gun.

"Let's go, Aaron," Slick Suit said with a sneer.

"Wait, I have to play this hand." He laid his cards down. "Four aces," which was a lie, but in the movement, he palmed Virginia's laser pointer.

"Everybody else just stay put." Dark Suit looked around at the group, all now standing, watching. Aaron stepped forward and one of the orderlies fell in behind him as they moved into an open room, heading for the ramps. Three men stood to one side, one holding a bat, the others two-by-fours. White King Sam stood opposite, rubbing his hands and staring at Dark Suit.

"Just stay where you are," the latter said, "or I'll hurt her."

"Then I get to hurt you," Sam said with a grin.

Aaron was behind and to the left of Dark Suit. He

knew Tontine was waiting for a diversion, just the
slightest chance—and Aaron aimed to create one. Blinding someone with the tiny laser was out; that chance had
passed already. One other chance was coming up. He'd
been teasing Merlin with the pointer again just before
the card game; now he hoped the cat had gone back to
one of its favorite observation spots atop a tall metal
cabinet they had to pass before getting to the ramp.
Please be there, Aaron prayed. His heart skipped a beat
when he saw the cat's crouched form as still as a
porcelain figurine except for one twitch in the tail.

All right, cat, don't be asleep. Pay attention.

Using his thumb as a guide, he aimed the pointer. The
dot slid up Dark Suit's back and danced on his cheek.

The cat reacted instantly, leaping onto Dark Suit's
shoulder, staggering him. In grabbing for the animal, he
let go of Marian. Feline reflexes took over; claws dug into
cheek and man and beast yowled. In the next second,
White King Sam hurtled in from the side, knocking both
down. Aaron caught a glimpse of cat streaking up the
ramp and Marian racing up after. Action swirled around
him: Tontine already had knocked Slick Suit's gun aside
and was slamming a knee into his gut. Sam slammed
Dark Suit's head onto the floor. Miguel wrestled with the
orderly. The other one started to raise his gun, but a bat
flying at his head forced him to duck. In an instant, the
boardholders were upon him. Black King Leo and Ken
raced down the ramp.

"Aaron!" Tontine barked. "Up! Go! Go!"

Aaron didn't wait, scrambling up the ramp. Eddie and
Kilkenny waited at the top.

"Marian?"

"Around by the back wall." Eddie pointed.

Aaron hurried over, found her sitting on the floor,
back to wall, stroking Merlin.

"Is he OK?" He slumped down beside her.

"Had some hair ripped out, I think, but otherwise he's
fine."

Aaron rubbed the cat's head. "I'm sorry, Merlin, I really am, but it was a desperation move."

Marian touched Aaron's cheek lightly. "It's all right. Pretty quick thinking."

The cat pushed itself out of Marian's grasp, took a few steps, shook itself, then sat and began licking its side.

"Cool cat."

Marian smiled. After a moment, she said, "Aaron—"

Gunfire erupted from below.

"Oh, God."

The gunfire turned out to be a couple more thugs who had raced in to help. They missed, giving manorites a chance to pile on the shooters. The kidnappers suddenly found themselves surrounded by angry people wielding bats, boards and knives. Both Dark Suit and Slick Suit barely could move from the beatings. Retreat had been the only option, a fast one, down the ramps and into the van and a car with bullet holes in the rear door. Some ex-manorites also fled.

And so, three weeks later—a nerve-wracking three weeks in anticipation of another attempt that never came—Marian and Aaron were preparing to leave. Albeit reluctantly.

"We'll endanger whoever we take shelter with," she had said in one of their innumerable arguments.

"True, but if we keep moving, the danger won't last. Plus, we leave this place, we'll be getting away from the abductors, too, taking the heat off Grid Manor."

"Well, I suppose."

Aaron watched as Marian opened a battered trunk near the foot of her bed and drop her backpack in.

She picked up his and did the same, closed the lid. She sat on it and looked back at him, seated on the narrow metal-frame bed.

"Doubts?" he said.

She shrugged. "All the time. I just wish I knew if we were doing the right thing."

"It's hard to know in any case. And it's hard to leave our friends behind."

She gave him a sharp look. "I can remember when you denigrated a lot of these people because they were jobless and liked it that way."

"That was my old self speaking," he said. "I owe my life to them, and I'm not sure I can repay them. Running away seems a bit . . . ungrateful."

"If what you say is true about deflecting the captors, you are repaying them, by leaving."

"Yeah." He looked at his hands in his lap, then back at her. "I am very confused, perhaps even more than I was after the change. And you're partly to blame."

"Yeah, like I was responsible for the Holn."

"You said something on Christmas Eve that got me thinking. When you wondered about the reactions of the people in the encampment as they watched the ship leave. All I thought of was money. You saw the other aspects. What was it? Hopes and dreams, probably unfulfilled."

She came over and sat down next to him, bright eyes looking into his. "'The unexamined life is not worth living.'"

Aaron held up a hand. "Socrates."

She smiled. "That's what you're going through."

"I suppose I am." He shook his head. "And if this hadn't happened to me, would I ever have examined it?"

"You're just looking for ans—" She stopped. Footsteps filtered in from the far end of the room, and someone whistled an old Beatles tune he couldn't remember the name of. They stared at each other a second, then stripped their jackets off and she stuffed them into the trunk, then rejoined him on the bed. A few seconds later, Ken appeared around the dividing curtain.

"Heigh-ho, you two, what's up?" he said.

"Just talking," Aaron said, *and trying not to look guilty.*

"I'm sure."

Aaron frowned. "What's that supposed to mean?"

"I think you'd better come with me."

The two shot a glance at each other.

"Why? Where?" Marian said.

"Down-ramp. Let's go."

They looked at each other again, got up slowly. Aaron's uneasy feelings were confirmed when they found at least eight persons waiting for them. Ken pointed to the same couch they sat on the first night they'd arrived. Tontine sat in a chair directly in front, Virginia off to his side.

"Your trip's been canceled," Tontine said.

"What trip?" Aaron said brazenly.

"Bus trip to Kansas City, Missouri." Tontine pulled out what looked like several bills folded over, handed them to Marian. "Refund of the bus fare."

She clasped the bills with two fingers, sighed and looked down, face flushing.

"What bus fare?" Aaron said.

"The tickets you went through the elaborate ruse to buy during the shopping trip last week."

"I see." Aaron pulled the tickets out of his shirt pocket. "Didn't work, eh?"

"Oh, it worked," Tontine said. "Damn near succeeded. Unfortunately, you bought them from a friend of mine at the bus station."

"Fuck," Aaron muttered as he tore the tickets in half and let the pieces flutter to the floor.

"We figured something was up anyway. Virginia got suspicious at the withdrawals from the account."

Marian sighed. "I thought I was being careful."

"Just what did you hope to accomplish?" Virginia said.

Marian rested an elbow against the couch arm. "Resolution."

"I was going to contact some people, friends, when we got to Kansas City, people I could trust, stay with them a while, then move on again—"

"You don't trust us?" Tontine leaned forward. "We're not capable of sheltering you, or meet—"

"That's not the point!" Aaron felt his face flush deep red. "It's about safety. Our staying here just puts all of you at risk. We thought that by leaving, we could spare you possible injury. Without us around, they wouldn't have any reason to hurt you."

"And we have no say in deciding this."

Aaron just looked at Tontine.

"Besides," Ken said from above Marian, "you were about to leave something precious behind." A ball of fur was thrust into her arms, causing the money to flip out of her fingers and join the ticket halves on the floor.

"Oh . . . Merlin would have been all right. You guys would have loved him." The cat turned and stared at her through unblinking eyes. "And I would have sent for you eventually, so stop looking at me like that."

"Mrow."

"All right, what's next?" Aaron shrugged. "Sent to our rooms? To bed without supper? Grounded for six weeks? A session with a belt, perhaps?"

"We ought to, I suppose," Tontine said. "There's been a long period of half-done or sloppy chores, short tempers and generally reckless behavior that's been getting on more than a few nerves here."

"Why haven't you said anything?" Marian said. "I didn't realize—"

"It doesn't matter, really," Virginia said.

"I—"

Tontine leaned forward. "What really hurts is the idea you two would plan this behind our backs. We are not your captors."

"But you do have power over us!" Marian blurted. "All well and good for you to cancel our trip and keep us inside here. You can do it. Like Dorothy said, we're just small and meek. You can push us around and order us around with impunity because we can't fight back, and you know it!" She buried her face into the cat.

"All right, you two listen to me." Virginia sat down between them. "We are not interested in pushing you around no matter what it looks like to you. That's just not true. Small and meek? Look at yourselves, you *are* small and—well, I wouldn't say meek. Small, though, and, yes, powerless. I know what you're feeling, really I do, although I certainly haven't been put in this extraordinary situation. Some of us have been, still are, in pretty powerless positions ourselves. Pain and frustration, fear and bewilderment, we've seen it in your faces, heard it in your voices—and we've felt it. So we have a pretty good idea of why you tried this.

"But as Tontine said, what angers us the most is your excluding us. We're your *friends,* for Christ's sake! Look at these people here. There's Carlos, who plays his guitar for you, and White King Sam and Black King Leo who taught you to play chess. And Maria, and Ella, and Anna. And Betty, your personal hair care expert, and Kilkenny, and Chastity, who's learned a lot about sewing from Marian, and Chris, who isolated himself from the rest of us until Aaron taught him how to make and fly a kite, and the others here in this room. They're your friends—believe it, you two. We had a meeting yesterday, discussed the situation, the danger to us—yes, we are aware of that, we are aware of the resentment our security measures have caused. And we had a vote—ask you to leave, allow you to stay." Virginia looked at Aaron and Marian each in turn. "The vote was unanimous: stay."

"Which is a miracle in itself." Ken rocked himself as he spoke. "Homeless people are notorious for their independence and rejection of most authority. Many live this way because they want too, because they're sick of rules and regulations and taxes and whatever. Not all, of course, some are victims of circumstances and others are victims of mental troubles, but even many of them will go their own way when the urge strikes."

Something is different here. Aaron studied Ken's face

as he spoke. The look in his eyes was sharp as he gazed back. His speech was clear and focused, and his hands were animated.

"Suddenly, you have this group, a rowdy bunch if there ever was one, coming together with a single purpose in mind. That purpose is to help you see this thing through. You have—temporarily, mind you—unified this place."

He's not drunk.

"That vote could get you killed," Marian said. "The attacks on the others, the violent deaths, the farce in the street, the near-success of the last one—don't they mean anything to you? Our captors are probably still after us. We can't ask you—"

"You don't have to ask," Tontine said. "It will be done if it becomes necessary. Don't argue. You can't go this alone. Both of you have been rejected, tossed out, thrown into the hands of strangers. But—you're among friends now. You need help, we will provide it."

"We know the reasons why you decided to leave," Virginia said. "We all agree this situation cannot continue. What we're asking is that you let us help you, let us work with you, to sort it out and find the next path. We're not so completely out of it we can't make rational decisions." She put a hand on Aaron's shoulder. "We do this because we love you." He felt a sloppy kiss smack his cheek.

"Eeyew," he said, rubbing it quickly with his sleeve as laughter peppered the room.

He looked across her to Marian and they regarded each other for a moment. "Why do I feel like a fool?" he said.

"Because you are," she said. "Unfortunately, you're not alone."

"Yeah." He looked at Tontine, inside feeling like the child his physical stature suggested. "If I've said anything derogatory or offensive, I apologize forthwith."

"Yes, please forgive us," Marian said, looking first at

Virginia, then Ken, then Tontine. "We have been blind and stupid, so wrapped up in ourselves we didn't . . . didn't recognize the true value of the friendships we've made here." She looked at Aaron, who nodded. "We accept your help. Again."

"Yes!" Kilkenny leaped over a table as the small group applauded. Tontine smiled, Virginia hugged Aaron. Ken, still rocking, said, "The signs were against you anyway."

"What do you mean?" Marian asked.

"Beware the Ides of March."

"That's today." She shrugged. "I guess my horoscope would be against me, too."

"And your tea leaves," Aaron said.

Conversation died into an awkward silence, except for a low rumbling from Marian's end of the couch. Aaron looked down at the cat sprawled in her lap.

"Man, I wish I could find that much contentment."

March 21

Miranda let out a long sigh, wishing Avram were more than an image on a twenty-one-inch monitor. Facing her in a colleague's office were Sumo and the Harpy, who'd come to Los Angeles but left Avram in Washington. It had to have been planned that way, and she had refused to meet with them until he had been contacted.

"Frankly, we are a bit disappointed," Harrison was saying. "We had hoped to see more progress than what has been achieved."

"The progress is there," Miranda said. "It's all in the reports. You have to read them to find it."

"That's the other thing," Radmilla said. "Your attitude. Nothing but sarcasm and an unwillingness to cooperate."

Miranda slowly stood up, suddenly certain she knew where this was going. "I get sarcastic when I get frustrated. I get frustrated when I am unable to complete my job because of interference from outside."

"Well, you won't have to put up with the frustration or interference any longer," Harrison said, lightly sliding his hands together. "We are removing you from your position on the Holn Effect Task Force effective immediately. We feel we should appoint someone who is more respons—"

"Pardon me," said Avram from the monitor, "but shouldn't you check first with the administrator of the project?"

"We felt we didn't have time to consult you because we are at a critical junction," Conroy said. "We are sure, when we present the facts to you, you will go alon—"

"Baloney, you big bag of jelly. You flew out there to fire her so I wouldn't be around—"

"Avram, don't push it—"

"Well, *I* will," Miranda said, turning on Harrison. "Being that it doesn't look like I have much to lose. Tell me why you're firing me. The true, unexpurgated, unadulterated, real reason."

"I told you, your lack of coo—"

"I will not be trifled with, Dr. Conroy. I'll tell you what the real reason is. It's because I failed to sweep this thing under the rug, to get it out from in front of the TV lenses. I failed to protect your precious president from being bumped off the air because of the group. It won't go away, though, will it? Every month, there's something else—someone getting killed, someone being thrown out of the house, someone being attacked. More and more, every month. And I have reports from the FBI about incidents not yet on TV. Two of the group are missing, guardians of two others have lost their jobs directly because they harbor group members, and there's a whole list of threats mailed, faxed, called, and sent in by rock. It's just a matter of time until someone finds out—and then it'll be more bad publicity."

"We did not consider that as a reason—" Radmilla began.

"No, it's more than that. Your policy failed, Radmilla, failed. And you want a scapegoat. You want to shift the blame so you won't have to wake up in the morning and feel guilty—"

"I categorically rejec—"

Miranda turned to her with such vehemence Radmilla stepped back. "Of course you reject it, but face the fact, Radmilla, if you had done what we suggested, Myra Caslon would not be dead and that family would not be grieving. But no, you bureaucrats had the answer. You wouldn't listen to us. What are we, just a bunch of eggheads? We did know there was going to be death and fear and hatred. And I refuse—*refuse*—to take the blame for that."

"You won't have to, Miranda," Avram said. He held two envelopes next to his face on the monitor. "In here is my letter of resignation. In here is a letter signed by every member of the Holn Effect Task Force. Not just the group leaders, but everyone. The letter says that if Miranda Sena is dismissed or demoted, all signees will quit immediately. My letter says the same thing."

"Blackmail, Avram?" Harrison snorted. "I thought you were better than that."

"Not when it comes to the integrity of scientific endeavor. We'd heard rumblings you were going to try this, and I and the other task force members have decided the stakes are too great. Now, consider this. The task force is not interested in the squabbles you people have among yourselves about who is responsible for the way things turned out. You chose not to listen to us. The consequences are out of our hands. However, if these squabbles threaten to overwhelm the scientific process, then it is over. And once free of the task force, you have no control over what the ex-members say or to whom. That's another part of the pledge: The moment the resignations are official, ex-task force members will hit every newsroom they can get to and make it clear what Miranda just did: A scientific recommendation was made but the government chose to ignore it. There are seventy-two members of the immediate task force, so I think you can imagine the resultant brouhaha."

"In fact," Miranda said, looking at her watch, "I'm going on the air live in ten minutes. *Nightline.* I'm sure Kevin Cooper would love to have the scoop on the firing of the scientific director of the Holn Effect Task Force."

"Avram, you can't do this!"

"We mean what we say, Harrison. Time to make a decision."

Miranda planted herself in front of Harrison, feet apart, hands on hips, eyes locked on his. "Well?"

When the producers had called, she'd said only if they came to her. To her astonishment, they did, setting up in her office. She realized she would have enjoyed spilling the beans about her near-firing, but it hadn't come to pass—yet.

The field producer raised a hand. "Five . . . four . . . three . . . two . . . cuing opening." As the show's theme song played, Miranda had a sudden thought and looked at the monitor of herself and tried to see what books were showing in the background. *A Brief History of Time.* Good. *Wonderful Life.* Appropriate. *Origin of Species.* Excellent. A tattered paperback copy of *The Human Brain* by Isaac Asimov, a book she had read a long time ago and that perhaps had gotten her started on this long trail. *Chuck Amuck.* Oops. So that's where that silly book went . . . too late now. . . .

"I'll, uh, I'll be watching you on TV tonight," Avram had said after Sumo and the Harpy stormed out.

"I might not be able to say anything, not with Lakewood and Sam Innes as the other guests."

Avram smiled. "You have our work cut out for you."

As she had feared, after a taped roundup on the status of the Rewound Children (not mentioning the missing two—Jack had insisted that be kept quiet), the host spent most of the early part of the show with van Kellin.

"Mr. Cooper and all the others had figured the story would have faded by now, but with all these things happening we can't seem to ignore it," the field producer said during a commercial.

"These things are happening because people are afraid, and they're listening to other people who are afraid, so we have an endless cycle going."

"Why don't you say that on the air?"

"When is your Mr. Cooper going to get me on the air?"

"Well, he wants to make some points—"

"You contact your Mr. Cooper and tell him if he has something to ask me, do it now, or I'll chase you guys out of here before the next commercial."

"Dr. Sena," Kevin Cooper turned his well-coiffed visage to her camera within a minute after the show returned, "what is your position on these Rewound Children? Do you agree with Reverend van Kellin that they pose a risk?"

"These are people, humans," she said to the flawless image. "They've been through an extraordinary experience, an experience like no one else has in the history of mankind, but that does not change their basic humanity one whit."

"I don't understand how anyone with one whit of humanity can sit there and say that." The Rev. van Kellin adjusted himself carefully in the monitor. "One of your own scientists, an eminent scholar in his own right and a known Biblical expert, has said many times these children are threats to humanity—"

"I have never said they should be killed, you bloated son of a scum-sucking gnat." Dr. Innes's expostulation caught everyone off-guard; before the switch could be made, viewers were treated to van Kellin's jaw dropping and his face going deep red. "I said they needed to be studied. I said we had to be aware of any changes that could presage a competition between human and other species. I said if that were the case, we needed to take careful measures to isolate and observe. I have never—*never*—advocated killing or otherwise harming those people." So deep was his voice it rumbled out of the small speaker on the monitor.

Miranda blinked. Dr. Innes was on the main monitor now, gray hair catching points of light, head and face erect on square shoulders. "You have been taking my words out of context and twisting them to suit your needs. Just like you accuse the liberal left-leaning media of doing. I have had enough of you, Lakewood, and I want it to stop *right now.*"

"Now just a minute," van Kellin said, matching the volume but not the resonance of Dr. Innes's voice. Miranda listened with half an ear; the rest of her mind was taken up with the turn of events. Dr. Innes had remained mute throughout the early part of the program, betraying nothing about what was going through his mind.

". . . science means we are searching for answers. Objectivity is our goal, but of course, we do not always achieve it. Things get in our way. Our beliefs. Our politics. Our humanity. Our culture. And now, the paradigm every scientist has learned in school and practiced through the process of being alive himself— that is, being born, growing up, aging, and dying—has been assaulted by this event. Small wonder there's dissension and disagreement among us. For Christ's sake, we are just human.

"It is much more difficult to be a scientist than a preacher. All a preacher has to do is make up his mind to believe. A scientist has to have proof, proof that will stand up to careful scrutiny of colleagues, many of whom are strangers."

"Now just a minute. It is not that easy—"

"Gentlemen, I believe the topic is the humanity of the Rewound Children, not the merits of science versus religion. Dr. Innes, how exactly do you think the Reverend van Kellin has distorted your views?"

"Very simple, Kevin. In his pronouncements of death sentences upon the children."

"I have never called for their deaths. It is a matter of survival of the human—"

"Would you like us to play tapes of your sermons when you talk about eradicating the devil's spawn? You pissant! You have not done a thing to help anyone come to terms with this. People turn to you for solace and guidance in a world knocked askew and all you have to offer is fear and loathing, to borrow a phrase. And you use *my* words, *my* research, *my* name, to do it! Damn you! Worm! Yellow-bellied coward! I denounce you, right here in front of God, Mr. Cooper, Dr. Sena, and all the people watching. I denounce you as a coward and your preaching as hateful and your beliefs suspect. You are *scum,* sir!"

The picture switched to van Kellin, who was a case study in apoplexy: red face, veins bulging, choking on his words, eyes wide. In the next second, the picture switched to Miranda, nearly making her jump.

"Dr. Sena, why do the Rewound Children spark these kinds of reactions?"

"Uh, Dr.—Samuel just said why. He talked about scientific paradigms being assaulted. Well, that certainly applies to all of us. It goes right to our very cores, the essence of our existence, does it not? As humans, as men and women—and as children. Everything we've been taught about ourselves, about growing up, reaching maturity, aging, preparing for death, the progression of life—it's all been tossed out the window. What these creatures did was challenge our conception of life, challenge us right out of our complacency. Of course, the idea of an ordered universe has been under attack before. Well, here's a new twist."

"It's a struggle, I can tell you." Dr. Innes rumbled again. He came back on the monitor as calm as if nothing had happened. "I have seen the task force people study the data, go through them line by line, bit by bit, searching desperately for answers, getting frustrated and losing their tempers and throwing things." In her office, off-camera, Miranda grinned. "It is a tremendous struggle, Mr. Cooper, more than most of you people will ever know."

Miranda felt a thrill shoot through her body. She didn't know why or how long it would last, but she was ecstatic to have Dr. Samuel Innes on her side.

"This also challenges us on how we think of our own children," she said out loud.

"How do you mean?" She was live again.

"Watch the video-return slots at your local video store. A car comes up, adult driving, passenger, a kid between the ages of six and eighteen. Who gets out to put the tape back, no matter what the weather, no matter how bad the traffic, no matter what the crime rate? And who stays in the cool/warm/dry/safe car, waiting? That's what I mean. Free labor, no rights, no pull against the big and powerful adults.

"And so when some adults are transformed into beings the size of children, we think nothing of stripping them of their rights, their responsibilities, their property, their savings, their families—their dignity—because that's how the culture thinks of little humans. Just things to be tolerated as long as they stay in their place. Then we have idiots like van Kellin telling us to fear them and that jackass Goth counting down their deaths and we act surprised when someone loses control and does some harm. What hypocrisy!

"What is going on here? Are we so afraid of these people we have to kill them all? For God's sake, they're the size of ten-year-old kids! Have we lost all our compassion? Have we lost our sense of wonder? Are we a nation of cowards now?"

Nineteen

March 29

Not so much head around the eyes. Flatter. Miranda leaned back, took a careful look at the Holn floating in her computer field. *Need to lower the tentacle group.*

When her number finally came up five years ago, she had prepared her list of questions, only to have most struck; redundancy was a waste of precious time. Still, that left a large hole, so she improvised others:

Do you understand the concept of art?

Do you create simply for the joy of it?

Do you create music, harmonic sound in rhythmic pulses, to soothe the mind or to feel emotions, or just because it is pleasurable? Do you sing to each other?

Do you create representations of other things in manipulative media, just for the pleasure of seeing or creating something beautiful, or of making a statement in metaphor?

Do you tell stories to each other? Do you act out these stories, taking the parts of the characters?

Three months later, she sat before the main screen in the communications building not far from the ship. The first half-hour the Holn representative and the human representative discussed her scientific questions—neuron structure, neuron firing rate, neuron pathways—

but then Alpha reached down with a big tentacle and hefted a flat, glasslike octagonal sheet. As she watched, colors flowed across the surface, shapes formed but changed constantly, swirling and breaking, making absolutely no sense to her.

"I created this," the voice from the speaker intoned carefully. "This is my imagination. It has no . . ." (she wondered whether Alpha was struggling for a definition) ". . . purpose . . . except I like to look at it. My friends like it. I am . . . proud . . . of it."

Most of the answers to the art questions were the same: "yes," except for music. A whole new line of discussion suddenly opened up. She rose in the hierarchy, evidently catching Avram's eye in the process. And now, her "personal message" was flying toward the receding ship—all because she got Alpha to show a side of the Holn no human had asked about before.

As she peered at the image through narrowed eyes, someone knocked at her door. Few did that, but one person always did.

"Come in, Samuel." She turned and watched as the broad-shouldered man stepped in. "I enjoyed our tete-a-tete on TV last night."

"So did I, Miranda, actually." Dr. Innes tugged at his already well-fitting coat as he came over to her desk. "I thought I'd—oh, did you draw that?"

"Uh, yes. A sketch I started in Albuquerque that got a little more complex than I'd expected."

"Would that perchance be the Holn you discussed art with?"

"The very same. I think. My memory might be fading on the details."

"That's your drawing, too, isn't it, of that rather remarkable-looking woman?" He nodded toward a picture on her desk.

"My mother, yes, I drew that."

He turned toward the wall behind her. "The landscape?"

"Yes."

"The style is obvious after seeing one in progress." Dr. Innes stepped over to the painting. "There were a lot of barbed comments about us scientific types ignoring the artistic side of human nature. They forget it was a scientist who gleaned that side of the Holn." He gestured at the painting. "Now I see how it came to be. I am discovering many delightful things about you."

That she almost blushed irritated her. "I learned something last night, too."

The craggy face frowned. "I am going to announce today I am backing off my position about these people not being human. Careful study of the available information—including Constance Peterson's data, I might add—has not shown that thesis to be correct. I apologize, I know my ten days have long passed."

"You didn't have to come here to tell me this. That's what the meeting's for."

Dr. Innes turned back to the painting, hands behind his back. "Do you know why I said those things last night?"

She studied his back, the gray hair, the tailored suit jacket. "Because you're afraid you're responsible for six deaths."

"Do you think so?"

"I do not and never have."

Dr. Innes turned and looked at her. "Thank you. I watched helplessly as what I was saying was being construed as a call for their destruction. Last night I had had enough. I should've taken action sooner." He took a deep breath, let it out slowly. "I used to admire Lakewood."

"I hope the bad publicity is not the reason you're modifying your position—"

"No. I am faced with incontrovertible evidence and therefore must reevaluate my postulates. It is the correct thing to do. While it does not erase my responsibility completely, I am grateful for your support."

"I am trying to keep a valued and esteemed colleague on the team." *And when did this happen,* she wondered. "One who should not have to bear the blame for everyone who distorts his conclusions for their own ends."

"An ancient tradition. We scientists often think what we learn is so obvious, so logical, we are totally unprepared for the distortion and passion those truths, so-called, can engender."

"That's because we are now so good at sorting data we tend to look at that process as the guiding force behind everything," Miranda said as she toyed with the drawing stylus. "Thanks to tools like this"—she jerked a thumb toward her computer monitor—"we can reduce everything to A-B-C processes. Human passion does not follow that order, often taking us empiricists by surprise."

"And that human passion is faced with its most important challenge since—huh." Dr. Innes turned his head aside. "I was going to say the birth of Christ." He turned his gaze back to her. "Lakewood's labeling me a Biblical scholar was a little exaggerated. I wrote on the Bible, arguing a scientific basis for some of the events described. For Lakewood, though, and many others of his ilk, this is a disaster. A disaster that started when we got the first signals from the Holn. Not just their world, but their whole universe and the structure it was founded upon is turned completely upside down. Lakewood and Brigman and their ilk are barely hanging on by their fingernails." He rubbed his face with both hands. Miranda thought she caught a glimpse of an old man just then. "I have read the Bible again during the months we have been studying this group. I am afraid I cannot find room for the Holn in it. And, God help me, I cannot find room for the seventeen, either."

"I don't quite agree," Miranda said slowly. "But then, I've been doing a good job of avoiding the question myself." She glanced at the clock. "I guess we'd better get to the meeting." She saved the drawing, turned off the computer.

"You're left-handed," he said as he stepped to her desk.

"Uh, yes."

"Two of the group are left-handed, did you know that?"

Miranda stopped, looked at Dr. Innes. "No, I did not."

"Handedness has been overlooked. I didn't know myself until a sharp-eyed left-handed graduate assistant pointed out Mr. Othberg using his left hand to play catch with some young visitors in a video shot at his nursing home. We looked at the other personal pre-event photos and found Mr. Fairfax holding an expensive pen, a gift from his bosses, in his left hand. We wanted to follow up to see if this characteristic had been changed, but videos of the two men post-event are not conclusive. We'd like to get with them to determine the outcome."

"We're working toward getting with at least some of them again, somehow." Miranda picked up her notebook and walked toward the door. "It'll be tricky because we've hit a good-sized wall in getting follow-up examinations. Only a couple have cooperated, and then in a very limited manner. Plus, Mr. Fairfax is still missing."

"Speaking of ways people are treated," Dr. Innes said as he held the door open for her, "I would imagine you have been rather upset with me."

"Let's just say a couple of headaches had your name on them."

Dr. Innes smiled. "I am sorry, Dr. Sena. As—"

Constance Peterson suddenly turned a corner. "Oh. You're together already. Well, I'll just run along, then. Uh, see you." She kept her word literally by dashing ahead.

"What was that all about?"

"I have no idea. I've given up trying to figure out the quirks and whims of this rabble."

They found out what it was about when they opened the door to the auditorium and the room erupted into cheers. The entire task force rose to its feet, applauding. Two men held up a banner that read WE SALUTE OUR HEROES, while another closer in waved a giant fax blowup of the lead headline from that day's electronic *Village Voice:* HOLN SCIENTISTS GETTING PISSED OFF. Miranda and Dr. Innes looked at each other. She shook her head as he laughed, the skin around his eyes crinkling.

Miranda stepped up to the podium, and after the noise abated, said, "All right, that's it. You're all fired." In the ensuing laughter she saw a familiar face, just arrived from Washington. "And that includes you, Avram Rolstein. *Especially* you."

The whole thing was silly, but she felt good, mostly because everyone else seemed to be in a good mood. "Wanda demanded she be given the first spot. So, here she is. Wanda Bettemeyer of NASA/JPL."

Wanda bounced up to the podium. "Gosh, what a thrill to be introduced by a genuine celebrity—"

"Oh, be quiet!" Miranda hollered as she sat down in the first row.

"Well, I guess some people just can't handle fame. Anyhow," she said as the laughter died down, "I'm here with some new data we believe will be a help. By the way, they didn't call themselves Holn, or the Holn. What they said in the initial contacts was 'We are from the home.' That's home, h-o-m-e, their name for the mother ship. Evidently someone on Earth either misunderstood or felt it needed jazzing up, so it became 'We are from the Holn.'

"This is significant because, to them, the mother ship *is* home. No other place carries that designation, not even their originating planetary systems."

Wanda turned some pages in a paper notebook. "In

our crash program, we threw everything we had from their visit into one humongous data base and let the big computers crunch it, then we fed that into the Nimbus FLS at the National Center for Supercomputer Applications at Illinois. The FLS part means fuzzy logic sorter. With this machine, we can set some fairly wide parameters and have the machine look for connections, no matter how tenuous."

She looked at the blank screen window behind her. "I have only one visual aid today, so you'll have to bear with me. Can I have image A-27, disk eight, please? Again, I'm going to skim the surface. Details are in the database." She grinned. "A monster database, I might add."

A graphic appeared behind her, a Holn in three sizes, largest on the left. "Here we have the three genomes of the Holn." She stepped over, pointed to the middle one. "The planet Earth genome as we know it." She pointed to the left image. "The original planet genome, a body three times as big and six times the mass of the Earth genome. An organism ideally suited for a planet with the gravitational pull around that of Neptune." She pointed to the one on the right. "The mother ship genome. Just over half as big and just under half the mass. This genome," she pointed to the largest, "was practically unknown to us because most of what we learned about the Holn is based upon the mother ship genome. This threw us off the track because some of the data they gave us was about the original genome, but we didn't catch on. In other words, they had been giving us two different sets of data. The difference got shuffled under 'stuff to know later.' Much to our regret."

She looked out at the rapt audience, then back. "You see, these are modifications. They modify themselves to match the place. This"—she pointed to the mother ship genome—"is the way they are ninety-nine percent of the time. Small, agile, able to live in a zero-to-half gee environment. When they came here, they changed their physical size, bulked up, as sportswriters say. And this was just a guess, an intermediate step if necessary. They could have bulked up to this"—she pointed to the original genome—"if it became necessary. They never had a clear idea of their destination until they reached Pluto's outer orbit, so they were prepared to match whatever they ran into. When they get back to the mother ship—home—they either will return to home size, or will already be in that state."

"Now," she said over the rustling that passed through the assembled group, "two things I want to emphasize. One, age. The lifespans Ben described last summer are for the original genome. Our friends here, as near as we can tell, are a little longer-lived. On the order of a thousand to two thousand Earth years."

Again the sound passed through the crowd like dry leaves rustling in a breeze. "Two. Look at the original genome. Something is missing. These, the large tentacles on the second segment. This is not a natural condition. The Holn evolved this after they joined the mother ship, but it is not the result of many generations of adaptations. They added them to themselves right away. And every Holn born since then has had this characteristic. You see? Not only did they add this appendage to help them get around in zero-gee, they added the coding to their genes to continue it in succeeding generations."

"Not to sound like a broken record," said a voice, "but how?"

"That's still speculation. It's one of the questions we keep beaming at them, hoping they'll find it in their three-part hearts to answer." She gazed at the image a moment, then turned to the audience. "Our best bet— and I'm sorry for having just a guess, we've tried to find out, honest, if you want to lash me with a wet noodle I'll submit—our best guess is still nanotechnology. The nanotech theorists are split into two camps, those who say the molecular machines were organic and those who favor inorganic."

She tapped the podium as she studied her notes. "At any rate, that's my main presentation. Questions?"

Miranda, as she headed to the podium, remembered a colleague once suggesting a room full of separate minds thinking alike could charge the atmosphere and send sparks leaping between each, reinforcing the emotions, forming a hydra of mind. At this point, she wasn't ready to dismiss the idea completely.

"Some nice bombs you tossed."

Wanda laughed.

Miranda turned to the group. "Where do we go from here?"

Dr. Innes stood up.

"A few months ago, I criticized some of you for looking upon humans as mere vats of chemicals. I argued long and hard for an alien aspect to these people. I am setting aside that hypothesis. We have these seventeen so far incontrovertibly human people in front of us—down to eleven living, I guess—and while I'm not quite willing to give up on the idea that something unique makes up the human mind, we must proceed with that as a basis. They, the Holn, had to have malleable material. It looks as though a cauldron of chemicals in human form is that material."

"In four days?" Lindsey asked as Dr. Innes sat down. "I still have big problems with that timing. Four days, actually three and a half if you consider the spacecraft didn't close until late morning, to take what they have learned and completely change a human."

"Remember, we gave them all we knew about ourselves," Dr. Innes said from his seat. "They had six years to analyze and formulate. This technology"—he gestured toward the screen still showing the three Holn—"suggests knowledge much deeper and advanced than our own. Child's play, I would think."

"Their expertise would go back even farther than six years," said Timothy Jenkins. "It would go back millions of years of travel, exploration. So we live in a different atmosphere. It wouldn't take much to adjust the reactions a bit. Think of the database they must have."

Anna Lowry, who'd been conferring with members of her staff, now waved a hand. "Lab reports on blood, stool, and urine samples on the seventeen just after the ship left last year showed heightened levels of certain substances. Phosphates, for example, and some unusual amino acids and other organic compounds. None of it harmful, but the thing is, the levels dropped within hours. We believe this is tied in with the process of recession."

"Wait, wait . . . um, OK, fine, all right, I'll assume they had molecular machinery," said Orlando Tousee. "What I'm still having trouble with is this whole idea of adults being turned into children. Yes, I've studied the reports on the children, but all I see are healthy kids. What I don't see, except in my mind, is the process, the change from adult to smaller adult to teenager to child. I have this vision of someone sprawled across a table like the evening sky as the poet says with tubes and stuff all leading to and from and liquids and gelatins flowing mostly out and the body shrinking like a balloon slowly deflating." He shook his head. "It is just so inconceivable."

"I know what you mean," Wanda said. "I didn't give it much thought until lately when we started talking about itty-bitty bugs. I suddenly envision the adults slowly immersed into this roiling mass of microscopic bugs, which are swarming and twisting like—like maggots on dead meat. Oh, lord"—she rubbed her forehead—"forgive me, I get goose bumps just thinking about it. It's just—in every square inch of skin, bone and organs, billions, trillions, skadillions of these things had to be swarming, moving at fantastic speeds to fulfill the program."

"And what a program!" Anna said. "Every cell, every nuclei, every piece of DNA, in every part of the body, these things move with solid purpose, taking apart, removing, restructuring and all the while keeping things functioning—heart, liver, pancreas, all of it. Swarming into a eyeball and shrinking it to just the right size and shape, redoing heart muscle so it still fibrillates properly, building a bladder that functions perfectly. How could they have built, reengineered, such perfect humans? Mind-boggling is woefully short as a term of description."

"What did we give them to work with?" Avram said. "A blueprint, but a blueprint of the *ideal* of a human, without bad teeth, or warts on the butt, or missing fingers or a lopsided spine."

"They could've done anything," Constance said. "They could've given them three feet or four arms, or a set of tentacles where neck meets collarbone, they could have changed their skin color, or their IQ. If they know so much about the human genome, the possibilities are endless."

"They did change hair color," someone in the back pointed out.

"Yeah, they did. And they practiced remarkable restraint if that's all they did."

"At least," Jake Skettles's Australian-accented voice called out, "they didn't leave us with infants, unable to talk, to tell us who they are, and give us some description of the place where . . . it happened."

"What about that?" Timothy Jenkins said. "Have we gotten any kind of conception of the place or procedure from the ki-people?"

"Nothing concrete," Olive said, removing her glasses. "Just generalities common to all descriptions: oval rooms, generally gray, a light source directly overhead, long armaturelike devices moving, a sound of chimes and whispers. Two of the group mentioned the surface of the room above or in front of their faces seemed close enough to touch. Wanda, a small space like this would suggest an immersion of some sort."

"Oooh," Wanda said, hugging herself. "I'm going to have a bad dream tonight."

Light laughter filtered around the room.

"Well, all this talk about what the group might have seen or not still doesn't answer the big question," Orlando said. "Why? Why did they do this?"

"We don't know the human mind yet," Miranda said, "and you expect us to divine an extraterrestrial one? My bias toward my field of study makes me wonder how they could keep the patterns of memory, personality and autonomic functions intact as they changed the mass and size of the brain. It seems to suggest those patterns aren't quite as dependent on physical structure as we'd assumed."

"I believe it's possible to at least get a basic idea on why," Matt said as he stood up. "Wanda, you said you gave the Holn the entire book on our physiology. What about the other half? What did you tell them about our culture?"

"Everything they asked about." Wanda leaned against the podium. "Human culture, the various types, the differing lifestyles, structure of community, the whole spectrum of human life on Earth. However, they seemed to show a greater interest in the developed cultures, ones with technology, complex infrastructure, and complex social patterns. This might be bias on their part, being a technological culture themselves. The great books, writings on religion and philosophy, both Eastern and Western, technological development—they got it all. And our popular culture, comics, movies, television, books, theater, the sports culture, the art culture, music, the whole enchilada. Mostly after our own Miranda Sena brought that part up, of course. If you remember, one of the most famous images to come out of the ship was of them watching an episode of *Star Trek*."

"Advertising?"

"Oh, yes."

Matt looked down at his foot doing something behind

the chair in front of him. "All right, here we are, an intelligent species, doing all sorts of clever stuff. In comparison to the rest of the animal kingdom, though, we look a bit immature. Well, after all, we are all born three months premature because our swelled heads won't fit through the female pelvis otherwise. So parents have an extra three months to watch their child develop.

"I'm sure all of you have heard of neoteny, where the adult retains juvenile characteristics: pushed-in face, big eyes, hairless body. As our brains have grown, humans have retained characteristics of young ancestors, and it's a big reason why we prefer puppies to the adult dog, kittens to the adult cat—even baby warthogs are sort of cute. This carries to our response to infants and children because the childlike qualities catch our inborn—"

"Oh, I think you're pretty cute right now," a female voice said from somewhere to the side.

The room exploded into laughter. Matt, frozen in mid-gesture and mouth open, turned slowly in the direction of the voice and cocked an eyebrow. He interlaced his fingers, brought the backs of his hands against his cheek and snuggled his head into the notch.

"You should have seen me when I was a baby." He batted his eyes. "I was so adorable."

More hearty laughter.

"Taking that as a cue, let's consider something," Matt said as the laughter subsided. "The Group of Seventeen, each individual. Except for Othberg, because of his age, but picture the others. How many here think these people look better now than they did pre-event? Leave aside the absence of wrinkles, the disappearance of acne, the elimination of moles, warts and other blemishes. Just consider the structure of the face. How many think these people look better now than they did before?"

He waited a moment as the room rustled. "Well, let me put it this way: How many here think they look *worse* than they did?"

No hands went up.

"How many here envy the group at least that?"

Hands appeared all over the room.

"Fine," Matt said, smiling. "I say there's more than casual connection between the action of the Holn and our relentless drive to stay young, to act young, to think young. What is our main pursuit in this culture? Youth. Our entire cultural milieu reflects that quest. Even in the great literature, there's a sorrow for the passing of time and degradations of old age. And look at the stuff today, the ads, the TV shows, the movies, contemporary books, all glorifying the physical ideal of youth even though the current population as a whole is older. That was the not-so-subliminal message the Holn picked up on."

He tapped his foot. "Turn seventeen people into children and fulfill almost a universal dream. Are they trying to tell us something?"

The buzz this time swelled into high volume.

Two hours, thirty-seven minutes later, Avram said, "Deep thoughts, Dr. Gunnarson, deep thoughts," as he, Miranda, and Matt headed back to Miranda's office.

"And I was amazed by the level of intensity today," Miranda said. "I haven't had such a freewheeling discussion with this group since it began. With perfect hindsight, we can say too bad Wanda's data were buried for so long."

"Except it casts these creatures as benevolent sages, traveling through the galaxy dispensing youth elixir."

"Perhaps that's what—"

Avram was cut off by a woman stepping forward. "Three people are waiting in your office, Miranda. One identified himself as Jack Theodoric."

"Great. Thank you, Bonnie." She picked up her pace.

"Did you find them?" she said as soon as she got her door open.

"What did I tell you?" Jack said to a woman and man

standing to one side. "I have nothing to report," he said to Miranda. "We've hit a dead end, we're stuck."

Miranda dropped her notebook on her desk. "Then get unstuck, damnit. You're FBI, for God's sake, you've got power."

"We're not giving up. I promise. In fact, the attorney general has authorized the bureau to supply security for the remaining group. He took this action unilaterally."

Miranda sighed. "Well, that's something."

"Now that we've got that out of the way, may I introduce representatives of the MacAlister Foundation. They've come with a proposal about the Rewound Children."

A woman in her late thirties, shorter than Miranda but not as slim, with auburn hair cut short and styled around a high forehead and round, friendly face, stepped forward.

"Hello, Dr. Sena, I'm Alexandria Roth, known as Alex," she said.

"Giles Lassiter." The man, probably in his forties, was tall and thin, with long fingers.

"Avram Rolstein."

"Good to meet you," Giles said.

"Please, have a seat," Miranda said, taking the chair at her desk.

"This is Wynona MacAlister's proposal, but we understand you made the suggestion first, Dr. Sena," Alex said. For the next hour, the scientists listened, read information on electronic notebooks, and asked several questions.

Finally, Miranda turned to Avram. "Are these people legit?"

"Wynona MacAlister and I go back a few years, and while I can't count myself as a personal friend, I do know whatever Wynona MacAlister decides to do, she does it with class and better than anyone else could," he said. "She is one of smartest, cagiest, and most powerful women in this country, and places beyond. I intend to give it my full support. It is an answer to a vexing problem."

"The question is, will the survivors go along?" Matt said.

"I don't want these people to become sideshow freaks," Miranda said. "I don't want them to become guinea pigs, I don't want them locked away forever. Six are dead and two are missing——"

"That is why the foundation is moving," Alex said. "Wynona and the board have been discussing it on and off for weeks, but after watching your impassioned plea last night, she's melted a few phone lines ordering us to get on the ball. She thinks she has a way to help and she won't let anything get in the way. Even so, however, she will defer to you and Dr. Rolstein."

Miranda sighed, sat back. "Avram, I'm going to follow your lead on this. If you think it's good, then let's do it. What do you want from me?"

"To continue your research," Giles said. "We, the foundation, will handle all the details. If you have any trouble with anything, call us. Wynona will use all the resources she has to clear the way."

"I will make myself available as a go-between," Avram said. "In fact, I'll go up and see the old girl myself, charm her a bit, then warn her that if she crosses Miranda she'll be hit with a firestorm."

"Thank you very much. That'll really endear her to me."

"There is one thing you can do," Alex said. "We would like to recruit one of the group to help us talk to the others. Any recommendations?"

Miranda looked at Matt.

"Five of the people are above-average intelligence," he said. "Tom Cathen, Earl Othberg, Cheryl Vroman, Marian Athlington, and Aaron Fairfax. Any of them would be good."

"Two are missing, though, right Jack?" Miranda said.

"Yes, they are, aren't they?"

"I don't quite understand how someone can just drop out of sight," Avram said. "Especially these people."

"It's not that difficult if you're underage," Jack said. "If you don't have a credit card, or bank account, or welfare account, or net credit, your name doesn't show up. And these people have been stripped out. They've been fired, so their contributions to Social Security have stopped, along with tax money to the IRS. Their bank accounts have been dissolved into someone else's, and their credit cards have been canceled. It's what you were saying last night, Miranda, about children. Until they become adults, the only thing that marks a child in the corporate and government nets is her Social Security number."

Jack rubbed an arm. "And that's all they have now. We have electronic watchdogs on the nets. If either number pops in, the dogs'll bark. So far, though, the only growls from either number since last June was a car-rental agency looking for the auto Athlington had used."

"What about relatives?" Avram said.

"Athlington's sister and Fairfax's ex-wife aren't talking, but we think they're involved in some underhanded dealings. Fairfax's sister, who lives in the remotest part of Alaska buried under tons of snow—at least according to the Alaskan agent who had to fly from Fairbanks, then take a two-hour snowmobile ride—says she has not heard a thing from her brother."

Jack changed position in the chair, told them about Marian's landlord and her surviving cat. "The hospital staff kept the cat for a few days, but some homeless veteran took it and an envelope of money the woman had shipped with the animal. The staff didn't know about the money, so now they're assuming the cat's gone and the money spent." He spread his hands. "And that, Dr. Sena, is as far as we've gotten."

The group sat in silence.

"Earl Othberg would be your best bet," Matt said suddenly.

"And where can we find him?" Alex said.

"Relax. He's in Hawaii, not Al—"

"Miranda!" The shout and the door slamming open came simultaneously. Wanda charged across the carpet. "The Holn! An answer! It's coming!" She stopped next to Miranda's chair. "They're answering!"

"What—"

"Ben called. They just got a precursor message. The Holn say they'll send a reply in about ten hours. They're—" Wanda stopped, looked around at the group. "Oh, am I interrupting something? I'm sorry." She grabbed Miranda's hand. "You have to come, Miranda, to JPL, when it arrives. Two A.M. tomorrow morning."

"Well, all right, that's great. I'll consider going—"

Wanda placed her other hand on Miranda's. "You don't quite understand. It's *your* message they're replying to. Yours, Miranda."

Twenty

March 30

"The short notice has enabled us to keep the veep level low," Ben grabbed a handful of M&Ms from the bowl on the table, began poking through them. "The Vice President of the United States isn't going to make it, I'm afraid." He dropped some of the candies back.

"You have a problem with the blue ones?" Matt said.

"An abomination." Ben examined what was left. "The short notice also caught us off guard on receivers. Fortunately, we got the VLA at Socorro primed. Barely." He tossed a few into his mouth.

Miranda picked up a blue M&M. Besides this group at her table, other members of the task force, scientists, engineers and execs from JPL, and three pool reporters ambled around the room awaiting the golden hour.

"Who's idea was it to stick my message on the wall?"

Ben smiled, shrugged. "Could've been anyone. Appropriate, though, don't you think, 'Miranda'?"

It had embarrassed her to find the framed missive hanging next to a Voyager 2 image of Uranus's most convoluted moon, also named Miranda. She'd written the message in longhand:

To the visitors:

We are humbled and honored by your visit. We have learned many new things, the most important being that we are not alone in the universe.

We are puzzled, however, by your actions just prior to your departure. The humans you studied emerged changed, regressed to the physical stage of human children. Outside of the physical changes, these people also have been hurt in other ways. Five are dead, slain by others out of fear and ignorance. What was the purpose of this deed? We have no explanation from you.

We do not ask out of anger, we ask out of concern for our fellow humans. All through your stay, you were kind and benevolent. Help us to understand the purpose behind this action so future generations will not look upon the Holn—and other visitors from other worlds—with fear and hatred.

Sincerely,
Miranda Sena

[interaction with Alpha, May 14, 2004]

"One thing has occurred to me lately, though, ever since those gentlemen on *Crosshairs* brought it up," Avram said after taking a sip of coffee. "Those Holn were incredibly brave. They landed on this planet with no guarantee we wouldn't open fire on them."

"Yeah, that came up in discussions here," Ben said. "They've done it before on other planets, so I guess they figured it was safe."

"Maybe they're cagier than we give them credit for,"

Miranda said, pushing the M&M around on the table with a plastic stirrer. "Maybe they deliberately chose an isolated landing place."

Ben and Matt suddenly straightened.

"Hell, yes," Matt said. "They knew the official places would be surrounded by armies and guns and whatnot."

"That's why they were orbiting, to see if they could find a less dangerous spot," Ben said.

"Possibly," Avram said. "When they landed, there were seven people from the astronomy club, three from the TV station and my wife and myself at the site. Hardly a threat. Nearly an hour went by before the first military chopper landed."

"And, meanwhile, civilian gawkers were jamming the roads," Ben said. "How long before the ground troops arrived in any strength?"

Avram nodded. "Seven hours. The Guard finally had to come cross-country, smashing through fences and across roadless terrain to get there."

"So the landing site might have been less of an impulse than we thought." Ben shook his head. "Or were led to believe."

As 2 A.M. approached, the visitors began gathering near a window overlooking the control room.

"How long will it take to translate?" Miranda asked.

"Not more than five minutes," Ben said. "Even if they send *War and Peace,* it shouldn't take long."

Miranda could see Wanda behind one of the consoles wearing a headset. She envied the JPL scientist slightly for being among the few who would first hear the sound of the message, even if it was just electronic buzz.

Ben turned, addressed the group. "After translation, the message will appear on the monitor to your left. Assuming they sent one, it should be on its way. Right now, the Holn are closer to the orbit of Uranus than Jupiter. They used Jupiter to get a free speed boost. At the velocity they're going now, barring any changes, they'll reach mother ship in about fifteen years."

A hush fell over the room at the top of the hour. 2:01, nothing but hiss over the speakers. 2:02, two or three people shuffled nervously. 2:03:12, "Signal capture. Confirmed. The Holn are talking."

2:03:41, "Signal ended. We have a clean capture. Translation initiated."

Miranda had to force herself not to hold her breath. Three minutes passed before the JPL logo on the huge wall monitor disappeared, replaced by a blue background. A white frame appeared, blank at first, but then words slowly scrolled top to bottom.

WE HEAR YOUR QUESTIONS[.]
ANSWER - WE DO THIS FOR YOU[.]
BEYOND 17[.]
YOU HAVE MADE CLIMB FROM NOT KNOWING TO KNOWING[.] WE UNDERSTAND CONFUSION [BUT<?>] REST IS NOW YOUR STRUGGLE[.]
HOW - SPECULATION ON <direct translation n.a., using colloq.>TINY<93% certainty> MACHINES CORRECT[.] ORGANIC[.<?>] DID NOT KNOW THIS WAS IMPORTANT TO YOU[.]
WHY - PHYSICAL LIMITS NOT BOUNDS[.] WHY DO YOU THINK OTHERWISE[?] MIND IS <one word - no known translation> [AND] MIND IS THAT WHICH SEES<54% probability; others: knows{37%}, understands{10%}, {other choices 3%}>[.] IF YOU WANT TO KILL 17 [THAT] IS YOUR CHOICE[.] LOOK AT<60% probability; other choice: TO{40%}> YOUR FUTURE FIRST[.]
<alpha string as received>MIRANDA SENA<end> WE DO NOT SING TO EACH OTHER[.] THE UNIVERSE SINGS TO US[.]

Miranda stared at the words, unaware of anything else around her. Emotions with roots back to her graduate days when first word of extraterrestrial contact hit like thunder worked at her. She closed her eyes, brought her hand to her face, but could not stop tears from trickling down her face.

> *"Copies of the message have been sent to every government, every university, every institution that has requested it. Plus, the raw copy is on the World Wide Web at WWW-NASA-dot-Holn-dot-gov. Everyone is invited to comment. We're still going over it but, except for that one word, it's pretty plain to us."*
>
> *"The 'one word' Danthen referred to follows the phrase 'The mind is.' However, in the next sentence, Danthen said JPL is tending to give more weight to the word 'understands' than the computer's choice of 'sees' in the phrase 'mind is that which.' This is the only response the Holn have given since they departed last June 14. It seems to be a personal response to a plea from Dr. Miranda Sena, the scientific head of the Holn Effect Task Force. The 'raw copy,' as Danthen described it, already is causing controversy, especially the suggestion the Group of Seventeen represents the future for humanity.*
>
> *"Rolf Treadwell, CNN, Pasadena."*

"Earl?" Walter said from the deck.

"Over here—yeow!" A Frisbee, spinning in hard and fast on a throw from Tom thwacked off his knuckles. "Ow! Dang!" He shook a finger at Walter. "You did that on purpose."

"Sorry." Walter suppressed a smile. "There's some people here to see you, but only one introduced himself." He looked at a business card. "Jack Theodoric of the FBI."

"FBI?" Lucas said. "What did you do now, Uncle Earl?"

"Nothing." Earl picked up the disk, tossed it at Jennifer with a flick of his left wrist, then hurried inside. The agent, in open-necked sport shirt and chinos, was flanked by a brown-haired woman in a smart suit with the just-proper-length dark gray skirt, and by a thin man about an inch taller, also neat in coordinated blue suit.

"Earl Othberg, I'm—"

"I remember you, Mr. Theodoric," Earl said as they shook hands, Jack's swallowing his hand.

"And these—" He was interrupted by the noisy entrance of the kids.

"Children, I think you'd better—"

"If this has something to do with Uncle Earl, we want to stay," Tom said.

"This has a lot to do with Mr. Othberg," Jack said.

"Well, all right, then sit and be quiet."

Jack finished the introductions. "This is Giles Lassiter"—Earl shook hands—"and Alex—Alexandria—Roth. They represent the MacAlister Foundation."

"I've heard of them. They go around giving away money."

"Won't you sit down?" Walter said.

The children sat on the floor, the two foundation people together on the short couch, Marcia and Walter on the long couch, Jack in a chair and Earl in the recliner opposite the foundation people.

"We're not here today to give away money," the woman said, "much to the disappointment of the children, I see." Muffled giggles came from that corner. "We are here instead with a two-pronged proposal. One, to ensure the safety of Rewound Children, and two, to begin legal action to overturn Alden Commission rulings and return some individual rights."

The foundation, she said, would start with an appeal of the original ruling declaring the group members children. At the same time, lawsuits would be filed against those people who seized property, funds, or guardianship.

"That won't be a problem here," Earl said. "Walter took over control of my finances and never has denied me a request, although he thinks I'm wasting a lot of it. It's just that he has to sign the forms before I can get my own money."

"That's one of the areas we want to correct," she said. "Personal control of your own estate, and in the end, your own life."

"I see." He rubbed the fabric on each chair arm with the heels of his palms. "How do you plan to protect us?"

"By bringing the group together in one place," Giles said. "A safe haven or, as Jack insists on calling it, a reservation. We have our eye on a failed resort in Marin County, north of San Francisco. The reservation would be guarded and patrolled, a place where you could live out of the public eye and away from fear. You would have complete freedom to live as you chose, and also to come and go as you please. All amenities would be provided, including housing and food. Recreational activities would be available, and as much media attention as you can stand."

"But we're not going to rip families apart," Alex said. "Anyone you wish to bring will be welcome—indeed, necessary. This way, the families can get away from the fear, too."

"It'll also put us in one place where the scientists can poke, prod, jab, stick, and peer at and drain blood from us and run us through their infernal machines and have us perform for them. And rip our pajamas off and take pictures of us and sell them to tabloids."

"I can personally assure you," Jack said, leaning forward, "that Dr. Avram Rolstein and Dr. Miranda Sena, the two head scientists of the Holn Effect Task Force, were angry as hell about that."

"As to your other concerns, Earl, that has been addressed also." Giles took out three business-sized envelopes from a jacket pocket. "The foundation wants the Holn Effect Task Force to remain in charge of the research effort. However, Dr. Rolstein and Dr. Sena know that there was some action taken before the task force was formed, and a few actions after, that have caused bad feelings—"

"That's certainly understating it," Earl said. "Why do I tell them to go to hell when they ask for follow-up exams? Because it's bad enough being treated like a mentally retarded child, but when they continue to think of me as a lab rat to experiment on, forget it. They want my cooperation, they're going to have to do more than 'feel bad' about the wretched treatment."

"Are personal apologies enough?" Giles separated two of the letters, held them out. "One each from Dr. Sena and Dr. Rolstein. Dr. Rolstein especially, because, as he put it, he was one of the gargoyles behind the masks in Santa Fe. For the record, Dr. Sena did not join until the task force was formed. She did not participate in any of the physical exams—"

"Studied us from afar, right?"

"As a researcher, yes. I think you should know she is quite upset at the treatment you have received and has given Jack hell for not—because he cannot stop the attacks. Believe me, Mr. Othberg, she is very concerned about the safety and well-being of every member of the group."

"Is that a fact." Earl gazed at the letters Giles still held out. Finally he stood up, stepped over and took them. Both were addressed simply to "Mr. Earl Othberg," one in a scrawling script, the other in a flowing, cursive style.

"This third letter is from Wynona MacAlister, administrator of the foundation, explaining exactly what she hopes to accomplish."

The writing on the third envelope was compact and elegant. "What do you want from me?" he said as he sat down.

"We need someone to help us recruit the others," Alex said. "You were recommended. Travel with us and help explain the project on a personal level. Help us persuade these people this is the best hope they—"

"Be a Judas goat, in other words. Lead the rest of the

group into the lab where they can be dehumanized and examined and studied. It's either this or be demonized by religious nutcases. Demonized and dehumanized. Some choice."

Alex leaned forward. "Neither of those are our intentions. If it's any help, Mr. Othberg, this idea is not new. Dr. Sena proposed something like this last summer, but she was overridden by the government. Wynona is trying to go one better and give you a place to live in safety while you sort out what happened and what you will do next. Scientific research, as important as it is, will be secondary."

"If this is any help, Earl, you have my word that what they say here is true," Jack said.

Earl watched his left hand tap the letters against the chair arm. The proposal would solve a nagging problem, but even so. . . .

"If this place lives up to what you want it to do, then I think a better name would be sanctuary."

Jennifer turned bright pink when everyone looked at her.

"That is a splendid idea," Alex said.

". . . CNN has learned that Health and Human Services Secretary Roberta Fletcher had ordered the dismissal of Dr. Miranda Sena, the scientific chief of the Holn Effect Task Force. The order was not carried out, and sources told CNN the reason was because the entire task force, all seventy-two researchers and technicians directly involved, signed a letter stating they would quit and take their story to every newsroom they could find, end quote. When asked to comment by CNN reporter Marinka Svoboda, Dr. Sena had only this to say":

"Don't ask me about internal politics. Ask me about progress on determining answers to questions."

"All right, how are things progressing?"

"Very well, thank you. That last message from the Holn has served as a collective bolt of lightning. We will be

*announcing some important results soon, and believe
me, Ms. Svoboda, they'll be a lot more important, and
interesting, than any internal bickering you might hear
of.''*

"No other member of the task force will comment.

*"Still, some officials are wondering why, ten months
after the extraterrestrials left the children on the hillside,
news surrounding the Rewound Children is still swirling
about. Here are three examples:*

*"In Chicago, Michael Thompson, brother of
Rewoundee Eddie Thompson, has had to sell his gym
and exercise club because of a declining customer base
he attributes to broadcaster Allan Goth's campaign that
cast aspersions on him and his operation. Michael
Thompson said the business, Windy City Gym and
Health, had been profitable because of his efforts to
create, in his words, the best damn gym in Chicago, and
the business had no debts or liens at the time he sold it.
However, Goth, who has a daily radio show heard coast-
to-coast, has said anyone who harbors a Rewoundee is a
traitor because the Rewoundees are enemies of decent,
God-fearing folk. Goth has mentioned Windy City Gym by
name and suggested anyone who is righteous and patri-
otic should not patronize the business. Michael Thompson had this to say''*:

*"First, I had to surmount racial prejudice in getting the
licenses and loans for the business. A lot of white folk
didn't want a black man owning a business, especially
downtown. So this is just another excuse to allow hatred
and fear to color one's outlook. As far as my brother
goes, he's my bro' and I will stand by him. I know the
word 'bro'' is overused, but he's part of my family and I
will help him and protect him as long as I can. Stick that in
your ear, Goth.''*

*"In Houston, the wife of Rewoundee Pablo 'Pete'
Aragon has annulled the marriage and gotten a court
order barring him from seeing their three children. In
addition, his sister, Angela Chavez, has lost her job as*

cafeteria supervisor at a local school district. School officials decline comment except to say a reason is, quote, bad influences, end quote. Chavez still has her second job with a catering service, but the owner, who asked that she and the name of the business remain off the record, says Chavez now only works in the main kitchen to avoid contact with customers. Chavez is the designated guardian for Aragon despite having three children of her own. Her husband, Joe, a commander of an anti-missile battery group, is in South Korea, having been deployed in the buildup of troops to meet the new emergency there.

"In Amarillo, Texas, police and fire units were called to the house of Dale and Sue Rithen after a Molotov cocktail ignited a fire. Damage was limited to the roof, but police say it follows a series of threats against the Rithen household. The Rithens have not one but three Rewoundees living with them: Dale's mother, Linda, his father, Jerry, and Paula Caulfield, who was ejected from her mother's household several months ago. Dale and Sue Rithen say they will move before asking any of the three to leave.

"Allan Goth has mentioned both the Rithens and Chavezes at various times in his program.

"These incidents, and others we have reported, bring up the question of how much longer can this go on? Six of the Rewindees are dead because of what one task force scientist calls simple, naked fear. How many others are going to die? In the end, who will be responsible for their deaths? And who is responsible for their safety?

"Rolf Treadwell, CNN, Washington."

Earl watched as a fine rain fell on the bright flowers of Marcia's garden. Two days had passed since the visit from the MacAlister group and they were still in town awaiting his decision. They'd stayed another two hours on the first day as Earl peppered them with questions and outright challenges. Last night, they'd been over for dinner at Marcia's invitation, and Earl spent three hours on the phone with Wynona MacAlister. She was as formal as her handwriting, but talked convincingly.

In his letter, Dr. Rolstein apologized for the bad treatment in New Mexico and tried to explain why.

We were dealing with the unknown again. We'd gotten complacent in the time they spent there doing nothing but talking. When the group was first captured by the Holn, we panicked along with everyone else. My God, what did we miss? Did we say something to anger them? Did we overlook something they had told us? Then we found you and the others—and we were at a total loss. This we did not expect. And we refused to believe it. We believe it now, though. We think we have reasons why and a method how.

Now we have to deal with the consequences.

Dr. Sena's letter was different right off—she wrote the whole thing by hand in her stylish script.

Cold hard fact often distracts us. We are so enamored of these facts we look upon them as the end-all, the sole reason for everything. In this case, we forgot the facts were based on people. People whose lives had been shattered and who had no inkling, at first, of what had happened. We won't forget again. I will make sure of that.

Are you still left-handed?

That last question both amused and puzzled him until he took a closer look at her writing. She might have practiced to get it readable, but it still had the slant of a lefty.

A hand holding a bowl of chocolate ice cream and sliced bananas coated with hot fudge suddenly appeared before him.

"Thanks," he said as he accepted the bowl and a spoon from Walter.

His nephew sat in the next chair. "How's the decision process going?"

"I guess I took longer than I should. Thanks for the time. I do think, though, it's the answer we've all been looking for."

"Indeed?"

"Yep." Earl spooned in a heap of ice cream. "Jack Theodoric really likes the sanctuary idea," he said after clearing the ice cream. "Simplifies the task of protecting us. I'm also looking at it from my point of view. And that of all the others. A place to be free of fear. A chance to remove danger, and hatred, from our loved ones. A chance to stand back and take stock of the situation."

For a few moments, the only sounds came from raindrops spattering on leaves and the house, a slight rustle of a breeze, and spoons scraping ice cream from the sides of bowls. Attacks on the house had lessened, but mostly because of the twice-daily drive-by of a police cruiser. Sharkjaw—real name, Nelson Francis Greggson—had stayed tough until a six-foot-three policeman with biceps the size of melons dangled handcuffs before the wide-eyed boy. His resolve dissolved quickly.

Walter had refused to accept money from Earl to help replace the windows ("That's what I have insurance for"). Earl did replace the *Enterprise* with a model so large Earl couldn't get his arm around the box. When finished, the thing looked spectacular, but Earl was hoping the activity had soothed fears in a boy who didn't quite understand the hate flowing around him.

Walter put his empty bowl on the railing, sat back.

"What do you want us to do?" he said.

"I want you to go on with your lives," Earl said instantly. "You've made a good life here. I won't ask you to give it all up just to watch over me. I'll miss you and Marcia and the kids, but you, and they, can best help me by being what you were before I got here and loused it all up."

"Well, it won't be quite the same. And it's all your fault, you know."

"What?"

"We made the final decision earlier this month. We're going to quit our jobs and open that pharmacy and grocery we were talking about. What you said about us falling into a rut and avoiding risk really rankled us for a while. Then we realized why: It was true. At least we can say we took the chance."

Earl studied the profile of his nephew in the muted light of the day.

"Now you're talking like an Othberg."

"You think so? Well, like I said, you're pretty much to blame for it all. So we're going to call it Earl's Market."

Twenty-one

May 17

"What made you choose science, Virginia?" Marian asked.

The stargazing session had turned lackluster because of the glow from city lights and the inadequacies of Betty's bird binoculars, so the gathering on the roof of Grid Manor had turned mostly to conversation.

"Physics class in my junior year of high school, I think. Our teacher, Mr. Daniels—Mr. D—took us to the old gym for his annual demonstration of motion, force, and gravity. This consisted of a blue-speckled bowling ball hung on a rope attached to a girder. He chose one student to stand on a platform against the wall. That year it was me. He brought the ball and jammed it under my chin and said if I understood the principles we had just gone over, I would know what would happen when he let go."

Virginia sat down on a stack of wallboard. "It swung out away from me in a nice, graceful arc, then started back. It got bigger, and bigger, and bigger—I think my eyes were getting just as big as it swung back. I pressed myself into the wall, but it kept coming, closer and closer, looming larger and larger and I almost ducked. But it stopped, without touching me, less than an inch from where it started, then began to swing back. I started breathing again. Mr. D told me later in the thirteen years he'd been doing that, I was one of three kids who didn't jump aside."

"Heck of a way to demonstrate science," Aaron said.

Virginia leaned back on her hands. "I think it was the certainty that impressed me, the fact that Mr. D knew no matter how many times he did the demonstration, no kid would leave the platform with a broken jaw."

Marian sat down on one of the lawn chairs that dotted the roof, actually an unfinished floor. The evening had a touch of coolness in it, a typical May evening for Albuquerque. Earlier in the day, they'd surprised her with a birthday party, complete with a lemon sheet cake and mint chocolate chip ice cream. The group gave her a nice purple sweater, which now warded off the evening chill. Aaron had his own gift for her.

"For Marian, daughter of the librarian," he'd said as he handed it to her.

She smiled at his use of the old family joke—and realized nearly twenty years had passed since she had heard it spoken.

"The Magic Mountain by Thomas Mann," she said after pulling the wrapper from the paperback book. "You know, I've never read this."

"One of the few books I really remember from college," he said. "It's about a guy who lets himself get into an absurd situation, full of interesting but strange characters."

She looked at him. "Apropos to anybody we know?"

"Of course not. *He* could leave any time."

As she sliced the cake, she asked about his birthday.

He waved an arm vaguely. "Back in February somewhere. It wasn't important."

She looked down at the slice she had just made. "You might be right."

The bottom line, two months after their aborted

departure, was that they were no closer to a solution. The heightened security and near-paranoia were taking their tolls—tempers flared more readily and the feeling that the four walls, as flimsy as they were, were closing in dogged everyone. A general agreement was taking form that the best course of action would be to contact the Holn Effect Task Force. Marian balked, though, remembering the isolation, the forced medical tests, the rough handling by anonymous beings swathed in green and Latex who hardly said a word, much less a kind one, to her as they demanded and demanded and demanded. She knew Aaron was remembering, too, from his silence when the subject came up.

"Virginia!" Tontine's shout broke the quiet.

"Over here," she shouted back.

A flashlight beam swept across the roof, catching the group, Tontine's figure at the source. "Fire below."

"What? Is it bad?" Virginia said as the trio ran toward the opening.

"Bad and getting worse," Tontine said.

At the next floor, they could smell the smoke; by the third floor down, the flashlight beam had become visible in the particle-laden air blowing up from below. By the time they got to the great room, smoke billowed up the ramp in great choking clouds. White King Sam was waiting.

"As you feared, 'Tine, the stuff's comin' right up the ramps."

"What about the others?" Marian said.

"We had plenty of warning bec—"

Black King Leo ran up the ramp shouting "No exit! No exit!"

A second later, Ken also charged up the ramp, running hunched over with a bundle under one arm like a quarterback scrambling for the end zone, shouting, "I got the cat! I got the cat!"

"Sidestairs, go!" Tontine led the way with his flashlight. They passed the couches and chairs and rugs that had made the room if not cozy, at least comfortable, toward an opening between plywood walls. They had to step carefully along a narrow space between wooden wall and the edge of the floor. At least the fresh air got the smoke out of their eyes and nostrils. Reaching a set of metal stairs, the group clattered downward to another set and another. On a flight of stairs with only a thin pipe as bannister, Marian lost her footing, but Black King Leo grabbed her from behind.

On the fourth floor, they were forced to retreat from roaring flames.

"Cut off," White King Sam said.

"Chain ladder," Tontine said.

They had to dodge detritus left over from construction to get to what would have been the back of the building. The heat and smoke increased, driving them in their flight. Security lights on the building across the alley illuminated the coiled ladder. Leo and Tontine rolled it out from the bolts securing it to the floor. Tontine kicked it over the edge, and Marian watched as it uncoiled and hit the asphalt with four rungs to spare.

"White, Black, go down. Give a shout if there's problems on the way and hold it for the rest."

"Right," Black King Leo said, placing a foot on a rung without hesitation. White King Sam followed, and a minute later shouted back up, "Fire on the third floor. Spreading." Another minute, "Second floor, engulfed. Be careful."

"Marian, pull your hair back. Put this on." Tontine removed his jacket and she slipped it on over her tresses, buttoned it up. "Ken."

Ken stepped out awkwardly onto the ladder.

"Put the cat down," Marian said.

"Can't. I have to save—"

She stepped to the edge. "Listen to me, Kenneth Polking. I will not have you sacrificing your life for my cat. If it comes down to your life or Merlin's, put the cat down. Do you understand me?"

Ken gazed at her a moment, then smiled. "Yes, I do understand." He started his downward trek.

"Mar—"

A crackling roar erupted behind them; flames licked greedily through cracks in the plywood walls.

"Go, go," Tontine urged.

She clambered onto the ladder. It had a tendency to jerk sideways, threatening to force a misstep. She had to concentrate but keep moving because Virginia got on five rungs above. Billowing smoke surrounded her, stinging her eyes, but she quickly learned to judge how far apart the rungs were and could hit three times out of four. The third floor still was more smoke than fire, but the second floor was a roaring storm, flames snapping and licking across the ceiling. Heat washed by in a rush of wind, blowing her hair and blasting at skin. Hot air burned her throat, and the rungs were uncomfortably warm to bare-handed touch. She stepped up the pace of her descent, but was surprised at the coolness below the first floor ceiling—no fire, no smoke. When she got to five rungs above the ground, she jumped.

"That way." White King Sam pointed.

Marian dashed to the mouth of the alley where Ken waited, still holding the bundle. A few seconds later, Virginia jogged over, binoculars bouncing on her chest. Flames surged out of the second floor, and Marian nearly panicked. Aaron ran up, stopped, put his hands on his face.

"Let me see," she said, turning him toward the light. "Yes, your eyebrows and hair got singed. Are you OK?"

"Yeah. Just trying to get my heart slowed down. Where's—"

Tontine and the two kings ran toward them, and as they caught up, the entire group ran across the street where a block away a bright-red fire engine screamed toward them. A dull *whump!* suddenly sounded above and blazing shards arced out over the street.

"Kerosine heater," Aaron said.

"Shit!" Tontine dashed off toward a fireman getting out of a truck. The others joined a small Grid Manor group, where Miguel wrote down their names.

"Tontine?" he said.

"Over there," Ken said. "The others?"

"All over around here."

"Watching our home go up," White King Sam said.

Thick smoke poured from even the top floor now, with flames beginning to lick out between walls and snaking upward, twisting and roaring until the whole center portion of Grid Manor was engulfed.

Tontine stepped up on the curb. "Had to warn them about the propane and kerosene stores."

He joined the lookers watching the pyre dance around the steel girders. The first stream of water rose and hit the fifth floor. Too late, though.

"I got the cat," Ken said, creating an opening in the cloth so Merlin could peer out.

"Mrow."

Marian scratched the cat's ears. "Thank you, Ken."

"I had to save him. He saved us."

"What do you mean?" She had to raise her voice over the din.

"Wailed like a siren," Black King Leo said. "Yowling I'd never heard before from any cat, especially from him. We ran down to find out what the hell he was doing. He was on the edge of the fifth-floor ramp just a wailin' and carryin' on. We smelled the smoke before we saw the fire."

"Regular little smoke detector he is," Ken said.

"How—" A new clatter cut her off. Kilkenny and Betty pushed her cart around the gawkers. Something with legs stuck upward from the main basket. Occasionally Kilkenny would pull an item out and hand it to someone. When he got to Black King Leo, he handed over a dark, rectangular box with a knight impressed on the lid and a chess board.

"Thanks," Leo mumbled. "My father gave me these."

"Kilkenny, did you risk your neck trying to save this stuff?" Tontine asked sharply.

"N-no. Just g-grabbed and r-ran." He grinned.

He pulled out a couple of backpacks from the lower rack. "Y-yours," he said, handing one each to Marian and Aaron.

"Met Betty on se-second floor, E-eddie and Tom helped me. R-ran down and ou-out far west side with s-stuff, got B-betty's cart by kitchen."

Betty looked up at him. "Chair."

"Y-yeah." He yanked the big item off the top of the pile, turned it over and set the rocking chair down in front of Marian.

"My God, you carried this down nine flights in a burning building?"

"Not me-me, F-fuller. New guy. Big f-fellow. Strong."

"This isn't even mine. It was here when I got here."

"Whose is it, then?" White King Sam said.

Everyone looked at each other. Kilkenny suddenly pointed at it with both hands. "Yours now."

Marian laughed, shook her head. "I guess so. But damn, nine flights?"

Kilkenny shrugged. "C-couldn't save c-cake."

She had a sudden picture of flames surrounding the cake sitting on the picnic table, icing melting and turning black. She also saw the three-legged couch burning, the sewing box aflame, plywood walls being consumed by roiling flames. . . .

Kilkenny and Betty began to move on. The cart wasn't empty yet.

"Wait, here's something of yours, Betty." Virginia unslung the binoculars and handed them to her.

Betty's head bobbed.

There wasn't anything else for the group to do but watch. By now, the fire had spent its initial rage by swallowing most of the shelter and now quietly was consuming what it could before being smothered in turn by the water streams. The smoke flowed in a great airborne river to the east, a tall signal to anyone wanting to know where the excitement was.

A bright light stabbed at Marian. She winced as a TV camera lens swept by. The light was gone in an instant, throwing everyone back into shadow.

"And now for a roundup of news around the nation. Police have charged Paul Mellinfield with first-degree murder in the death of his wife, Sandra. Sandra Mellinfield had been one of the Rewound Children, and her death last October had been ruled a suicide from an overdose of sleeping pills. However, investigators now say the medicine was given to her without her knowledge, but evidently that's not what killed her. The medical investigator has issued a short statement saying Ms. Mellinfield was drugged at the time of her death, but the cause likely was asphyxiation, probably by having a pillow pressed into her face. Mr. Mellinfield is an executive with the Global Bank of Commerce, and his second wife, Carla, is pregnant with their first child.

"Meanwhile, several hundred women protested the new anti-topless ordinance in Miami Beach today by removing . . ."

Earl's mind drifted from the television. So Sandra might have been murdered after all. Six dead for sure, perhaps eight—no sign of Aaron and Marian. At least he knew why he'd never heard from them—and that gnawed at him constantly. He had visions of them buried in a shallow grave near some dump, left there by persons unknown. He could see Aaron, the man-boy with thick hair and sardonic sense of humor; and Marian, with those blue eyes and gossamer hair framing that delicate face. . . .

He cursed. *Where the hell* are *they?*

At least the rest of the project was going well. In the month since he'd agreed, Earl, Jack, Giles, and Alex had traveled to see every other member of the group—and every one of them had said yes with a palpable sense of relief. Pam Yolbin's mother, Pete Aragon's sister, and Eddie Thompson's brother all had agreed to come, thereby assuring a nutritionist and physical trainer for the group. Tom's companion had agreed also, especially after the foundation promised to help in a legal battle brewing over Tom. Linda and Jerry's son practically had his job resignation written before the end of the conversation.

Earl's brain started slipping into sleep. On the TV, something was being said about a fire . . .

He sat bolt upright, stared, then jumped up.

"Jack! Gilac—Jale—Giles! Alex!" He ran into the suite's dining room. "I saw them! Aaron and Marian! On TV!"

"Where? Doing what?" Jack practically shouted back.

"I didn't catch it. There—there was some story about a fire somewhere, and there was a crowd shot, and they were there, I know it was them!"

"What were you watching?" Alex said as she headed for the sitting room.

"A news channel." Earl and the other two men followed her. "A roundup or something."

"Headline News," she said. "In a half-hour, they're going to repeat everything."

"We should record it, though, so we can get all the info," Jack said.

"The gift shop has blank tapes for sale," Giles said, heading for the door. "If they're still open, I'll get one, if not, I'll go elsewhere."

"You have twenty-five minutes," Alex said.

"Right."

The shop was open and Giles was back in ten. The three real adults sat on the couch, Earl on the floor in front. Giles wielded the remote control.

The story about Sandra Mellinfield came on. "God," Alex breathed.

"This," Earl said.

"Tape started," Giles said.

". . . of suspicious origin chased about forty-five homeless people out of a temporary shelter inside an unfinished building in Albuquerque, New Mexico. No one was hurt in the blaze but—"

"Come on, come on," Earl muttered. "There! There!"

"Keep the tape going," Jack said.

The news went on to something else. "Now."

"Rewind, rewind," Earl muttered.

Giles stopped it just after the report started. "About . . . there."

"Freeze!"

The image froze on a girl half in shadow, face blocked by long hair. Earl moved closer, heart racing. "Can you do frame by frame?"

"Yep."

Earl grimaced as, at first, the figure was lost in shadow, but a few frames later, someone moved and light fell flat on two children, both of whom suddenly looked straight out of the TV.

"Freeze!"

"Them?" Alex said.

"Them!" Jack exulted. "Where?"

"Albuquerque," Giles said. "Where it all began."

"Right." Jack jumped up, went to a phone. "I'll get us on the first flight. We've got to get there fast 'cause someone else might have recognized them."

"Look at the T-shirt he's wearing," Alex said.

"'I survived the Holn,'" Giles read. "That's great—"

Earl moved toward the large screen on his knees. He placed his left palm on Aaron's image, right palm on Marian's.

"They're alive." He didn't bother to check the tears welling up in his eyes or the constriction tightening his voice. "Goddamnit, they're alive."

Twenty-two

May 18

In the distance, the blackened skeleton of Grid Manor rose like the remains of some prehistoric beast as Aaron approached behind Ken, Marian next to him with Virginia behind. They had just been to the library, where Virginia could return the books Kilkenny had saved from the fire—and explain what happened to the ones he hadn't. Now they were going to pay a quick visit to what was left, just out of curiosity. Tontine, Black King Leo, and Kilkenny had gone ahead to make sure no one was lurking at the site. Clouds in the west threatened a shower, but for now the sun was blazing, which had prompted Marian to don T-shirt and shorts, leaving her hair free.

"The hell with it," she'd said, "if they're still looking, then here I am."

Actually, her brash statement seemed to reflect the general attitude after the fire, as if the brush with death had energized everyone. Tontine's careful planning had paid off—injuries had been kept to minor cases of smoke inhalation. No one had been hospitalized, but everyone lost something in the blaze—Kilkenny couldn't grab it all. Half the night had passed before they found shelter, a run-down motel far out on Central Avenue. The fire

department provided transportation, taking everything
that had been saved, including Marian's chair and Betty's
cart. Tontine drove his old Ford, which had escaped
unscathed. Arson was the suspicion, and of course, Aaron
and Marian were probably the reason.

Just as they rounded a corner two blocks from the site,
Tontine, Black King Leo and Kilkenny rushed over.

"Not a good idea," Tontine said, slightly bushed.
"Guys in suits are poking around."

"Guess we'd better head for the car," Virginia said.
"Sorry, gang."

Aaron shrugged. "Ah, well. You've seen one burned
building, you've seen them all."

"Buncha guys in suits, eh?" Ken said as the group
headed away.

"Yeah," Leo said, "three or four. And a coupla cops."

"And b-boy," Kilkenny said.

"Yeah, the boy."

"What boy?"

"Some redheaded kid—

Aaron and Marian spun instantly as if on cue.

"Red—"

"Who—"

They looked at each other, Aaron indicating she
should go ahead.

"You saw a redheaded boy about our size?"

"Yeah."

"Tontine, I, we, have to see him."

"Could be dangerous. He's with the guys in suits."

"I have a hunch I know who it is," Aaron said.

Tontine nodded. "Leo, come with us. The rest of you
head on over to Civic Plaza."

They approached cautiously, keeping something in
between as they came within a half-block. They huddled
behind a set of dumpsters and peered at the wreckage.
Some of the blackened girders had twisted in the heat,
and the interior structure had burned out completely. In
the alley, the deployed chain ladder still dangled.

"Still there," Tontine said. "The kid, too, by what used to be the first stairway."

Aaron peered through a gap between the two dumpsters. He focused on the boy's white T-shirt, blue shorts—

And flame-red hair.

He moved aside for Marian. "See what you think."

In an instant, her body tensed. "Earl."

Aaron nodded.

Tontine and Leo knelt beside them.

"The kid with red hair is Earl, one of us, a Rewoundee," Aaron said. "I don't know if he's a prisoner. He doesn't look like it. He's all by himself kind of kicking through the stuff. I'd like to get a mess—"

"Someone's talking to him, a skinny guy in a suit," Marian said.

"Can you tell how they're getting along?" Tontine asked.

"Just talking," she said. "Now they're leaving, looks like. Yes, headed for a red minivan."

"Not white?" Aaron said.

"No."

"Does it look like he's leaving voluntarily?" Tontine said.

"Evidently. The man isn't even touching him." She turned to them. "Out of sight now."

"You want to talk to that ki-person?" Tontine said.

"Yes, I want to know his status," Aaron said. "I haven't heard a thing about him all year, and he's a friend, I'd like to think. And I'm curious as to why he's in Albuquerque."

"And poking around Grid Manor," Marian said. "It's more than coincidence."

"Yeah," Tontine said. "Leo, follow them. The rest of us will wait at Civic."

"Right." Leo stood, hurried around the dumpsters.

At Civic Plaza, the group stayed in a tight knot, Marian and Aaron in the center. Talk was spare, but the wait was short. Leo came over a grassy knoll barely twenty minutes after leaving the group.

"The Hyatt," he said, pointing to a hotel rising high across the street.

Aaron looked at Marian.

"Miguel," they said together.

"Kilkenny, does Miguel work today?" Tontine said.

Kilkenny hesitated a second. "Y-yes. Convention catering, ten to six."

"Let's go."

The entire group followed him around to the employee's entrance. Tontine, Ken, Marian and Aaron went inside. Various manorites had worked there off and on, including Tontine and Ken, so they were allowed through the huge kitchen to a door opening into a large room. About a dozen men and women in snappy turquoise short jackets with tails and dark trousers carefully placed floral centerpieces on tables covered with white cloths.

A woman in white blouse and long dark skirt approached. "What's up, Tontine?"

"We need to talk to Miguel. It's urgent, but it'll be brief."

"All right."

She wound her way around the tables and spoke to Miguel, who hurried over.

"Que?"

"There's a man—boy, whatever, we think is staying here," Aaron said. "He's one of us. He's our size with bright red hair. His name is Earl Othberg. We must get a message to him and him only."

"His name again?"

"Earl Othberg." He spelled it.

"The message?"

"Tell him, tell him, Aaron says it's time to throw off the disguises and take over the planet."

"Oh, that'll be real helpful if someone hears it," Marian said.

"That's all right, they won't get it out of Miguel even if they torture him."

Miguel raised an eyebrow.

"That's for identification, so he'll know it's real. Tell him also we need to see him as soon as possible. Somewhere."

"How about the employees' entrance, about eight?" Tontine said.

Miguel nodded. "I will get the message to him."

Earl felt the cool evening touch him as he stepped through the doorway. The scent of rain still lingered, and water from the quick shower had pooled in a low spot in the sidewalk. He'd been alone in his room scanning e-mail on his electronic notebook—a gift from the foundation—when the soft knock came. The slim, dark youth in the waitperson's uniform had delivered a startling message.

He stepped over to the puddle, tapped it with the toe of his athletic shoe. The ripples distorted the reflection of the buildings around him. He stomped on it hard, splashing water on the parking meter pole and the car next to it.

"Mister Othberg, you're acting like a child."

Earl spun. Aaron stood next to an entrance to the underground garage wearing jeans and a T-shirt.

Earl leaped forward. "Aaron! Damn, it's good to see you!"

Aaron moved toward him and they met about halfway, grasping each other, then they embraced and slapped each other on the back. They stepped apart and gazed at each other. Aaron looked well, grin creasing his face. "How did you know I was here?"

"Saw you playing in the ruins of Grid Manor this afternoon," Aaron said.

"Grid Manor? You mean that homeless shelter?"

"Yeah. You look fit."

"Lots of swimming and biking. You don't look so bad yourself. Where's Marian, is she OK?"

"Marian's fine. What are you doing here?"

"Looking for you and Marian. I have a proposition for both of you."

"You're doing this of your own free will?"

Earl studied Aaron a moment. A wariness had suddenly settled into his features. "Yeah. Um, I brought some friends. You remember Jack Theodoric?"

Jack stepped out of the door.

"The FBI man? Sure, from that first day." They shook hands. "You were most kind."

"I'm very happy to see you well. I, uh, we brought some other friends."

At his gesture, Alex and Giles came out of the door. Aaron stepped back.

"This is Alexandria—call her Alex—Roth and Giles Lassiter." Jack said. "They represent the MacAlister Foundation."

"The genius grant people?"

Alex sighed. "The same."

"The foundation is making all the arrangements—"

"What arrangements?"

"I'd like to outline it with you and Marian together."

Aaron studied his shoe a moment, glancing twice at Earl. Earl, for his part, was a bit surprised; he hadn't met this kind of reticence before.

"Earl, can you trust these people?" Aaron burst out in a rush. "Can you personally guarantee neither I nor Marian will be hurt?"

What the hell has happened to them? "Yes to all your questions. I have put my own safety and life in the hands of these people. And the other members of the group have agreed to do the same."

"The other members?"

"All of us."

Aaron studied him a long moment. "I'd like you to meet a friend of mine," he finally said. "Tontine?" A tall, solid man with black hair just going to gray, grizzled beard and sharp eyes stepped around a corner. The way he stood, Earl got the impression of a coiled spring. "This is Tontine. He and some others have watched over us for a year. I trust them." He indicated the three behind Earl. "Can you say the same about them?"

"Yes," Earl said without hesitation.

Aaron looked up at the man. "I guess we should at least hear what they have to say."

The man nodded. "You yourself talked about Mr. Theodoric. I think they deserve a chance."

Aaron looked at something across the street.

"OK. Tontine, the limo, please."

The man snorted. "Right. Limo. Sure."

The "limo" was a beat-up old sedan. Jack and Earl rode in the back seat while Giles and Alex followed in a rented minivan—"Red," Aaron had said; the other man had nodded. During the drive, Aaron told Earl about the "clinic" and subsequent events.

"Do you have any idea who these people were?" Jack said.

"Nada. They were very careful not to say anything in our presence." Aaron had to peer between the seat backs to see them. "Except for Nurse Ames, and just before the Lexus got shot, she called Slick Suit Curt."

Jack tapped his teeth and looked out of the window. "And the gun?"

"Local police should still have it," the dark-haired man said.

"It'll be a start."

Earl found Aaron's descriptions of their reactions to Harold's and Alisa's deaths fascinating.

"I didn't see it until reruns the next day," he said. "I started watching standing up, and the next thing I knew I was on my butt on the floor with Walter's family bending over me. I guess it just knocked the stuffing out of me."

"Yeah." Aaron scratched an ear.

The rest of the trip was made in silence, with Earl beginning to understand Aaron's caution. And that friend—taciturn and wary, but Earl had the feeling little was escaping the dark eyes.

The friend steered the car into a parking lot surrounding a motel that charitably could be called run-down. Earl got out and stepped over to Aaron's side and waited as Alex parked the van.

"Upstairs," Tontine said and led the way up a concrete-and-metal staircase. The light in the room caused Earl to blink. Two of the standard rooms had been combined into a sort of living room. Little was done, however, to lessen the hardness of the concrete-block walls or soften the garish light from overhead fixtures. The carpet was faded and threadbare, and the shabby furniture looked about ready to collapse. This feeling was exacerbated by the sight of several people crowded into the room, sitting on the rickety tables and chairs, all watching him as he stepped inside. It took a moment to separate out a coffee table placed nearly in the center of the room, and next to it, a sturdy rocking chair, out of place in the midst of tackiness. Seated in that chair was a lithe girl with extraordinarily long hair. In the next second, she was out of it and had thrown her arms around him.

"Oh, Earl, it's so good to see you," Marian said into his ear.

"Double back on that," he said, hugging her tight. They released each other, both smiling. Her eyes managed to sparkle even in the harsh light.

"Oh, Earl—God, you look great," she said.

"You look pretty smashing yourself."

In his peripheral vision, Earl caught a glance of Aaron, eyebrow arched, half-smile on his face.

"Come, sit down."

"Uh, you remember Jack Theodoric of the FBI?"

"Vaguely, yes. Hi, Mr. Theodoric."

"Jack, please. May I also introduce Alexandria Roth, AKA Alex, and Giles Lassiter from the MacAlister Foundation."

"Yes, we are the ones who go around giving money to

smart people," Alex said rapidly. Then, conversation-
ally, as she shook hands with Marian, "I am very glad to
meet you."

"I, too," Giles said.

"Well, thank you all."

A couple of the people got up and moved four chairs
over. Giles, Jack and Alexandria arranged theirs in a
semicircle as Earl moved his next to the coffee table not
far from Marian. As he sat down, a large brown-and-
white cat ambled over.

"Do I pass muster?" he said to it.

"Merlin, behave." Marian curled back into the rocker.
"So, what's—"

Jack stepped over to the coffee table and stared down
at the cat, who looked back and said, "Mrrow?" Jack
snapped his fingers and pointed at Tontine.

"*You* took this cat from Lovelace Hospital."

"Yes," Tontine said.

"Oh, damn, hell! We were that close and didn't follow
up—fu—damnation!"

"What is it, Jack?" Alex said.

"Remember I was telling you about Marian's cat that
disappeared from the hospital? This is it. And that
gentleman over there was the quote, 'scruffy veteran' who
took it. Instead of following the cat trail, we dropped it,
assuming the scruffy man had stolen cat and money."

"That's what you were supposed to believe," Tontine
said evenly. "Especially if you were someone out to hurt
Marian or Aaron."

Jack shook his head. "Very nicely done," he said as he
sat down.

In the silent minute that followed, Aaron sat on the
end of the table next to Marian. The cat padded over to
him, and he reached out and began to scratch it behind
the ears. "Earl and these people have a proposition they
want us to hear."

"It's about our future," Earl said. "Short-term and
long-term."

He outlined the MacAlister proposal. Neither Aaron nor Marian interrupted while he spoke.

"And the others have agreed to this?" Marian said when he ran down.

"Every single one," Earl said. "And some are bringing their families." He listed those he knew. "You and Aaron will be allowed to bring anyone you wish to."

Giles gestured at the room. "Everybody, if you want."

"To a 'sanctuary.'"

"I've been to the place. A thousand acres of beautiful forests and meadows. It's a resort that failed, and one reason it did was because of the money sunk into it. There are two lakes, one a swimming lake where the water is conditioned and treated and kept crystal clear. The cabins are the latest in solar and wind technology and are cushy as hell. Gymnasium, tennis courts, hiking trails, satellite TV, equestrian center—the works. This is the place the foundation is proposing we live in. And grow up again in."

Marian rocked in the chair as she studied Earl. "And these people? Can we trust them?"

That suspicion again. "I'm staking everything I have on it. I have talked with Wynona MacAlister, and while it was on the phone, I believe her when she says she's doing it for us. Before we all get killed."

"Too bad she didn't do it earlier—" Aaron began.

"Yes, she regrets it very much," Alex said.

Marian rocked. Aaron continued to pet the cat, which by now had draped itself half over his lap.

"Excuse me, but I don't quite understand your reluctance," Alex said. "Everything Earl has said is true—"

"You care to repeat what you told us in the car, Aaron?" Jack said.

Aaron did, and when he finished, Alex sat back.

"Do you know who did this?" Giles said to Jack.

"No. We have suspicions, nothing proven."

Alex leaned forward. "Now I understand. I will tell you right here and now we are not those people and we will not treat you like that. No, I—" She just shook her head.

"Kilkenny," Aaron suddenly said, reaching into a pocket and pulling out something. "Go to my room, look in my backpack. Bring the object wrapped in plastic, please." He tossed a key and a wiry youth whose hair was combed impossibly neatly snatched it.

"R-right." The youth fairly leaped to the door and charged out.

"When do you hope to have the place ready?" Marian said.

"Work has been progressing very well," Giles said. "We'll be ready for tenants by the end of June. The uh, the task force wants to bring you all together to make some, uh, some measurements before then."

"I'd like to get some measurements myself," Aaron said.

The young man leaped back in, handed the object to Aaron, who struggled to pull off several layers of plastic wrap. "This is still around because of Kilkenny, who saved it from the fire." Kilkenny grinned and stuck a thumb up as he returned to his spot. "Give this to one of your friends, Earl."

Earl handed it to Alex, who read the label on the edge. *Star Trek: The Third Generation."*

"You'll find a couple of episodes at the beginning," Aaron said. "About halfway through, you'll find the good stuff. I taped the conversation I had with Janessa and her shyster. I don't know if it'll be any help, but I thought I'd get it down on tape."

"You're sneaky. I'll have to remember that," Marian said. "Maybe you'll get your Maserati back."

"Afraid not," Jack said. "The man Janessa married wrecked the Maserati this last winter. Spun out on I-635 and hit an overpass abutment. He walked away, but the car was totaled. Insurance refused to pay because they had questions about transfer of title."

Aaron laughed. "Serves that asshole right."

"You trust us with this?" Alex said.

Aaron shrugged. "We have to start somewhere."

"All right, I'll make a deal." She indicated Earl. "Anything we do with this tape will be done in his presence."

Aaron nodded.

"Is there going to be a school at this place?" Marian said as everyone stood up.

"One of the first things we thought of," Giles said. "Then we remembered we're dealing with adults, not children who need to be educated."

"I wouldn't go that far," Marian said. "Perhaps offering college courses would be appropriate."

"It's under consideration, yes," Alex said.

"If it does happen," Aaron said, "then I would recommend for a staff position Dr. Virginia Barker."

Earl saw a woman sitting in a corner react as if shot.

"Medical doctor?" Alex asked.

"Uh, no, uh, doctorate," said the woman. "In particle physics. I sort of stopped. I'm not sure I could. Uh, teach, I mean." She glared at Aaron. "I'll get you for this, Fairfax."

Laughter echoed in the room.

"Normally, I'd arrange for a security detail," Jack said. "However, your group did a pretty good job protecting them, Tontine. You think you can do it a couple more days?"

"No hay problema," he said as he shook Jack's hand.

Earl's group led the way out. Outside, Marian and Aaron joined him.

"How's your nephew?"

"Oh, doing fine. They plan—huoof."

He suddenly found himself being pushed firmly along the balcony by the pair. They didn't stop until they reached a corner well away from the rest of the group. A yellow bug bulb cast a sickly light on Marian's hair.

"All right, Earl Othberg," Aaron said, "I'm asking you again, and I want the plain truth, the whole truth, out of earshot of those who control y—"

"Nobody controls me—"

"Oh, sure," Marian said. "And if you get out of line they slap you down damn quick because you are as powerless as a child."

"The scientists are going to be there, aren't they, with all their probes and tubes and stuff?" Aaron demanded.

"Yes, but with a different attitude. You should read—"

Marian jammed a finger into his chest. "I will not be a lab animal again. I *will not,* do you understand? I got away from that once and I will not—"

Earl grabbed her shoulders. "Marian, Marian, listen! That will not happen here. I have the personal assurance of the leaders of the task force." He let go, ran a hand through his hair, distressed at the difficulty he was having in breaking through their fear and distrust. "Look, Dr. Rolstein, Dr. Avram Rolstein, was one of the faces behind the masks at Lovelace. He's apologized to me about the treatment, in a letter and in person, and he's vowed to personally apologize to every member of the group. I had the same skepticism about the whole thing as you do. Well, maybe not completely, not having been sold and all, but I'm telling you this might be our only chance. For ourselves and for the people we love. You should see the others. They're frightened, really frightened. And you should've seen the looks on their faces when we told them about the sanctuary. Linda Rithen, tough, down-to-earth Linda Rithen, wept." He took a deep breath. "The one you really need to talk to is Dr. Miranda Sena. She's the scientific chief of the task force, and she's been riding Jack hard about you two, demanding he find you, and making him quail every time he's had to call her to tell her he's failed again. You'll like her. She's a warm, sensitive person who likes to draw pictures. She's human, too—"

"She's never talked to me—"

"Because you've been missing. Look, all I have to offer here is my word. The foundation is for real, the proposal is for real. I've seen the sanctuary site and it's a good place." He raised his hands in a supplicating gesture. "Trust me. That's all I can say."

Marian's face was in shadow because the light was behind her. Earl could see Aaron's face only in profile as they looked at each other. They stood like that for several seconds, and Earl realized how quiet things around them had become.

"All right, Earl," she said softly. "You have my trust." She leaned forward and kissed him on the cheek.

He pulled her to him, reached out for Aaron and the three embraced there in the corner under the yellow light.

Miranda found it peaceful in the three-sided ozone shelter that not only blocked UV light but cut some of the noise around her on the beach. This was not the most elaborate shelter; it was made to be portable and go up in a hurry. It belonged to Matt Gunnarson, and she found it amusing she was sitting in his shelter.

Just as she'd found it even more amusing to find herself in his bed that morning. They'd gone out for a pre-birthday dinner the night before, and then to his apartment, where she discovered first, his wall of trophies won in triathlons and marathons and such, and second, his collection of 1930s–40s big band records. "Had to pay a fortune to find a turntable with 78 rpm still on it," he'd said as he put Glenn Miller on.

In the ensuing evening, she'd discovered how compassionate Matt could be. And passionate. . . .

She shook her head. *Don't get into that mood now.*

The resonant mood had deeper roots, though. The message from the Holn still galvanized the task force, giving enough clues to send them off into frenzies. Answers at last seemed within reach.

Matt ducked inside and sat next to her on the blanket,
muscles in chest and arms and legs tensing and relaxing
in a coordinated, smooth dance of perfect symmetry—

"Give me that." She grabbed an iced tea from his
hand. "I need it to cool off."

"Why?" He straightened, flexing shoulder and chest
muscles. "Something making you hot?"

She glared at him. "Would you like to wear this?"

He laughed, relaxed. "You have a lot of gall, sitting
there in your form-fitting one-piece backless beach wear,
exposing long shapely legs—"

"Be quiet. The beach patrol frowns on too much
physical activity."

They both laughed. "Thirty-four years old today, and
I'm acting like a schoolgirl."

"Why not? You've been under a lot of stress. Physical
activity is a good way to relieve that tension."

"Mmmm," she said, sucking in the cool herbal tea.

"I'll take you on a ten-mile hike with full backpack.
That'll—"

A trilling cut him off. He raised an eyebrow as she
closed her eyes and drank more tea. The trilling sounded
again. She hunched her shoulders. Again.

"Blast!" She set the tea down, reached behind her and
yanked out her electronic notebook. She jabbed a button
to PHONE and popped the screen open.

"Sena here," she snapped.

"Jack Theodoric," the voice said as his image formed
on the screen. "I just wanted to let you know we've
found the last two of the group."

A wave of dread passed over her and thumped in her
stomach. "Yes?"

"They're fine, Miranda. We met with them last night.
They're not dead, they're not hurt, they're not prisoners.
They're healthy as oxen and as sharp-minded as ev—

"Dr. Sena? Miranda?"

"Give me a minute." She took several slow breaths,
trying to get her heart to stop hammering. She felt a

strong grip on her shoulder and looked into gentle eyes in a face close to her own. "I'm all right now, Jack. Unexpected good news is a little hard to take."

"I can understand. I felt like jumping up and down and hollering when I saw them myself."

"Where did you find them?"

"In Albuquerque, right where we were in January. I'll save the tale of how we bollixed the cat connection for later. Aaron and Marian have been living with a homeless group for several months. Two nights ago, their shelter burned down, and we saw them on TV. That's how we found them, not through any clever detective work."

"That's terrific—"

"There's a little more you need to know, Miranda. It seems Mr. Fairfax has been dragging around a videotape all this time, a tape he made of his wife signing divorce documents. He made the tape because he thought she was up to some chicanery with her lawyer. He was right, but that's not the best part. He didn't even know he had the rest of this because he'd been locked in the laundry room.

"He recorded the sale of himself to a drug company, Tydings APR, one of the biggest. A lawyer for the company came in and they discussed terms right there in front of the camera they didn't know was on. The idiot lawyer even boasted about their other purchase: Marian Athlington. We've got enough evidence to charge the lawyer, the drug company and its CEO with trafficking in human lives. We're also going to nail Marian's sister and Aaron's ex-wife. You will be hearing of arrests later this week."

"God in heaven," Miranda muttered.

"That's a truly amazing piece of news, Mr. Theodoric," Matt said.

"This has been a truly amazing year, Dr. Gunnarson."

Miranda folded the notebook shut, looked over at Matt.

"Happy birthday," he said.

Twenty-three

"... taken into custody were Arlene Bermond, seen leaving federal court in Des Moines, Iowa; and Janessa Williams, here being escorted into federal court in Kansas City, Missouri. Both were arraigned this week on charges of trafficking in human lives and violations of constitutional rights. Bermond, the sister of Rewound Child Marian Athlington, allegedly sold custodial rights to Athlington to the drug company Tydings APR for two hundred fifty thousand dollars. Williams had been married to Aaron Fairfax, also a Rewound Child, at the time of the Holn incident and she allegedly annulled the marriage and sold Fairfax's rights to the same company for four hundred fifty thousand dollars. FBI spokespersons say the international drug conglomerate was interested in determining if the procedure used to make the adults into children was commercially viable._

"Also facing charges are the president and CEO of Tydings APR, Richard Salcido, and the company's chief counsel, Bucklin Corstain. As a result, Tydings stock value began to fall on international markets ..."

So that's what I was worth to Janessa. Aaron looked over at Marian, who stood rigid, hands clenched into fists, face frozen into a mask. He started to put an arm around her, but she turned her back to the TV.

"Forget her," she said more to herself. "She's in the past. Let her stay there." She fixed Aaron with a sharp gaze. "Why are you worth more than I am?"

"Probably because Janessa is a harder bargainer than your sister."

She jerked her head as if trying to dislodge something. "Let's go. We don't want to be late to our appointment with Dr. Sena."

"We do this because the government won't. Look at the release we gave you people. It's a copy of a memo from the Vice President of the United States to the secretary of Health and Human Services suggesting the latter, quote, push the whole thing under the rug, end quote. Now I would suggest that started the whole chain of events that led to six Rewound Children being killed and the others suffering from attacks physical and mental. Did you know, for instance, that this very thing had been proposed by Dr. Miranda Sena nearly a year ago? It was promptly shot down.

"As far as the lawsuits are concerned, we will file to redress injustices done to the Rewoundees through seizure of property and denial of rights—"

"Ms. MacAlister, didn't the Alden Commission settle all this?"

"I don't think so, and I have a coven of constitutional lawyers who agree with me. A commission is not a court. There is no legal precedent for such a thing. Our challenge will start at the federal district court level and move up to the Supreme Court. We'll see what Justice Alden does then, won't we?"

"Your whole attitude, Ms. MacAlister, seems to be that the government hasn't done anything right—"

"It hasn't. Let me tell you people something: start digging. Find out who really has been controlling the situation. The Holn Effect Task Force is merely the public body, nearly powerless. Find out who are the ones moving in stealth behind the scenes, the ones wanting to

push it all away. It hasn't been possible despite their best efforts, and it's probably because you people have kept the news about these people alive. Congratulations. Now, dig and find more dirt. There's lots more where this memo came from."

"You really think the government is that bad?"

"In this case, yes. Partly because the people involved didn't realize how serious this was. They were all too busy trying to get reelected. When they did realize the impact, they got scared. When governmental types get scared, they try to shove the blame off on someone else. People inside this government have made some terrible decisions that led to some horrible deaths. Problem is, they won't recognize their culpability. They'll deny it to the day they die. Well, I don't intend to let them. Now, that's all. I don't want to miss the task force's press conference this afternoon, and neither do you. It'll blow your socks off."

"Well, that's the end of the press conference by the rather outspoken Wynona MacAlister as we watch her leave the room, where she announced her famous foundation was establishing a sanctuary for the Rewound Children in California. The project was kept secret until three days ago, and by then, the foundation had bought the land, started renovations, and had contacted the children. In addition, the children had been moved to secret quarters in Los Angeles two weeks ago for what the task force has termed follow-up examinations.

"Her actions are getting support in the United States Senate, where a bill has been introduced that will give federal status to the sanctuary and also transfer control of the Holn Effect Task Force from the Department of Health and Human Services to the National Academy of Sciences. The measure is sponsored by two members of the American Alliance party, but the Senate majority leader is reported to have said the bill has a snowball's chance in hell.

"Yesterday marked the one-year anniversary of the finding of the Rewound Children, and a lot has happened in that year. A lot more seems to be happening today, what with one press conference so far and the one Ms. MacAlister mentioned by the task force later today. That one is the subject of much anticipation.

"Browning Wells, ABC/USA Today Information Center, Los Angeles."

For the tenth time, Miranda checked her notes, trying to ensure everything she wanted to say was somewhere on the white cards. Whether the press would let her say it all was another matter, but she would try. At least she would not be facing the pack alone this time; Dr. Innes and Matt would be with her. Avram uncharacteristically had stepped back from delivering the latest, and most important, results.

"My job is political," he had said. "The scientists directly involved should be the ones behind the words this time."

"Come in," she said automatically to the knock on her door as she double-checked an information sheet.

"Dr. Sena, I presume?" a childlike voice said.

She turned. "Aaron Fairfax and Marian Athlington, I presume back."

"At your service."

She noted the dry humor as she extended a hand. Both of theirs were small in hers, but with firm grips. Aaron wore a white shirt and dark trousers, Marian a light-blue blouse, dark-blue skirt. Her flowing hair was pulled back, cascading down her back to her knees.

"Please, be seated." Miranda pulled her desk chair over and sat down. Marian sat in the chair next to the desk while Aaron pulled an armchair closer.

Subjects do not have the motions of average children, she had read in one of the reports. *Now that they have had time to adjust, they are more confident about their orientation and do not display hesitancy or misplaced gestures often seen in children this approximate physical age.*

"I know both of you pretty well on a molecular level, but I'm ashamed to say I know little else. Even though you've been here a couple of weeks, I still couldn't seem to find time to see you."

"We know you a bit from TV," Aaron said.

She grimaced.

"Earl spoke highly of you," Marian said.

"Earl is one of the more unusual members of the group." Miranda said. "Oh, by the way, Aaron, here's the book you'd asked for." She handed it to him in a sack. "Alex asked me to give it to you. She says it's only a 1996 edition, but it was the only hardcover she could find."

"Oh, great." He slid the book out of the sack, glanced at the complimentary bookmark. Then he handed it to Marian. "It's for you, actually. *Magic Mountain,* to replace the one lost in the fire."

"That one was only a paperback," she said.

"This one's nicer."

Miranda studied them during the exchange. Matt was right; they were good-looking children. But their eyes held more depth, more intensity, than a "normal" child's would have. And their body language carried other meanings as they leaned toward each other and touched each other lightly. Could they be in love? Possibly, and Miranda felt that something about the two together made sense, like two lost pieces of a puzzle just found and not to be separated again.

"I want to apologize," Miranda said. "For the suffering, the pain and the sorrow."

"You sound like you're taking the whole burden upon yourself," Marian said, closing the book. "It's not your fault the Holn came and did this."

"Unless you gave them our names," Aaron added.

"That's part of the trouble. I didn't know your names

until much later. You were just numbers crunched into visual data dancing around on my computer screen. By the time I got curious enough to find out about the humans behind the numbers, it was too late. You had vanished and three others were dead already."

"How would you know," Marian said, looking down at her hands, "that my own sister would sell me for medical experiments?"

"I have been accused of being that coldhearted. Just another heartless scientist seeking knowledge without concern for human suffering."

"A few weeks ago, I might have agreed, Dr. Sena," Marian said, fastening a direct gaze back on her. "In the days when we were bitter because we didn't understand what had happened to us and it seemed the rest of the world thought we were better off dead. Or in a lab."

"And now?"

"During the year, it became clear that one voice kept speaking for us, taking our side, pleading our case," Aaron said. "That voice was yours."

"Perhaps because I finally stumbled upon the real stakes here. I should say we. You have no idea what your cases have done to the studied aloofness of scientific detachment. And we find ourselves slightly bewildered by it, too." She glanced at the clock. "I've got to go. The press will not remain docile for long. Thanks for the visit. I hope we can do this again soon."

"You know our address. Come up and visit. As a friend."

"Thank you, Marian. I will."

After the door shut, Miranda returned to her desk to gather her notes. *Why did I get so emotional when they were found? Now I know.*

"Good afternoon, ladies and gentlemen." Miranda looked out over the field of faces that jammed the auditorium. "I am Miranda Sena, scientific director of the Holn Effect Task Force. At the podium to my left is

Dr. Samuel Innes, a member of the task force and an eminent neurobiologist from the University of Florida. On my right is Dr. Matthew Gunnarson, another eminent scientist, this time in genetics, from Princeton." Each stood at his own podium. She tried to stand as straight as possible between the two men. "We'll start with a general statement, then answer any—well, most—of your questions. We hope by being willing to do so the message we want to get across eventually will."

In a corner to her right, leaning against a wall behind two reporters wearing bored expressions, she saw Avram Rolstein smirk.

"It's one day past a year since the Holn visitors left the changed seventeen human beings on a hillside. In that time, much has happened, some of it tragic. Some of it avoidable, but we don't want to get into that."

Miranda straightened the white card on the lectern.

"We are here to announce two main conclusions of the research of the Holn Effect Task Force. These are based upon on our own studies, some of which have been confirmed in part by the last message from the Holn.

"First, the mechanism the extraterrestrial visitors used to cause these changes was a form of molecular machinery, machines the size of molecules that can rebuild, remodel, remove, and otherwise remake cells. The Holn confirmed this, also stating the machines were organic in origin. The procedure was done whole-body; that is, all organs, bones, tissues and glands were done at once. The few memories the individuals have of oval rooms and spidery—probably mechanical—armatures, serve to reinforce this hypothesis."

She took a breath, wished for but put off a glass of water. "Second, all surviving members of the Group of Seventeen have shown growth. These include increases in height, from just under two to about five centimeters. The uneven rates are what you'd expect among differing individuals. Bones are lengthening and ribs are reossifying at the proper junctions. Tendon and muscle tissue are expanding and keeping up with the bone-growth rates. All growth is within parameters we would expect in the immature human genome.

"We believe all members of the group are growing up again, if you will, and they will be able to live normal, healthy lives once again."

"I already knew that," Earl said. Around him, the group had gathered to watch the news conference on one of six video screens. Across the room, a lavish buffet was being attended to by some of the medical and security staff.

"How did you know?" Jerry Rithen said.

"A rambunctious teenager remembered what they said our height was after the ship let us go. She and her siblings measured me and lo, almost an inch taller."

"Now why the hell didn't we think of that?"

"I firmly believe now they are human." Dr. Innes placed his hands on the edges of the podium. *He doesn't look as aged,* Miranda thought. "My group and the task force in general have found nothing to indicate otherwise. No mechanical contrivances, no foreign—if you'll forgive the term—bodies, no systemic changes in any organ are indicated. This includes the brain."

"But hasn't there been some rejiggering of their genes?" someone yelled out.

"Yes," Matt said. "And from what we can determine, the changes are for the good. A stitch in a DNA pair to decrease susceptibility to a disease, for instance. The most famous, of course, is the change that lessens the risk of inherited breast cancer in one of the women. And I'm sure we'll find others. Preliminary results suggest the Holn discovered a way to boost immune systems—"

A clamor cut him off. "You mean," a reporter finally managed to shout above the din, "that they made them immune to disease?"

Earl Othberg sprang to Miranda's mind again. One

report had said he spent much time in the Hawaiian sun, swimming, bicycling, skateboarding, in scanty clothing and without protection from UV exposure. He reported no sunburns, confirmed by family members, and his skin had tanned only slightly. This flew in the face of a family history of skin susceptible to sun damage.

". . . I want to stress that probably ninety-nine percent of an individual's DNA has been left alone," Matt was saying. "If they had a weakness for chocolate before the Holn incident, they still crave chocolate now.

"I would, however, caution everyone not to denigrate human science and attribute all the good stuff to the Holn. In the last forty years, we have made tremendous strides in understanding our own organism. We've identified many of the areas where miscued genes cause a host of life-threatening conditions, including colorectal cancer, breast cancer, Huntington's disease, multiple sclerosis, some birth defects, and many, many more. How else would we know what the Holn did to these people? There's an unfortunate tendency, however, to say the Holn came and cured everything. I don't think that's quite true. I don't think these people are going to live the rest of their lives without catching another cold. They're still at risk of cancer from exposure to toxic substances. And aging—well, we'll have to wait another generation now to find out what the changes did to the natural processes of aging. Someone younger than me will have to do those studies."

One shout rose above the others: "Can you be saying, then, they have created the Superman?"

"No. I don't think you'll see a super race walking the Earth in the next ten years."

"A nurse asked me about colds and flu at Grid Manor." Aaron leaned back in an overstuffed chair. "I told her there were plenty of colds and stuff around, but it all seemed to skip over us. She said, 'Our point exactly.'"

"Yeah, I got the same response from someone else," Eddie Thompson said. "I wonder if we have been changed. Made super or something."

"That's the whole problem, isn't it?" Cheryl Vroman, on the couch next to Marian and Linda. "We don't know yet."

"How's your arm?" Marian asked.

"Huh? Oh, it's fine." She absently rubbed the spot where it had been broken. "My doctors said it healed almost perfectly and much more rapidly than they exp—" She stopped, stared at Marian.

" 'Our point exactly,' " Aaron said.

"You said molecular machinery was used as the means to effect the metamorphoses?"

"Yes," Miranda said, setting down a pitcher of water, "although I don't think metamorphosis is the word we should use here."

"Do you think this has applications on Earth?"

"Oh, yes. Nanotechnology, as we refer to it, is a definite research goal here. The Holn machines are a little different in that they're all organic. The Holn devices resemble proteins more than vacuum cleaners, and can be eliminated from the system as regular organic waste."

"This is based on one line in a cryptic message?"

"No, they said 'we confirm' and 'organic.' We found remnants of unusual compounds in each individual, compounds that gradually dissipated over time. The relevant groups in the task force are pursuing this, hoping to find clues to the structure of these devices. What probably will remain the mystery is the step-by-step procedure, the details. Actually, though, that really isn't important."

"I see your prediction came true," Aaron said as Tom sat down on the couch arm.

"Yeah."

"What prediction?" Cheryl said.

"The state wants to remove me from the home of a homosexual. They say the Holn might have fixed me so I'm not gay anymore and they don't want bad influences to corrupt me again."

"Jesus. Well, I'll tell you, if I were still a lawyer, I'd offer my services."

"Thanks. The ACLU has jumped in. And the foundation." He stroked his chin. "Of course, it's not just the state. A gay AIDS activist told me I should've had AIDS, or at least been HIV positive, so the miracle cure would have been worthwhile."

"God," Linda said. "What did you say?"

"Mark decked the guy before I could."

"Good for him!"

"Ah, Paula," Pete said as Paula and Pam joined the group. "Been to any Wal-Marts lately?"

Paula laughed softly. "If you ever need a place to stay . . ." She shook her head. "I just don't believe I did that. God."

"Good thing we ran out of toilet paper when we did," Linda said. "I was—"

She was interrupted by a security guard accompanying a stocky UPS driver in brown shirt and shorts carrying a box. The guard pointed to Aaron.

"Aaron Fairfax?" the driver said. "This is for you. They X-rayed it before they'd let me deliver it."

Aaron accepted the signature pad but had to change hands so he could sign with his left. The box was heavy, and he glanced at the return address: The Astral Dance, Sedona, Arizona.

He smiled. "I know what it is."

The smoky quartz crystal was well packed.

"Wow," Cheryl said.

"Neat," Jerry said.

"Uh—weighs a ton," Marian said as Aaron handed it to her.

"At least thirty pounds. There's a note. 'Dear Mr.

Fairfax. It wasn't until several weeks after it all happened before I grokked you were one of those people on the ship. To think what they did to you—it's mindboggling. I remember your interest in the crystal, and as time went on I realized it belongs with you. Please accept it with my blessings. May the vibes it puts out give you peace and harmony.' Signed, Argon Donnell."

"Why change adults into children at all?"

"Now we're into the essentials of the matter," Miranda said. "Look at that line in the Holn message: 'If you want to kill the seventeen that is your choice. Look at your future first.' Future? As children? No. What did they say at the beginning? 'We do this for you. *Beyond* seventeen.' They're talking to *all* of us. They acknowledged our rise from instinct to reasoning beings and now they have set out a new challenge for us, the challenge of finding out how to remake ourselves—"

"What good is that knowledge?" Allan Goth, *the unshutupable,* Miranda thought. "What good does it do to turn adults into children?"

"You're missing the point again, Mr. Gulp." A few titters crackled around the room at Dr. Innes's quip. "Turning them into children is just the illustration, the example. Understand? First, the Holn rather spectacularly demonstrated we can defeat diseases and debilities that shorten our life span, disable us, hobble our minds, make us weak and ineffective. Second, they suggested we don't have to be limited by the physical limits of our bodies. They even wondered why we think it's necessary. No, as Dr. Gunnarson pointed out, we were well on our way to solving many of these problems ourselves. In many cases, for reasons political, financial, and cultural, we often hesitate at the brink of success, making progress slow and painful.

"This entire incident is about possibilities, Mr. Goop, and if jackasses like you would get the hell out of the way, we can get on with it."

"Oh, now you're going to start insulting me like you did Reverend van Kellin—"

"I am no longer interested in the worthless rantings of a paranoid old fool."

"Fine, but stop avoiding the issue, and that is whether the aliens the people have been turned into—"

"They are not alien, Mr. Goof, I just got through stating that," Dr. Innes said.

"I'm sorry, but I think—"

"Who the hell cares what you think!"

Matt and Dr. Innes looked over at each other. Both had uttered that last statement together, word for word. Matt walked over to Dr. Innes and both slapped palms in a high five. Laughter filled the room. Miranda just smiled, shook her head as Matt returned to his podium.

"OK," Miranda said as the laughter died, "there have been a lot of changes in the last year and you have just witnessed one. Now, if there are no more questions about the subject at hand, we will close the confer—"

The place erupted into shouts as reporters waved hands clutching electronic or standard pens, a few caps and even a white scarf. Avram disappeared behind the frantic shouting of the two now-lively reporters.

Of all the tasks Miranda ever had to face, one of the hardest she ever did was right at that moment as she struggled to keep her face bland despite the grin of triumph threatening to break free.

"I have some news," Marian said as she sat back down next to Earl on the couch.

"They have a whole news conference for that," Aaron said, still in the same chair. The others had drifted away as the press conference droned on.

"Not that," she said. "I was just talking to Jack, and he told me they got Slick Suit and Nurse Ames."

"Well, hallelujah. Still at the clinic?"

"Oh, no, they shut that down mid-March."

"What! You mean we've been fearful of leaving Grid Manor all that time and they'd already flown the coop?"

"According to Jack, the corporate guy in charge got nervous when Slick Suit and Dark Suit planned a big direct assault and he pulled the plug."

"Hell. What fools us mortals be." He grabbed a pillow and buried his face in it.

Marian let out a small laugh. "That's not all."

Aaron lifted a corner and peered at her. "Now what."

"Jack says we weren't the targets for the arsonists in the Grid Manor fire. A businessman hired a couple of thugs to set it to force everyone out so the owner would have to sell it. The businessman didn't know we were ther—"

Aaron sat up. "Wait. You're telling me we stumbled down dark stairs in thick black smoke and dangled in front of an open fire threatening to get roasted like a weenie because of a *business rivalry?*"

"That's it."

Aaron tossed the pillow, fell back. "Jesus H. Christ on a rubber crutch."

"You guys lead such interesting lives," Earl said.

"So how come we weren't invited to join the Holn's mother ship?" Kinsea Lee looked as dapper as ever.

"Humans could not survive on the Holn ship because their atmosphere is poisonous," Matt said. "It would take much reengineering of the ship to accommodate us." He paused a moment. "But you know, that *is* a good question."

"Have you figured out what the missing word is in the Holn transmission?" The Japanese television reporter had to stand on a chair to be seen.

"JPL says the best they've come up with is 'solitary,'" Miranda said. "Now what does that mean? Separate from the body? Is there a quality that makes the mind coherent beyond its physical structure? As Dr. Innes pointed out, the Holn seem to think so. We're still struggling with that one."

"Dr. Gunnarson, does your hypothesis about the Holn keying on our worship of youth still stand up in the light of the recent message?" The questioner was George Johnson of the *New York Times,* the only one who had pursued the matter.

"Yes, because they regressed the adults into children. Why? Wouldn't Mr. Othberg, say, have been satisfied with the body of a thirty-year-old man? Probably, but going back to the genome of a child really grabbed our attention. We don't have to carry it that far, but, by God, look at the possibilities. That's the message there."

During the pause, Miranda scratched an itch above her eyebrow. Her mouth was dry, sweat trickled down her back, her leg muscles were rebelling. The press conference had been going on an hour and a half, and fortunately, it looked as though the reporters were running out of questions. She glanced at Dr. Innes and Matt. They'd planned this, rehearsed it and expected to be scorned for it, but, as Dr. Innes had said, "the critics can take their little tushies to hell."

"We've been talking in general terms about the consequences of the Holn actions, but we want to emphasize some points, particularly about the consequences to humanity in general and specifically the people you've"—*not me*—"dubbed the Rewound Children."

Matt took the baton. "The Holn came here out of curiosity. In the process, they answered two fundamental questions we had about ourselves. One: No, we are not alone in the universe. Two: No, we are not locked into the life cycle evolution has left us with. We are on the doorstep of a whole new world. I know that's a tired cliché, and it's been said many times before, such as when the Berlin Wall came down, or when the Republicans took control of the House and Senate in '94, or when China and Taiwan finally merged." He dismissed all with a wave of a hand. "Child's play."

"The challenges are horrendous." Heads and lenses swiveled to Dr. Innes. "And our history is atrocious at the times we've been handed the keys to each new world. Such as the moment in 1945 when we announced the nuclear age with spectacular fire and sound. Fear has driven everything connected to the atom since then. What we lack is wisdom—and lord, do we need it now. We have acted abominably toward the Group of Seventeen. Well, there are eleven left. We still have a chance to redeem ourselves. The Holn seem to think we're going to kill them all. I pray we can prove them wrong."

"And what about these individuals?" Miranda tried to focus on faces, not video equipment. "What does the future hold for them? How many times have we all said to ourselves 'I wish I could do it all over again'? How many times have we said to ourselves 'If I only knew then what I know now'? Well, these eleven people *can* do it all over again, and with the knowledge and experiences of one lifetime already. They don't have to make the same mistakes again. They can go on to do whatever they wish, start again, find a better life, learn new things, fall in love again, start new families, live a fuller life than they—or any of us—ever have dreamed about. This is what the Holn have done for these people.

"Last year, we had a presidential election, but little was said about these momentous events. Candidates grew angry because the Group of Seventeen was stealing their TV time. What foolishness. If you think these eleven people—and the six dead—were the only ones affected by the Holn visit, you are sadly mistaken.

"'Look at your future,' the Holn said. Are we brave enough—and wise enough—to live in that future?"

Aaron, feeling like a kid heading to the principal's office, followed Alex, a PR man, and an FBI agent toward the auditorium. Reporters weren't satisfied with all they'd just heard—now they wanted to hear from a Rewoundee, the one who spoke on the hill last June.

"Me and my big mouth," he'd muttered. On stage, he jumped a couple of times and waved, trying to see over the podium. A chair was brought for him as laughter filled the room.

"I am Aaron Lee Fairfax, I am forty-four years old and I used to own a Maserati. I don't anymore, but neither is it important anymore.

"We are not devils, we are not angels. We are not here to take over the Earth and subjugate everyone, although that does have its appeal. We are people, humans like all the rest of you, who became random subjects of an extraordinary series of events." Big words again coming out of such a small mouth.

"Now that we know we are going to grow up again, we have new hopes and dreams. As Dr. Sena so eloquently explained, we have second lives to live, and we wish to live them as best we can. I cannot say we will do a better job this time. We are still human, we still make human mistakes, we are still driven by the same human passions and desires. But we will try. We will go on, but with a whole new load of questions about ourselves and our future.

"And we will live with the memories in our hearts of the six people of the group who are not here. They were among us, and they were our friends.

"And humans do not forget their friends."

Twenty-four

July 4

Miranda put her bare feet up on a chair and leaned back, snuggling into a long, silk robe, a gift from Matt. Below the hotel balcony, San Francisco Bay glittered in the early morning sun, sounds of the city reaching her only in muted tones.

"Ah, my lady, fresh-brewed coffee, courtesy of the hotel." Matt, in sweatsuit, set two steaming mugs of coffee on the small wooden table. "You look quite elegant in that lovely garment."

"I feel like a queen. What did it set you back?"

"Tush, tush, one does not ask the value of one's gifts. I got it on sale."

Miranda laughed. "How enchanting."

"Part of the reason you look so good, I think, is the rest you've gotten on this break despite yourself. Good ol' Avram. Knows when to call a halt."

"Yes, but there's still some work we need to do before the task force scatters—"

"There you go again, talking like the mother hen." Matt took a drink of coffee, looked at her. "Perhaps you're too close to your subjects."

She sat up. "Nonsense."

"Oh?" He got up from the table, disappeared into the

331

room. When he came back, he carried a good-sized painting, which he placed on the arms of his chair, balancing it with a hand. "Explain this, then. Avram says take a couple weeks off and you spend most of it working feverishly on this portrait. Not too close, you say?"

Marian Athlington gazed out of the portrait, long hair cascading over bare shoulders. Behind her left side, the constellation Orion shone through an open window; behind her right shoulder, a hefty cat sat imperiously on a bookshelf, green eyes mirroring the sharp look in the blue eyes of the main subject.

Miranda looked into the reflection of the sky on the surface of her coffee. "An artist does not have to explain her inspiration."

"In this case, you don't need to." Matt set the painting on the floor, leaned it against the balcony wall. "But I am curious as to why her."

Miranda straightened. "That image is based upon a database I used last December when I finally got curious about who I was studying instead of just why. It was a lifeless image, a collection of number-based pixels, based on those idiotic photos they took last year. It stuck in my mind for a long time. The only way I could deal with it was to do that. I needed to infuse some life into it. The life I know she has in her."

"In my humble opinion, you have succeeded." He stepped back, gazing at it. "Is the cat artistic license?"

"No, Alex Roth had some friends of Marian's in Albuquerque take pictures of her cat and send them to me." She stood up, stepped over to Matt's side. "Why am I getting the third degree here?"

He took her hand. "I'm trying to understand a little more about the woman I love. I assume we're taking this to Rewound Ranch today for more reasons than you just want to show off."

Miranda gently touched the painting edge with a finger.

"It's a gift. I want her and the others to know I believe

in them beyond numbers and molecules and alien encounters."

"Could this be the last report about the Rewound Children? Is this the last time we'll mention these people, the last time what they do will make the news? Probably not, but perhaps the nature of the news will change. Instead of reporting about their deaths, we will be able to report about their lives. Marinka?"

"This afternoon, the Rewound Children will be joined by the Holn Effect Task Force at Rewound Ranch—the sanctuary's unofficial name—for a Fourth of July picnic and fireworks bash. As big as the ranch is, it still will be pretty crowded; the entire task force is bringing families to join the group and whatever of those families have come along. Dr. Avram Rolstein says the events are planned as a celebration—of life, of friendship, and of freedom. All of the surviving members of the Rewound Children are now living on site. The MacAlister Foundation has hired several members of family and friends of the group to help run the place. Rolf?"

"For instance, Dr. Virginia Barker has been appointed chairperson of the extension school the University of California is establishing there. Dr. Barker is a particle physicist who lost her job seven years ago and ended up in a homeless shelter in Albuquerque, a shelter that eventually took in Marian Athlington and Aaron Fairfax, two of the rewoundees. Her first official act was to hire Mark Adams, spouse to rewindee Tom Cathen, as a professor of English. Angela Chavez, sister to rewindee Pete Aragon, has been hired as a nutritionist, and Michael Thompson, recently married brother of rewindee Eddie Thompson, will work as a physical trainer. Other hirings are expected soon. Marinka?"

"Two of the rewindees themselves are reemployed. Tom Cathen has been rehired by UC-Berkeley as a professor of humanities. He will complete his studies on the social structure of the mother ship inhabitants that he

*began before he was transformed. Meanwhile, Golden
Gate Associates, the prestigious law firm in San Francisco, has rehired Cheryl Vroman. Spokesmen say she will
participate in lawsuits related to the Rewound Children,
and have hinted at a possible appearance in court for oral
arguments. Rolf?"*

*"So it stands now—the group is in a safe haven, each
member making plans for his or her new life. They have
no more idea what will happen now than do any of us in
our own futures. As Mr. Fairfax pointed out, they still must
grapple with the same questions about life we all do. Only
they, as the scientists have pointed out, might be har-
bingers of a new, but exciting, world.*

"This is Rolf Treadwell . . ."

". . . and Marinka Svoboda, CNN, San Francisco."

Aaron studied his hand at the end of his arm. Now
that he knew for sure all the other cells in his body—not
just fingernail cells—were dividing again, promising
growth back to what he had been, a weighted shroud had
lifted from his mind.

He tried to center himself in the infinite distance
where moons orbited planets, planets orbited stars, stars
orbited in galaxies, galaxies moved in stately grace in
neighborhood groups, the entire structure of the universe moving—where?

He heard bare footsteps come up behind and a body
drop down to his left, limber legs joining his in dangling
over the pier end.

"Penny for your thoughts," Marian said.

"Show me the penny first."

She spread her hands. "Do I look like I have a penny?"

"No. You look quite fetching, actually." She wore the
same he did: a pair of swim trunks.

"Don't get fresh, Mr. Fairfax."

"I wish I could."

She smiled at him from under a thatch of wayward
hair. "Just be patient."

"Patient, she says," rolling his eyes. "I'll show patience." He ran a finger up her side.

She twisted sideways and fell against him. "Stop it," she said, looking directly into his eyes, smiling slightly. "I'll have to retaliate."

"Just be gentle," he said, stroking her jawline lightly, then down her neck and across her chest. She reacted as the touch traveled, then pushed herself up, still gazing at him. His hand found hers.

"So," she said with a shake of her long hair, "put the penny on my tab and tell me what you were thinking about so seriously."

"Just my place in the universe."

"Still?"

"And I suppose you've got it all figured out."

She took a deep breath. "No." She pushed a long lock aside. "Those damn Holn. Do this to us and then run away."

"Maybe they aren't running away. Maybe they're just biding their time, waiting for us to grow up. Meanwhile, they're preparing Earthlike quarters on the mother ship—it takes time because, remember, they can't handle an oxygen atmosphere—and when we mature, they'll come back for us."

"That's an interesting thought." She looked at him. "Would you go?"

"Probably. You?"

"I don't know." She turned her gaze across the lake.

"Actually, I'm here for a more prosaic reason," he said. "I need to let the air currents flow around my left auricle in order to boost the cooling effect—"

"What are you talking about?"

He rubbed his ear. "Adrienne called this morning."

Marian arched an eyebrow.

"Just let me have it. Chewed me up one side and down the other. In essence, I'm a dope because I didn't turn to her for help, and when I tried to explain how I couldn't allow my problems to intrude upon her life, she lit into

me again about how we are brother and sister and how
she would have found a way to help and how worried she
was when the FBI told her I was missing and she told me
I was obstinate, stubborn, mule-headed, pig-headed,
oxen-headed—"

Marian giggled.

"Well, you get the drift." He sighed. "The upshot of all
this is that I seriously, *seriously* misjudged my sister."

"It's too bad you were so wrong, but I'm glad you
were."

"You'll be able to judge for yourself. She's bringing the
family for a visit later this month."

"Oh, Earl's family will be here, then."

"Great. Their kids are about the same age."

They looked out over the swimming pond of clear,
treated water over a sandy bottom. The other lake, a real
body of water about five times the size, was about a mile
away. To their left and on top of a rise stood Holn Row,
large and luxurious cabins, each with its own kitchen,
parlor, large screened porch, and up to four bedrooms,
all furnished right down to the shower soap. Pete Aragon
and his sister's family took the one on the far north end
closest to the main lodge; Pam Yolbin and her mother in
the next; then Eddie Thompson and his brother; Linda
and Jerry Rithen with their son's family (wife, boy and
"cutest little granddaughter," according to Joanna
Yolbin); then Tom Cathen and Mark Adams. Earl and
Aaron were sharing the next-to-the-last with Tontine,
and Marian, Virginia, and Ken took the southernmost
cabin. Cheryl moved in with Pam and Paula stayed with
Linda and Jerry.

Tontine used a grant from the MacAlister Foundation
to trade in his dying Fairmont for a "halfbreed" utility
wagon powered by electricity for the city and com-
pressed natural gas for the highway. He, Virginia, and
Ken packed up what few things they had—including
Marian's rocking chair—and drove out from Albuquerque, bringing along an extra passenger.

"How's Merlin?"

"He's found a spot on the porch where he can lie in the sun and watch all that's going on."

"He's going to get fat. And lazy."

"Watch how fast he moves when the fireworks go off tonight."

Virginia went through a metamorphosis of her own, getting her hair styled, buying some snappy clothes, and shucking off her dowdy appearance like a butterfly out of a cocoon.

"Don't look so surprised. I *am* a professor, after all," she had said.

Ken got a haircut and some new clothes, grumbling about it the whole time. His last job was as a campus landscaper, so he was put in charge of the resort grounds.

"Jesus, would you look at the size of these lawns?" was his response.

Virginia and Ken also announced an August wedding.

"How's Tontine?"

"He shaved. Chin as smooth as mine."

"That's worth seeing."

Soon after their arrival, Aaron had found Tontine sitting in a chair in a darkening room, staring off into space.

"What's the matter?" Aaron asked.

"I am useless here."

"You're not responsible anymore."

Tontine leveled his sharp gaze on Aaron. "What do you mean?"

"At Grid Manor, you shouldered everybody's burden, took a personal interest in their safety, set up the structure of the society to make the place run smoothly, to make it an island of calm in an uncaring society. You don't have to do that anymore, Tontine. You can ease back, let most of the burden fall on someone else's shoulders. Now you go on your own personal quest to find what you want, what you are."

He'd kept that piercing gaze on Aaron a long time. "A personal quest, huh?" he finally said. "Sounds . . . interesting."

In the last week, he discovered a well-equipped carpentry shop in one of the maintenance buildings. He'd asked a few questions, touched some of the machinery, fingered lengths of wood. Something seemed to be stirring behind those dark eyes . . . or so they hoped.

"Promise me something," Marian said on the pier.

"What?"

"Promise you'll help me dig out Tontine's secrets. We'll have to be careful, but we have the time, now."

"We'll start with his real name," Aaron said. "Gimme five." He raised his hand and Marian slapped his palm, laughing.

"By the way," he said, "you'll be happy to know I'm not worth two-hundred thousand more than you."

"Oh?"

"Yeah, I talked to Barbara Carlson last night, my successor. Part of the money was a kickback for inside information Tydings wanted. The SEC is all over Thagg, Morgan, and Edwards and half the staff quit." He shook his head. "I worked so hard to keep the shadow of scandal out of that place. God *damn* it!"

She bumped his shoulder with hers. "You did what you could. Money corrupts."

He snorted. "I ought to know."

"At least one person we know can handle money. Miguel."

"Yeah. That kid is amazing."

Miguel, it turned out, had saved nearly eight thousand dollars. Unfortunately, his fiance had jilted him, but instead of mooning over it, he bought a house in Albuquerque's South Valley with foundation help. The property included a small guest house, and Betty and Kilkenny moved in.

"Virginia talked to him last night," Marian said. "Betty's already gotten a couple of neighborhood customers, and Kilkenny is going into the lawn-care business."

"That's great."

Ken had been right about most of the people at Grid Manor. Even after Alex and Giles had announced the foundation would offer help in any form to the people who had been in Grid Manor most of the year, only a few had accepted anything, mostly using services to find jobs and better shelter. The group began to drift apart. Indeed, to their sorrow, White King Sam and Black King Leo put the chessmen away, folded up the board and faded away into the night, unobserved by anyone.

Aaron sighed. "'Lately, it occurs to me . . . what a long, strange trip it's been.'"

"Amen."

They were not aware of the footsteps coming up behind them until the last second.

"Look out," Aaron said, ducking.

The figure of Earl hurled over them, curled into a ball and hit the water with a tremendous splash.

"Oh, Earl," Marian muttered as water droplets rained down.

Earl's head broke the surface with a swirl of water.

"What're y'waiting for?" he shouted. "You guys have been sitting there like bumps on a log. Enough talk. Get in here and swim. The water's great. Worry about tomorrow tomorrow."

"Earl the swimming philosopher," Marian said.

"Duck," Aaron said again as more feet pounded down the pier. Eddie shouted as he leaped, followed quickly by Cheryl. Two splashes and more cold drops dotted their skin.

Marian stood up. "I'm getting soaked just sitting here."

"Yeah. Buncha ill-mannered children." Aaron stood up, and they started heading up the pier. Two more shouting figures ran at them, Pam with Pete at her heels, then two more splashes. Aaron and Marian didn't get very far when Jerry thundered by, followed by Linda and Paula.

"Will you look at that," Aaron said. "He's being chased by two females."

"Jealous?"

Splash-splash-splash.

"Not yet."

They both stopped and watched as Tom approached rapidly.

"SorryI'minahurry," he muttered as he dashed on down the pier.

Marian gazed after the figure in bright yellow trunks. "Is that any way for a professor of humanities to act?"

Splash.

"Hey!" Earl hung off the end of the pier. "Last one in is a rotten egg!"

"Don't need it," Aaron shouted back.

"Names will never hurt me," Marian said.

"You're both rotten eggs, then."

"Childish," Aaron muttered as they continued walking. "Of course, you realize it would be a moot point anyway, on who would be the rotten egg, I mean. It certainly wouldn't be me."

"I beg to differ with you, Aaron Lee Fairfax. I don't remember everything about Christmas Eve, but I do remember staying well ahead of you for several blocks."

"Well, sure, you had a half-block head start. If you hadn't pooped out, I would have caught you eventually."

"Pooped out? *Pooped out?*"

"Yeah. Just ran out of gas."

She turned and faced him, legs apart, hands on hips, hair flowing over arms and chest. "That is an untruth, sir."

"Not so." He faced her. "If I were inclined to do so, I would leave you in my dust. If I were so inclined, you understand."

"If I were so inclined, I don't think so."

"If I were so inclined . . ."

"Yes?"

"If—"

In an instant, both were hurtling down the pier.

"Clear the LZ, here they come!" Earl shouted and disappeared.

Aaron's feet pounded the ersatz wood and air brushed across his body. He leaped at the pier edge and soared weightless over the shining surface, watching as the water rose at him. It stung him as he smacked through. He quickly pushed toward the surface. He broke through to air, cleared the water from his eyes and spotted Marian doing the same three feet away.

"Ha, ha, Marian, the rotten egg."

"Liar! Take *that.*" She smacked water into his face.

"Why you—take *that.*" He splashed her back, then was hit in the side of his head.

"Sneak attack eh? Take *that,* Linda."

She laughed, returned fire, and was splashed immediately by Earl, who got hit by Paula, who was splashed by Tom, who got it from Cheryl. Soon everyone was splashing everyone else and water flew everywhere.

Sound waves originating in vibrating vocal cords powered by expulsions of air reverberated off the water, bounced off rocks on the shore and shot up over the land to echo off natural and manmade structures.

To any human ear within range, it sounded very much like the laughter of children.

About the Author

TERRY D. ENGLAND was born in Los Alamos, New Mexico, in 1949. After a stint in the U.S. Air Force, he attended the University of New Mexico, where he earned a bachelor's degree in journalism. He later earned a master's from St. John's College in Santa Fe. A journalist, England has won an Associated Press award for a science-based article and currently works for the *Santa Fe New Mexican,* a local daily newspaper. He lives in Santa Fe.

AVONOVA PRESENTS
AWARD-WINNING NOVELS
FROM MASTERS OF SCIENCE FICTION

BEGGARS IN SPAIN
by Nancy Kress   71877-4/ $5.99 US/ $7.99 Can

FLYING TO VALHALLA
by Charles Pellegrino   71881-2/ $4.99 US/ $5.99 Can

ETERNAL LIGHT
by Paul J. McAuley   76623-X/ $4.99 US/ $5.99 Can

DAUGHTER OF ELYSIUM
by Joan Slonczewski   77027-X/ $5.99 US/ $6.99 Can

THE HACKER AND THE ANTS
by Rudy Rucker   71844-8/ $4.99 US/ $6.99 Can

GENETIC SOLDIER
by George Turner   72189-9/ $5.50 US/ $7.50 Can

SMOKE AND MIRRORS
by Jane Lindskold   78290-1/ $5.50 US/ $7.50 Can

THE TRIAD WORLDS
by F. M. Busby   78468-8/ $5.99 US/ $7.99 Can